FEVER CHART

by

BILL COTTER

McSWEENEY'S BOOKS

SAN FRANCISCO

www.mcsweeneys.net

McSweeney's and colophon are registered trademarks
of McSweeney's, a privately held company with
wildly fluctuating resources.

ISBN: 978-1-934781-41-8

For Carly Nelson,
and for Marcio Coello

FEVER CHART

I

In the kitchen of my new apartment, Mr. Kline and I sat on two milk crates on either side of a paint-spattered sawhorse. I gave him a money order for $265. He handed me a house key and a mailbox key and a grody, dog-eared paperback entitled *Shuffle*, whose cover was adorned with a photo of a Zippo-brandishing monk sitting Indian-style next to a can of gasoline.

"Son," said Mr. Kline, "I've quartered a number of you Boll dischargees before now and I have come to learn that they will occasionally, and with no alert, do themselves in, often without due regard for their surroundings."

Mr. Kline owned a half-dozen Section-8-friendly apartments on Onion Street in the middle of town, and was (according to Mina Purvis, the head social worker at the Boll Compound for a Variety of Disturbances) sympathetic to the plights of the melancholy, the obsessive-compulsive, the manic, the bulimic, the merely crazed.

"And the *other*, too, Jerome," Mina had said during my Boll outtake interview, winking at me while playing cat's cradle with the giant green rubber band that she used to hold my file together. "The *other*."

Mr. Kline stared at me.

"I'm pretty sure I won't be committing suicide," I said.

"Good, because it's just plain rude to commit a suicide, especially a messy one. But if you just have to do it, please be tidy," he said, stabbing a short, Band-Aided index finger at the jacket photo of the author, a certain Quentin Bohner. "I think the most neighborly way would be Pharmaceutical Method Number Sixteen, the one with the nerve pills in the mashy potatoes. That's how I'd go if I went nutso or got quadriplegized in a ski-doo crash. Another good way's Bohner's Easily Obtainable Lethal Vapors Number Six. Just get schnonklered and tape a plastic bag over your head. See?"

The injured finger indicated a cartoon diagram of an asexual individual on a couch, head swaddled in a trash bag. A tipped-over bottle on the floor read XXX. I'd always considered this method déclassé, but maybe it was experiencing a revival.

"But maybe the best way is Number Twenty-Two, same chapter. The old CO."

"CO?" I said.

"Carbon monoxide. Car and hose and duct tape. See, look here at the drawing. Just run the hose from the tailpipe up to the crack, there, in the window. Tape it down snug."

He looked closely at the diagram.

"Looks like a Pontiac," he said. "Who wants to go in a goddam Pontiac? Christ. Well, it doesn't matter. Got a car, son?"

"No," I said, a little depressed now. "No car."

"Well, good," said Mr. Kline. "Cars are more trouble than they're worth anyway, and they always crash. Anyhow, whichever one you pick, just don't get any blood or matter on anything. And don't stick your head in the oven. One can't turn off an oven if one is dead."

Mr. Kline wrote out my lease agreement with an unsharp Sharpie.

"Sign there, and there, initial there."

I signed, I initialed.

"Good. Call if you have problems with the potty or the radiator."

"I will."

"And here." He handed me two stamped postcards: one addressed to him, the other to the county coroner. "If you decide you do want to push up your own daisies, please write down the particulars and drop them in a mailbox. There's one up the street by the Dome Restaurant."

My apartment needed occasional maintenance.

I didn't like to bother Mr. Kline, so I always waited as long as I could to call about the flushlessness of the toilet or the moody radiator or the scuttling noises beneath the floor. When I could stand the privations no longer, I'd call Mr. Kline and leave a timid message on his machine, and an hour later some maintenance gorilla with oily knuckles would come by and pour insecticide between the floorboards or snake the toilet or whack the oil-filled radiator with a wrench.

A couple of months after I moved in, during the deadest, shortest days of winter, Mr. Kline died. His daughter Pat took over the management of the properties, a period I experienced as one of spotty maintenance and surprise inspections—conditions much like those in the hospital I'd recently left. The rent went up. The power often failed. All the drains would occasionally organize an apartment-wide clogging. The refrigerator micturated coolant in the night. A long crack shaped like the coast of Alaska appeared in a wall. A bizarre, purplish smut began to grow in a kitchen cabinet. The linoleum squares of the bathroom floor unstuck themselves and curled up like scrolls.

I could handle all that. But the radiator... that worried me. As winter deepened, it radiated less and less and less. Soon, I was forced to install my toaster oven on the bedside table, and construct at the foot of the mattress a berm of hot-water bottles fashioned from empty cranberry-juice jugs.

I called Pat often with my no-longer-timid complaints. They all went unanswered.

Meanwhile, I went faithfully to work—three hours a day guiding a 2.0 horsepower Mister Wobbler brand buffing machine over one or another bit of flooring in a community college down the road. Afterward, I went to the loathsome day program that was one of the conditions of my discharge from the Boll. It was conducted at a defunct social club in the middle of town, where the day-programmers chain-smoked and muttered harmlessly, or, for a change, took turns at the game table with Murray Pupino, an old guy in pink seersucker Sansabelt overalls who enjoyed obliterating people at Scrabble and Boggle and Othello. He liked to remind one of one's lifetime record against him in various contests, whenever one happened by.

"Othello: Murray, 41; Jerome, 0. Scrabble: Murray, 66; Jerome, 0," he might say, as you were wandering across the room to see if there was anything interesting in the trash.

On a terrifically cold day a few weeks after Mr. Kline's death, I nearly beat Murray at Othello, but he had a "seizure" and knocked the game board off the table. He "recovered" from his "seizure"—which also carried symptoms of "amnesia"—and promptly set up the Othello game again as though nothing out of the ordinary had occurred. Then he lit a Carlton 100 and invited me to try my luck.

"Othello: Murray, 42; Jerome, 0."

I stomped around the day-program room for a while after that, wishing I hadn't quit smoking. If you didn't want to play games with Murray, there was absolutely nothing else to do except smoke. You weren't allowed to sleep. There was never anything interesting in the trash.

I sat down next to Terry Gold on the wicker loveseat across from the game table and glared at Murray. There were hours left until I could go home. At least it was cozy here.

Then Blaise, one of the day-programmers who was usually in the bathroom cat-napping in a stall in order to baffle the no-sleeping rule, raced into the room and announced that we were all getting sent home early because there was a weather emergency in effect.

"Snow?" we said.

"Temperature," said Blaise.

It was twelve below and not even dark yet.

When I got home, it was only a few degrees warmer inside my apartment than outside: the radiator had finally quit altogether.

My toilet wasn't working either. It had always needed a whack and a snaking now and then to keep it operating at capacity, but I didn't have the experience or finesse that Mr. Kline's old maintenance gorillas had had, and so the toilet had fallen into neglect, the most odious symptom of which was its reduced appetite. Stragglers often reversed to reappear in the main pool.

This morning's straggler, I discovered, was trapped precisely in the center of an ice oval.

I was appalled, and very concerned. The spectacle was horrifying, but the consequences were what concerned me: *I needed my toilet.*

Take away my meds, leave me outside in the cold, sic violent pets on me, batten me to a gurney, but please don't separate me from my toilet. I could never, ever, ever be more than a few hundred yards away from a toilet, a good, clean, private lavatory, with an exhaust fan, some sort of high-decibel white noise, the essential side items, and a nonwobbling ceramic commode with suction like an airlock on a space station.

I took a deep breath and called Pat Kline-Dooley again. Pat Kline-Dooley did not return my call.

That night I slept in my clothes, with two sets of long johns over them, my coat over the long johns, and an outer wrapper of blanket, bedspread, and a smelly acrylic afghan I'd stolen from the day program. I took my nightly fistful of pills (dry—the pipes were frozen and the refrigerator contained nothing in a liquid state except salad dressing, which had been there since the day I moved in), then wedged myself between my two mattresses. I was tempted to turn on the stove, but the fire often went out by itself, filling the apartment with natural gas and mercaptan.

One of the more massive pills didn't go down all the way. Instead it lodged in whatever conduit runs just under the breastplate, where it slowly dissolved, and burned like lye for most of the night.

The next day I blew off floor-buffing, as well as *Embolden!* (the day program), because I was really pretty comfortable wrapped in blankets and sandwiched between two mattresses. The stalled pill had finally been metabolized. The day program was probably closed anyway—judging by the sparkling hoar on the walls, the temperature was still dangerously low.

I dozed, comfortable and hidden. Even my alimentary processes were in slumber.

Then, with a rowdy *ktank*, the radiator went on. It hissed and groaned reassuringly.

I luxuriated. No day program. No shellacking by Murray. I wouldn't have to call Pat again. Soon the tiny skating rink in my toilet would thaw and I could send the oddment to its septic grave.

Warmth. I unwrapped myself and went to go pee.

The edges of the ice-oval had indeed begun to melt. I tried the water in the shower. A trickle! A tiny trickle, but a trickle!

I ate some gherkins and a bag of Swedish Fish for breakfast. I made a cup of instant coffee with sugar and Cremora powder, lay down on the bed, closed my eyes, and lost myself in the hiccuppy cantata of a functioning forced-oil radiator.

It began to get a little too warm, so I got up and twisted the valve at the base of the heater.

It spun freely, with no effect.

No matter; I cracked a window a quarter inch.

My apartment got warmer and warmer.

I opened all the windows that were not painted shut. I put an old fan in one of the windows and set it on HI to pull in the subzero air. I took off everything I was wearing. I took a cold shower. The radiator clanked and blew. Finally the heat forced me outside.

I stood by the sidewalk wearing a pair of shorts and a T-shirt and some thick wool socks. It was as cold as yesterday, maybe colder, but I didn't plan to stay outside long.

The radiator cranked and burped, loud as a garbage truck. Shimmering, foundry-hot air emerged from one of the windows.

Two little kids, boys or girls I couldn't tell, upholstered to the nose in quilted dark green down coats, waddled down the sidewalk across the street. They looked like hand grenades. I looked like a lifeguard in booties. They glanced my way once or twice, then faced each other. Icy, bleating giggles.

My stomach started to cramp. I needed to use my toilet. Stupid Swedish Fish. Down the road, at least ten blocks away, the Dome Restaurant glowed dully. I'd be in trouble by block six, if not before.

I paused, clenching. Sudden, awesome visions of eighteenth-century French sewers and Ex-Lax overdoses and upended Porta-Potties. At the last possible instant I raced back upstairs.

The paint was actively peeling off of the walls. The wall I shared with Rhea Donni, the neighbor who'd been living next door since her discharge from the Boll Compound in 1946, was entirely denuded—no paint remained on the slick, warping plywood. Hitherto dormant insects, evidently fooled into thoughts of spring by the sudden warmth, had emerged from their papooses or whatever and been consequently roasted crisp. Their crunchy carcasses were scattered here and there.

I ran to the toilet. I sat down on the hotplate-hot ceramic seat just in time to safely squitter the by-products of coffee, pickles, Swedish Fish, and the inactive ingredients of oral psychotropic medicines. I flushed, burning my finger on the handle. But instead of disappearing, the contents rose, as if the Devil himself were squeezing them out of Hell.

I scooped up my coat, jeans, boots, and a flannel shirt, and then ran downstairs. Something hot in the bundle of clothes I held to my chest burned my neck. My belt buckle.

I dropped my clothes outside on a little mound of hard black snow. Behind me the Onion Street Horror moaned and spat.

My clothes were at my feet, but I was still too hot to put them on. When the sweat on my neck started to rime over and crackle when I moved, I got dressed.

I wanted that Winston-with-the-filter-broken-off nicotine-and-sulfur burn in my throat more now than I could ever remember.

But Marta wouldn't have approved.

It began to get dark.

o

I had been several months away from discharge when Marta was admitted to the Boll Compound. She had come from Louisiana.

The story was that she had quit taking her Eskalith against the strident objections of her shrink in New Orleans. Marta then took off on a road trip in a rental car she did not plan to return.

Her arrest occurred on the catwalk of a Skyy vodka billboard overlooking the MassPike in the Allston-Brighton section of Boston while in a deep, buck-naked embrace with some pseudo-punk hitchhiker named Tommy whom she'd picked up somewhere near Hartford and then effortlessly and irreversibly seduced. The Massachusetts state police separated them with threats and pepper spray. Tommy climbed down from the catwalk unaided, eyes streaming and blinded shut, and Marta fell into a forsythia bush festooned with enough trash to break her fall. They stuck Marta in the Nashua Street Jail, and Tommy was committed to Taunton State for a few days before being sent home to live with Mom and Dad in some Hartford suburb.

Marta wound up at the Boll.

The first time I ever saw her, she was in one of the indoor phone booths across from the Boll smoking room, a foul box lined with asbestos furniture and buckets of sand, where I spent a great deal of my time smoking and smoking and smoking.

I had been pretending to read an article about snells in *Crappie World*—the only reading material available in the smoking room except for an old, coverless *Redbook*—but I was in fact covertly watching this new oddball patient chatter inaudibly into the phone.

She had the blackest hair I'd ever seen. Maybe even the blackest *anything* I'd ever seen—completely nonreflective across the spectrum. It was touching the floor, because she had arranged herself in an improbable and likely uncomfortable position on the tiny seat, with her legs crossed and her feet on top of the pay phone and her arms folded under her back, like a sleepy gymnast doing a shoulder stand. She stayed like that for more than an hour.

And then, with no warning, she twisted around to look through the yellowed plastic of the phone-booth door into the smoking room. She screwed up her face, pinched her nose, squawked into the phone, and laughed for five full minutes, winding locks of her supernatural hair into the helix of the phone cord.

Finally she came out of the booth, stretching. She was barely five feet tall. Snug blue sweatpants that appeared to be made of the same substance as men's dress socks rode low on her wide hips. Dust and dirt clung to the ends of her space-black hair.

She stopped and squinted for a long moment into the smoking room, where I was sitting with Buck Chalmers and Miriam Selig. Miriam had just lit the wrong end of a Doral and Buck the right end of a pipe. Marta grimaced, squawked in that peculiar way, and ran off down the hall.

Presently she returned. She had in hand a large white rectangle of plastic, which I recognized as the dry-erase board from the dining room on which the kitchen staff scribbled the menu for the day. Marta fanned it vigorously at the smoking-room trio.

"Diz! Guz! Ding! Diz! Guz! Ding!"

Then she was gone. The wind she'd stirred up ruffled my hair. The air in the venomous smoking room even cleared a little. I buried my half-finished Winston deep in the little beach of sand next to the sofa, and left.

I went to therapy later that day and asked my shrink for NicotiNo, an experimental nicotine gum engineered for hard cases and available only in a few research hospitals, including Boll. Boll always received the rawest batches of test drugs, the kinds that, if successful, were still twelve years from the market, and if unsuccessful... well, you never heard about those.

Dr. Boone was a preposterous Jungian caricature who always sat with his back to a large unshaded window during our therapy sessions, and so was only visible in silhouette. It was months before I saw him in normal lighting. He was tall, had a tombstone-shaped head, and often stuck his little finger in his ear and twisted. He loved to write prescriptions.

Dr. Boone also liked to hear about my dreams, and whether I massaged myself.

"Massage?"

"Yes."

"You can't easily massage yourself, can you?"

"No, no. Masturbate. Do you masturbate, Jerome?"

"Oh."

"Any *dreams*, Jerome?"

Lately, Dr. Boone had been trying to get me to commit to a single word that might sum me up.

"Would you say you're an *enigma*, Jerome?"

"You mean like Rasputin?"

"Yes."

"No."

I'd love to be an enigma. Brooding, poetic, dangerous, hypnotically powerful. I was none of those things.

"Perhaps you are *idealistic*."

"No."

"Perhaps you are a *rescuer*."

"No."

"Perhaps *you* might have an idea, Jerome. Perhaps consider your predominating emotional state. However, let us try to avoid words like *depressed, suicidal, tormented, sleepy, bored, lonely*."

We sat in silence for a moment, while I pondered and he screwed his ear with his pinkie.

"Homesick, I guess."

"For where? Jerome? Where do you consider home?"

Nothing came to mind. Nothing. I couldn't even coax my imagination to produce a generic architectural structure or a specific city on a map. Maybe home is the woods? Or a meadow? No, those didn't feel right. Space? No. A tidal pool? No.

"I don't think there's anywhere in particular."

However, the more I thought about it, homesickness was *precisely* my dominant feeling.

"Perhaps, then, you mean not homesickness, but nostalgia, or perhaps longing. *Sehnsucht.*"

"What?"

"Nonspecific desire accompanied by melancholia."

All of my desires were quite specific. Cigarettes. Warmth. Doritos. Love. Coffee. And—fresh to the roster—Marta.

"It really feels like a branch of homesickness," I said. "Homesick *for*, but not for any specific place. What's the word for that?"

"Perhaps there isn't one."

"So my feeling isn't common enough to have a name?"

"Do you wish to be special, Jerome? Not common?"

"I just think there should be a word."

"Then perhaps you can coin one," said Dr. Boone. "A private word, which you may use in your mind when the feeling overcomes you. 'I, Jerome, am feeling *blank*.'"

"The feeling isn't a good feeling."

"Then let us try Dagbaptogaktinublin, fifteen milligrams *bis in diem*, to start."

"I want to quit smoking, too."

"Let us try NicotiNo."

I had my last cigarette and my first dewy lozenge of nicotine gum at 7:35 that evening. I also chose that moment to begin praying that Marta would notice me. The newer, fresher, non-ashy me, the infatuated but respectful, the shy but vivid, the curious but unstalkerlike me.

She didn't notice. She was always on the phone. The message board next to the phone booths was shingled in tacked-up pink-paper messages— almost all were for Marta. Many were from Tommy.

When she wasn't inverted in the phone booth, Marta liked to crouch on her hands and knees with her nose a fraction of an inch from that day's edition of the *Boston Herald*, which she spread on the floor in the hallway that led to the crafts room. Anyone that wanted to get by her had to guess the word she was looking at; if they guessed right they had to kiss her ass, which would be stuck up in the air and elastically covered by the snug blue sweatpants she wore every day.

Those who wanted to kiss her ass of course guessed likely words: *Kennedy, snow, gridlock.* Those that didn't want to kiss her ass—or those afraid to admit the truth—did the opposite.

"Hapax."

"Wrong. You may pass."

"Pitcairn."

"Incorrect. Pass."

"Jerkoff."

"Pass."

Nobody, whatever their desires or needs, kissed her ass.

I made only two trips through the hall the week she was preoccupied with this particular safe-conduct riddle. I was terrified I'd have to kiss her ass. Kissing her ass would have been the highlight of my life, but I wouldn't have survived the elation. But I *had* to go to Advanced Pipe Cleaner class with Nurse Heinecculus or face discipline, and past Marta was the only way you could go.

"Qiviut?" I said, terrified.

"No. Pass."

Nurse H had a big dictionary on a shelf behind her desk in the crafts room. I brought it over to my workspace, and while I manipulated pipe cleaners (I'd been working on a Reign of Terror diorama, complete with crowd and guillotine and Robespierre on a tumbrel), I flipped through the appendix of "prefixes and suffixes."

After class, I stepped into the hall. There was Marta.

"Ignodomia?"

"Wrong." Then, without looking up, she said, "What's that?"

Her black hair seemed deep as a lake.

"Similar to homesick."

"Oh. Are you ignodomic?"

"Yeah."

"All I know is I'm homesick for New Orleans. You may pass."

I carefully squeezed past the guardhouse of her bottom.

Dr. Boone approached, heading in the direction I'd just come. A tiny pink and green bowtie peeked over the neck of his macadam-colored wool sweater, which shone with lanolin.

"Hello, Jerome," he said.

"Hi, Dr. Boone. Hi."

He passed me. He stopped and looked confidently down at Marta. "Ouagadougou?"

"You are correct!" shouted Marta. "Plant 'er right there!"

Marta slapped her bottom. It shook, hard muscle covered in baby fat. Her dusty sweatpants were stretched to the limit, and the cool, dark pink of her skin shined through the weave.

Dr. Boone retreated quickly without planting anything anywhere. He hurried past me, the naphthalene perfume of lanolin swirling in his wake.

I learned later that Dr. Boone was also Marta's doctor. I didn't tell Dr. Boone that I'd massaged myself imagining his kissing Marta's ass in the hallway to the crafts room while she slapped my head and hollered *Correct Correct Correct*!

One summer evening after a rain, the robotically antisocial Harry Bampfylde and I were playing UNO in one of the Activity Chambers. I chewed nicotine gum and swatted mosquitoes, while Harry drew and drew and drew, his handful of UNO cards fanning out thickly. The occasional mosquito passed through Harry's breath and perished, dropping into his ever-present tumbler of prune-ale. Harry took some psychotropic horse pill whose principal adverse effects were an uncontrollable asinine grin and insecticidal halitosis.

I'd been routing Harry all evening, because I could see his cards reflected in his glasses. I was about to shout *UNO!* again when suddenly Marta came into the room dressed in a knee-length *The Coneheads* T-shirt. She found a Twister game, untouched for decades under a pile of pastoral jigsaw puzzles and imperfect backgammon sets, and announced to Harry and me in a lusty stage whisper that she wanted to play Twister *right this minute*.

Harry immediately grew little cerise hives all over his neck and chin. He began to shake his head vigorously.

"Ohh, yes, my happy friend!" said Marta.

Marta grabbed the Twister set with one hand and Harry's ear with the other, pulling him into the center of the room. Still gripping Harry's ear, she dumped the contents of the game onto the floor.

"Serf! Spin!" she said to me. I jumped up and found the Twister spinner.

Marta squawked and laughed and radiated quintillions of sex quarks into space.

Harry was surprisingly talented at Twister. I started to worry I wouldn't get a turn with Marta. Which meant I'd have to play Harry. What if he breathed on me? What if he had a hard-on?

No problem—I would secretly manipulate the spinner. It seemed to me that Harry could not possibly do Left Foot Blue and retain his balance.

But before I could put my plan into action, Marta poked Harry in the solar plexus, causing him to collapse on her in the classic missionary position. She squawked and chortled and wrapped her legs around him and kissed his hives while he huffed and sweated, his badly pilled chamois shirt gathering up around his armpits.

At that moment, the usually staid and implacable day nurse Barb Lutz came in and screamed. She wreaked Harry with a yellow Wiffle ball bat until he rolled off Marta and bolted, the corners of his medical smile touched with something that might have been real joy.

Barb Lutz gave chase. Marta stood up, took the Twister spinner away from me, sat in my lap, and kissed me.

I had a wad of NicotiNo gum tucked back behind a wisdom tooth, which she found with her tongue and began to chew as if it were hers, while still kissing me. Then she stopped. She looked at me for a second, and then engulfed my entire nose in her mouth. Then she jumped off my lap and ran away.

The wad of NicotiNo was stuck to the end of my nose.

It turned out I wasn't special—she kissed all the nonsmokers. She also sat in laps. And pantomimed blow jobs on the finials of the group-room chairs. And escaped. And hid. She broke into doctors' offices; overturned games of Go that had been in progress for days; cried. She tipped over a fruit-juice machine and robbed it. She would leap, and, in midair, fart in a convenient face. She once shot a well-licked suction-cup arrow at Luna Kinsky, which stuck right in the center of her forehead. Luna pulled it off with a loud, cartoonlike *twop*. It left a violet, three-week hickey.

The only times I ever saw Marta sitting still were when she was reading. Peter Straub, Stephen King, Dean Koontz. And Anne Rice. Lots of Anne Rice. Homesick for New Orleans, I guess.

When she read she curled up tightly on a couch by the dining room, wearing her sweatpants, big fuzzy skull slippers, and a flannel nightgown on which she'd Magic-Markered a likeness of the Vampire Lestat.

But even then she wasn't really still. Both her knees bounced; she scratched her elbows and peeled calluses and gnawed at a wart on her palm. She twisted and pulled out her eyebrow hairs. She winced and blinked. She could interlace her toes perfectly.

I preferred short biographies and long romance novels, but I took up the horror genre myself, in case Marta and I ever had a conversation. I wanted to be able to discourse suavely and intelligently on the subject. (I would never have told Marta this, but except for *Interview with the Vampire*, which was great, Anne Rice was terrible.)

I felt that the best place to assay conversation without seeming like a lout or a stalker was the dining room, so for some weeks I took to sitting closer and closer to her, ready, willing, hoping that she'd pick me to engage in a one-eyed staring contest, or to throw ham at.

One evening in the middle of January, I armed myself with a hardcover Anne Rice novel, went to dinner early, and sat across from where Marta usually sat. I opened up to one of the many disappointing pages of *Lasher* and furtively watched for her to come in. I drank coffee, ate forty or fifty fish sticks, and pretended to read. Harry, the only other person around, had finished eating and was on his knees in the middle of the dining area trying to pick up a quarter Marta had glued to the linoleum.

The patients came and went, but Marta did not occur. I read the same paragraph a hundred times. It got late. The kitchen staff came out and scraped the deltas of uneaten spinach and beet loaf out of the big metal basins into a portable dumpster. It looked like Marta wouldn't make it to dinner. Maybe she was being disciplined for something.

I was idly watching Bert, the garbage manager, wheel the dumpster around the dining room when Dr. Khouri and Barb Lutz came into the dining room and announced to the few of us left that there'd be a special meeting in a few minutes.

"Attendance required," said Barb Lutz, staring at Harry through her yellow-tinted trifocals.

The Announcement Theater was filling up with patients and nurses and doctors, as well as a few gloomy, board-of-directors types I'd never seen before. Even the maintenance guys were there, unfolding folding chairs and placing them wherever there was room.

Everyone was seated now, except Dr. Boone. He began:

"Thanks to all for attending a special all-hospital meeting. It is with great sadness that I must tell you all that one of our residents has very suddenly and unexpectedly passed away. Marta Day was killed in an auto-mobile accident last night."

My neck and scalp went cold. Harry yelped. He had his fist at his mouth and was grinning wildly. After a moment he began to wail. A single, plangent *aah*.

Barb Lutz kneeled next to Harry and held his hand. I sat down at a lit-tle card table and shuffled the sweat-soft UNO cards. I chewed NicotiNo. The meeting was over.

Marta had snuck out and gone drinking with one of the kitchen gophers, a vindictive headbanger with beige teeth and a pillowy mullet he kept balled up under a hairnet during work hours.

Barry Miner always got off work at eight p.m., at which time he would go out to the parking lot and let his unmuffled Firebird warm up while he shed his apron and plastic shoe-bags and examined his hair in the rear-view mirror. Then he would squeal off into the evening to do whatever it was he usually did. Practice bass, deal pot, tailgate somebody, whatever.

The night before the meeting, Barry and Marta had gone out together. They'd snuck out through the kitchen. A few townspeople later said they'd seen Barry driving his Firebird with less care than usual. Marta and Barry had last been seen at Limm's, drinking Long Island iced teas and playing darts. The bartender at Limm's said Marta threw darts with less skill than anyone he had ever seen, at one point releasing a Bottelsen steel-tip during her windup, which sent it in a direction opposite to the dartboard, right at a pool player who was spared a pierced church bell by a slender pool cue that just happened to be precisely in the dart's flight path.

With that, shadows fell on dart fun at Limm's, and Barry and Marta were ejected.

Later a pumpkin farmer called 911 to report an explosion in one of his fields. Barry and Marta had crashed into a cottonwood tree. The Firebird blew up. Barry and Marta were killed and burned to ash.

o

I stood rock-still on my hillock of black snow, dying for a cigarette. One of those purely medicinal French kinds, humid, heavy as a Tootsie Roll.

It was almost dark. Behind me, my apartment shot steam out of the windows. Black flakes fell around me. Ashes.

I had dressed but was getting so cold that a trip back into the apartment was starting to look like a good idea.

I hated the outdoors. I liked being inside, under ceilings, in rooms. Sheltered. But here I was, standing between the road and the sidewalk at the mouth of a short dead-end street no one ever drove down except to dump garbage, or, once, before my time here, the lower half of a body.

After about thirty minutes of indecision, I decided to head up the road toward the Dome Restaurant.

I had just stepped off my snow hill when a blue Pontiac with its trunk held shut with a bike chain drove past me and down to the cul-de-sac, which was occupied by a ziggurat of snowplowed snow nearly twenty feet high. The car turned around and crept back toward me. It slowed and stopped.

The automatic passenger window started to roll down, but after about two inches its servo gave out and it began to make a struggling *hukn hukn hukn* sound.

"Hey?" said a girl's voice through the crack. "It's the only window that works."

I couldn't see much inside the car. But I could smell cigarettes. Not the pungent, mouthwatering sulfur and saltpeter spike of a freshly lit cigarette, but the dirt of two decades of spent ones. It was a smoking-room smell.

I squinted into the crack.

"Hi."

"I'm trying to find an address," said the voice in the Pontiac. A flash of white inside, and the sound of paper. "Um, this is Onion Street, right?"

"Yes."

"Does it start up again someplace beyond the dead end?"

"Just woods back there."

It was woods as far as I knew. And a ropy, PCB-thickened stream which in the spring churned with deformed water-boatmen.

"Oh," she said, still invisible through the three inches of open window. "So there's no 9813. No 9813 Onion."

"Not in this town. This street only runs a few blocks. Can I see your paper?"

A tiny hand illustrated with a mehndi vampire pushed a scrap out of the crack.

"I think you're looking for 98 ⅓," I said.

"Oh."

"That's my address."

"You're Jerome Coe?"

"Yes. Who are you?"

"Aren't you cold? It's fucking fourteen below."

A low, powerful *krrnk*, and all the lights on the block went out.

"Yeah."

"Is that your place?"

My apartment, lit an eerie green-orange from the inside, suddenly spit blankets and shreds of steaming mattress out of the windows.

"Yeah. It was."

"You knew Marta," said the girl.

"Yeah! You too? Oh, she was so—"

"Get in."

II

A few days later I parked the blue Pontiac in front of a big blue house on Iquem Street in New Orleans.

I inventoried my luggage (one ancient Braniff flight bag) and shook my injured hand to test the pain. Not bad. A little crunchy maybe. And the Tushies diaper I was using as a bandage needed changing—blood had seeped through in a few places and had dried black-cherry black. The long slice across my back stung from the trickles of sweat that had found their way inside, but it wasn't nearly as deep as I'd feared.

I climbed out of the car. The heat was breathtaking, and I took a deep breath of it. It reminded me of my apartment, rattling and whistling like a kettle. At least that little over-mehndied monster of a travel companion was history.

In the front yard of the big blue house was a metal desk with an orange Igloo perched on the edge. A man was sitting there, dispensing a lavender fluid into a *Little Mermaid* promotional cup. The desk, a government-issue thing, drawer-free, its paint weathered down to salt-pocked stainless steel, had clearly been a feature of the yard for a long time: blue morning glories were climbing its legs. The man himself looked like he'd been there long enough for morning-glory scouts to consider climbing him, too.

"Excuse me," I said, from the street side of the front yard's white-washed iron fence. "Is—"

"Surely it is," he said, his voice rich and musical, as though he had extra vocal cords that vibrated in harmony. "Gatorade. Cold. Want some?"

"No thanks," I said. "Is—"

"That a Huggie?" he said, gesturing at me with his *Little Mermaid* cup.

"Oh. Uh, no. Tushie. I had some bad luck."

"I bet what you *meaning* to say is that one of you lady friends stick you, probably over some *other* lady friend."

"Wow," I said, feeling a little like I'd been caught at hide-and-seek. "That's an awfully good guess."

He had lots of scars. Little and big. Knotted and old. Pink and shiny and new.

"That mean they *love* you, chief," he said. He laughed and drank some Gatorade. "But you want me to tell you something? You need to change that thing."

"I'm afraid to see what's under there."

He laughed again. I laughed, too. I felt naked, legible.

"So," I said, "is this the youth hostel?"

"Mm-hmm," he said, tipping the Igloo toward himself to get the last few drops of Gatorade carafed therein. "They about full up, though. Half of Denmark here."

Inside the hostel, just beside a pathogenic-looking couch and in front of a huge pair of barred, painted-shut French doors that led to a veranda, was a woman sitting behind a low desk of the same species as the one outside, though this one had not had its paint, a cheerless smaze gray, bullied off by the clime.

She was hunched over the desk, pulling long dirty-blond strands of hair from a plastic hairbrush. On the wall behind her was a large patch of soot, teardrop-shaped and stretching fifteen feet up to the hammered-tin ceiling.

"What happened?" I asked, nodding at the big soot drop. "Fire?"

She stopped, mid-pull, without looking up. She remained that way for three full seconds, then placed the hairbrush on the desk and raised her head.

"What's your name?"

"Jerome."

"Carolyn. Yes, a fire."

I smiled. Carolyn smiled back. A tiny dimple formed in the tip of her nose.

I hated smiling, and didn't if I could help it—I have curious teeth, and have been told my smiles are suggestive, if not downright leering. I'd practiced wholesome smiles in the mirror, but they just made me look like a cult leader.

"Eighteen bucks a night," said Carolyn, the smiling over, the fire talk over, too. "Locker key's a twenty-dollar deposit, refundable. Pillow's on the bed. Need sheets and towels?"

I did. I gave Carolyn thirty-eight dollars. I signed my name on a clipboard register she dropped in front of me with a clatter. Under ADDRESS I wrote "Massachusetts." Not very precise, but true. She looked at the clipboard register, then gave me a key to the front door, a thin stack of linens, and a short oral brochure on the dangers of the city.

"Massachusetts? Nice. Safe. But here? People like to murder each other. Last year, we were America's Murder Capital. Four hundred twenty-one killings. And it's looking like 1995 is going to repeat. Often it's a drug thing, or an unfaithfulness thing, but lots of times it's just a flaring temper. A tip: if you, as a pedestrian, get a sense that an oncoming person is about to flare their temper, just cross to the other side of the street."

"But—"

"What if there's a temper on the other sidewalk? Just walk down the middle of the street. You'll see that a lot."

"B—"

"What if there are tempers everywhere, you ask. Well. Consider acquiring one of these."

She reached into her backpack and pulled out a black object. It took my brain a moment to verify the object as a gun. She cocked it and pointed it at the acme of the soot drop.

"Okay," I whispered. There weren't many guns in Boston. Not that I ever saw, anyway. I wanted to tell her to put that thing away, but she didn't look like she stood much contrariness. She was nearly six feet tall and had long, springy muscles in her neck. She didn't look like she stood anything she didn't want to stand. And she was armed.

Then the gun was gone, returned to her backpack.

"One of the residents here got mugged in a cemetery," continued Carolyn, as though no firearm had been on precarious display. "Then, while he was in the waiting room at Charity, a lady dressed up in a nurse's uniform stabbed him in the arm with a mechanical pencil. So stay out of the cemeteries," she concluded.

"I promise," I said, trying to imagine getting stabbed with a mechanical pencil. Instinctively I brought my bad hand up to my other arm to massage the pencil wound I'd so successfully imagined.

Carolyn looked at, but did not comment on, my darkened Tushie. I hid it behind my back again. She bent over to inspect the room-vacancy chart on her desk.

"There are four beds in your room—two bunk beds—and three are taken. You're the fourth. You just filled the hostel, Mr. Jerome Coe."

She turned around. On a big world map tacked to the wall by the soot drop, she stuck a blue pin in the middle of Massachusetts, right in Quabbin Reservoir. Her hair fell in shallow waves to the middle of her back. There was a big dry oak leaf tangled up in there.

I was the only pin in the United States. About thirty other pins, all blue, were crowded into Europe, most in Denmark. There was only one other pin apart from those: in Quito, Ecuador. A pink pin.

Beneath the powerful odors of mold and sweat and magnolia blossoms, which persisted throughout the hostel, my room also had its own signature scent: a humic musk, like composting laundry.

I occupied the top bunk of the left bunk bed. The other beds were linenless and piled with sports bags, mossy bath towels, and Ziplocs filled with preening gels and disposable razors. Scattered on the floor and on the bunk under mine was a thin topsoil of European jockey shorts and funny socks that were likely the source of the paralaundry smell. There was also a selection of pornographic magazines evidently published in the low countries. One was called *Größte Pfosten* and featured on the cover a teutonic Adonis whose *Pfosten* were indeed signally *Größte*.

This was home, for now.

It was January, but the heat was astonishing. I had been issued a barf-colored blanket and a gray sheet by Carolyn at the front desk, but it was far too hot to cover up with the blanket, or even lie on it, so I folded it up and stuck it under the thin, flaccid pillow, which was really more like an oven mitt.

For a while I lay there, unable to sleep, and listened to insects bounce off the screen of the only window in the room.

These insects, I'd noticed, were on both sides of the screen: those outside seeking shelter, and those inside seeking freedom. The inside ones were numerous, biologically diverse, and loud. They scuttled and ratcheted, and occasionally dropped from the ceiling and *tk*ed on the floor like pistachio shells. I didn't want to lie directly on the "mattress," but even less appealing was the idea of insect life falling on my body, carapaces down, waving appendages and trying to flip themselves over while I slept.

So I covered myself with the sheet, tucking the ends under my feet and the top of my head and the edges under my body, to limit direct contact with the mattress, which was studded with metal buttons and randomly scaped with starchy patches.

I pulled my sheet taut. I surely looked like an overturned canoe. Louisianian creatures bounced off the fabric stretched across my open mouth. My eyes adjusted to the light coming through the sheet from the meager floodlamp in the yard of the hostel. Beings, large and small, alighted on my sheet and promenaded across it. I flicked them from underneath and listened to them land in other parts of the room.

I dreaded the arrival of my roommates. I prayed I would fall asleep before they got back from wherever they were. I didn't want to have to smile. I didn't want to listen to anyone masturbate in Danish. I wanted to lie here under my canoe and consider pink pins and nose-dimpled desk clerks with brown leaves in their hair.

Even though Carolyn had said I'd filled the hostel, there seemed to be no other inhabitants. No snoring, or music, or creaking bunk beds. Just my pistachio shells. I was alone.

So, with care not to open ingress to my canoe, I reached down and pulled off a sock, a white ribbed sports sock that I'd worn for much of my drive down here. It wasn't essential—I had another pair in my bag and two more down in the car. I slipped it over my hand like a mitten, pulled open the gap between the elastic lip of the sock and my palm, and inserted my erection (it had always been quick to recognize opportunities). Then I went silently to work in the traditional manner.

○

At a hospital near Boston, some time before I was sent to the Boll Compound, I'd been in a situation similar to the present one—in bed, in the dark, hard-on in a sock—but that time I'd had no replacement for the object sock. I had one pair, and that was it. No way to launder it afterward. But such had been the urgency of the matter at that moment that I would've sacrificed all of my clothes and my shoes and my TV privileges in order to masturbate without limitation.

In fact, the only obstacle at the time had been Tod, my roommate: I had to wait for him to drift off to sleep—a state of being, for him, evinced by somniloquy. When he finally began chattering unintelligibly about his sister and a skeleton key and something about kiddie pools, I went ahead and extravagantly ruined the sock.

The next morning I stuffed it in a Styrofoam coffee cup, put a lid on, and placed the rude parcel on a cafeteria tray to wait for the kitchen staff to carry it out of sight. Well done!

Regrets quickly gathered.

I had no visitors and no money—in short, no way to get a replacement sock. I was forced to wear my shoes with one sock, or none. My sockless shoe and foot began to smell. In votive to symmetry, I spent the other sock. Now I had two smelly feet. I could wash my feet, but not so easily the leather sneakers. After a week of an increasingly pungent tang, I asked for some baby powder at the nurse's station. I sprinkled it in both shoes. But the powder amalgamated into a gray dough, which, rather than absorbing odor, preserved it, in the manner of a pomade. Within a few days, my condition had the power to nauseate me via three channels: odor, texture, and sound. Walking with dough in one's shoes makes a pianissimo whoopee-cushion sucking noise that brought up images of open-heart surgery.

But shoes were de rigueur at this hospital, as at most.

I tried to fashion two socks from the sleeves of an expendable shirt, but I was not allowed a needle and thread to close the ends, so the "socks" kept working their way out and up my shins, like leg warmers. In an environment where body odors were common and sharp, I began to emerge as a special case. Within a few weeks, I knew, my atmosphere would awaken indignation in the other patients, some of whom had indignation that had lain dormant for years and years.

But that never happened. Instead, I was informed that I was being transferred to another facility.

"My feet?"

"No," said the informing nurse. "More doctors at the new place."

I'd been at the sock hospital for months and months and had never even been assigned a doctor—there were never enough to go around. All I'd received the whole time was that unwashable stink, like fish-gutters get. Maybe at the new place they'd give me some socks without arguing that if *I* got new socks, everybody would want new socks. You never knew—some places were more tolerable than others. In the end, though, they were all far more alike than they were different.

They transferred you in an ambulance in those days, no matter what. They didn't just stuff you in a cab or on a bus, or get a nurse to run you over to your new hospital. You had to go by ambulance.

It was cold and snowing on the day of my transfer. The wind blew, and the tiny snowflakes stung like midges. Out in the cold, my feet didn't seem to stink as badly. I guess the wind blew much of the odor away.

The inside of the ambulance was warm and calm. I climbed up and sat on the gurney, and the two EMTs climbed in behind me.

"Gotta lay down, pal."

One of them crawled up front and started the engine. The other strapped me in.

"Christ, what's that smell?"

"My feet. My shoes."

"Jesus."

We shot down the MassPike toward my new home. Me, the EMTs, and my feet.

"You got a fungus or something?" my EMT, Teddy, asked after a while.

"I don't know. Probably."

"You ought to wear socks."

"Wow, why didn't I think of that?"

"What, you don't have no socks?" said Teddy.

"No."

"Nobody to bring you some?"

"I don't know anyone around here I'd like a visit from," I said.

"You ain't from here?"

I shrugged.

"Dino!" my EMT called up front. "Get off at Allston!"

"What the fuck for?"

"Coffee!" said Teddy. "And socks!"

They stopped at a Dunkin' Donuts in Boston and bought me a sweet, hot coffee—one of the ten best cups of coffee I'd ever had. Then they stopped at a St. Vincent de Paul, and all three of us went in. They took quite a risk, letting a patient out of the ambulance.

"Get some shoes and a couple pair a socks," Teddy told me. "I got about seven bucks. Get a move on, though."

I found a pair of old steel-toed boots that appeared to be entirely odor-free, and two new pairs of wool socks in perfect condition. They were still hitched together with filaments of clear plastic, even.

"That was fast," said Teddy.

"Yeah. Thanks, Teddy."

"Shit, I did that for me, not you."

Dino was openly gawking at a punk girl by the coatrack. She was tall and had a split lip cobbled with messy black stitches. Green eyes, red hair, and dirty, fingerless white opera gloves. She was trying different army jackets on, one after another. To gauge a proper fit, apparently, she was trying them on without a shirt or bra underneath.

By this time, she had not only Dino's but also Teddy's and the proprietor's attention.

"Listen, give me thirty seconds to take a piss?" I said to Teddy.

"Yeah, okay," said Teddy, as best as he could with his jaw slack like that.

I found the bathroom just inside the storeroom, which was heaped floor to ceiling with clothes. At the end of the storeroom, behind a clothes dumpster, was a freight door, slightly ajar.

I took off through it, barefoot, my new boots and socks in a paper bag, into the snowy streets of Boston.

o

Alone, in the hostel, I carried on for a while, building pressure, getting noisier. The hostel bunk bed didn't squeak, but rather made a ducklike sound with each upstroke. After a few more minutes of accelerating vigor, I gave up trying to be quiet. The bed quacked, and now with each down-stroke released a soft *pit* sound: *pit quack pit quack pit quack pit.*

I was beholden now. Committed. If I'd been suddenly transported at that instant to the front of my seventh-grade math class, with Corey Czyz and Nadia Mundy in the front row, I wouldn't have been able to stop.

I wheezed. The sheet had worked its way off my head and feet. I cast it aside and completely gave in, bouncing on the bunk bed, chewing my biceps.

The sock worked as expected. My heart beat so hard I felt the squeez-ings of blood in my brachial arteries. It had been a real thumper.

I rolled up the sacrificial article and dropped it behind the bunk bed. The sweat on my body began to dry and cool. My eyes adjusted to the dark. Danish sports bags and dirty clothes covered the floor and the beds. The upper bunk across the room from me was piled particularly high with the burdens of travel.

But then it moved. The crap on the other upper bunk *moved.* Then it snorted, changed positions, and blew an involuntary nose-whistle. An empty oilcan of Foster's Lager fell off the bed and landed softly on the low range of shit on the floor.

I froze. I stayed frozen, listening for clues that my roommate had either been genuinely asleep or fully awake while I was busy with my massage.

Then, a gentle snore, followed by a whisper that certainly seemed like a lyric of deep sleep. Eventually I relaxed and fell asleep too.

The following morning I woke confused—spatially, temporally, psycho-logically. A ceiling two feet from my face. I was varnished with sweat, through which rose stinging welts. Somewhere below me was choral snor-ing. The air smelled like a saltworks. What the hell was going on?

I couldn't remember if I was depressed or not, if I was in the hospital or out. Had somebody died? Was I broke? In love? Lost?

I lifted up my bandaged hand. I looked down at my sockless left foot. Oh. I remember. Long drive. The Ertzes, and those *dogs.* The ice. Marta, in the sky. The cinnamon-roll bakery. My injured hand. New Orleans. Hostel. Carolyn, the desk clerk. Pink pin. Not really so depressed, come to think of it. Brokenhearted, sure, but just in a general sort of way, as always. Not flush, but not broke either. A disability check would come on the third of the month, just a week away. $92.90, available at any ATM.

And I was free—that was the main thing. Ready to start again in a place where it did not snow. Free!

Of course, I'd furiously jacked off in the presence of some Danish fellow in the deep of night—there was that.

I cautiously looked over at the other top bunk. Still piled high, but it seemed now like no one was there. I sat up and peered over. Deserted. Just a hollowed-out spot among the clothes and junk where someone might've been, now occupied by a half-empty bag of Zapp's Cajun Crawtater chips and a guide to the New Orleans cemeteries, thick with Post-it notes. Had I slept next to the unlucky stabbed guy? Dotting the crap on his bunk was a panty here and a bra there. He must have been a highly virile Dane. I hated him. I was glad he was gone. Maybe he got mugged again, while pursuing innocent virgins.

On the lower bunks, however, were two men. The man beneath my bunk was huge. The man on the other lower bunk was barely half his size. Their mattresses had been laid bare—the absurd European Dopp kits and wooly towels and laundry boluses that had so densely populated them had been swept off without concern into the middle of the room. Both men were naked except for tight, bright yellow briefs. The men were facedown and white as aluminum siding, except for their necks, which were scarves of angry vermilion. I wouldn't have been able to sleep with a sunburn like that unless I was full of lager, which they apparently were, since the lager cans all over the room were empty. The lager had to be someplace, and logic suggested it was in these two men.

I slid off the top bunk and attempted to leap quietly to the floor, but somehow I hooked a toe in the string anchorage of one of the little metal mattress buttons. I landed headfirst in the sodden belongings of my roommates, neither of who awakened or even stirred. An inch from my nose were the *Pfosten* of Werner Eidotter, the *Größte Pfosten* cover model.

I got dressed. My eye hurt where I'd hit it on a roommate's weird plastic shoe. My toe hurt from being snarled in powerful string. And my bad hand still hurt, too.

It was light out, but I had no idea what time it was. Downstairs in the lobby, the clock said 5:45, but it could have been morning or evening. I guessed morning—the look on Carolyn's face was certainly one of someone at the end of a double shift.

"Still here?" I said, with a familiarity I hoped she would return.

"Yeah," she said, with only a couple PPM of familiarity. "Thirty hours and counting. I'm usually five p.m. to five a.m., but my relief did not relieve me."

"Jeez," I said, looking at the clock again. "It's quarter to six in the *evening?*"

"Looks like you slept for twenty-four hours."

Carolyn piled her hair on top of her head so she could scratch vigorously at an itch on the back of her neck. In the process she smudged the charred spot on the wall behind her with an elbow.

"So," I said, leaning on the steel desk as if I were a kindly barkeep. "I'm curious. What caused the fire?"

"Lighter."

"Wow. Accident?"

Carolyn said nothing. Instead, she closed her eyes and opened her mouth, obviously preparing to sneeze. But, an instant before its climax, she suppressed it, so that the only sound she made was a feeble *sqwnch*. Much tearing of the eyes followed.

"Bless you. I wish I could do that."

"Practice."

"Okay," I said, as if she'd given me a command rather than an explanation. She might have. An arcane silence followed. I studied my feet. I was wearing brand-new socks, because my other pair had been half-ruined. A florid blush, starting at my solar plexus, rose like carbonated jam to my scalp, stopping at my right eyeball socket to throb.

"Been in a fight with your roommates already, have you?" asked Carolyn, observing the throb.

"Oh, no. I'm not a fighter. I'm a fleer. I fell out of bed. On my eye."

She quickly consulted her laminated sleeping arrangement chart. "You fell out of the upper berth?"

"Well, I jumped. But I got caught on something on the way down."

"You look like you get caught on things a lot," she said, nodding at my bandaged hand.

"Oh, this one wasn't my fault," I said, and it hadn't been. I hid my hand behind me.

"What about that dent in your head?" she challenged, eyes brightening.

I did in fact have a dent in the side of my head. Rather, a hollow, or a lowland, I chose to think. That *had* been my fault.

"Never mind, sorry, not my business, don't mean to pry," she said, holding up both palms as if to shield herself from any personal facts I might issue.

"I'm hungry," I said, like a kitten in an illustrated children's book.

"Then by all means, feed! Monstrelet's. Walking?"

"Yeah."

"Ask Batiste how to get there. The guy in the yard. He owns the hostel. And remember, while you're walking, keep your hands—hand—out of your pocket and run if you feel threatened and don't go down Doyle and don't forget to cross the street if approached by a temperamental sort."

"Okay."

"And change that fucking diaper."

On the way to Monstrelet's I stopped in a bookshop that sold autographed Anne Rice books. I thought about getting one inscribed to Marta, with the idea of solemnly burning or burying it.

"Thirty-two hundred," said the affable guy behind the counter. "For personally inscribed copies of *Mummy* or *Queen*. Anne no longer signs *Lestat* or *Interview*."

"Can I bring in my own copy for her to sign?"

He laughed heartily.

"Oh, no. No, no. Got to buy the books here, in the shop."

Instead I bought a pocket-size Cajun-English dictionary and a plastic-coated map, and continued on to Monstrelet's.

In the un-air-conditioned diner, at my sticky, wobbly table, I sweated freely, but so did everyone else—a mixture of locals, Tulane students, aggressive hipsters, and tall, slouchy waitresses with war-dead stares and sloppy, crooked mouths. There was a group of uniformed Catholic-school girls smoking, drinking coffee, and exchanging cruel stares with the slouchy waitresses, who might have been their older sisters, alumnae of the same school. Everyone sweated like actors in a John Cassavetes movie. Shirts stuck to backbones, armpits radiated tidal rings, crossed legs slid oilily over one another, every square inch of décolletage glistened. An occasional yelp could be heard when a drop of sweat rolled suddenly down the forehead and into the eye. My horrible hand, which I kept under the table, steamed in its diaper. Maybe I should've followed Carolyn's order and changed it, but I really didn't want to see what was under there.

A waitress appeared.

"Four cinnamon rolls, please," I said. It was what I'd been jonesing for more than anything else since Tommy and I had parted ways in Alabama.

"They're big," said the waitress.

"Okay."

My waitress, after placing my order, embarked on a break. She sat alone at a booth in the back corner and began to work a crossword. Occasionally she pushed wet tongues of black hair off her cheekbones.

She reminded me of something—a thing so recent that it felt like déjà vu. Quarterways through a cinnamon roll as big as a tournament Frisbee, I suddenly realized what seemed so familiar: she resembled, uncannily, those heavy, wet, lascivious flowers that were growing out from under the iron fences and lolling like whores along the buckled sidewalks I'd traveled on my nine-block journey to Monstrelet's from the hostel.

My waitress stabbed at the crossword with her ink pen. She lit a cigarette, blew a perfect torus of smoke, winked at a large round man with a hectare of red beard, filled in another crossword answer, then yawned, dropped her cigarette in a coffee cup, lay down on the long seat, and went to sleep.

The whole diner seemed lulled by her catnap. I noticed for the first time that the symptoms of withdrawal from all my psych meds had almost completely disappeared. I would never take them again. I would never put myself in a position where I might be prescribed them, ever again. That shit was *over*.

This city just might be the right place. A place where the lethal, frosted past can't cross the Huey P. Long Bridge. All at once I felt the possibility of relations without obsession, friends without fear, adventure without danger, sex without agony. Craziness without insanity. Love without rescue. I felt able. I felt home.

Then, another feeling, far dearer: I needed to know where the bathroom was.

I stood up. My waitress woke at the same instant and looked at me. Without my saying anything, she pointed to the trafficky entrance to the kitchen.

"Through there," she said. "Watch your step."

In the kitchen a vast short-order cook was smoking and rolling sausages on a grill while a scrum of slouchy waitresses wheeled around him, picking toast out of toasters and forks out of baskets. The floor was positively frictionless from condensed grease and humidity. No one paid any attention to me as I cut through.

In the tiny bathroom I sat, got comfortable, and opened up my little plastic folding map. I decided I'd later go buy three colors of Sharpie felt pens at the K & B drugstore I saw on my walk over here. Red, black, and blue. I'd make a little dot with a Sharpie on my map for every bathroom I found in New Orleans. Red dots would denote the worst bathrooms, the don't-use-except-in-an-emergency shitclosets; blue dots would mark the average fast-food-restaurant facility; and black dots would indicate spotless, leisurely suites.

I was sitting in a definite blue. Fairly clean, as long as you declined closer inspection of any surface or its fissures. Fanny ribbon was in bounty, but it was about as soft as emery paper. The toilet itself was a slight product, designed for occasional domestic use only. It had no place in the big leagues. At least there was a plunger.

I pored over my map for a promising part of town to dump the goddam Pontiac. I didn't really need a car in New Orleans, and I sure had no attachment to this particular shitwagon. Besides, it wasn't mine, and I did not like to think about the trouble I could get in for driving it.

There was a spot on the map that had a bunch of railroad tracks crossing each other. From TV, I knew that convergences of railroad tracks meant hobos and loitering and abandoned cars. I'd drive the car over there, file the engine numbers off, leave the keys in plain sight, and then take a nice leisurely stroll home, breathing in the delivering heat and the musk of the whoring flowers along the way.

o

"Is it really minus fourteen degrees?" I asked the girl with the mehndi vampire on her hand, while I hunted around for the seat belt in her car.

"Give or take," she said tonelessly.

Behind us my apartment glowed like a kiln. Then, the big meow of a fire-engine siren.

"Oh well," I said, finally finding my seat belt. "Hope you don't mind if I ride around with you until I figure out a place to live! Ha ha!"

"I don't care," she said, still toneless, as though she'd never learned how to inflect. "Where can we eat? Drive-thru only. Way too fucking cold to get out of the car."

"McDonald's is all there is," I said, unsure of how to be with this person. "The old Burger King got shut down by OSHA. Norwegian rats."

"Direct me. I'm not from here."

I noticed the dome light was on. She noticed that I noticed.

"Won't go out when the car's on," she said.

"Go left at that pile of snow with the shopping cart stuck in it."

"I hate that shit," she said. "Marta loved it."

"Shopping?"

The girl turned my way as though she'd just realized she wasn't alone. She stared, maybe auditing me for clues to my nature. She was small and round, but her face was thin. Her upper and lower lips mirrored perfectly each other's gibbous shape and raw-tuna cast. Her head was recently shaved but growing out, the roots brownish, the ends blond, almost clear, probably from a powerful oxygen bleaching. Below the stubble, barely visible, was a tattoo of a Celtic knot.

"Snow, man."

"Oh," I said. "I didn't know her all that well."

"She ever mention me?"

"Who are you?"

"She never mentioned her best friend?"

She turned and looked at me again, hard, as if she was expecting a lie.

"I don't know," I said. "I never talked to her that much. She told me once she was homesick for New Orleans. Bear left at that big pile of snow."

"Really. And what else did you talk about, down there at the Boll Compound."

She stared intently, the surfaces of her little brown eyes disconcertingly dry. Her eyelashes, illuminated by the dome light, reminded me of Venus flytraps. She wasn't watching the road as carefully as I would've liked. I hadn't expected interrogation, antagonism. I had a few questions of my own. Marta had been my friend, too, sort of. We'd *kissed*.

"Not much, really," I said, crossing my arms, feeling defensive and protective of Marta. "How did you know that I knew her?"

"She might've mentioned you."

"Me? Really?"

"She said she thought you might've had a little crush on her. Read the same Anne Rice books she did. She thought you might've even quit smoking to impress her."

Wow!

"Ho," she said, again looking at me instead of the road. "Looks like you *were* crushing. You're red as a human lung."

"Everybody liked her," I said. "Everyone at Boll. And everywhere else, too, apparently—she was on the phone all day."

"All day?" she said, drawing her lips back from her teeth, which were slick dun pebbles. "With who?"

"She got tons of messages. Most of them were from Tommy, Tommy, Tommy, who was this hitch—"

"What do you mean 'most'? Who were the other messages from? And what the fuck were you doing looking through her private shit?"

She squeezed the steering wheel with a small, pawlike hand, stretching the intricate henna vampire.

I was suddenly scared. This girl was between me and the black cold, the kind of cold that would turn a spray of hot water to snow before it hit the ground. The kind that freezes the hairs in your nostrils. And beyond the cold was my uninhabitable apartment. I had nowhere to go. I was officially homeless. Boll wouldn't take me back—they had discharged me because they needed the room for other disturbees. They had a goddam *waiting* list. The idea of getting sent somewhere else was even worse than living outside: state psychiatric hospitals were the only places where I felt trapped and homeless at the same time.

"I would never look through her stuff," I said, backing off. "They tack the messages up on the board. So everyone can see."

"Oh."

She relaxed.

"It's just past that big pile of snow."

"Yeah, thanks, I can see the giant fucking yellow *M*."

She stopped at the McDonald's intercom and cracked her window just enough to yell out her order.

"Big Mac, do not put onions on it, please, do not get an onion any-where near it, please, big Sprite, big fry, apple pie, big coffee. Annnd... hold on." She looked at me. "What do you want?"

"I'm all right," I said, feeling cheap and lost.

"What, no money?" said my companion. "I'm not eating alone. I'll pay. Hurry."

"I guess I'll have a small french fries."

"Jesus," said the girl.

I wanted to go home.

"McNugget Happy Meal, Sprite," she shouted at the intercom.

At the drive-up window, she slipped a twenty through the car-window crack. The clerk had to reach out to get it. When the food came, my com-panion opened the car door for an instant and snatched everything at once.

"Here," she said, handing me my Happy Meal as we drove off. "Eat."

My fries were brown and soft, and formed not discrete fried-potato quanta but rather a homogenous, cooling mound. My McNuggets were stretchy. My Sprite was Diet.

My companion and I looked at each other's food, and then at each other.

"Who *are* you?"

"Tommy, you idiot," said Tommy, her mouth stuffed with Big Mac.

"Oh," I said, feeling simple, small, tired, alone. "I—what do you want exactly? From me?"

"Well, Jerome, I do in fact have a very specific request."

"What?"

"I want you to go to New Orleans with me. A pilgrimage to Marta's birthplace."

I hadn't been expecting that.

"I'm kinda broke."

I was. I always spent all my extra floor-buffing pay on paperbacks.

"Figured. But I'm not."

"Why me? You don't even seem to like me a whole lot."

"I don't want to go by myself, and I need somebody to share the driving. You're the only Boller I could find."

"When are—?"

"Now. Well, shortly. After you tell me where motherfucking Farm-to-Market Road 1199 is."

"Wait! Now? Really?"

"Yeah, now. What, you want to go home and pack?"

She giggled. It sounded like a small breed of dog sneezing. I didn't say anything.

"So," she said. "You going to tell me where 1199 is?"

"Uh. Well, I guess that's kind of an east–west road, we probably should get on US 7 South in order to—"

"You want me to drop you off someplace?"

"Huh? Uh, I, well, there's—"

"You have nowhere to go, do you?"

Tommy and I headed in a general northwesterly direction along 1199. The roads were deserted.

"I don't think we're heading south," I said.

"The first stop on our pilgrimage is local. I want to see her cotton-wood tree."

It took me a moment to figure it out. She meant the one Marta'd hit.

"Are you sure you want to see that? I'm not sure I want to."

She ignored me. She leaned over the steering wheel and squinted at the dark road. Fields surrounded us. We drove up and down shallow hills. Every so often a tree, marking the corner of a property, appeared in the headlights. Tommy would slow, then stop, then study the tree, her chin on the steering wheel. After a few moments she would drive on until another tree appeared.

"They all look the same in the dark."

"Hey, I might need a restroom soon," I said.

"You couldn't go at Mickey D's?"

"I didn't have to go then," I said. Stupid Happy Meal french-fry burial mound. Stupid nuggets.

It was warm in the Pontiac. The heat had been on full since we'd started out. I'd been sitting cross-legged on the bench seat, my boots off, my wool-socked feet snugly tucked into the crooks of my knees. Climatically speaking, I was as comfortable as I'd been since this morning, during the brief hour between winter and summer in my apartment, when I'd been wrapped in blankets and comforters and wedged between my mattresses.

But digestively speaking, I was having some discomfort. A sound like an unclogging drain tremoloed in my gut. If I had to, I'd go in the snow, but I'd rather not. I'd really rather not.

"Maybe we can just run back to that Price Chopper?" I said. "They're open all night. They have a bathroom I could use."

"I can hold it for hours," said Tommy, conversationally. "Days. Can't you piss in the snow? There's nobody around. I won't watch."

"I think I need a bathroom. It's sort of a little problem I've kind of got. Please take me to Price Chopper?"

"Oh, Jerome. I see. Number two. Why, the snow won't know the difference."

"Your front seat might," I said, feebly. "Come on, Tommy, I'll be quick. I'll buy you a Sprite while I'm there. I could sure use one myself."

"I've had plenty of Sprite," said Tommy. "Hey, does that look like a cottonwood?"

She slowed the car on the deserted road. She pointed the headlights at a tree, and stopped.

The tree shone like aluminum in the headlights. The cooling engine *ik-ik-ik*ed.

Long strips of bark had peeled off, like the skin of a flayed martyr, the bone and muscle of bare wood underneath streaked white and yellow and gray. A single broken branch, blackened and twigless, stuck out from the snow cover by the trunk. About ten feet up the trunk was the branch's charred stump.

"How can a tree survive that?" said Tommy.

"It's such a little tree," I said.

We watched the tree for a while. My breath condensed into wisps.

"Can you turn the car back on? I'm freezing."

"I want to make a descanso," said Tommy.

"A what?"

"You don't know what a descanso is?"

"No. Make whatever you want. Just please turn the car on. Please."

"You know those little crosses with wreaths or drawings you see along the side of the road sometimes?"

"That's what those're called?"

"Help me make one," said Tommy.

"You'll never be able to stick it in the ground."

"C'mon. Then I'll take you to Price Chopper."

Tommy climbed into the backseat, which was full of junk. Clothes, car fix-it stuff, brittle plastic rope. A huge dictionary, nearly cubic. A wooden clog. But mostly clothes.

I reached back to hunt through the mountain of old laundry. Deep inside, it was warm. I left my hands in there, pretending to look for descanso ingredients.

"Ah!" said Tommy. "I think I found the perfect thing."

She pulled up a crowbar/lug-nut wrench—a perfect cross, with one end sharpened. She also pulled up an old blue scarf, covered in salt and mud, from a decade's worth of dirty winter boots crushing it into the floor mat.

Tommy wove the long scarf under and over the crossed bars.

"Come on," she said. "And bring that big shoe."

As cold as it was inside, it was nothing compared to the interstellar vacuum outside by the maimed tree. The air was motionless. Even my plumbing slowed. In a way, it was pleasant. My shoulders and ankles relaxed. Sleep begged. Just lie on top of the glass-hard snow and

"Help me, man!"

I jumped. The cold hit. My guts started to knot.

"Stand it up," she said.

I did what I was told, though I knew the ground was as tough as a safe.

"Fuck, hold it steady, Jerome. Jesus."

Be quiet, quiet.

With the wooden clog she sledged at the wrench again and again. I held the iron cross as steadily as I could, but it didn't pierce the ground. It didn't even *scratch* the ground.

Tommy paused, then threw the shoe into the dark.

"Lean the crowbar against the tree," she said.

I did. Tommy turned to go get back into the car. On the spur of the moment, I took my belt off and wrapped it under and over the arms of the wrench. I jogged back and jumped into the car. Tommy started the engine as I shut my door.

"Wow, we better go, I can't hold it much l—"

"Shh," she said. "A moment of silence."

She rested her forehead on the steering wheel. Then she slowly raised her head and stared out at the tree.

"What," she said, "is that?"

"What?"

"On my descanso. Is that a belt? Is that your *belt*?"

"Yeah, I—"

"Go take it off."

"Why?"

"Take it off."

"Well, no. I want it there."

"It's corrupting my memory of Marta, so go fucking take it off."

"I could say that your crusty scarf is corrupting *my* memory, but I didn't. Besides, you said you'd take me—"

"Get out. Outta my car."

In her tiny mehndied hand she held one of those big barrettes you see in the hair aisles of drugstores.

"What?"

"Get on it, Jerome. The big road trip's off. Out in the snow with you, my friend."

"Are you kidding? This is nowhere!"

She had just told me get out the car on the coldest night since the nineteenth century, and for some reason was also squeezing a big barrette.

She peeled her teeth like a ferret. A confetti of brown lettuce was stuck between a canine and a molar. She leaned into me and hissed in my face. She struck at me with the barrette, which I deflected with my hand.

"Jesus! Okayokayokay! You're fucking crazy! You psycho! You don't have to hit me!"

She hissed again, in a tone that humans can't easily make. Only aliens and ghouls.

I scratched and tore at the door handle until it opened and I fell into the road. She drove off with the door swinging. The taillights disappeared over one of the hundred million low, frozen hills.

I screamed once, but the silence of the emptiness after the scream died out was so spooky I didn't do it again. I stood in the silence for a moment, waiting for my eyes to accustom themselves to the darkness. Soon the snow cover became visible, and then Marta's tree. An ancient stone property fence led up a hill, and behind me I could see a black shape, maybe a barn or a stand of trees, far away. I hoped it was a barn.

The only sound was the occasional pistol-crack of the brittle snow cover.

But soon I became aware of another sound. Taps. Little hollow taps, like BBs falling on a dinner plate.

On the snow cover, small, hard, black teardrop-shaped objects, hundreds and hundreds, bounced and tumbled and rolled away from me and down into a depression in the snow at the foot of Marta's tree by the descanso, where they came to rest.

They were coming from my hand.

An extra finger, below my pinkie, had grown out of the side of my palm. It gently curved, like a frond of an aloe plant. The little black objects were jumping out of it. Oh good, I was having a psychotic break, too. Why not go crazy, right? This was the perfect time for a neuropsychiatric light show! Why not die hallucinating strews of magic beans shooting out of my hand!

Oh, I see. Not beans. Blood. Drops, freezing hard before they hit the ground.

That strange barrette, she did something dastardly, something magic with it. A conjure. Blood dripped and hopped. The accumulation of black blood pellets was deepening. I was losing a lot of blood.

Hands are very vascular, I remembered a doctor once saying.

I lost control of my insides.

Then Marta appeared, a delicate, shimmering lacewing-green, hovering over the cottonwood tree.

Above her head spewed a white ribbon that after a moment settled gently into a bubble. A comic-strip thought bubble. It was my brain's preferred method of announcing that it was about to acquit me of sanity.

Inside the bubble, hundreds of Scrabble tiles, letter-sides down, materialized.

Three flipped over.

SIT

I did. More tiles flipped over and arranged themselves at the bottom of the bubble.

A MOTHER BIRD SAT ON HER EGG

I remembered this one. P. D. Eastman. Kitten, cow, steam shovel.

THE EGG JUMPED

"I'd rather not sit through this thing," I told Marta. "I've heard it like, a million times."

OH OH

o

After my meal at Monstrelet's, I walked quickly back to the hostel and started up Tommy's car, my plastic map up on the dashboard.

The railroad switching yard turned out to be as menacing and deserted as I'd hoped. I parked and lifted the hood. I had no idea where the engine numbers were, and truthfully I wasn't even sure what part the engine was, though I assumed it was the big thing in the middle with the tubes and cables coming out. I saw no numbers on it, though, and in any case I didn't have a file, so I shut the hood, looked one last time in the car, rescued the rest of the Tushies from the floor of the passenger side, and left the keys in the ignition. I turned to head back to the hostel.

Soon I was lost. My map proved useless, as many of the streets had had their signs stolen, or perhaps had never had signs, or even names, in the first place.

I sat down on an anonymous corner and squinted at my plastic map, angling it this way and that so I could read it in the growing dark.

"Fuck this," I announced to the deserted corner. I stood up, kicked at nothing in particular, and then hurt my injured hand trying to wad up the plastic map, which merely sprung back into shape. Inside my Tushie, fresh warmth and a marrow-deep ache.

"And fuck this."

I stood up and headed toward the brightest horizon.

Street after street of dark houses, wishy-washy streetlights, and inert cars with cracked windshields. The glow on the horizon that I figured was the French Quarter did not seem to get brighter.

A working streetlight. I paused and examined my bandage. A bright new spot, moist and Kremlin red. I *must* change this, I thought, no matter how terrified I was to see just how badly Tommy had cut me.

The phone pole that held the streetlight had two signs, neither legible. I reached for my map.

The streetlight went out with a *ptch* and a modest display of sparks.

"Dammit."

Down the street was the light of a diner.

The glass door to the Smart Harriet Food Restaurant jangled when I opened it. I stood just inside the door for a moment as the jangling subsided. The restaurant was almost silent, unlike the strident din of Monstrelet's. It was—also unlike Monstrelet's—air-conditioned, unhip, and lit as bright as a dentist's office.

I sat down in the first booth, which had tall, green-vinyl seats and Formica tables, their designs worn away by hundreds of thousands of sliding coffee cups and plates of pancakes.

I pulled a laminated menu from between a crusty bottle of Crystal hot sauce and a labelless jar of small pickled ovoids of some kind. Apparently a decision-maker at the Smart Harriet had decided to change the menu, and had penciled the new selections on strips of masking tape stuck over the decedent items. I peeled up a piece of tape that said FACON 2 PCS; under it was BACON 15 STRPS.

A voice said: "Ioanna, what's this 'fassone'?"

"That's 'Facon,' with a long *a* and a hard *c*, Coryate," answered another voice—Ioanna's, I supposed. "It's a portmanteau of 'fake' and 'bacon.'"

"Oh."

"Want some?"

"No I do not."

I leaned out of my booth. A small man in a corduroy sports coat sat at the counter, studying the menu intently. His feet didn't reach the floor. His trouser cuffs didn't reach his feet. I couldn't see his face, but a tight, dense, black buzz cut stuck to his skull like iron filings.

"So no more bacon?" said Coryate.

"No more bacon," said Ioanna, who was visible on her hands and knees under a table, apparently dewobbling it by wedging a pocket calculator under one of the feet. "I'm experimenting with healthier fare."

"Well, what's this here 'veggie beans and rice'? Beans're vegetables and rice is vegetables where I come from, and that's Lake Charles, USA, by God."

"And they're vegetables here, too," said Ioanna. "They're just not cooked in bacon grease and mixed with sausage."

"I'm concerned about the wording here," said Coryate. "Beans and rice is vegetables, so why put 'veggie' up front like that? That don't make it healthy."

"The 'beans and rice' in 'veggie beans and rice' refers to the dish, not its vegetable components," said Ioanna, crawling out from under the now-stabilized table. "'Veggie' qualifies said dish, which is made with lard and soy paste rather than grease."

"Grease counts toward meat?"

"Well, it's not a vegetable."

"Neither is feldspar, or hydrated silica," said Coryate.

Ioanna appeared at my booth with a plastic glass of iceless water in one hand and a cup of coffee in the other, both of which she held by their rims with two fingers. She had freckles on her arms that disappeared under the short sleeves of a loose black blouse with tiny pearl buttons, and reappeared in greater numbers on her collarbone. She leaned over and placed the coffee and water in front of me.

I accidentally bumped the table. Both the coffee and water spilled. They commingled, forming a muddy little river that made its way slowly to the edge of the table.

"Another one?" said Ioanna. "I'll fix it for you. Don't move."

She got down on her knees and crawled under the table.

"Don't expect anything," shouted Coryate, turning around for the first time.

His face and hands were randomly smeared black, as though he'd been in a charcoal-briquette fight. He wore a long, millimeter-thin mustache that seemed to function as a plinth for his nose, an oily bulb that appeared to be pulling all of his other features toward it. His iron-shard hairline stopped low on his forehead and his ears stuck out like shutters in the wind, threatening to slam shut over his eardrums.

"Ignore him," said Ioanna from under the table. She hammered at some-thing, presumably another defunct calculator. My refreshments jumped. "You need to change that bandage."

She came out from under the table.

"I guess I'll have some pancakes and some Facon, please. And some biscuits."

"Is that a diaper? I spy Velcro strips."

She was younger than I'd thought at first, maybe forty-five. Her brown hair was tied up in a utilitarian bun. Now I could see there were also tiny freckles that climbed over her collarbone and up her neck to pool on her cheekbones. One of her earlobes had a healing cut, as if an earring had been torn out.

"Say, is there a phone I could use?"

"Only blood from a fairly serious injury would soak through a commercial disposable diaper like that."

I kept my hand under the table.

Coryate and his oily bulb came over.

"What injury?" he said. "Come on, let's see it, son."

I was trapped. I sighed, and put my hand on the table.

"You ought to run over by Charity and get one of them emergency-room people to change that," he said.

"Don't like doctors," I said, sounding like a wet piccolo.

"Come with me," said Ioanna.

"Ah, uh," I said.

"Coryate, stay out here."

She turned around and headed to the back of the Smart Harriet. On the way she shouted into the kitchen.

"Facon, cakes, biscuits!"

A practiced snarl and a crash came from deep within. Ioanna turned back and glared at me.

"Come," she said, pointing at the restroom.

She sat me down on the lid of a toilet and balanced a cafeteria tray across my knees.

"Hand on the tray."

I obeyed. Ioanna kneeled in front of me on a dishcloth. She had several more in her lap. Next to my hand was a mess of first-aid supplies: iodine, cotton balls, tequila, Band-Aids, paring knife.

"Sit still."

Ioanna peeled the Velcro, a long, careful *rrrt*. She unwrapped the diaper until the dried blood held it fast. She eased the paring knife between two layers and sliced it open like a catfish.

"I don't want to see it," I said.

"Have a little tequila."

"Is there a worm?"

"No, it's an uncommon bottle of tequila that has a worm these days. This is a drugstore-bought spirit, purely functional."

I had some. She pulled firmly but carefully on the diaper, like it was a weed whose roots might break off and remain stuck in the ground. In my hand something gave, a stubborn bottle cap finally yielding. Then the familiar, almost comfortable, almost urinary warmth of freed blood.

The diaper came loose. Before I shut my eyes I caught a glimpse of the contrast of my moist, bleached-gray palm with the butcher-shop pinks and marbled reds of my sliced and crushed and reopened hand.

Vinegary fluids.

"You need a doctor."

"It doesn't hurt."

"Should. That's why you need one."

Then the dry, slightly abrasive touch of gauze, getting tighter as she wrapped it around my hand. I opened my eyes. Blood was leaching along the mesh of cotton fibers as quickly as she could wrap. A shallow pond of thin blood, spiraled with peroxide and iodine, had collected at a corner of the tray.

Coryate came in. He had a coffee cup in his hand.

Ioanna turned around.

"Damnation. Did I tell you to stay out of here or did I just say it in my head?"

"But I need a cup of coffee, dammit. All the pots are empty, and I don't feel like waiting for you to finish playing doctor."

"Get out."

"You can have mine," I said, taking a sip of tequila.

"Hum. Okay. Thanks."

"Sure."

"Hurry it up anyway, woman," said Coryate. "This fellah's cup won't hold me long."

"Get out, you mosquito."

Coryate did not. Instead he unzipped and took a long, noisy piss in a urinal behind Ioanna. Then he left.

"You can come back and have pancakes and Facon and biscuits," said Ioanna, "*after* you see a doctor and get that mess cleaned and sewn back up. Now go."

"I don't really know where I am. I'm not from here."

"Where do you stay?"

"A youth hostel. On Iquem Street."

"A fair distance. Is there somebody there can come fetch you?"

I thought about it.

"Well, yes. I think so."

An hour later Carolyn pulled up in an old brown Chrysler—her mother's, I learned later—and came inside.

"Can't make a habit of this, Jerome," she said, looking completely wiped out.

"Sorry."

I wasn't a bit sorry. I was delighted. I liked Carolyn, though I wasn't sure how, yet.

Ioanna—whom I also liked, though I wasn't sure in what way either, except that it felt filial—did not acknowledge Carolyn.

"C'mon, Jerome."

Carolyn headed for the door. The leaf was still in her hair, an inch or two lower.

"Come back sometime, Mr. Jerome," said Ioanna.

She never asked what had happened to me.

Carolyn was quiet on the ride back.

The floor of the passenger seat was deeply hidden by what felt underfoot like books and papers and shoes and tennis balls.

"Sorry about all the crap," she said, when we were almost back to the hostel. "I'll clean it out one day. I think there's a five in there somewhere."

As though I were drawing for a raffle, I reached into the mess and pulled out a random object. It proved to be a small hardcover book, sans dust jacket. I squinted and angled, but couldn't read the title page in the dark.

"Put that back," she said suddenly. She snatched the book away just as we were driving under a bright streetlight, and I caught one gilt word on the spine.

Shuffle.

"Sorry," I said.

She skyhooked the book over her shoulder into the backseat. This sure beat driving around with Tommy. Who, officially, no longer mattered—my last connection to her was parked in a dead zone, waiting for a new owner.

Carolyn and I drove on in silence. Not an uncomfortable silence, like we'd shared earlier that day, but rather a tranquillity, a peace de luxe of the sort that comes from the *kensho* that you're not alone.

I never did go to the doctor. But I did take Ioanna up on her invitation to come back and visit. Indeed, I went to the Smart Harriet nearly every day, a new bandage on my hand which I'd wound myself over the sink, eyes closed, in the moldy, slick bathroom of the hostel.

"How's the mitt?" said Ioanna one afternoon, skidding a plate of pancakes across the table.

"Getting better every day," I said, a falsehood. It didn't look like it was healing well at all.

"Mm."

"Ioanna, will you hire me on here? I'll wash dishes, mop, whatever you want. I can make good grilled cheese sandwiches."

Ioanna looked me over for a moment.

"Harriet will say no."

"There really is a Smart Harriet?"

"There is," she said. "You wouldn't like it here, anyway."

"You seem like you like it here."

"I was born here. I was born a waitress, and I'll stay one, like it or not. But listen. I know a woman who might take you. I'll telephone her and let her know you might stop by, and that you make outstanding cheese sandwiches."

Ioanna scribbled something on a green diner bill and handed it to me.

MRS. (NOT MISS) HEBERT AT ERRIL'S FASHION DEPARTMENT STORE.
PRACTICE GRILLING BEFORE YOU GO.

o

After I slipped away from Teddy and Dino at the St. Vincent de Paul and into the Boston winter that day, I ran twenty zigzag blocks barefoot until I was far enough removed from the possibility of recapture to pause in an alley and put on my new boots and socks. I couldn't feel my feet. I washed them in the snow. There were cuts and smears of blood on the soles, but nothing serious. I dried them on the lining of my jacket. I put on my new socks, both pairs, and then the boots. My hands were so numb I couldn't tie the laces. I left them alone, long black streaks like ink squirted in the snow.

I looked around. I was behind a bar or liquor store—crates of empty pint bottles of Knickerbocker beer were stacked by a service door. I stood up. The thrill of unexpected freedom was starting to evaporate; it was quickly being replaced with the dread of an uncertain future in the hostile outdoors of a part of town I didn't know well at all. I was also penniless.

I walked, inland, keeping the harbor wind at my back.

The landmarks became more and more frequent. Ah, there was Grippick Manse, my old halfway house. And there: the L-Bo Room!

Months and months earlier, I'd become infatuated with a bartender who worked at my neighborhood tavern, Duke's L-Bo Room. Leigh Marrat, the bartender, was reputed to like only dangerous men, bad boys, and in accord with this reputation, was in possession of an abnormally undersized but still awfully scary boyfriend, Bill Izzoli, who'd robbed more than two hundred and fifty liquor stores from here to Poughkeepsie, or so he claimed. Eventually, Bill discovered my infatuation, addressed it, and that was the end of that.

I remembered where Leigh lived, so I headed that way. Besides, she was the only person in the whole city I cared to see. I prayed she still lived there. And I prayed with reverence that she wasn't seeing Bill, armed robber nonpareil, anymore.

On the intercom of her old apartment building was a button labeled in light-green felt-tip: L. MARRAT.

"Hello?"

"Hey, Leigh?"

"Yes? Who's this?"

"Hey, it's me, Jerome Coe? Remember me?"

"Drone Gold?"

"Coe? From Duke's? I used to sit at the end of the bar and drink Cokes and Michelobs and eat Andy Capp's Hot Fries?"

"Uh huh."

"I used to run with old Dewey and Jeff?"

Both Dewey and Jeff had been semi-friends and Duke's regulars. Dewey Martin was a gloomy philatelist who liked to complain about the Bruins and tap garlic salt into his beer, and Jeff Dahmer was a state-secessionist who, for mystical reasons, was obsessed with the idea of war with Connecticut. (An entirely different Jeff Dahmer, an encephalophagous Milwaukeean, wasn't to become known to the world for another couple of years. His debut—which occurred well into my stay at Boll—must have been quite a complicated day for our Jeff.)

"Mmmm…"

"I had a zit on my forehead that wouldn't go away?"

"Oh! Oh my God, Jerome! Come up here right now! Can you come up? I'm so glad you came by. You know, I've been thinking about you. Let me buzz you in."

I could have collapsed with relief.

The heavy glass door rang like a fire bell. I pushed it open. Above me, through four floors of sagging banisters, Leigh, tucking her hair behind her ears and grinning magnificently, waved like a castaway.

"Jerome!"

She hugged me so hard and with such coverage I could feel the little bow at the cross-your-heart point of her bra through her T-shirt, and also what might have been a pierced-belly-button ornament. I looked over her shoulder into her apartment: no movement. No Bill. Asleep? No, Leigh probably wouldn't have let me in if Bill was here, no matter his state of consciousness.

"Let me look at you." She took me by the upper arms and adjusted me until the light was right. "Looks good, Jerome. Maybe a little pockmark."

"Like a dimple?"

I'd always wanted a dimple. If it was on my forehead, fine.

"Yeah. It has character. Everyone should take my advice, without question. Like you did. Oh Jerome. Come in."

I looked around her apartment. I saw no particular evidence that Bill'd been here recently. No beer-can pyramids, no hunting knives, no balled-up tens and twenties with blood drying on them.

The dozens of Michelob and St. Pauli Girl and Knickerbocker bar mirrors on the walls reflected Leigh and me standing together. No Bill stood between us. My joints loosened at the profound relief. I sat down right where I stood.

"Jerome, are you all right?"

"Oh, I'm fine. Tired. I, uh, got evicted."

"I command you to lie on the futon and rest."

I obeyed, making my way slowly around the many, many obstacles.

Hundreds of LPs lined the walls. A fake Victrola with a tape deck and graphic equalizer stood partly blocking the door to the bathroom. There were clothes everywhere, covering every surface to a depth of several inches. Close-fitting faded pastel T-shirts emblazoned with pop-culture emblemata, fancy jewellike panties, washed-out grayish workaday panties, jeans in every state of erosion, a web of stockings and tights. This upper crust of garments covered a lower mantle of denser, larger articles, which occasionally poked through in the form of a promontory or mesa. Shoes of every conceivable fashion hazardously studded the entire matrix.

Some clothes I remembered. There, hanging over the corner of a Hamm's Beer lamp shade, was the light-blue cowboy shirt Leigh often wore, whose vagrant pearl buttons used to sometimes pop off and land on the bar. And over there, spread across the rows of LPs, was an oversize black ultra-fuzzy turtleneck sweater that looked exactly like the one she'd been wearing when I'd gotten my first hug. The ultra-fuzz had made me sneeze, which she had found hilarious.

A big futon against a wall under the lone window was the only surface not covered in clothes—it was instead crowded with magazines and paperbacks and two or three knots of blankets and sheets. There was also a big stuffed pumpkin and a few rarefied pillows. And a big purple flashlight.

"Lie down," said Leigh. "Hungry? Guess what. Hot Fries!"

I sat on the futon. Leigh bounded over the clothes moguls like an impala and landed in the kitchen. Presently she came back into the room and gently tossed me a bag of Andy Capp's.

"Wow, thanks!" I said, tearing the thing open like a nine-year-old with a birthday present. "Hey, how's old Bill?"

"Oh it's so sad," said Leigh. "Bill's been in jail for a while."

"Oh, darn, Leigh. I'm sorry."

"But his mom is going to bail him out tomorrow around noon."

Leigh must have seen something in my face, because she added: "But don't worry, Bill's super-duper mellow these days. I talk to him on the phone once a week."

She gave me a look I could not interpret, except that it seemed expectant, or as though the look itself were distressed that it wasn't being understood. She held this inscrutable mask for several seconds. Then she said, "Jerome, stay the night, wouldya? I mean, you know, to rest. If you don't have anywhere else. Hang out till Bill gets here so you can say hi."

That look again.

"Uh," I said, imagining Bill catching me here, gouging my eyes with his tiny thumbs, popping my testicles with his little jackbooted feet, hammering my kidneys with his itty-bitty fists as hard as railroad spikes, crushing my windpipe with his terrifying mulberry teeth. "Uh, I don't know how much Bill would like me being—"

"Oh pooh. He'd love to see you. Promise?"

"Well, sure."

The look vanished. Her regular being, always dominated by a summery smile that made me think of marigolds, returned.

"I can't wait to see him, but I'm not looking forward to dealing with my sister," she said, plucking tiny socks out of the topsoil of garments, evaluating them, and throwing them back.

"Dee, right?"

"Yeah," she said. "You probably never met her—she never comes to Duke's. We look a lot alike except Dee's cuter, thinner, taller, *morer*, in every way, plus she has a beauty mark on her cheek."

I recalled that Bill had always had a thing for both Marrats. And that both Marrats had a thing for Bill Izzoli. Whenever Bill was in jail—which was often, but never for very long, it seemed—Dee took up with Jeff Dahmer. Jeff was such a puddle of love for Dee that whenever Bill got sprung and Dee raced back to him, Jeff simply piled himself on a barstool in wuthering humiliation until Bill got busted again. This had been going on for years.

I opened my mouth to point out to Leigh that everyone seemed better off whenever Bill was in jail, but instead I crunched Hot Fries and tried to imagine a *morer* version of Leigh. I could not.

"Oh Jerome," she said, locating a pair of balled-up yellow socks that

looked like Peeps. "Bill's been wanting to have both of us—me and Dee—
I mean he wanted us all to go to bed together. He said me and Dee could
make up that way. That freaked me out. I love Bill so much and I know he
meant well, but me all naked with a naked boy *and* with my sister naked,
all doing naughty stuff?"

"Gross," I said. "I mean, you know, not *you're* gross, I didn't mean that
of course, or that Dee's gross, or for that matter that Bill's gross, but..."

"I know. I told him no, and he got so upset he stole Jeff's Pacer—you
remember the one he was restoring and trying to supercharge into a hot
rod?—and drove it through the window of a mattress store. Symbolic,
I guess. Poor Jeff. His car's totaled, and tomorrow Dee will dump him in
order to concentrate on Bill again."

Leigh swallowed that last word, the way people do when they might
cry. But she didn't. After a moment, she sat in the middle of her clothes-
field and pulled on her Peeps.

"Was he hurt?" I said, with such bogus yet convincing concern that
the ever-present shame cloud over my head busted open and rained shame-
drops down on me.

"No, he's fine. But that's why he's been in jail for the last two months.
Dee blames me for everything that happened. She hates me. But I love her,
and I miss having a little sister."

I could tell she did.

"So it's been just me and Shelton for a while," said Leigh, uprooting a
couple of galoshes from somewhere.

Leigh gestured to the far wall where a drift had formed, composed of
a leopard-print robe, latex corsets, a terry-cloth romper, and a huge beach
towel. Shelton, blending in like an army jeep in a jungle, lay across the
ridge of the drift.

"A cat."

"Oh yes! That's Little Shelton." Leigh bent down and tom-tommed her
thighs as a summons to Little Shelton. "Come here, L'il Sheltie! Come over
here! Meet Jerome!"

I'd never seen a cat come when called, unless the caller was also waving
a grouper filet around. Leigh had no grouper filet. Shelton did not move.
So Leigh forded the sea of clothes to bring Shelton to meet me.

"This... is Shelton." Leigh hefted Shelton into my arms. He felt like a flight bag full of chili. "Now, don't you two go anywhere. Eat what you want. You still look hungry. Oh Jerome. I'm so happy you're visiting. Listen, don't answer the phone or the door while I'm gone. I'll be back at three a.m. or so. Do you smell a foot smell?"

Leigh grabbed her right foot and pulled it up to her nose to sniff.

"I... where are you going?" I said, alarmed. I was getting tired of being gripped by alarm.

"I gotta go," she said, stepping into her galoshes. "I can't wait to talk. I gotta be at Duke's ten minutes ago. Covering for Winnie, whose mom slipped on a Pop-Tart. Oh I love you, Jerome! Gotta run. Pah!"

I was alone with Shelton. His languid style had obviously been an act to please his mistress: the moment she left he suddenly sprang free with a needle-clawed, raking contortion, and was soon busily wedging himself under the futon.

I walked through the surf, avoiding spiked heels and underwired bras, then squeezed past the stereo into the bathroom, also deep in textiles. The door wouldn't shut all the way, blocked as it was by a spill of clothes and a few puddled towels.

I found a towel by the sink. I folded it on the toilet seat and examined the interior of the phone-booth-sized stall. It was clean, with a Shower Massage showerhead and a fairly modern temperature-control system. A translucent orange beauty bar. Dr. Bronner's peppermint castile soap. I turned on the water. The little bathroom began to fill with steam.

I scrubbed and shampooed. I sat down cross-legged and scrubbed my feet until my arms hurt. I leaned back and let the water run over me.

For the first time since that afternoon—really, for the first time since I'd been committed to the sock hospital—I felt safe. Nobody knows where I am, I thought, except a beautiful girl who's been thinking about me and who loves me. I think she even *needs* me; I think she wants someone to be with her tomorrow when Bill comes over.

Maybe she wants me to protect her.

My vagus nerve flexed, radiating nauseated fear.

If only the miniature bastard were in jail forever.

Back when I was a regular at Duke's L-Bo Room, I hadn't been alone in my crush on Leigh. About ninety thousand other locals, men and women alike, embraced meager hopes that her affection was something more than just part of her personality or part of her job, that it was more than just friendly barkeep banter. That she really liked *you* best.

It was hard not to think Leigh liked you when you got her attention. She was moistly flirtatious and aggressively huggy. Only the wide walnut bar kept her from apportioning full-melt frontal hugs to everyone, but she still reached as far over the bar as she could and draped her arms over your shoulders and kissed your ear. If it was really crowded and even the wiliest sidling couldn't get you close enough to the bar for a hug, then Leigh would wink and *pah* and gesture in zingy semaphore until you felt like a celebrated wit and lover instead of a glum beer drone. She smiled with such stretch that you could see the pink of her innermost gums meeting her innermost cheeks, and when she relaxed her mouth, plump little vertical creases formed in her lips where the lipstick was not elastic enough to follow the expansion and contraction of her smile. The whole light show of her stayed bright even when she wasn't around.

But she always forgot you. You might come into Duke's, accept your hug and kiss, then duck out to get a pack of Kools, come back in after five minutes, and get the whole pageant of welcome again. Indeed, there were plenty of people who did just that, in and out, hugs and kisses all day.

Leigh might remember a mustachioed toreador with a metal hand who only ordered Rob Roys and tipped uncirculated Morgan silver dollars, but she would never have remembered someone who sat wherever there was a vacant stool and ordered Cokes and beer and was thin and short and wore characterless outerwear, such as myself. Unless there was an unignorable feature to lodge in the subconscious, my kind were not recalled. We were not filed. Certainly, I always got a hug and a kiss or a wave and wink, but so did everybody. I could not be distinguished.

Until I got my zit.

It was probably listed in the literature that comes with prescription medication, under adverse effects. Blurred vision, smelly urine, furry tongue, etc., etc... and Gleety Facial Eruptions.

The zit had been idling subcutaneously for at least two weeks before it surfaced. It was just a tender spot in the lower middle of my forehead until it debuted as a modest pimple.

But then I started to worry it, which just made it mad. Within a few days it was a crimson alp, so large that in a raking light it cast a shadow. I could even see it without a mirror, out of the corner of my eye. It was a profane bindi, and it hurt.

Leigh noticed, even in the smoke and bar-dark of Duke's. Bill had been in jail for a while—this may have had something to do with her feeling comfortable enough to address a beerbot like myself on a genuinely personal level.

"None of my business," she said, in a tone of voice I'd only heard her use with her actual friends, "but I had them like that one time, all over my face. I still have the scars. See?"

She leaned over the bar and tilted her head back and to the side. I could only look at her lipstick crevasses and her long nose. I blushed so hard that I'm sure my zit was comparatively diminished.

"I think I see," I said.

"I had them on my neck *and* on my chest. But listen: go get Accutane and Cleocin T. Miracle drugs."

I carried a little notebook in my back pocket that I used to scribble nonsense in when out in public so as to not appear vagrant. "Let me write that down," I said, pulling out said notebook.

"Write that down," she said, handing me a pencil of the sort used for scoring miniature golf that she kept stuck under a scrunchie in her hair. The pencil was warm.

"Okay."

"Okay then."

"Right."

"Righto!"

Then she leaned in and gave me a hug that lasted a fraction longer than usual, and patted me on the cheek.

I borrowed sixty bucks from Dewey so I could buy new clothes and get a becoming haircut.

"When're you gonna pay me back?" he said, holding three twenties over his head, out of my reach.

"End of the month," I said, stretching, grasping at air. "When I get paid at the tire store."

I worked just enough hours at a nearby used-tire lot to buy beer and paperbacks and satisfy the employment requirements of Grippick Manse: twenty hours a week. Or back to the hospital you went!

"You better," he said, stuffing the money into my shirt pocket. "That's my goddam philately cash."

I began to go to Duke's earlier and earlier in the afternoons, when fewer people were there, and always occupied the same stool. I was always magnificently groomed and appointed. My hugs and kisses from Leigh really started to feel special. Distinguished. Leigh would examine my forehead and tut-tut or otherwise remark on the progress. I was a friend now, or at least an acquaintance. When the bar would close for the night, I'd go home to the halfway house, lie in bed, and beg God for sleep so morning would come that much quicker and I could go back to Duke's L-Bo Room.

Saturdays after closing were the worst. Bars were closed on Sundays, and the only thing to do was walk around the vicinity of Duke's in hopes I might see Leigh go in to work to slice limes or clean pint glasses or something.

I nursed my zit, meaning I worried it and worried it, keeping it florid and pulsing. I squeezed and picked, rubbed and torqued. I once tapped it with a ball-peen hammer, which hurt so bad I thought I might barf. Dr. Somer, Grippick's on-call shrink, wrote me out prescriptions for Accutane and Cleocin T, but I never filled them.

"Are you sure you're taking Accutane twice a day?" Leigh said when it had been a few weeks and still the zit was a monument to the affliction.

"I really am!"

"Forty mgs morning and night?"

"Two little brown pills like footballs, right?"

Lies! Lies! Lies!

"Yup," she said. "But you know you gotta wash your face every day, all the time."

"I do," I said. "I don't know what's up."

I started to get a reputation, partly because of the zit, which became an object of light barroom ridicule, but also because of the favoritism that Leigh showed me. Competitors began to show up with hammered fingernails or split lips, wearing whiplash doughnuts or homemade casts, limping, sneezing, trembling. One guy, Joe College, went so far as to proliferate artificial chicken pox all over his body, fashioned from the tapered ends of hundreds of candy corns and stuck down with double-sided tape. It was an arresting sight, to be sure, and I think he's still dating one of the women at the bar that night who decided she wanted to nurse the helpless, pocked wreck back to health.

Still, no one got the same amount of attention that Leigh paid me.

But then, one day, the zit started to look a little better.

No matter what abuses I heaped on it, it continued to shrink, and eventually it matched in luster and hue the rest of my forehead. Leigh and I had less and less to talk about.

The day finally came when there was nothing to talk about.

That afternoon I was drinking beer and flipping Hot Fries into my mouth, cursing my loathesomely healthy forehead, when Leigh, who had been by the coffeemaker cautiously sewing a pearl button onto the breast pocket of her cowboy shirt, began to squeal and jump up and down. She ran toward me, the needle and thread still attached to her button and whipping back and forth across her shirt. In a rush of momentum she jumped, sat on the bar, spun on her rear end a half turn, and then vaulted off and into the arms of a goateed elf in combat boots.

"Bill Bill Bill Bill!" she cried into the top of Bill's head.

Bill Izzoli had brought his own beer, which he held at arm's length while Leigh hugged him and whimpered into his large bald spot.

"Ho! Yo! Ho! The fucking beer, woman!"

"Oh Bill."

"Need to watch the beer. You always flail."

"Oh Bill."

"Now, blow out these turds and shut this bar down! It's Pah Tee Time!"

"Oh Bill."

Jeff Dahmer, Joe College, Dewey Martin, and I, the turds, were efficiently scuttled with Bill's swift kicks, one of which popped Jeff's billfold out of his back pocket. Bill caught and kept it. The bar door slammed behind us. We turds stood in the snow. Shrieks and giggles and tigery roars vibrated Duke's L-Bo Room.

I didn't want to hear anymore. I went home to Grippick, leaving Jeff and Dewey to contemplate a parking meter. I didn't go back to Duke's for a while after that.

Sometime later, though, I met Dewey in line at the post office, where it was my job to collect the halfway-house manager's mail. Dewey, who worked as a nurse's aide in the geriatric ward of St. Elizabeth's, was there to buy a sheet of commemorative stamps for his collection.

"Got my sixty bucks?"

"Shit." I said. "No, I forgot, sorry. I'll get it, though."

Dewey sighed.

"All spent in vain, Coe," he said, shaking me by the shoulders. "The boil's gone now. Got to admit, that was one lucky blemish."

"I tried to make it last," I said. In retrospect, there were so many things I hadn't tried. Picric acid, thorium, spells.

"It was bound to happen, boil or no," said Dewey. "No one can keep her attention, man. Not to be discouraging, but fucking forget about her. Bill's here now.

"Sheet of twenty-cent pickles, sheet of airmails, the ones with the atlatls, three plate blocks of that brown stamp with the guy on it," Dewey added, addressing the postal clerk.

"What the *fuck*'s he got?" I said, too loudly.

"And a sheet of those new dollar stamps," said Dewey. "Oh. Wait. Cancel that last one, Mister Postal Clerk, I didn't bring enough *money*."

Dewey glared at me.

"I said sorry!" I said. "I hate Bill Izzoli!"

I stomped my feet. At the time I had my green and white leather Stan Smith tennis shoes—the ones I later killed at the sock hospital. They were not ideal as winter footwear, so my feet were usually numb. This allowed me to stomp hard when I felt like it. Wondering what an absurd dwarf convict had that no one else had made me want to stomp.

"Calm down, Jerome," said Dewey. "Leigh likes dangerous fellows. Robbers and safecrackers and guys with switchblades. Some girls are like that. One day you'll catch one that likes sad-sack orphan weirdos. But forget Leigh, man. You're just not the dangerous type, even with all the mental-patient shit."

"I'll buy a sword, a samurai sword, and wear it across my back. That'd get her atten—"

"Man, what're you after anyway? Pussy? There's chicken in Duke's who'll screw anything."

"No! I—"

"Marriage and babies and swing sets and Sears charge cards?"

"No. Well... yeah. We'd take good care of each other."

"C'mon. Look at you. You can't stay out of a nut ranch for more than a year at a time."

"Yes I can! Once I was—"

"Never mind. Okay. Do what you want, Coe. Jesus."

A few days after that I went back to Duke's. There were several people at one end of the bar eating beer nuts and watching the Patriots drop the ball in the snow and get flags and skid into the shotgun mikes on the sidelines. Leigh was tending bar, but not looking nearly as happy and affectionate as usual. She smiled and waved at me, but bestowed no hug. Nobody else that came in got one either.

Bill came in. Leigh jumped and spun in the shiny depression on the bar and vaulted into his arms. She didn't seem quite as giddy this time, though.

Bill began playing pool at a tiny pay-table by himself. Every time he missed a shot, which was often, he quietly whipped his cue in the air like a sword. I glanced at him every so often in an old mirror over the cue rack. Whenever he was lining up a shot, up on his combat-booted tiptoes, squinting at the object ball, I took the opportunity to glance at Leigh.

Leigh brought me a Coke. I quickly monitored Bill, who had just launched the cue ball into the men's room and was now busy stomping on a cube of blue chalk. I smiled at Leigh, who smiled back warmly. I quickly looked back at Bill, who had apparently powdered the chalk to his satisfaction, because he was now occupied with watching me in the mirror. He had discovered my infatuation. He stared right into my eyes with a look I never forgot.

Bill disappeared. The bar filled up. I drank a little too much. I'd spent most of my money. I overtipped Leigh with what was left and went out into the night. It was lightly snowing, and cold.

A moment later I turned down the alley shortcut that led to Grippick Manse to find a few people moaning in the snow. Dewey. And Jeff. Joe College, Danny diSimone, Cândido Braz, Patty Cork. All bloodied and crumpled, each covered with slightly more or less wet snow. Before I could react, I found my own self on the ground. A heavy boot came down on my knee. I got one good look at Bill Izzoli before the tiny, boys-department-size combat boot, with slush and blue powder trapped in the zigzag tread, came down on my face.

Some weeks after the beating from Bill, I got fired from the used-tire store for napping on the toilet. I didn't tell Dave, the halfway-house manager, that I'd lost my job—I just made sure I was out of the house for the required twenty hours a week.

I did a lot of loitering. One warm afternoon, while doing so on the banks of the Charles, a man in a tennis outfit approached me.

"Jerome?"

"Yeah?"

"Shit. You look just the same, like a little kid. Remember me? Hugh? From Bannerman Place?"

Hugh Moustakos and I had been at the same home when we were seven or eight or so. At that age—when one's cuteness is gone but the ability to manipulate strangers into believing otherwise has not yet fruited—the chances of getting picked up were not very good. Nevertheless, a man and a woman came by one day, and even though Hugh smelled like a basement and looked like Roy Orbison, the couple picked him up.

"Jeez," I said. He didn't look the same at all, except for his small hazel eyes. "Hi. How are you? How'd that family turn out?"

The woman had been wearing a heavy camel-hair coat with big brown leather buttons. At one point, she crouched down in the hall of the home and spent a long time going through her purse for something she never found. A few days afterward, when Hugh was gone, I found a ChapStick in the hall near where the woman had been.

"Pretty good," said Hugh. "I'm a dentist. You?"

"Well, you know, this and that."

When I was nine Bannerman shut down and scattered the kids everywhere. I went out to a frightful Christian gulag in Detroit.

Hugh gave me his business card.

"Come by for a free filling," he said. "Anytime."

Just following my encounter with Hugh, there passed a short but active period richly salted with my old, familiar thought bubbles, themselves freighted with subterfuge and wile and rotten advice. One afternoon, while waiting for a train at the Maverick T station, a bubble over the heads of a couple of Red Sox fans waiting on the same platform reported that *now* was the time for me to realize my ambition of sexual contact with the third rail. I got a running start, but the Red Sox fans caught me prae flagrante delicto and pinned me to the concrete. The cops escorted me back to Grippick Manse, whence I was immediately expelled into the remand of the Sock Hospital, q.v. above. There, while the bubbles slowly diminished and their dialogue grew meaningless, I passed the hours until the snowy day months later when the kind EMTs Teddy and Dino bought me coffee and footwear, and I immediately repaid them by withdrawing from their custody.

Then: Leigh. Again.

After the water in Leigh's shower started to run cold, I got out and made myself comfortable on the futon. I tried not to think about Bill, about tomorrow afternoon. I fell asleep, though for how long I had no idea. I woke confused and without any meaningful memory, but that was soon scattered by the warm, comfortable recollection of Leigh, which itself was immediately cut to bits by the specter of Bill. The apartment was cold, but dread was what really chilled me.

It was one in the morning. Leigh would be back in just a couple of hours.

By the futon was a big drawing pad that had a colorful drawing of a mandala on the open page. Next to the pad was a scattered selection of Prismacolor markers, and the scores of magazines Leigh'd swept off the futon so I could lie down.

I leaned back on the futon and my elbow hit something hard under a pillow. Oh—the big purple flashlight.

I looked closer. It turned out not to be a flashlight, but rather a long nubbed baton of purple shock-resistant plastic that was probably an advanced kind of vibrator.

It was recharging. There was a little LED indicator that suggested it was not yet finished doing so, which in turn suggested it had recently been used. It had a power cord that was piped under a yard of clothes and plugged into the wall. It had a button, a dial, and two switches, each with three unmarked settings.

I lay transfixed with lust. I tried to ignore my erection. I thought about sunspots and planaria and frozen locks. I tried to recall what the *I* was in *ROY G BIV*. But it was no use—the erection advanced, obstinately trying to bully its way through my underwear and burst through my jeans to stare at me, demanding attention.

I sacrificed one of my brand-new wool socks. I stored it in my coat pocket.

I lay there, warmer but disgusted and ashamed. I considered blinding myself with a rose-gray or fawn Prismacolor and running around like Oedipus.

Shelton emerged from under the futon. He decided to make friends with me, probably because I was the warmest thing in the room. He sat on my chest, kneading and purring, then went to sleep there. He was heavy and warm.

I surprised both of us by suddenly starting to cry. He jumped off my chest when I swallowed my tears wrong and began to choke. I curled up on my side, breathless and understanding absolutely nothing about why I was here, but everything about why I could not stay. *Coward!*

Then, Leigh's key in the door. I pretended to be asleep. Leigh went right to the kitchen and rattled some dry food into Shelton's bowl. Dainty crunching followed. Leigh climbed onto the futon. She patted me on the arm. I smelled cigarettes and ammonia and road salt.

The room grew silent. Shelton had finished eating. Was Leigh looking at me? My lids fluttered—I couldn't fake sleeping very well. I yawned and opened my eyes, pretending to wake.

But Leigh was asleep, her mouth open, her long nose pressed against the bare futon.

She flipped over on her side, facing the other way. Her saddle-shaped waist, and the T-shirt and red skirt that met at the bottom of it, moved with the slow roll of her breathing. My throat dried out.

Shelton came out of the bathroom licking his chops. He went over to Leigh and made himself comfortable against her belly. He watched me, pupils contracted, with a suspicious malevolence, like a seer. It reminded me of Bill in the barroom mirror the night he stompered eight people, one at a time, as they came out of Duke's. I had been the seventh, and the luckiest.

I rolled over, picked up the pad of drawing paper, and wrote in big letters with a currant-red marker on the first blank sheet: *Thanks Leigh, for Everything! You're the Greatest! Love, Zits.*

I'd spent five full minutes deciding to sign it *Love* instead of *Luv.*

I spent another fifteen reading and rereading my message, wondering if somewhere in those nine words Leigh would be able to see just how terrified I was of Bill.

Quietly, in a terrible yellow lumpen shame, I left. I left her alone. And I was out in the cigar-ash snow of Boston, again.

I didn't have anywhere to go. I couldn't go to Duke's because I was broke, and bars frown on the broke, as they cannot buy spirits or beer, or even spend quarters in the cashew machine. Besides, I doubted I knew anyone there anymore—after Bill had left me and the other Duke's regulars moaning and hemorrhaging in the lightly falling snow, he had apparently gone back to the bar in a sunny, generous mood and bought the last call for everyone remaining, then told Leigh that anyone who had ever looked at her longer than it took to order a beer was forever persona non grata, *and* eligible for a hospital beating.

So I stayed outdoors. And, as the days went by, I began to look more and more like that was where I stayed. I hadn't had my medicine since Dino and Teddy came to fetch me, and for several days I'd been feeling submerged and lockjawed. In the evenings I snoozed in different T stations until midnight, when the trains stopped running and the bulls threw you out. During the day I ate pizza crusts, stockpiling as many as I could in a briefcase I'd found under a mailbox. Pizza crusts are the landlubber's sea biscuits. Inland hardtack.

Finally the chemicals metabolized. I found a dumpster behind a stationery shop in Somerville that never had anything in it but cardboard and paper. No broken glass, no corroded rebar, no medical waste, no bags of mulching organ meat. A spot like that should've been stuffed full of bums. But it was all mine. Warm, safe, secluded, clean. Mine.

One night it was gone. Why did they take dumpsters away sometimes?

To knock the dents out? Repaint? All I knew was I was exhausted and my house was gone.

I headed to the Boston Public Library. I'd fall asleep on the steps, and in the morning I'd go in and spend all day there, dozing and drinking from the water fountain and reading newspapers from other lands.

I woke up too late—all the other bums had hied to the library way before me and hogged all the chairs and good foreign newspapers. Even the other domestic papers were in use. All I could find was a Cinnabon-smeared day-old *Herald* on the floor, opened to a page covered with mattress ads and foreclosure hear-ye's and estate-sale announcements. At the bottom of the page, to the left of a notice about the cancellation of Gallagher's World Wide Fart Tour, was a small two-column-inch crime item.

BEER-BOTTLE KILLER IN COURT

BOSTON (AP) Guillermo I. Izzoli, thirty-four, of Taunton, was arraigned late yesterday in South Boston District Court in the death one month ago today of twenty-nine-year-old Leigh Bellechasse Marrat, of Allston. His Honor Judge Epes Warrick, Jr., accepted Mr. Izzoli's plea of "guilty as hell" to the charge of murder in the second degree. On the morning of Feb. 10, Mr. Izzoli beat Ms. Marrat to death with beer bottles, following his discovery of an alleged affair the victim was conducting with a certain Mr. Zits. The crime occurred in the deceased's apartment on North Beacon St. just hours after the accused was bonded out of the Suffolk County Jail, where he had been held on unrelated charges. Mr. Izzoli has also pleaded guilty to animal cruelty in the death of Ms. Marrat's cat. He faces a possible sentence of life behind bars for the murder of Ms. Marrat, and a fine of $2,500 in the death of the pet. An evidentiary hearing has been scheduled for early next week.

I read it again. Then again. I stood. The people in the library all looked at me at once. I ran outside. I slipped on the steps, fell, hit the back of my head. I got up and ran down Exeter toward the Charles. The tourists and shoppers and locals stared at me. Each of their bubbles contained a word or two of the news item. I covered my eyes, still running. I hit something and fell hard. I tried to sit up, but a shiny black shoe was stepping on my hand. I looked up. A cop grinned at me from under a nicotine-stained mustache.

Guilty

"Pop that bubble!" I said. "I am Mr. Zits, you know!"

Another cop came out of nowhere and soon I was in the back of a cruiser, where I howled.

"What!?" said the two cops in front.

"I'm Zits!"

"Pissah for you, pal."

"I was afraid he'd pop my testicles!"

"Pissah, wacko. Now shutthefuckup."

They took me to Mass. General. I had two broken fingers. They straightened them out without removing the handcuffs. They took an X-ray of my head, commented on the chaos therein, asked me what the metal plate in the back of my skull was.

"None of your beeswax!" I screeched. "I signed it *Love!*"

Then, without further questions or ceremony, they jitneyed me over to the state facility I had been on my way to when I skipped out on Teddy and Dino exactly one month before.

o

The admissions staff at the state hospital didn't care that I was Mr. Zits or that Leigh was dead or whose fault it was. They cared about blood pressure and drug allergies and whether I was going to bolt. They took my clothes and looked at my broken fingers again and then slid me into restraints for a night or two. Then they let me up and led me to a large iron bed in a dark room.

I slept, I ate the pills they brought, I got out of bed only to go to the bathroom. A shrink came once a week and sat in a corner of the room for an hour or so and left. She asked questions sometimes.

I occupied the long, prone hours altering history: I don't write a note in currant ink; I don't leave, but stay until she wakes; I say to her *I'm glad I'll be here when Bill comes over after jail*; she says *Me, too*; I fry us some bacon and scramble eggs in the grease and make cold-water biscuits and cowboy coffee; we wait for Bill; I tell her I love her; I give Shelton his amoxicillin pill because Leigh doesn't like to do it; we get sweaty playing indoor badminton with a wadded-up ped. Bill comes to the door. Leigh tells him she's through with him so go fly a kite. He comes in with empty Genesee pint bottles in each hand. He swings at Leigh but I catch him and he falls. I hit him with his own bottles. There's a wine bottle and I hit him with that. There are empty gallon jugs of Mott's apple juice, I hit him with those, there are bar mirrors, I pull them off the wall and rain them down on him, the ceiling opens, plate-glass skyscraper windows fall from the clouds and bury him in slivers, Leigh and I go to Legal Sea Foods and eat shark steaks and drink Japanese beer and

Some nurse came in and told me to get out of bed, that it was time to go to Deaconess. I couldn't get up, so he hefted me into a wheelchair. I signed a form consenting to something. Then, an ambulance, swaying orange tubes and fluid-filled bags hanging from the ceiling. The ride ended, and they wheeled me into some place. Then I was lying down, looking up at a nurse, a woman with peach lipstick. She told me when I felt the cold in my vein to start counting backward from ten. I told her I knew, that I'd done this before. I'd never gotten below seven in the past, but I counted down to three this time before the thiopental hushed up everything.

I woke up with a powerful headache, a great fitter's vise shut on my skull from chin to crown. Back to my room at the hospital. More hours saving Leigh, killing Bill. A few days later, the same, a trip to Deaconess, a headache, worse this time. They gave me the gift of Fiorinal. The shrink asked, Is the ECT helping? but I was too tired to move my mouth. Back to Deaconess once more. When I woke up, the headache was so bad they gave me morphine. They told me I'd clenched my teeth and cracked a couple molars, that it shouldn't have happened, highly irregular, I must be resisting. Back at the hospital, I ate their pills and slept. Nurses' aides with steel flashlights checked on me every fifteen minutes, all day, all night, while I saved Leigh and murdered Bill, Leigh and Bill, Leigh and Bill.

One night: Bill fights back. He hits me with his bottles. I try to fight but my hands fall off like ripe apples. He hits me. I break into pieces—arms, legs, head—and fall among Leigh's clothes, disintegrated, able only to watch. He catches Leigh, he hits her again and again until the bottles break, but he keeps striking, cutting her, blood spattering on pads of newsprint. He slices Shelton in two and leaves. I watch the dripping room and the red jags of Leigh's body for an unblinking lifetime.

The doctor came again and sat in her chair. She said there won't be any more treatments, that she's going to try something else. I'm not sure if I said anything.

Now Bill always comes, and he always shatters me and then cuts up Leigh and Shelton. All day, every day, over and over, the same. I never save her. I tried thinking of other things, but, like a song stuck in my head, Bill always comes back, swinging, slicing.

A nurse came with a Dixie cup of water and some pills. I sat up and took them. He left.

Bill bangs on the door

I waited for the flashlight to come and go. It did.

I can't help myself I let Bill in

I eased out of bed. I pulled off a sheet and tied it to the crossbar at the foot of the old, heavy, iron-frame bed.

My hands fall off ripe apples He hits me I break up

I flushed every drop of adrenalin into my bloodstream, and then lifted the foot of the massive bed until it stood on end.

He breaks his bottles on Leigh

In the floor were two small, shallow, circular dents where the bed legs had stood. With the sheet in hand, I lay down on the floor and positioned my temple on one of the circles.

He sabers her with them She opens up new moons of butcher-shop red

I pulled steadily on the sheet until the bed tipped and began to fall.

Bill stops midslash and looks at me, and with blood in her mouth Leigh says Jerome you

"There're easier ways to retire, guy," said the MD, peering into my right eye with a whatever-that-is.

"Yeah," I said.

By chance, I was in precisely the same Mass General exam room I'd been in six weeks ago when they'd set my broken fingers. This time I was there with a linear skull fracture, the kind there's not much treatment for, except patience.

The room was small, bright, and smelled like Werther's Originals. The doctor was a short, broad-shouldered man in his sixties who looked like

Harry Houdini. His hair was brilliantined and parted in the middle. Calluses covered the palms of his huge hands, as though he volunteered as a lumberjack in his spare time.

"Tell me when you can see my... don't move your head, guy. Tell me when you can see my hand."

He stared at me and moved his left hand into my field of vision.

"Now," I said.

"How's your pain?"

"Okay," I said, and it was. Dropping a bed on my head had not only *not* killed me, but had cured my ECT headaches.

"What're you in the hospital for?"

"You don't have my file?"

"Yeah, but I want your opinion," he said, running the handle of his reflex hammer along the sole of my foot.

"Just general bananas, I guess."

"Now *that's* a *divot*, Lanny Wadkins," he said, squinting at the bed-leg dent in my head. "Looks like somebody chipped a Titleist off your ear. Mood?"

"What?"

"I'm asking about your innermost feelings, guy."

"Oh," I said. "Not bad at all, come to think of it."

"Not uncommon after a suicide attempt."

"Maybe they could make it a treatment."

The doctor stuck a couple of X-ray films of a head on the wall-mounted lightbox.

"What's that?" he said, pointing to a black rectangular spot on one of the films and staring at me like he'd caught me lying.

"A steel plate," I said, bending over and tapping on the back of my skull. "I slipped and fell when I was little. Running around a pool. A lot of doctors have said that was when I started to... deviate."

"You've been in the system a long time."

"So what?"

A nurse came in and gave the doctor a manila envelope. She looked like a "nurse" in a dirty movie, with high heels and seamed stockings and a soft little scallop of bra just visible.

"Mr. Coe," said the doctor, studying the contents of the folder. "Looks like the powers're going to run you out to bowl."

"Really? That's pretty weird. Candlepin?"

"No, no, guy. Boll. The Boll Compound. It's a facility."

"That hoodoo-guru place in the boonies? What'd I do? What for?"

"Officially," he said, "alternative treatment."

"And..."

"Politically? The state system wants to be shut of you. Suicides fuck up their funding."

"I can't pay for anything like that!"

"Boll still gets some state—and federal—funding, guy. You won't have to pay."

"Jesus. *Boll.*"

"The place isn't all that fruitcake. There're still drugs and group therapy. It's just a looser place, calmer. Good food."

"Well," I said, slumping. "Do I have a choice?"

His big face split with mirth.

"What're you complaining about? Where would you go if I let you out the door right now?"

"I can take care of myself."

"No, guy, as a matter of fact, you can't."

"So, when?"

"A few days here, then a two-hour ambulance ride west."

The sexy nurse came in with a wheelchair.

"Czynthia, roll Mr. Coe here up to gen. psych."

I rested, ate rice pudding, drank coffee. A goth girl named Melmoth who'd lost an eye from a gunshot suicide attempt taught me to smoke. Bill and Leigh still featured in my thoughts and dreams, but the colors of her murder were softer, the sounds attenuated, the action farther away, as though I'd moved back a few rows in the theater of it all.

A week later I was transferred to the Boll Compound for a Variety of Disturbances, where I spent nearly three years smoking and pacing and eating experimental medicines and tolerating Dr. Boone as he did his best to proof my life against neuroses and other -oses and the crouching ambuscades of guilt.

Then, one day, Marta appeared in a phone booth outside of the smoking room. Soon after, she, too, was gone.

o

I sat on the alabaster-hard New England snow cover while blood drops fired out of my hand and shit froze to my skin, and Marta floated over her cottonwood tree like ball lightning, reading in the Scrabble language.

THE HEN WAS NOT MY MOTHER

She brightened, pulsed, then fissioned into two Angels, one Marta and one Leigh, both shining blinding greenish-white light, both sharing one great bubble over their heads. Marta held a Twister spinner. Leigh had a great purple flashlight. They cried out my name. They batted me over the head with their symbols and wailed indictments in Scrabble.

"I'm sorry!" I cried. "Oh!"

They moved toward each other and resolved again into a single Angel. They began to blacken and shimmy at the edges, swarms of desperate, coked-up tadpoles.

"Oh help me, I'm sorry!"

You're having a heart attack they said, using my voice.

I grabbed my heart and yelled—it's what you're supposed to do if you're in cardiac arrest.

"Stop it!"

"Aah!" I yelled.

"Quit that! I didn't mean to cut you! I was going to come back, I swear. I didn't even know I'd gotten you until I saw the mess all over the car door."

I stopped yelling. I squinted at the silhouette of Tommy's whiskered skull in the headlights.

"In my eyes! Tadpoles, black, millions! My heart! Pellets!"

"Fuck, man. Calm down."

"Tommy? What happened?"

"Jerome, get up. Come on. Gotta get you to a doctor. Upsadaisy."

I sat up.

"Christ it's cold. What're we doing out here? I have snow—ice down my pants."

"Come on," said Tommy.

"Did I faint?"

"I think *so*, Jerome. Come on," she said, pulling me by my hand. I stood up with a lot of effort. None of my parts worked.

She helped me to the car. We set off with great speed.

"Get something out of the back and wrap your hand."

"What?"

"Where's a hospital?"

"I don't even know where we are," I said.

The car was warm, too warm, and a trifle nauseating. My nose ran. The ice in my pants was melting.

"What's that smell?" said Tommy, flying over the black hills.

"There's ice in my pants," I said. "I mean... not water ice. I think it might be dark ice."

Tommy leaned her chin on the steering wheel.

"Fuck, Jerome. I just meant to spook you. You were being such a dick."

"Well, you spooked me. I told you I had to go."

"Jesus, look at you," she said, rolling her window down a bit. "We need a hospital. This is your part of the world, man, where are we?"

"I need a pair of pants and a shower, not a hospital."

"You don't think you need stitches?" she said.

"Stitches? For what?"

"*For what?* Where do you think all the blood is coming from?"

I observed for the first time that I was covered in thawing blood. A piece of meat like a slice of inch-thick flatiron steak was hanging off the side of my palm. There was absolutely no pain.

Oh, I remember now. The magical barrette.

"Oh god!"

I shut my eyes and tried to ease my flopping avulsion back into place.

"So," said Tommy. "Where's a hospital?"

"Oh Jesus! I thought I'd imagined this!"

I leaned over and put my head between my legs so I wouldn't faint.

"Hold on. You're not going to upchuck, too, are you?"

I wanted to die. Crash into a cottonwood and get torn into calcined bones and scorched meat. I whimpered.

"Jerome, it was an accident, man," she said. "I said I'm sorry. Want me to say it again?"

"Woooh."

"Fuck. Please don't cry. Fucking *Christ*, man! The reeeeeeek!"

Wait. Why *not* faint? I loved fainting. It was one of my very best things. So I sat up. I fainted.

I woke to sharp cuffs of metal on glass.

Tommy was standing outside the car, banging on my window with a key attached to a foot-long wooden ruler.

"Up!" she said. "Out!"

I sat up. We were parked at a Citgo station. I remembered my hand just in time to not look at it. The stink was so bad the car could've served as a nausea test-chamber for spacemen. I got out, cradling my cut hand against my stomach as if my very guts were spilling out. It hurt now.

"Here," said Tommy, tucking the key, a big wad of clothes, and a bottle of Windex with Ammonia D under my arm. "Bathroom's around the corner. Clean yourself up. Clean up good, man. I mean fucking *cleanse*. Then I'm taking you to my parents. In Hartford. My dad's a doctor."

"Don't like doctors," I said. "Don't need a doctor."

"It's on the way," she said.

An alien but vital urge to bite off Tommy's nose suddenly began to buzz in my gums. If I hadn't been so trembly and weak—not to mention humiliated—I just might've.

The bathroom wasn't nearly as cold as outside, but still below freezing, so I quickly stripped to nothing, spritzed myself with Windex until my trigger finger ached, and then, using a Joe Cool Snoopy pajama top (the softest article in the clothes wad Tommy'd given me), wrapped my hand up without looking. I wiped myself down with another clothes-wad member (a Christmas-tree skirt), repeated the process (enormous daisy-print Vera apron), then dressed in the remainder of the clothes wad: women's white jeans, SKI BUM acrylic sweater, exhausted suede cap flocked with woolly little snowmen.

I pulled on my boots (which had survived the dark-ice adventure largely ungilded), rescued my billfold, and went back out to the car.

"It's only about forty-five minutes," said Tommy as we pulled out of the gas station. "Can you hold your asshole shut that long?"

"What kind of doctor is your dad?"

"Butt. Oh, by the way, my mom makes hot chocolate—have some, or she'll get her feelings hurt."

"Another, Jerome?"

"Okay," I said, holding up my mug, trying to ignore Tommy's five dogs jumping up on my chest and growling subsonically. Mrs. Ertz, Tommy's mother, who reminded me of Captain Steubing, poured hot chocolate from a double boiler into my mug, which was emblazoned with a skinny, beardless, malevolent Santa Claus of an Eastern European make.

"How was your shower?" Mrs. Ertz said, letting the largest of the Ertzes' dogs lick a dribble of chocolate off the bottom of the pan. "And Christine's robe? Comfy?"

"Oh, yes, fine, thank you, yes, comfy, appreciate it."

"Tommy's sister doesn't like just anybody to wear her good things," said Mrs. Ertz. "But Christine won't be back from Williams till next week, and what she doesn't know..."

She winked and laughed brittlely, and put the pan on the kitchen floor so the chocolate-eating dog could have full access.

The animal seemed friendly, or at least not unfriendly, but he was so big he could have stood on his hind legs and drooled in my hair, if he so chose. The middle-size dog, a certain Bumper, did not stop baring his fangs and nipping at the hem of my robe, his eyes watering and his red, tumid penis alert beneath him, like a tiny wet gnome hat.

"You don't have to worry about old Bumper," said Mrs. Ertz, bending over to squirt something in one of Bumper's nostrils. "He looks scary, because he had to have his lips removed, but he's a sweetheart. He likes to hug, and have the backs of his thighs pinched."

"Oh ho!" said Dr. Ertz, Tommy's dad. "Who doesn't. Say, that hand sure looks bad, Jerome. Are you *suuure* I can't dress it for you? I'm gentle as a lamb. Got all the tools of the trade right here, too."

He plonked a red plastic tackle box down on the table.

Dr. Ertz had eyelash-like eyebrows and wide, dry eyes the color of unpainted aluminum siding. His hands looked like pink hothouse ferns, and his purple-red mouth seemed to pinch at its lining of teeny, carious teeth. There was no way I was going to let him touch me.

"Oh no, it doesn't hurt at all."

Joe Cool was caked in brown blood. I hadn't had the courage to take him off in the shower, so I'd just stuck him out of the shower transom. I wiggled my thumb and the other three fingers, but I couldn't wiggle my storm-colored pinkie. It, in fact, did not hurt. It was entirely numb.

"Suit yourself," said Dr. Ertz, pouring the rest of his hot chocolate into his puncture of a mouth. A thin, frothing brown line ran down his chin.

Then he was suddenly on the floor, wrestling with the three other dogs—greyhound triplets that barked and pawed and nipped and seemed to be everywhere at once, like a gas.

"You can stay up in Christine's room—that's the one in the middle, see?" Mrs. Ertz pointed to a door along an open hallway on the second floor. The door had a NO FOOKIN ADMITTANCE sign on it, with a picture underneath of a leprechaun being electrocuted. "Or you can just stay with Tommy if you want, of course, in the basement."

"I guess Christine's room?" I said.

"Go right on up," said Mrs. Ertz.

"Or go down," said Dr. Ertz, still down on the floor with the dogs.

"Dad, will you just shut up? He's not my fucking boyfriend," said Tommy, who was stretched along the couch watching *The Real World: Lvov* or something. "Mom, I need some Motrin and the Cheez-Its. Please."

"Cheez-*It*, said Dr. Ertz. "It's singular in construction for singular and plural. Do you need money, darling?"

"Yes, please, Dad. Cash? I don't have time for a check to clear."

"Oh? Leaving so soon?" asked Dr. Ertz, rocking on his heels, his hands in his pockets.

"Tomorrow, early."

"Where are you young people off to?" the Ertzes asked simultaneously.

"I'm off to Poland to fuck her," said Tommy, pointing to someone on *The Real World* who looked a little like Marta, except calmer, with a flat, expansive forehead and a cigarette in a holder.

Tommy surfed off *The Real World* to avoid a news brief by Kurt Loder about somebody that found Elvis's Diners Club card under a merry-go-round. She paused on a show about parachute failures.

"Thanks for the pig sandwiches and chocolate, Dr. and Mrs. Ertz."

Dr. Ertz was counting a pile of cash. Mrs. Ertz was in the kitchen.

"'Night, Tommy," I said, on my way up the stairs.

A rainbow parachute collapsed. Tommy surfed on.

I lay on Christine's bed, which was park-bench-hard and canted sharply toward the middle of the room. If I fell asleep, I would roll off and land, probably avulsion-first, on her shaggy four-leaf-clover rug.

I fell asleep anyway.

Later I woke, clenching the bladder muscles.

I lay unmoving for about thirty minutes, until the pressure in my bladder got to be painful, then I sat up slowly. The bed creaked. Immediately the dogs started grunting and scrabbling outside my door. I lay back down.

Thirty minutes later, the pressure was bad enough that I really had no choice but to face Bumper and Bitsy and whatever the greyhounds were called.

I got up without making the bed creak and went to the door. All was quiet. I reached for the doorknob. All was calm. I touched the doorknob. All was calm. I turned the doorknob.

Snarling and rutting and foaming. It sounded like a gazelle being torn apart. I went back and sat on the edge of the bed, looking around the room for an idea.

I undid the old latches on a casement window and pulled with my good hand until it finally popped up a few inches. There was no screen to worry about. I stuck my dick over the sill and held the window up with one hand so it wouldn't come guillotining down and really make things complex. I relaxed the muscles. A waxing gibbous moon lit the room a chalky, shadowy gray.

I peed like a superhero. Urine Man.

But the urine splattered back. A storm window, now streaked. Pee ran into the casement, mixing with a century of mummified gypsy moths and decayed foam insulation. I clenched the object muscles—possibly the single most difficult act of abstinence of my life—and the flow shut off.

Desperately I looked around the dark room for anything, anything in which to decant. The dogs yipped and scrabbled. Bumper had forced her snout under the door.

I turned on the light. There was a closet with sliding doors. A bureau.

Stuck to the mirror over the bureau was a picture of Bono with his mouth open. There was a rocking chair with a leprechaun doll relaxing in it, the sort of horror-movie doll that wanders around at night cudgeling sleeping people.

Nothing under the bed at all. Nothing in the bureau drawers except green sweaters and green panties and green jeans. The closet doors were locked.

I curled up like an infant and lay on the rug, panting. Bumper, snout bloodied, watched me under the door. I counted sixteen dog legs pacing behind him, yowling for meat.

Above me, on the wicker rocking chair, Lucky stared.

I got up, picked up Lucky, clamped him under my arm for leverage, and pulled on his head. It came off with a crunchy pop. I filled him full of pee. I plugged his head back in, then made him comfortable again on his rocking chair.

I woke in the morning to Dr. Ertz sitting on the edge of the bed. He smiled monstrously. In one hand he balanced a tray with orange juice and toast and bacon and a cup of coffee, in the other he had a big Filene's bag. Lucky watched us from his chair.

"Tommy's dressing and preening," said Dr. Ertz, placing the tray across my thighs. "And Triffica—that's Tommy's mother—went out first thing and chose you an outfit for you two's trip. Sit up and eat your breakfast, my friend. Up! Up! Fortify! There you go. Pillows behind the head. When you're done, try on your clothes. The dogs are all in the oubliette, so don't worry about them."

He slapped my shin through the thin blanket.

"Last chance—want me to look at your hand?"

I shook my head. Think what those pink ferns have probed!

He left, leaving the door open.

I ate. In the Filene's bag were two pairs of boxers (sleds on one, sushi on the other), a couple pairs of dramatically bell-bottomed jeans three sizes too large, each pocket of which was embroidered with big, loopy copperplate Fs, a green flannel shirt, a blue flannel shirt, four pairs of white ribbed sports socks, and a tremendous dreadnought coat, heavy as a dump-truck tire. I dressed, put my old "clothes" into the Filene's bag, and rolled up my new ones.

In the bathroom medicine cabinet I found an old unfinished prescription of Beepen-VK. Probably wouldn't prevent an infection, but it couldn't hurt. I ate a few, pocketed the remainder, then went downstairs.

Tommy was at the kitchen table, counting money. *Live and Let Die* was on TV. The jazz funeral scene.

"Hi," I said.

A man on the street in the French Quarter watches the Dixieland funeral procession. He is sweating.

"Where are your folks?"

Outside, fog and snow. My pinkie was still numb, but the rest of my hand, my wrist, and my forearm ached like fractures.

"Out someplace."

"Your mom bought me some new clothes."

"I know, I couldn't stop her. Nice fucking pantaloons."

I hitched up the roomy jeans. I wished I had a belt.

"Your mom's pretty cool."

"Take her. Please."

"Where're the dogs?"

"In the hole, probably. You ready?"

"Whose funeral is it?" says the man to a bystander.

"Uh," I said, from under a sudden but familiarly smothering terror: I was broke. I was homeless. Injured. It was winter.

"Uh *what*, man?"

"I don't know, maybe we can stay here for a while?"

"No."

New Orleans looked warm on TV. I could be broke and homeless in a warm place.

"Well," I said. I could put up with Tommy for three days. She was hateful, but she hadn't meant to hurt me.

"Well... what?" said Tommy. "Fuck, man, know any sentences?"

Besides, I could not think of a single alternative.

"Okay."

"Go to the bathroom."

"Leave the razor here," I said.

"Yours," says the bystander.

"Let's go."

o

Through the rear window of Tommy's Pontiac, fog ate the buildings of downtown Hartford.

"Haven't you ever loved anyone so much you'd travel across the country for them?" Tommy asked me when we crossed the state line into New York.

"No, I guess not," I said.

"That's lucky," said Tommy.

"It doesn't feel lucky."

"You'd feel a lot unluckier if your only love was dead and you weren't asked to the funeral and you're driving two thousand miles just to see if you can get one more taste of her before she's completely gone, to see the bars she went to, the hospital she was born in, the sky she looked at."

Most of the time, Tommy drove.

It wasn't long before the symptoms of psych-med withdrawal began to manifest. Tics in the muscles of the forehead; pyrotechnic prisoner's cinema; a nearly irresistible urge to crush my own Adam's apple. These would all pass. Since meds had never done me much good anyway, I had plans to never take them again.

We ate from convenience stores. I was content with Slim Jims and Cokes, and Tommy subsisted on refrigerated sandwiches. Each time we ate, I had to ask her to stop an hour later so I could use a restroom.

Tommy had started to repeat many of the anecdotes she had about Marta, adding a little, cutting a little each time. Polishing. Now they'd spent several days together instead of three hours; now they'd met on a train instead of in the ladies' room at a New Bedford Jack in the Box; now they'd made secret love in the cozy coat check of the Ritz-Carlton on the Common instead of groping on a billboard catwalk; now they'd been separated from each other in the Isabella Stewart Gardner Museum when Tommy'd fainted with emotion before the empty frame of a stolen Vermeer and been rushed to a hospital while Marta, unknowing, was strolling in the snowy garden by herself, instead of their being separated like dogs by cops and chemicals.

I did not challenge her embellishments. I just wanted to get to New

Orleans, then say so long forever to Tommy and her malevolent narcissism.

I did more and more of the driving the farther south we went. By the time we crossed into Tennessee, I was handling most of it. I was content with this: Tommy was quieter as a passenger. She slept a lot.

Somewhere in northern Alabama, after more than a hundred miles of silence between us, Tommy startled me by saying, "You know what, Jerome?"

"What?"

I waited, but she didn't say anything. It was four or five in the morning. I was driving sixty-five down a narrow, deserted two-lane road. The massive trees on either side of us arched so snugly over the road it was not hard to imagine the car as ordnance firing through the bore of a huge cannon.

I didn't ask Tommy *what* again, because I didn't want to know and maybe she'd forget she'd said anything at all.

"I wish that that guy was still alive, that's what," she said finally.

Far ahead of us was a brighter spot on one side of the road.

"What guy?"

"That kitchen guy," she said, sitting up and looking down the highway. "Look, if that's a store up there, stop. I'd kill a cocker spaniel for a nuked Hot Pocket calzone right now."

"What a weird place for a store. What kitchen guy?"

"Jerome, let me tell you a story. A kitchen-guy story. It's a fable. Wait, do you smell that?"

"I didn't do anything at all, I swear!" I said. We were approaching the bright spot in the road. "Oh, wait. I do smell it. Wow. What is that?"

"Cinnamon rolls. Pull into the lot."

A single streetlamp illuminated a small gravel parking lot occupied by a delivery van that read on one side BAKED GOO (a ghostly outline of the DS barely evident), and a low building set at an angle to the road, as though it had been erected on a giant lazy Susan and rotated 45 degrees. The perfume of the tiny bakery before us was so intoxicating as to be nearly sexual. Who would've thought northern Alabama was the world's Parnassus for come-fuck-me cinnamon rolls.

"Do you think they're open?" I said, charmed dreamy by the aroma.

"It's a fucking bakery. Sparrowfart-early is when bakeries bake, Coe. C'mon. Let's eat."

Inside was a single room, no larger than a garage. At the far end was the kitchen, at our end a glass bakery case with a cash register on top. Right in the middle of the room stood a card table covered in secondhand tools and utensils and junk, each tagged with a price. Next to the tool table stood a museum-grade glass vitrine filled with three racks of cinnamon rolls. Suddenly I got my first food-related boner ever. I hadn't even known they were possible.

"Yo!" shouted Tommy, idly picking up an old claw hammer from the card table. "Service, please!"

"Yes, please? There is no need for shouting. Hello! Hello! How may I help you?"

Just behind the register sat a woman watching a tiny black-and-white TV freeze-framed on the stony profile of Rutger Hauer. She did not look away. With the steadiness and concentration of an optic surgeon, the woman was scissoring away tiny bits from a precise one-tenth-scale black-paper silhouette of Rutger.

"Yeah. Dozen of those," said Tommy, indicating the vitrine with the claw hammer. "You have coffee here?"

"Sorry! Sorry. Those rolls are on hold. But there are some in the Blodgett oven, let us just wait for the timer to tone! Minutes away. And no coffee, sorry, sorry."

With a *kenk* Tommy dropped the hammer back onto the card table between us.

"Anyways, Jerome. Let me tell you my little kitchen-guy story."

She picked up a large cast-iron spokeshave.

"A couple hours before I rescued you outside your on-fire apartment, Jerome, I broke into the Boll. What the fuck is this fucking tool?"

"You broke *in*?"

I picked up a kind of industrial whisk ($1.99) and bounced it gently on the edge of the table.

"Not the main building, where be loons. The annex. The doctors' offices. I busted a basement window. Found Marta's doctor's office and took a big, crazy shit right in front of the door. You would've been impressed, Jerome."

A buzzer sounded. The woman dropped her silhouette project, jumped up, and scuttled to the back of the bakery, yodeling "Rolls! Rolls! Rolls!"

"Jesus, Tommy," I said, putting the whisk back onto the table.

"Just a little payback."

Poor Dr. Boone.

"Why blame her doctor? Jeez, I know him, he's a nice man."

"Because the dead guy, the mullethead who murdered her, the fucking kitchen guy, is dead. If he'd survived, I'd be—right this very instant— torturing him to death with HCl and X-Acto knives. So the only one left to punish was her doctor."

"You have to blame somebody, I guess."

Only six hundred miles to New Orleans. God help me.

"Are you making fun of me?"

"Cooling period!" yodeled the baker woman as she scuttled back to her silhouette-cutting station by the register. "Ten minutes."

"No, I—"

"Good," said Tommy, picking up a big, dull auger bit and pointing it at my neck. "Because you're goddam right I have to blame somebody."

"She snuck out on her own, Tommy. She did it all the time. Barry Miner—the dead kitchen guy—snuck her out through the kitchen. I saw her leave a few times. Giggling and dressed in all black like a ninja."

"You saw her?"

Tommy's eyes, arid and matte, like those of a carved ebony fetish, corrupted the steaming, narcotic promise of my cinnamon rolls, now only six or seven minutes away.

"Well, everybod—"

"Oh. I see."

"She—"

"You didn't tell the staff though. Did you."

"Well, no, but Marta was so slippery, I didn't think it—"

"They could've stopped her? If they knew?"

"Yeah, I supp—"

"Put her somewhere safe, some quiet room?"

"—"

"Kept an eye on her?"

"Everybody snuck out now and then," I said. "It was a kind of secret camaraderie, you know, among the patients."

"So you *let* her go. You."

"Barry Miner took her out, Tommy, come on, she wanted to go."

"And now," said Tommy, "she'd dead."

On the table, under a delaminating Ping-Pong paddle, I discovered a tight coil of leather. A belt! $2.25! I leaned across the table to claim it. Tommy brought her auger bit ($13.99) down on my bad hand so hard every object on the table jumped a foot.

I screamed and fell back against the bakery case.

"You."

Tommy flipped the card table. Tools and junk rained down on me. She waded through the mess toward me and hacked at me with the auger. I blocked it with a boot but she kicked me in the mouth, wedging the toe of her filthy blue high-top in almost to my molars. I bit down as hard as I could. She howled and tried to yank her shoe out of my mouth. She chopped at my ribs with the auger until I let go. She fell back, shattering the vitrine of cinnamon rolls and dropping the auger. We both scrambled to stand up. A scream, *Stop now!* followed by a loud pop. Tommy grabbed a linoleum knife from the mess of tools on the floor. I ran out the door. She followed, roaring like a coke furnace. I pulled the keys out of my pocket, dropped them, heard and felt the linoleum knife open a long slit in the back of my coat, through my shirt, and deep enough into my flesh that I yelped. I kicked the keys as hard as I could. They went all the way under the car to the passenger side. I vaulted over the hood but Tommy couldn't lift her body high enough and smacked the fender, falling back. I found the keys in the gravel and unlocked the passenger door and jumped in just as she came around the front of the car. I yanked the door but she jammed her knife into the crack before the door could latch. I held it shut with one hand while she got her fingers in around the edge of the window and tugged back. Holding the door closed, I stretched back across the bench seat and with my bad hand put the key in the ignition, but couldn't turn it. Tommy was winning the tug-of-war with the door. I suddenly let go, hoping she'd fall back, but she'd been ready for that trick and merely stumbled back a step or two. But it was just long enough for me to reach back with my good hand and start the car. I kicked at her as she clawed at me to get inside. Still lying on the seat I pulled the gearshift into R and jammed down the gas pedal with my bad hand. The tires kicked up so much gravel it strafed Tommy's face and broke the passenger-door window. She grabbed my leg. The tires caught and the Pontiac launched itself backward toward the road, Tommy hanging on to my leg. We fishtailed. Tommy yanked me to the floor. I held on to the steering wheel with one hand, the car doing violent doughnuts in the gravel lot. Tommy began to climb up my leg, using handfuls of denim and flesh as rungs. But my jeans, extra-roomy as they were, couldn't hold fast under Tommy's pull, and they suddenly came down and off, over my boots, leaving Tommy rolling and screaming in the gravel parking lot, still holding fast to the jeans her mother had kindly given me.

I drove at least ninety-five miles per hour for two hours, every second checking the mirror to see if Tommy had carjacked somebody or stolen the BAKED GOO van and come after me, but I never saw another vehicle, coming or going. I turned down an unlikely road and drove a couple more hours until I reached another two-lane highway. Soon a truck stop called the Shoulder Lily appeared.

I parked, nose out, between two trailerless sleeper semis.

The whole bench seat, the steering wheel, the gas and brake pedals, and my entire body were sticky with blood. I carefully pulled my slit-open dreadnought coat and shirt off and over my bad hand, whose Joe Cool bandage was loose and lead-heavy with soaked-in blood. I could not think of what it must be like under there. The slice in my back was not as deep as it felt, but it was deep enough to be the source of much of the blood.

On the floor of the passenger seat Tommy's backpack lay crumpled. Inside were an A.N. Roquelaure paperback with a tasseled plastic bookmark of Nick Cave inserted, another straight razor, a bottle of Motrin, about two hundred in cash. A few liters of water. A squeeze-bottle of Anal-Eze. A small black rubber penis covered in crumbs and dirt and hair.

I climbed into the back and rooted around. I found an old but unopened package of Tushies diapers. I climbed out with the diapers and backpack and a change of clothes. Behind the car I took off my boots and socks and boxers. I washed with Tommy's bottled water, scraping the old blood off me with the edge of Nick Cave.

I unwrapped my hand. Something deep in it crunched, like sand in the gears of a Tonka truck. Blood literally fell out of the cut and splashed on the ground. I squeaked with the pain and threw up, but didn't faint.

I wrapped my hand back up with a Tushie, got dressed, picked up Tommy's razor, and walked over to an old Chevy Malibu that was parked nose-in to a dense knot of cattails and assorted other water weeds at the edge of the parking lot. I squeezed between the front bumper and the forest of weeds, boots in the mud, and crouched down. With the razor I unscrewed the front license plate, a Georgia tag from Oconee County. I took off the Pontiac's plate, jammed it into the backpack, and whipped the whole thing into the cattails. I screwed on the Georgia plate, wiped mud on it, and got back into the car.

I headed southwest. In a few hundred miles I would be on the front porch of a youth hostel in New Orleans.

III

Erril's Fashion Department Store was probably not the oldest department store on American soil, but it was certainly the oldest that had never been remodeled or modernized or cleaned. The floors were the worn, flecked, putty-and-bean color of junior-high-school hallways. The walls met the floor not at a sharp right angle but with a little ramp of oily, packed dirt studded with price tags and cigarette butts. The sales floor was dusk dark, illuminated only by low, shaded light fixtures, like in a noir pool hall. But instead of wiry felons and pompadoured hustlers, the place was alive with tiny old ladies in cataract shades slaloming sock racks and girdle displays. Erril's was also likely the last department store in the country with a lunch counter.

The Luncheonaire's low stools were all unoccupied. On the counter were clusters of standard diner complements: mustard, ketchup, and mayonnaise squeeze bottles, Tabasco, salt and pepper shakers, sugar cubes, tiny cream tankards, and large jam and jelly caddies with wire handles. On the end of the counter was a pie spinner spinning pies. Behind the counter but in front of the soda fountain was an old electric cash register partly mummified in silver duct tape. Just beside it stood a tall, skinny woman, her graying hair tied up in a ponytail. She looked pretty much the way Ioanna had described Mrs. Hebert. She was stabbing a two-quart can of orange Hi-C with a steak knife.

She left the knife sticking hilt-deep in the can, and turned her attention to me.

"Let's find a menu, unless you know what you want," she said.

The stool I sat on was so low and the waitress so tall that I had a sudden vivid memory of being in the bathtub as a child when a lady at the home I was at walked in with a box of Mr. Bubble and sprinkled it in the running water, smiling down at me.

I thought it was best to eat first, before stating my mission.

"Set me up with a menu, bay. What's good?" I said in my best easygoing voice, which I'd started to affect a day or two after arriving in New Orleans. Later I learned that most newcomers here do the same thing, sometimes unconsciously, but often actively practicing the music of the accent, then testing it out on native New Orleanians to see if it passed muster. It never did—you just got giggled at.

"Nothing to speak of," she said, handing me a menu.

I thought I'd get something like a po'boy or gumbo or étouffée, to mask my origins, but there was nothing of the sort on the menu. There were Reuben melts, hamburgers, butt-steak sandwiches, ham, and ham with pineapple circles. Under ACCOMPANIMENTS were french fries, milk, and coffee. Dessert was a roster of pies, and "Candy."

I ordered a hamburger and fries and a Coke. Safe enough, and it sounded good.

She disappeared for about five minutes, then emerged with my lunch. It was the largest hamburger I'd ever seen. A slice of onion an inch thick stuck out on all sides like a ring of Saturn. There were four french fries, each a half of a potato. The Coke came in an aquarium of crushed ice.

"Ioanna said it was good eatin' here," my full mouth said.

She stopped consolidating half-empty Tabascos with a foil funnel and turned to me, a hand on her hip.

"*You're* the cheese-sandwich man?"

"Yes ma'am."

"Well, get on back here and grill me one while I examine your technique."

I did. My technique, and the resulting sandwich, were perfect.

"This is a reasonable product," said Mrs. Hebert between bites. "But I'm concerned that that mushed breadhook of yours will fail you during the lunch stampede and I'll be left overworked and unassisted and a robber'll seize the opportunity to run off with my gratuity jar."

She tapped on my bandaged hand with a grilled-cheese crust.

"Oh no," I said. "A minor cut, getting better every day."

"Your timing's good, I'll grant you that. A colleague just quit me."

"I can start immediately!"

"Alrighty," she said after a moment. "But I need you to work as a scullion for a day or two first. Major left a mess."

I was the first new employee there in fourteen years, since Major Robey, the day-shift short-order cook and store mouser whose grinning pictures papered the wall over the dishwasher, had quit Erril's to enjoy a career in wager management, specializing in Pop Warner football. The workday started at nine in the morning and went until the evening cook, Grouchy Torrance, who was grouchy and had a Parkinsonian shiver, relieved me at five.

Every time I got home to the hostel after work, I'd check the big world map to see where the new people were from. It hadn't changed much during the month I'd been here. The pink pin in Quito was still there, but she was one person I hadn't met. I'd encountered many of the Danes, but never my two lower-berth roommates, not formally at least—they were always passed out on their bunks in some stage of drunkenness, or recovery from same. I only ever saw their dorsal sides banded with snug primary-colored jockey shorts. And I never saw my last Danish roommate, the one who may or may not have been present while I ruined my sock.

I couldn't tell if Carolyn felt the same kind of peace around me as I did around her, but she didn't seem to mind my hanging around and lying on the vector-borne couch in the lobby of the hostel after my shift at the Luncheonaire while she talked on the phone and monkeyed with her hair and made sport of the hostelers.

"A while back," she said one afternoon after I'd come in from a long day of grilled-cheese grilling, "one of the Danes scored some weed from someplace and decided he wanted to make a New Orleans–themed bong, and asked if I had anything he could use. All I could find was a ukulele with a Cabildo sticker on the back. 'How's this?' I said.

"'Ja nok!' he says, and, with some kind of little canvas roll of tools he kept in his pocket, he transformed the uke into a bong in I swear under half a minute."

"I tried a bong once," I said, "but I didn't do it right. I thought I was supposed to blow, not suck."

That had unintentionally come out with at least two entendres. I blushed, but Carolyn did not seem to notice.

"This guy didn't do it right either. He flicked his Bic, and then *floop!* the lacquer on the ukulele suddenly caught on fire."

I looked at the big soot stain.

"I'm surprised the whole place didn't burn down," I said, gesturing at the black teardrop. "Look how high the flames went."

Carolyn turned around and looked.

"Oh," she said. "*That*'s from a *different* fire."

"Serious? Do you have fires all the time? Are they scheduled or something?"

"It was this chick Francie," Carolyn said, her voice suddenly flat. She picked up an *Archie* comics digest on her desk and idly thumbed through it.

"Francie?"

Francie, Carolyn explained, was a lottery-ticket vendor at Tip's Grocery a few streets over who had come into the hostel one afternoon about a year before and pitched a Cricket lighter overhand at another hostel clerk's head. Francie missed the clerk, just barely, but the lighter hit the wall behind him and exploded, as Crickets, when pitched, will do, lighting the clerk's hair and nearly kindling the hostel itself.

"Random?"

"No," she said, drawing out the syllable and elevating the pitch at the end. "Not random."

"The other clerk wasn't hurt?"

"Terence?" she said. "Not really. Got his left-side dreads burned off."

"Oh, I've seen that guy. Working on weekends. I always wondered why his hair was like that. I get an urge to even it out."

"He would object."

"Yeah. Did they catch Frances?"

"*Francie.* Yes."

"I bet she went to jail."

"She sat in the back of a cop car for a few hours."

"That's all?"

"Her dad grounded her, too," said Carolyn.

There was something terminal about the way she said *too*. We were quiet for a while. Then, as if she'd been searching for the topic of conversation furthest removed from fire, she said: "Had a chick here once who lived in Antarctica."

I shifted on the couch so I could see her. She was sitting and tugging at her hair with an old plastic brush with black bristles. One knee was bent and pushed up against the rim of the gray metal desk. The denim covering it was pale and thinning. If she were to lean forward, the taut cotton strands might *snap snap snap*, revealing her skin and releasing the tiniest puffs of cotton dust.

"I didn't think anyone was from there," I said.

"She was, or so she said. She wanted to sleep with me. She said I looked warm."

That was the first time Carolyn had referred to sex. Incredibly, no uncomfortable feelings beset me. Not jealousy, lust, love, propriety, blues, shame, unrequitableness. Just that same weird peace. *I have a friend!*

"Did you?"

"Did I look warm?"

"No, I mean…"

"You know," Carolyn continued, "it only snowed here once, and I fucking missed it. It lasted three hours and was gone by noon. You know why? Me and my Antarctican were in bed at the Guesclin Hotel sleeping off a slivovitz hangover."

"What's that?"

"Czech white lightning."

"I bet it snows a lot in the Czech Republic," I said.

"Worse in Denmark. Believe me, I've heard stories."

"I wonder how bad it is in Quito?"

"No telling," said Carolyn, looking over her shoulder at the pink pin. "It looks like it's in the mountains. You oughta ask her next time you see her."

"You know, I don't think I've ever seen her," I said.

"You're kidding."

"Why would I kid?"

"She sleeps with you, man."

"What're you talking about? I'm not sleeping with anyone. I'd remember."

She smiled and snorted, as if she couldn't stand pretending for one moment longer that I wasn't an idiot.

"Not *with* you, you pervert. Next to you. The other top bunk? The Spanish didn't tip you off?"

That could not be. I looked at my socks.

"That's a girl?" I said.

"She doesn't look like a girl to you? Long black hair, kissy lips? She looks like a girl to me, Jerome," said Carolyn. "I mean, she's a *girl*."

"I've never seen her!" I said, sitting up straight, a bloom of pathogens rising from the couch. "I've never seen anyone in that bunk!"

"She does sleep during the day, come to think of it," said Carolyn. "She parties all night, with your other roomies."

"I've never met *them*, either," I said. "But, she's, I mean, you mean... are you saying that girls and boys can sleep together in the same room?"

"If the hostel's crowded, yes, Jerome, boys and girls can room together. Your other roommates are gay, anyway. They're good friends with her. And you're..."

"What? What? I'm not gay," I said, not really sure of it—the muscular calves on those Tour de France guys always gave me a boner. And I had strange, pelvicentric feelings regarding Daniel Day-Lewis's Adam's apple.

"Did I say gay? I was going to say that you're safe-looking."

"Safe."

"Safe." said Carolyn. "You're a very safe yet excitable young straight man."

"What's her name?"

"Miranda," said Carolyn.

"Miranda," said I.

I never saw Miranda. Her bunk was always empty, except for the scatter of panties and empty cans of lager. Now I wondered if the spring triple issue

of *Größte Pfosten* had been hers rather than one of my other roommates'.
I hoped it wasn't hers. I could never measure up to Werner.

It didn't matter anyway, because I had to move out of the hostel. I couldn't
earn enough making cheese sandwiches to pay eighteen bucks a night for a
place to live, even though I was quite skilled, and becoming locally famous.

I began spending my lunch hour and the hours after work apartment-
hunting. But after a while I realized I was looking less for apartments and
more for girls with long black hair and kissy lips. There were an awful lot
of them. But none were Miranda: I queried them all.

One apartment, just a couple of blocks from the Smart Harriet, had
sounded promising in the ad but proved to be unsuitable, because of the
antsy junkie squatters there who objected to any changes in the tenancy.

"Fuck off!" they said.

I fucked off and went to the Smart Harriet.

"You smell like grilled cheese," Ioanna informed me.

"I make a lot of them. I'm quite famous."

I wondered if Miranda had heard of my sandwiches.

"Famous? Are you getting rich?" Ioanna asked. "Are you going to
buy a mansion and lease me a wing so I can live out my spinster years in
seclusion?"

"I would, but I can't even afford to stay at the hostel anymore."

"I'll rent you my tub!" shouted Coryate, from the counter. "No pets!"

"No, that's okay," I said.

Coryate yelled for a refill.

I'd learned that Coryate was an artist who made his living doing charcoal portraits of tourists in Jackson Square. Reputedly he was also a sketch
artist for the cops, and occasionally accepted small thank-you gifts in return
for little changes here and there to his sketches so that they more closely
resembled persons the police did not like but whom they otherwise had no
good reason to arrest.

"How's the hand?" he said.

"Better," I said, looking down.

I still kept it wrapped in gauze and an Ace bandage. It just would
not heal properly. It hurt. I should've kept my word and gone to a doctor long ago. I'd have been able to make world-famous grilled cheeses
a lot quicker if I'd had full use of both hands. It was the one chronic,

concrete reminder that there had been a time before these pacific New Orleanian days, a period of frost, blood, locks, misinterpretations, briarthicket loneliness. I imagined the relief I'd get by hacking it off with a big pork cleaver.

I promised myself that once I'd found a place to live I'd go to the doctor and have this rotting gash taken care of. I didn't want to repulse Miranda, after all.

Carolyn telephoned later and told me that she had a friend who'd finally gotten so fed up with the surprise reversals of fortune that in his view so characterized New Orleans that he just up and got on a Greyhound back to his homeland.

"Homeland?" I said, still a little fuzzy from having a positively Kodachromic daydream interrupted: me and Miranda in a pile of autumn leaves, locked in a promising tickle fight.

"Canada. And his place is now available."

"That's great! Who…?"

"Terence, the poor bastard. Got wasted and fell asleep too close to a gas heater. Burned his right-side dreads off."

What a relief. Terence's place was cheap and only about fifteen blocks from the hostel. I still went to see Carolyn every day, partly—muchly—in hopes that Miranda would turn up. But she never did. She'd either just gone out or had just come back and gone to bed.

"How's Terence's shithole shotgun?" asked Carolyn when I came in one afternoon.

She quoined a whole giant SweeTart in her mouth and bit hard. A little chalky rocket shot across the room.

"Pretty fair," I said.

And it was, except for the next-door neighbor, Mr. Murdoch, a slick Romeo in his fifties who lived with his mother.

They fought a lot, this mother and son, mostly about the son's womanizing. He often had sleepover dates, and the mother would sometimes bust into the son's room while the dating was in progress, to warn the woman that she'd better watch out or she'd catch some AIDS. I knew this because *everything* radiated through those desiccated plaster walls.

"His mom? And he's *fifty*?" said Carolyn.

"Yeah. She's cool. I don't like the son, though. There's something of the player/masher/predator about him."

I would occasionally hear him promising a conquest his indivisible fealty, and then, sometimes within hours, promising another lover the same thing.

I had another damn good reason not to like the man, but I didn't feel like explaining it to Carolyn: my toilet was structurally connected to his—they were back-to-back, with just a thin wall in between—and if I was on my toilet when he sat on his, I seesawed into the air.

"I never went to Terence's place," said Carolyn, wrapping the telephone cord around a pencil. "But he tried to get me over there all the time, probably in order to fill me with absinthe and snip off my clothes with electric scissors."

Carolyn made an electric-scissors sound and scissored her fingers down the front of her T-shirt.

"Wow," I said.

"I think he thought that absinthe restored heterosexual lust in dykes."

"Does it?" I said, not sure if she was being sarcastic.

"Nope," she said. "Beer could, though. How's the water pressure?"

"Not bad," I said. "I'd say forty percent of ideal."

"Any charm? Everything in this city is supposed to be charming."

I thought about it.

"Well, in the kitchen over the counter there's a big black wooden thing stuck to the wall, like a Louise Nevelson sculpture. But tighter scrutiny revealed its true nature to be kitchen cabinets. A long bank of them, painted shut. I tried chipping away at the paint, but it must be a half-inch thick."

"Probably a body in there. Or maybe just heads. That's charming, I guess. Notice an odor?"

"No, just the—" I looked past Carolyn. I think I turned red, or maybe white.

"Wha?" she said, a giant SweeTart puck stored in one cheek.

"The girl from Quito's gone," I said.

I moved my head from side to side, to see if I'd just caught the light the wrong way. No, there was no pink pin there. I felt like I'd been hit in the back of the knees by a medicine ball.

"Yep, Miranda's gone," said Carolyn. "Checked out this a.m., before I came on. A surprise. I thought she'd stay forever. Oh, they do get some bitch snow in Quito, by the way. We chatted a little yesterday after she came in late from some kind of X-rated crab-boil puppet show in the Bywater. I told her about your snow stories, and how much you hated snow, and how you left Massachusetts because of it. That made her laugh."

"She laughed about snow?"

"Giggled. I think she liked you, Jerome. She said she watched you sleeping all the time. She said you have a cute philtrum."

"Me?" My esophagus dried out and the arches of my feet started to sweat. My whole skull was steaming and my ears seemed to be furling and trying to retract into my skull. "A cute philtrum?"

Carolyn looked at me very happily, like I was a torpid dummy who had just surprised the community by finishing ninth in a spelling bee, earning an item in the local paper.

"I think so," said Carolyn. "She also said you looked just like a tiny baby sleeping, that you curl your hand up into a tiny baby fist. She wanted to miniaturize you and carry you in a pouch to keep you cozy and protect you from harm, and feed you little bits of flan and lettuce and french fry."

"Oh my."

"What?"

"You're making all that up!"

"No, I'm really not. And judging by that rosy blush, it seems that the news pleases you."

"Not me," I said, squeaking, panicky, suddenly desperate to find her. "It sounds like she was flirting with *you*."

"Right," she said. "I wish. I never get femmes."

Carolyn was suddenly gloomy. For a few moments she focused on licking clean the inside of her Giant Chewy SweeTarts wrapper. Then she cheered up again.

"If I'd only known sooner," she said. "I could've won her for you, Jerome. Cute philtra are really irresistible to the Pacific South Americans."

"Really?"

"I'm sorry she's gone, Jerome. She was a fire-fucking-*work*. Except for the glasses."

My muscles withered under my skin. I felt like I was wearing a beef-jerky suit.

"Did she go back to Quito?"

"Doubt it. I think she was planning to stay."

"Where? You know, just curious."

"I don't have the slightest idea."

"Someone has to know," I said, considering running up to the room just to make sure she wasn't still there. "What about our other two roomies?"

"Gone, too."

"Dammit! Are you sure you don't have just a really slight idea?"

"I don't *know*, Jerome. Are you really hooked on someone you haven't met yet? Or even seen?"

"No, I certainly am not, how ridiculous."

I crossed my arms and tried to appear bored.

"Damn, you are. You really should've told me. A long time ago. I love matchmaking."

Truth was, I hadn't known until now.

I scanned the map as if it might hold a clue to her whereabouts. I was ready to go anywhere.

"If she comes back," she said, "I'll snag her for you."

"No you won't," I said, using a dismissive, woe-is-me tone of voice which over the years I'd tuned so finely that I could always count on a contradictory response from whomever I was addressing.

"Yes I will."

"No you won't."

"Just watch."

I was coming in the gate to the duplex when my neighbor Mr. Murdoch, the lothario whose mother interrupted his nightly gamboling to preach against communicative disease, emerged from a shed in his tiny side yard and began to vigorously run a rusted manual lawnmower back and forth over a square foot of weeds, shredding them. He was sweating and his black socks had fallen down to his shoes. He wore dark glasses, and a thin cigar stuck out of his mouth. I waved.

"I've been meaning to come over by the Luncheonaire for a meal, Mr. Jerome," said Mr. Murdoch grandly, pulling up his Bermuda shorts one side at a time.

"Seems like I'm there all the time," I said, not caring one way or the other. What was important at the moment was the possibility that Carolyn could find Miranda and explain to her that I was an agreeable, devoted sort and would make an excellent life companion.

"Come pay us a visit sometime," he said.

I wondered whom he had in his bed right this minute. Some credulous flower he'd plucked out of a dance club, probably. When he finished weed-shredding, he'd go in and have his way with her.

Later, I heard Mr. Murdoch's grave scapegrace chuckling next door. My brain unexpectedly engineered a scenario in which he was trawling the French Quarter with a big nylon purse-seine and caught Miranda. He declared his loyalty to her, brought her to his place, and stowed her in a box with air holes under his bed. And on nights when he had no luck finding gullible virgins on the streets of New Orleans, he chuckled—like now—then pulled her out and... *used* her.

Shaking my fist like Mussolini, I hissed at the wall.

"Never!"

Over the next few weeks, any workaday doings—sleep, job, food, bills, health—that didn't directly concern my pursuit of Miranda, I either shirked or forgot or just zombied through. Carolyn's assistance was largely technical or strategic—apart from the occasional brief prowl or stakeout, she didn't often do actual fieldwork. She did, however, try to cheer me up whenever I suffered an especially dispiriting search.

"She probably doesn't like me anyway," I said.

"Miranda didn't just see you sleeping, Jerome—a passive happenstance—but had *watched* you sleep. So chin up."

"I'll never, ever find her, and I bet she's forgotten me already."

"How can you have such a debilitating crush on someone you've never even met?"

"I'm not debilitated," I said.

Carolyn and I were sitting across from each other in a booth at the Smart Harriet. Ioanna was in a cold mood. She had taken our orders without comment, and had merely nodded when I reintroduced her to Carolyn. When she brought our food, she skidded the plates along the table so that they tapped the salt and pepper shakers at the far end. There was some sloshing of coffee. She gave Carolyn my pancakes and me Carolyn's waffles.

"You *look* debilitated," said Carolyn.

I sat with my elbows on the table, my forehead in my hands, staring at my pancakes, which had been placed on the same plate as my eggs and bacon, an arrangement I'd always found intolerable. If my syrup touched my eggs or bacon, I couldn't eat anything at all. And Ioanna knew that. She thought it was charming, or a symptom of Asperger's syndrome. Either way, she *always* made sure my sweets and savories arrived on two separate plates.

I glanced over at Ioanna to see if I could divine, from the way she swept out, wiped down, or swatted at things in the diner, just what I'd done to displease her. Maybe it was because she knew I hadn't gone to see a doctor yet about my stupid hand.

"Maybe *flummoxed* is a better word," said Carolyn. "And your bitchy mother over there probably doesn't help much."

"She's not my mother."

"Mother figure. Maybe the combination of your unpleasable mother figure and your unlocatable dream-girl figure has flummoxed and debilitated you."

Ioanna was stuffing napkins into a chrome napkin holder, far more napkins than the napkin holder was designed to hold, making napkins nearly impossible to remove, except in tiny shreds or in groups of one thousand. Most of the regulars brought their own.

Ioanna was really cramming one. Cords popped out on her neck. She bent over a little, and some cleavage became visible. Carolyn leaned toward me, watching Ioanna.

"She's hot, for forty-nine or whatever," said Carolyn. "Oh, but we're talking about your love life, Jerome. Sorry."

It felt different than love, this smothering mudslide of desperation and longing. It was an old feeling. Old as in preverbal, or even atavistic. But I didn't try to explain that to Carolyn.

I pushed my forehead harder into my hand so that my eyelids stretched. I moaned quietly.

"Please don't fall in love with her," I said. "I can't handle my friend figure lusting after my mother figure."

"You know what I think? I think your world is crowded with mother figures."

"Noo!"

"Would you just eat your food and quit groaning like that? You sound like Chewbacca."

"I can't. I hate this."

"If we can't find Miss Ecuador, I'll find you a girlfriend. I know lots of beautiful girls that won't have me. And they're sheep for nice philtra."

"But I want Miranda."

I moaned some more and squeezed my hair, while Carolyn ate lustily and Ioanna ignored our empty coffee cups.

"You know," said Carolyn, "I think your Ioanna there doesn't like me. She doesn't *approve*. She didn't like me the first time. I don't think she was expecting her little special man to befriend a coarse hussy."

"Guh."

"Maybe I'll be your girlfriend, Jerome."

Carolyn pantomimed a blow job. It was as shocking and obscene a performance as anything I'd ever witnessed. Then she initiated a game of footsie.

"I'm confused," I said.

Carolyn seemed amused by it all, and somehow my agonies made her expansive about her own sexual misadventures. She fell in love easily, she said, and became obsessed as deeply as I did, albeit with people she'd actually met at least once.

"Some of those girls out there nearly killed me," she said, as we drove down North Rampart after our meal. "The younger they are, the slimmer, the meaner, the smarter, then the darker the relationship becomes, until I'm a puddle of need, and then they leave me for someone that's even meaner and smarter but also has a tremendous bosom."

Carolyn swerved around an old man in a tracksuit doing a variant of the Riverdance in the middle of North Rampart. Carolyn and I often drove around aimlessly, drinking beer and wasting gas and avoiding eccentrics performing in the roadways. But this time I had the feeling we were aimed someplace.

"Where are we going?"

"We are going to look for your goddess. We are going to feel the curbs of every likely street until we find her. Or until it gets dark. I promised you I'd help, but I haven't been doing such a hot job. So. Here we are. Peel them eyeballs."

We drove up and down the long east–wests of the Bywater, slowing down now and then for closer looks at strollers and loiterers with Miranda attributes. As the false positives mounted, I grew even more despairing than usual.

The traffic slowed, then stopped. A rusted, ruined freight train was stalled ahead, blocking the road. Not quite stalled—it would jolt, then creep forward a few feet, then stop with a shudder, then jolt again and move a few feet in the other direction. There was another train on a parallel track doing the same thing, but to a different rhythm. Carolyn reached into the backseat and pulled a beer out of a big ice-filled cooler.

"Here."

"What's up with these trains?" I said, taking the glass quart of Miller. "I feel like I'm in a movie about doomsday."

A woman began to climb out of a hopper car. She hoisted herself over and then hung on to the lip of the car with one hand while she studied the ground. The cigarette in her mouth she tossed down onto the rail ballast. She wore a high-waisted white silk slip a shade or two paler than her skin and the spectral opposite of her short, chaotic, plum-tinted hair. She was backpacked, barefoot, and brass-knuckled. She let go of the hopper and dropped at least six feet, landing without a wince on the sharp rocks of the ballast. She picked up her cigarette, gave it a hard suck, then looked around.

"Is she what you meant by young and slim and mean?" I said.

"Don't point."

"I'm not pointing."

"Yeah," said Carolyn, sighing greatly. "She's what I mean."

The woman flicked her cigarette at least thirty feet, then ducked under the train and was gone.

"It was a bus wreck, my last relationship," said Carolyn, unsteadily, clearly affected by the short cinema of the feral freight-hopper. "It started so great, but got bad fast, then crashed. All because of a misunderstanding. That time, *she* was the one obsessed over *me*—can you believe that? But I was obsessed over her, too. We were perfect for each other."

She said that last without any irony that I could detect.

"Someone you worked with?" I said. "I read in *People* that that's asking for trouble."

"No. Well, kind of," she said wearily. "She wasn't really officially employed at the hostel. She was just there a lot, and kind of helped out some."

Finally, the trains slowly moved off, and we headed toward Arabi. We had started our second Miller quarts. It was getting dark.

"It was bad, though, huh," I said, not wanting the dialogue on love to fizzle. "It must have been very painful."

I sounded like Dr. Boone, for chrissake.

"Okay, it was Francie," Carolyn said suddenly. "The chick with the lighter."

"Oh. Ohh."

"The misunderstanding was that she thought I was cheating on her with this guy who worked at the hostel who was always coming on to me. But I wasn't. She threw the Bic at him—Terence, the dreadhead. Turned out later that *she*'d been cheating on *me*."

"Ak."

"Getting cheated on sucks," she said. "It's the mind's eye that does all the torturing. You know, picturing her with someone else, especially fucking someone else, doing it in that position that was just mine and hers, those little scream-hisses when she came that were *her* gifts to *me*, now she's giving them to someone else… you know what I mean?"

I noticed we were being ambitiously tailgated.

"Hey," I said, looking over my shoulder. "I think—"

"Maybe you don't," she continued, seeming to take no notice of the large car trying to spelunk our tailpipe. "Well. It hurts. And you can't not watch. The brain won't allow it. You see *A Clockwork Orange*? Remember the Ludovico Technique? Like that. The mind's eye, held open with little metal clips. Films. Over and over and overnovernover."

"You better let this guy around, he seems—"

"That, my friend," she said, still oblivious, "will never happen to me again. Never. Just talking about it now makes me want to drive off a cliff and die. Did you know I haven't hooked up with anybody since Francie? Know why? Just to avoid those films. They'll kill a girl. Kill."

"Carolyn! This guy is really close!"

"Oh. I see. Put your feet up on the dash, Jerome, I'm gonna stomp on my brake. I think I'm still insured."

But then we noticed it was a cop car, because of the sirens and flashing lights and the bullhorn commanding us to pull over.

"Fuck," said Carolyn.

We both had open quart-bottles of beer in our laps. Mine was almost full. Carolyn's was nearly gone.

She pulled over in front of a social club busy with people coming and going. I was in a panic. I had a full beer between my legs, and I was in a car, and soon I would be in a jail, where they'd run my name and see there was a bench warrant for me as a car thief and cinnamon-roll-bakery destroyer, then beat a confession out of me and throw me in solitary forever.

On the dashboard there was a blanched Monchhichi doll that must have been there for a decade. I grabbed it and forced it headfirst into the neck of my Genuine Draft. I carefully placed the bottle on the floor of the backseat just as the cop walked up.

"License and proof of insurance, please," said the cop.

"What'd you pull me over for?" said Carolyn.

My hand jumped to my heart.

"License and proofa insurance."

Carolyn yanked her backpack out from behind the seat and rifled around for a while until she found her billfold. She still had her quart of Lite beer between her legs.

"Here."

"Mm. And what you got there?" the cop asked.

"This is Lite beer from Miller."

"Let me see."

Carolyn handed the bottle to the cop, who held it up by the neck and peered through the liquid at the streetlights. There was about an inch of beer left.

"How much you had to drink tonight, ma'am?"

"Well, whatever's missing."

"Okay, then." He gave her the bottle back. "Get both those taillights fixed and your left directional and don't drive around this neighborhood this time of night, unless you bring you a bigger boyfriend. With two working hands."

"He's tougher than he looks," said Carolyn. "He's just lovesick right now. Besides, I have a .38 in my backpack."

"Okay then," said the cop. Then he went back to his cruiser and drove off.

"Wow," I said, sweating lather. "That jangled me up. I thought we were going to jail."

"What for? Busted taillights?"

"DUI and unlicensed firearms possession and smart-aleckiness and..."

"There's no DUI or gun licensing in New Orleans and I was perfectly polite and respectful."

We headed back west. Presently I caught the smell of the sea. Faint, but there. On a map, New Orleans is nearly surrounded by water. A lake, a river, the Gulf, bayous.

"I tried to kill myself after Francie," Carolyn said, her voice startling me.

"Jesus. Carolyn. Don't tell me that." I imagined Mr. Kline, my old landlord in Massachusetts, giving Carolyn a stern talk on the etiquette of the matter.

She turned on the dome light, and, without slowing down, rolled the right short sleeve of her shirt up over her shoulder. Through the stubble under her arm ran a short, fat scar right over the profunda brachii.

"I obviously missed the artery. Wasn't even close. Fucking hurt, and it didn't even bleed much. I didn't mention it to anybody."

"Fuck, Carolyn."

"I know."

"I command you to take good care of yourself!"

"You've never had anyone cheat on you. I envy you, you and your Miranda crush. I *run* from crushes now, not that I have them much. Or, more precisely, allow myself to have them. No more relationships for me. Just crushless sex. I'll take my relationship-forming urges out on you and your absentee Ecuadoran."

"This crush doesn't feel enviable."

"You didn't care about Miranda all that much till you found out she'd watched you sleep. That's kinda off, Jerome. A little kinky."

"Where is she now? Francie, I mean?"

"I don't know."

Quiet and a little drunk, we headed out on the old Airline Highway. Thunderstorms had been threatening all day. It was hot. The air was like meringue. I reached in the back and pulled a cold beer out of the cooler. I ignored my warm beer with the Monchhichi sticking out of it—likely both were ruined.

"Where are we going now? Stake out the airport lounge?"

"Watch planes."

The airport appeared ahead of us. Its cobalt-blue lamps lined runways that stretched off to vanishing points all around the circle of the horizon. The air-traffic control tower with its eerie green eye-panes looked out over the flatland.

It was late, but planes were still landing, probably delayed by the thunderstorms surrounding the city. Carolyn drove up to the top tier of the long-term parking garage and parked the car facing the runways. Ours was the only car up there.

We watched 737s land for a long time without saying anything. The only sound was the scraping roar of engines and the *brt brtbrt* of tires hitting the tarmac.

Carolyn climbed out of the car. She reached down and pulled the release on her seat back, which fell forward and lay flat. Then she jumped in the backseat and put her feet up. On the floor below her, among the beer bottles, was a snap of warm light: a gilt *Q* on the spine of a book. Quentin.

I recalled the chapter in *Shuffle* on arteries and veins. It was adorned with romantic little drawings of rococo daggers and distressed maidens in candlelit jacuzzis and persons from history who had tapped all their five quarts of blood. The drawing of Diane Arbus dying in her tub had looked like Peter Fonda asleep in a bumper boat.

"Comfortable?" I said, trying to forget *Shuffle*, at least for the moment.

"*Uuut. Ut.*"

She'd had more beer than I had. After a minute I climbed in the back too, and put my feet up on my pushed-forward front seat. The cooler of beer was on the floor between us.

We watched for planes, but there hadn't been any in more than an hour.

Carolyn leaned into me a little, then scooted over and put her head on my shoulder.

"Protect me from bad relationships," she said, an order. "And I promise I'll get you your black-haired snow bunny."

I felt an earring through the material of my shirt. A lone strand of hair poked at my earlobe. I adjusted slightly and put my arm around her shoulder. Perfectly natural. Because she was a lesbian and I was her friend, and we'd had some deep talks about love and such. Even thus, I grew a stratospheric, glowing erection.

"Deal," I said.

My heart chugged. Carolyn's hair, lighted by the glow of the airport, jumped every time my heart beat, or hers. After a moment of paralyzing discomfort, Carolyn gracefully half twisted toward me and suddenly she was lying face up in my lap. She reached up to pull me to her. I could hardly move, let alone bend over, even for a kiss, due to the erection. So I pulled her up to me.

She whimpered and cried and ran her hands over my face, kissing me lightly, almost without touching. She tasted of salt. I held her by the waist and under her shoulders. I slid down in the seat to get closer. I closed my eyes. I imagined Miranda, her kissy lips.

Then Carolyn stopped.

"Back in a few secs."

She climbed out, headed unsteadily to a concrete pillar, and disappeared behind it. A rivulet of liquid snaked from behind it, as black and shiny as blood under the sulfur arc lamps.

She came back.

"I have to go, too," I said.

I went over to the same spot she'd been. I saw where she'd crouched down, the spatter.

After some effort I undid my belt and zipper. My erection was the otherworldy, unbendable sort that I used to get in high school. And it was clearly not going to subside and allow me to pee in the accepted fashion (earthward). So I undid my jeans and just let go. I peed in a high arc over the city of Kenner, Louisiana. The last plane of the night cleared the thunderheads and landed between the long arrows of cobalt lamps.

When I got back to the car, Carolyn was stretched along the backseat, deep in sleep. Both disappointed and wildly relieved, I climbed in front, and soon I was just as dead to the world.

The drive back from the parking garage the next morning was generally silent. My clothes were damp with sour sweat. My head was a microwaved pumpkin. Carolyn pulled over in front of the First Impressions Bar and threw up out the window. Much of the barf went down inside the car door, where a rolled-down window waits to be rolled back up again.

"That's better," Carolyn said, driving off again. "I feel much better."

"How are you going to clean in there?" I said, grossed out.

"Smell goes away after a few days. I've been through this before."

I said, "Remember you said that beer just might make you like boys for a few minutes! Haha!"

"It does," she said. "But you spent those few minutes tinkling. Missed your chance."

She pulled up to my apartment.

"Besides," she added, "you need to reserve all your chang for Miranda. The Pacific South Americans like their boyfriends to be filled with chang."

Exactly what she meant by "chang" I wasn't sure, but the way she said it made me blush and sweat at the same time.

"I need a shower," I said. "And some bacon."

"Come by the hostel when you're clean and proteined, and we'll discuss your projected chang accumulation vis-à-vis Miranda."

I nodded.

"We'll return to our stakeouts and canvassing," she said. "Maybe we'll offer a reward for information leading to her capture. Now go."

"Promise? You'll help me make flyers?"

"Go away now, Jerome."

I climbed out, and Carolyn drove off.

There was Mr. Murdoch sitting on his porch. He had black mud on his shoes. He'd probably been out all night tiptoeing up to the windows of young maidens and then Peeping Tomming them. Window shopping.

"You got them driving you around," he said, smiling.

I don't like you, I thought.

o

From down on the linoleum floor of the Luncheonaire, I craned up at the underside of the lunch counter, trying to chip off seven decades' worth of gum wads as hard as snooker balls, using a lock-blade pocketknife Carolyn had given me for self-defense. The chore not only put me in a bad mood, but also made my injured hand (it had *just* begun over the last few days to exhibit little areas of shy, pink healing) wake up and howl.

Most of the gum deposits were blackened, anonymous fossils, decades old. But there were plenty of newer deposits, too, some even recognizable. Huge, nauseating oysters of Dubble Bubble; hemorrhoidal knots of Big Red (which, O horror, were still fragrant when chipped at); tiny gray clots of Juicy Fruit and Teaberry. The Bubble Yum family was well represented.

I paused for a moment to go in back and show Mrs. Hebert my Ziploc full of gum chips. She had just finished rolling coin.

"Find anything?" I asked.

"'58, maybe VG," said Mrs. Hebert. "That's it, though."

Mrs. Hebert liked to go through the business change looking for numismatic treasure: sleepers, she called them. When ordering coins from the bank to fill the register, she always requested at least twenty rolls of pennies, which she spent a good part of her shift examining. Then she sent the chaff back with the nightly deposit and ordered pennies anew in the morning.

"That old boy down at the Hibernia Bank knows to send cents over that I haven't been through already," said Mrs. Hebert. "These here I analyzed last week."

She showed me her '58 wheatback cent. I'd learned a good deal about scarce pocket change from Mrs. Hebert, and had gotten into the habit of examining dates and mint marks myself. A '58 was nothing. A spender.

"Let me know if you find any coins among the gum wads," she said. "And mind you don't slip and fall on that sword of yours and lance your islets of langerhans."

I was working on a revolting hemisphere of Fruit Stripe gum when two customers came in and sat at opposite ends of the counter.

The smaller of them had a big flat nose shaped like a moccasin. He was wearing a strange polo-type shirt, but with a cricket or maybe a wheelbarrow as the emblem. It was buttoned up to the neck. His collar was turned up and coated in a stiff balm. His nose-moccasin flared.

The other was similar, at least in his peevedness and general hue, but he was twice the size of his companion. Maybe a powerlifter, or a Greco-Roman heavyweight. His head was huge, easily a third larger than a regular head. His earlobes rested on his shoulders like tiny bookends on either side of an undercooked turkey.

He spread two fantastic, starfish-like hands out on the counter, blew his yellow-blond bangs off his forehead, then stuck out his tongue at the other man, who parried with a freezer-burn stare. Then they turned away from each other, swiveling their entire bodies on the squeaky stools, shutting their eyes, sticking their noses in the air, and crossing their arms, like Hanna-Barbera characters.

I know these guys!

"Hey, are you…"

"Hello, Jerome," said the little one. "You have not met me, but I am Knops, from your room."

As much as both Carolyn and I had been watching for and talking about Miranda, there had been no breaks in the case at all. Until now.

"Yes, and *that* is Dik," said Knops, pointing at his partner and snarling.

"Yo," said Dik.

Where is she? Take me to her now!

Be patient, be polite.

"We have read about your sandwich, here," said Knops, dropping a long maroon book on the counter. "You are famous, and we want to be a part of your fame and make you our friend."

My reputation had made it into *Zagat*. I was quite proud, and worked it into every conversation I could.

"Thanks, you two. A couple of grilled cheeses?"

"I will command ham," said Dik.

"Hamburger and the fries," said Knops. "Pronto."

"No grilled cheeses?" I said, my feelings a little hurt. "How about something to drink?"

"Floating Coke," said Dik.

"Ice and milk," said Knops, more loudly.

"So, you guys were friends with, mmm, what's her name... our fourth roomie?"

"Yes, Miranda she is named," said Knops. "She says you have an exciting philtrum."

"It *is* becoming," said Dik.

"Really?"

"His is gross," said Knops, indicating Dik's philtrum.

"No, yours," said Dik, pointing back.

They volleyed judgments for a moment longer, and then, apparently realizing that I was following their shots like a puppy watching tennis, paused to fill me in on their bicker's spark: just a few minutes earlier they'd started arguing in the Sheets and Shams department about where to go on vacation. Knops wanted to go to Athens, Georgia, to meet Michael Stipe and jam, and Dik wanted to go to the Galapagos and ride a turtle.

"Turtles are gaybone," said Knops.

"You are a silly bald man," said Dik.

"Why don't you just stay in New Orleans?" I said. "Miranda and us can all be friends."

"City has too much vomitus," said Knops.

"Too much hankypank," said Dik.

Growling, snarling, gimlet-eyeing.

It turned out they had been getting tired of New Orleans, but the shine really wore off when Dik threw up in a Bourbon Street strip club that he and Knops had gone into out of a sense of fun and adventure and derring-do. Dik was ejected by the management and had to continue his infirmity in the street among tourists, who thought it picturesque. Meanwhile, Knops had stayed inside the club to watch the strippers perform beguiling sleights with their nethers.

"I often vomit," said Dik, enjoying another Coke float.

"Why?" I asked.

"Nerve storms," he said pleasantly.

After recovering from his Bourbon Street barfing, Dik had gone back to their motel on St. Charles, alone, and had gone to bed.

But Knops was still stressed about Dik and the scene he'd made. As payback, Knops made friends with an attractive man in Jackson Square. Soon, they'd walked all over the French Quarter together.

The man asked Knops if he wanted to see the cemetery where Marie Laveau was buried.

"Of course," Knops had said, anxious for a spooky New Orleans tryst. Knops had never had sex with a black man.

But instead of trysting, the pair got stompered and robbed by a youth gang.

"Like the Warriors," said Knops. "Ajax and Swan."

Knops, bleeding freely, had taken the streetcar back to the motel. Knops told Dik he'd been stompered and robbed, then Dik apologized for barfing, and so Knops confessed his infidelity, and then Dik barfed again, but Knops forgave him.

"Dik, you vomit when under stress, and Knops, you sleep around?" I said.

They nodded enthusiastically, as if no one had ever understood the complexity of their relationship before.

"So you will be our homie," said Knops.

"Me too," said Dik.

"Okay," I said. "Friends."

Knops stood and stuck a palm in the air for a high five.

Without thinking, I tried to give him one with my bad hand, but I was way off target—I'd never been able to do a nice clean high five—and we hooked pinkies instead. It took a squirt of pure adrenalin not to barf from the agony.

"Yay!" said Dik and Knops. "If only our Miranda was present, we would have four for bridge."

"Maybe we can all meet here for cheese sandwiches," I said, my hand growing pleasantly numb and my head pleasantly heavy, as if both were filling with Stelazine-infused mud-bath mud. "She's still in town, isn't she? Right?"

"Miranda has returned to Quito to be with her beloved Dagoberto the fierce pelota champion and ravisher of maidens forever," said Knops.

"Yo," said Dik.

The pleasantness vacated, and a new kind of pain, rich in nettly venom, spread through my hand and up my arm.

"Look, Dik," said Knops, one-eye-squinting at me, my new kind of pain apparently visible on my face. "He is having a puppylove on Miranda."

"Poor chap," said Dik, in an excellent Cantabrigian non-rhotic. "Come pay us a visit someday when you are through with your cheese, and we will comfort your sick love."

Carolyn did not seem deterred by Miranda's not being on our side of the equator.

"She'll be back," she said, with a delicious confidence.

I shared none of her conviction. The buried-in-a-rockslide feelings I'd endured before I learned Miranda had emigrated were a sugary, Valium-drip high compared to how I felt now. Before the Danes' news, I was—or so it seemed in the present darkness—all moonlit with the assurance that my blood-on-ice history was history; that the ghostly love I was chasing would, this time, prove catchable and earthly; that New Orleans really was the last, best stop.

But now? Who cares? She was gone. Another flitting ghost.

When Carolyn was unavailable to salve my abject lovesickness, I would visit Knops and Dik, even though they did not provide the level of sympathy I'd hoped they might. Nor did they offer any practical advice. In fact, they appeared to enjoy being obtuse and slippery about the matter. Like a hobby. And this hobby, along with their desire to ride on the coattails of my cheese-grilling celebrity, soon formed the very essence of our friendship.

They'd rented an apartment in the French Quarter, right over a tourist-trap bar on Bourbon Street called Gumbeaux that sold hurricanes and something called a budmug, which was a rum-based drink concocted in an empty beer bottle. Potter's 151, milk, and cascabel peppers were merged with a pickled crawdad. Pickled crawdads will not sink in rum/milk/pepper slurries, but instead remain buoyant and clog the neck of the bottle. Perforce, the only way to drink a budmug is to turn the bottle bottoms-up, chug the whole thing, then suck the crawdad out.

One afternoon after work Dik and Knops ushered me inside and handed me a can of Foster's. I sat on the floor of their apartment. The pulse of the Gumbeaux downstairs shinnied up my backbone.

"Feel that Gumbeaux, bra!" said Dik, swaying to the thump.

"We and Miranda partied often down there," said Knops, pointing at the floor. "What a blast. Many, many budmugs!"

"Miranda, it is too bad she has fled," said Dik.

"You guys are absolutely certain she won't come back?"

"Dagoberto has tremendous thighs," said Knops from his perch on the windowsill, where he was avidly people-watching.

I wished I hadn't come. My mental IMAX looped Dagoberto using those thighs to give Miranda lusty squeezes, her face hidden by black hair and a huge, cloudy budmug, while he pumped her like a bellows, eroticized sweat gathering in his divine, peerless philtrum, deep and wide as the Mariana Trench.

"Best not to fall in love with her, my home," added Knops.

"I think it's too late."

"Surprise in water closet for you there," said Dik, pointing to the bathroom's wood-paneled door. One of the Danes had made it homey by shellacking it, horror vacui, with dozens of magazine pictures of Corvettes. "Two-ply Quilted Northerns, just for your bottom."

"Thank you," I said, remembering that a discussion of bowel processes had come up between the three of us the last time I'd visited. We had all announced our favorite brand of toilet paper. The Danes liked Pro-Klenz, the thin, untearable stock akin to newsprint principally offered in public stalls. Quilted Northerns for me. Miranda, they said, had refused to reveal her brand.

"You are welcome!"

"Why did she keep her brand a secret?" I said.

"She is coy. She says it is a wonderful soft secret for only her."

"C'mon. Can't you tell me anything? Is it imported?"

Dik and Knops quietly conferred. Finally they broke the huddle.

"Put on your red shoes, Jerome!" Knops shouted. "Dance and I shall tell you her toilet paper country."

And so it was in this way I learned about her. The Danes would make requests of me, and then reward me with tantalizing, incomplete facts. For the nation of her toilet paper's manufacturer (Japan), not only did I have to dance the Bondepigen, I had to let them enumerate all my scars, in situ, with an ink pen; for the knowledge that she slept in red long johns with a buttonable transom at the seat designed for convenience in the bathroom, like in cartoons about hillbillies, I had to orate the circumstances of my first boner (I'd been eight, in a mall in Evanston, Illinois, perched on Santa's knee, drinking in his never-fulfilled promise of a Christmas-morn wrist rocket); for the locations of Miranda's New Orleans dalliances (Possum Pelt Bar & Grill, the Office Depot packing-material aisle, Airline Books), but not with whom they'd happened, I had to learn an endless and unwinnable card game called *Hjerterfri* using some dollhouse-scale cards that Knops got in the Kastrup airport duty-free shop, *and* I had to tell them if I'd ever walked in on my parents doing it (I hadn't; when I was three they'd given me a Barbie suitcase filled with diapers and Lincoln Logs and put me in a cab by myself to the Bannerman Place and then vanished); to find out if she had ever been depressed or hospitalized or on psych meds, I had to recount my experiences with cunnilingus.

"No! Choose something else."

"No. Reveal."

"I have little experience."

That was very true.

"Spill! Spill! Spill! The! Beans!" they chanted.

I told them about Rizette, the psychiatric nurse at Taunton State who was a generation older than me and who insisted on sneaking me into the nurses' station bathroom to conduct our short affair. She had labia like ears. She tried to teach me an oral vibrating technique that demanded the mastery of a nasal hybrid of humming and whistling, as well as an unnatural tongue shimmy. Rizette suggested I practice on her off-days with one of those squeeze-open plastic coin purses. Mine was from Bay Bank, and had an irritating burr on one flap. Rizette finally gave me an F and broke it off. She immediately took up with Ricky, who was in on a three-day commitment after snipping off his big toe with airplane shears. His perfect hum-whistle was audible from the dayroom. I hated Ricky.

And Emmanuelle, a bowling-shoe-rental girl at Fast Lanes I met on a group trip from some psych hospital, liked for me to wear an adjustable headgear assembly that was reined at the ears in order to give her perfect control of my head. And she liked me to periodically refrigerate my face with a dedicated bag of ice cubes. I performed absolutely no cunnilingus—she rubbed herself on my unmovable face—but I got credit for it, and Emmanuelle always seemed dreamily pleased after an orgasm.

"And Ellen? Very responsive," I told Knops and Dik, who had crowded around me, bad-breath-close, in the European style, drinking Foster's and pointing at my mouth while debating something in Danish. "She could have a dozen orgasms in a row, and would call me at all hours to come and service her. She once hired a livery cab to drive me from Albany to New York City just so I could give her oral sex in her star's dressing room in a Broadway theater."

Ellen was fictional. Rizette and Emmanuelle were the extent of my experience.

"Eject tongue," said Dik.

I stuck out my tongue. Dik and Knops pointed and gestured in a detached, professional kind of way.

"I understand one must concentrate," said Knops finally. "One must chill, and study manuals, then one will master the art soon. It is not easy. This is what I hear, from my many many many women friends around the world."

"I am expert," said Dik, drawing a sharp look from Knops.

"At pussy licking?" I said.

"Certainly!" said Dik. "Back in closet. Dresda Ver Bouts. From Maastricht. She squeal like teapot. She tell her friends, and they look at me in town square and point. I stick tongue out, and they giggle and scream and flee."

With a surgical strike of an empty beer can, Knops hit Dik on his funny bone.

"Av!" said Dik, clutching his elbow.

"Okay, quit it. Now tell me if Miranda has any psychiatric problems."

"She takes little green pills like torpedoes. And some red pills like Ferrara Pan Cinnamon Imperials."

"What for?"

"Depression moods."

"What kind?"

"Jimi Hendrix kind."

"Oh, manic?"

"Yes, that kind."

"Poor Miranda."

She was of my people!

Manic depressives often do irresponsible things, and do them suddenly, like abandon their tremendous-thighed lovers and go to Mariscal

Sucre airport and fly to America in their nightgowns just to get one more budmug, or gaze at an exceptional philtrum, or feed somebody a magical shrinking-philter and then carry that somebody forever in a breast-high leather pouch. A lotto-scale probability of occurrence, but it gave me hope.

o

Business had tailed off a little lately, so Mrs. Hebert started telling all the tourists who came by for a taste of my sandwiches that I had just returned from the World Cup Cheese-Off in France, where I'd taken the gold in two categories ("Cabécou Freestyle" and "Sate the Shepherd").

"Where're your medals?" said some skeptic who wandered in one day, ordering only water and bragging about being from New Hampshire.

"Banque Degroof Luxembourg," said Mrs. Hebert, before I could open my mouth to sputter something dense. "Safe deposit."

Even though I was a little annoyed that I had to work so much harder to support Mrs. Hebert's fibs, I did enjoy the fame. And it kept my mind off Miranda.

The Tuesday following my visit to the Danes, the Luncheonaire was as busy as it'd ever been. Knops and Dik visited and brought along dozens of compatriots, all trenchermen with deep stomachs for cheese sandwiches. Carolyn visited and brought a few of her hostel coworkers. And my neighbor came by.

"Mrs. Hebert," I said, "this is Mr. Murdoch. He lives next door."

"How do you do," said Mrs. Hebert.

"I do just fine, now," said Mr. Murdoch.

Toward the end of the day, the *Times-Picayune* stopped by to take a couple of pictures for the paper's Living section.

"Are we really going to be in the paper?" I asked the photographer. Maybe Miranda had a subscription to the *Times-Picayune*, receiving a month's worth of issues all at once, which she would read in secret redoubt from Dagoberto.

"Probably," he said, playing with the f-stop dial. "Unless the O.J. verdict comes in. That'll get every square inch of the whole paper. Sorry."

Carolyn pointed a pickled jalapeño at the photographer.

"Better not give me red-eye."

He snapped a few shots of the whole group. I tried to relax my philtrum so that it looked natural, unposed, but it felt like an electrical fire.

Everyone left afterward, except Carolyn and Mr. Murdoch.

He and Mrs. Hebert sat on either side of the counter by themselves, leaning over a scatter of change between them. They whispered and scooted coins around. Mrs. Hebert would occasionally pick one up and hand it to Mr. Murdoch, along with a loupe. Whenever she examined a coin herself, Mr. Murdoch carpe-diemed and enjoyed good long looks down her blouse.

"I can't stand that guy," I whispered to Carolyn.

"So you've said," she whispered back. "What are you so worked up about him for? He's plainly harmless."

"He'll break her heart."

I scraped the grill and eavesdropped, while Carolyn yawned and ate pie. My boss and Murdoch were all whispers. Even his whispering sounded rutty.

There were a couple of hours still until the end of my shift, and I was having trouble finding anything else to do, at least that didn't require sandblasting or a hazmat suit.

"Why don't you go along home, Jerome," said Mrs. Hebert, finally, shooing me away with a rag.

He better not put my Mrs. Hebert in a whimsy box and store her under his bed. I loathed myself for introducing them.

"C'mon, Jerome," said Carolyn, pulling me by my bad hand. "They need to be by themselves so they can pretend they're not in lust."

"I cannot think of Mrs. Hebert that way," I said, gently peeling Carolyn's fingers off my hand.

IV

The weather grew cooler.

There were still hot days now and then, but violent electrical storms quickly snuffed them. During the summer even the long, vivid thunderstorms would cool off the city only for their duration—the moment the storm stopped, the roads boiled the rain and the air stagnated with bacterial vapor. The following day glossy bugs and weeds as tough as fishing line would emerge from the cracks in the city.

One afternoon, Dik and Knops stopped in the Luncheonaire. They had silly, excited looks, as though they'd just seen *Milo and Otis*. Without any foreword, they began to recite verse:

> *Roses are red,*
> *Violets are blue,*
> *MirandajustarrivedhereintheBigEasy,*
> *Woo woo woo!*

I demanded to know where, but they didn't know; they'd just gotten a postcard from her announcing her visit.

I ran to find Carolyn. When I told her Miranda was in town, she yawned so large I could see her wisdom teeth.

"Right on. Good hunting."

"But I need you!"

As the days went by with no Miranda sightings, Carolyn grew more and more distant. Less talkative. Bored. Sleepy. But all in a passive, daydreamy way, tinted with exhaustion, perhaps from tremendously gratifying sex: she was often tousled. I never asked about it, and I never saw her with anyone. I seemed to no longer exist for her, except as a style-cramping no-see-um.

I hoped it was just sex, not a relationship. The razor scar under her arm was a large enough presence in my mind that it turned up occasionally in my dreams as a red and black pillow splitting its seams.

Whatever had happened, I was glad for her, but I couldn't help feeling a little lonesome. Unappetizing. Like one of those abnormal cafeteria desserts with raisins and rice pudding mixed together that no one chooses even if all the Jell-O and pudding and carrot cake is gone.

No. I changed my mind, just now. I was *not* glad. She was dumping me as a friend, and it hurt. Just when all of our preparation and conference about Miranda seemed most critical, Carolyn was dropping out. I needed her for this—she'd promised me.

I went to the hostel after another rotten day at the Luncheonaire, hoping that Carolyn had tired of her new lover and told her (him?) to run along now; hoping we could relax into a conversation about Miranda and lovesickness, just as if we'd never been interrupted by Carolyn's own romance.

She was on the phone. She didn't look up. Her shoeless feet were up on the desk. I couldn't hear what she was saying, only the words' chirping lovey-dovey score. She was wearing a strange top I'd never seen before. Way too small, too cute, too sporty, too *purple*. It couldn't have been hers.

I lay down on the couch. On the floor next to me was a Sambo's napkin. I wadded it up and lobbed it at her. It landed in her lap. She looked up for an instant. I smiled and stuck out my tongue. Rice pudding. She looked back down. I sat there for a while. Then I left.

I visited a couple more times. The last time, I brought a six-pack of fancy beer, in reddish-brown bottles. She wasn't on the phone, but rather engaged in writing something with a chrome fountain pen on ivory-colored paper.

"Hey!" I said. "Spartzvongrumbacher!"

I opened a beer and set it next to her elbow.

"Fuck, man!" she said. "Don't spill that on this!"

"I didn't spill it, Carolyn, jeez. What are you writing?"

"I don't know."

On the back of her writing hand was a red-ballpoint drawing of a vagina smoking a joint.

I sat on the couch. I poured a beer down the raisin-and-rice-pudding's throat.

"No sightings, I guess, huh?" I said, knowing before the sentence was even half uttered that there hadn't been any and that she did not care.

She wrote a word or two, then looked up.

"What do you want me to do, man? Call the fucking Ecuadoran embassy?"

"You probably *would* have, a few weeks ago."

"What's that mean?"

"Nothing."

"What are you always hanging around here for?"

Mrs. Hebert gave me a few more hours at the Luncheonaire, which aired out the loneliness a little. And the anger. But she refused to talk about Miranda.

"Love is at war with the practical matters," Mrs. Hebert said one morning as I came in. "I need you to wipe down those salt and pepper shakers. And put some rice in the salt. Use the big rice, though; the little rice gets through the holes, and someone's liable to bite one and stub a molar and sue Erril's into bankruptcy. And then what would I do?"

"You could become a rare-coin magnate," I said.

"I'm working on just that. I just don't want Erril's to get sued into bankruptcy or collapse into a sinkhole until I've got a good coin inventory built up.

"In fact," she added, "they opened a Frost Bank branch on Loyola, and I'm going to look into their rolled coin right now. Wish me *bon chasse*."

"Break a leg."

"You might well grow famous from grilled sandwiches, but I'm anticipating renown for my global domination of the rare-coin trade. Look what I have."

Mrs. Hebert produced a small blue box. Inside, on a pillow of cotton, was a penny.

"Indian head. Worth fourteen dollars. Found it in a roll of nickels."

"Wow!"

"And those're 1991 dollars," she told me. "Adjusted for inflation, it's $17.6525."

"Are you going to sell it?" I asked.

"I went down to Popski's. He offered me four-fifty in store credit."

"That doesn't seem fair."

"It isn't. I mussed up his hair and took his SORRY WE'RE CLOSED sign. Popski is one of those folks who looks especially funny with mussed hair." She paused. "In the beginning, I'm going to market my coins here, in with the pies. Everybody contemplating pie can contemplate rare coins in the meantime."

"I bet you get rich."

She leaned over and began to whisper.

"That Mr. Murdoch seems to think so. He's an expert in numismatics *and* marketing."

"Is that right?"

"That is right," she said.

"I'll use the big rice," I said.

I hated Mr. Murdoch.

Knops came into the Luncheonaire later on that day, exotically depressed. His hair was an oily blond tonsure, and he had not shaved. His whiskers were blond also, nearly the same tone as his skin, which made his chin look not stubbly but merely blurred.

And he was wet. There had been a cold rain all day, the kind that made my hand's chronic ache more acute. Fizzier.

"Say," I said, "any sign of—"

"No!"

Knops ordered fries and three cheese sandwiches. He peeled the top layer of bread off the lowermost sandwich on his plate and peered inside.

"I will have a wheel of tomato here," he said, indicating the tomato-free gap.

I brought him a slice of tomato, which he slid inside his lower sandwich. Then he took out his billfold, a grimy Velcro type, and tore it open. An accordion of plastic sleeves filled with photos unfolded.

"He will not let me have a tomato when I want!" he said, harshly poking at a photo of a large man kneeling next to a truffle pig at some kind of Danish 4-H club.

"Wow, that's Dik?"

He looked like the product of Laverne DeFazio times Butterbean divided by a snowman. He was in his early twenties and appeared happy and mischievous.

"That is the chump," said Knops. He looked like he might cry.

"Say, you didn't happen to get a picture of Miranda, did you?"

It was suddenly crucial that I knew *exactly* what she looked like. My heart rattled and squished and secreted anxiety at the idea of an actual image of her. No more riddly half facts. No phantom to idly worship anymore. No foggy guesswork. I needed an icon.

"No pictures," said Knops.

"Damn. Would you describe her? Please? And no mysteries like at your apartment. I'm getting desperate. I know she has black hair and kissy lips and manic depression. But that's all."

"Dressed with pants and little shirts. Small shirts."

"Small shirts? Like... tight?"

"Small... these," said Knops, tom-tomming his chest.

"Small breasts?"

"Yes, flat boobies. And a dot, here, like Ginger, remember that person?" Knops indicated a spot on his cheek.

"A dimple?"

"Yes. No, beauty mass. Very chic. Oh, fast, too, at chowtime. Chompchompchomp."

I reduced the bust of my ideal image, took off the Catholic schoolgirl outfit, and dressed her in a black skirt and a white T-shirt. I inked a little beauty mark on her cheek with my mental Sharpie. I sat her down at a table. I sat myself down across from her, and we raced to see who could finish off a can of sour-cream-and-onion Pringles first. I won. Miranda wiggled my ears and gave my philtrum a salty wet smack.

"Oh, and the spectacles, yes. Similar to war criminal Henry Kissinger's."

Mrs. Hebert came in at that moment, looking rankled. It turned out that the Frost branch received all their coins, brand new, from the Federal Reserve.

"Freshly minted specie is of no use to the antiquary," she said, dropping a skeletonized five-dollar umbrella into the trash. "But I did find this."

She boosted a large canvas bank sack with a dollar sign like in a Richie Rich comic on the counter, which made the silverware bounce and the revolving pie case stop for a split second.

"Took a chance and drove out to an unpromising Hibernia over in Marrero."

"Yay," said Knops, furling his pictures.

Mrs. Hebert walked around behind the counter, regarded both Knops and me for a moment, then picked up the sack and went into the back.

I heard her noisily ripping kraft-paper wrappers off of rolls of coins. Knops stuffed about 70 percent of a grilled-cheese sandwich into one side of his mouth, which made him look like a squirrel, or a tooth-abscess patient.

From the back Mrs. Hebert called out, "Mr. Knops, you fighting with Mr. Dik again? You better settle down or he's going to drink lye in a romantic suicide. And you don't want that on your conscience. So go home and make up and pour the lye down the sink before Dik commits a romantic suicide because of your stubborn ways.

"And please pay with coins if you have them," she added.

Knops stood up, found a wet ten in a pocket, and threw it down on the counter. It slapped like a slice of baloney. Then he stalked away. He'd made it all the way to Parfums when I got an idea.

"Wait! Knops!"

Knops stopped and flapped his arms impatiently.

I ran into the back.

"Mrs. Hebert can I go home now I'm tired and it's raining no one wants a grilled cheese today besides we're out of bread and I dropped my spatula behind the stove again so can I go home do you think?"

Mrs. Hebert was on the phone, grinning and blushing like a teenager. It reminded me an awful lot of Carolyn.

Covering the receiver she said, "Fine. Go. Don't you go having a romantic suicide either, though. Mardi Gras is on the way, and I need my cooks."

"Is that Mr. Murdoch you're talking to?" I said, wrassling with my jacket.

"Now, what makes you say that, young man?"

It was!

"Sorry. See you tomorrow."

I caught up with Knops and told him I needed a favor.

"I am no longer interested in your sickness," he said. "I have my own shits to deal with."

"Please? God, Knops, please?"

We headed to the French Quarter. We walked the long way to Jackson Square, giving Knops and Dik's apartment a wide berth, as Knops suspected that Dik was there, sogging the property with barf and watching for Knops out the window in order to beg him for forgiveness or to bemire him in abuse and blame.

Under a big canvas umbrella in Jackson Square sat Coryate, with a sheet of paper masking-taped to a panel of Masonite he held on his lap. Across from him was a boy, twelve or thirteen maybe, wearing an ultrasuede blazer spattered with rain, sitting perfectly still. He had hair like Björn Borg. A woman, probably the boy's mother, stood behind Coryate looking like she'd just been handed a leaflet of illustrated anti-abortion literature.

Coryate ripped the drawing off the Masonite and handed it to Björn. The mother paid him, and Coryate waved them away. Then he gestured for Knops to sit, which he did.

"Thirty color, twenty charc," said Coryate.

"Mr. Coryate," I said. "Do you remember me? From the Smart Harriet?"

"Ah," he said. "Ioanna, the slow waitress with the gritty coffee and variable customer service. Yes. Your mother, right? Sorry. No offense. Nice lady. Good with wounds."

Coryate leaned forward, squinting, apparently confounded momentarily, as a visual artist, by Knops's blurry chin.

"She's not my mother," I said.

"Cop sketch," said Knops, baring his teeth at the squinting Coryate, who recoiled. "You shan't draw me, bra. Draw Miranda. I will describe."

I couldn't watch. I walked around the fence surrounding the statue of Andrew Jackson. Tarot readers, cards weighted down with round river stones, preached and pointed, their quarry nodding and hugging themselves;

a secretariat of tourists huddled under a balcony to escape the light rain; crust punks, in pairs and trios, sat on canvas backpacks, feeding their dogs muddy beignets and palmfuls of vodka.

Coryate finished. Knops paid him with more sopping banknotes. Coryate sprayed fixative on the charcoal sketch, then gave it to me.

Oh, it hurt. My hand went immediately to my heart. Don't stop, please don't stop.

"Heart attack?" said Knops, anxiously, as I clutched my new charcoal drawing of Miranda in one hand and my heart in the other.

"That's no coronary," Coryate said to Knops. "That's *love*, pal."

"You are lucky," said Knops. "I have no love."

Coryate packed up his umbrella and supplies and trudged off, muttering about coffee. Knops trudged in the opposite direction.

I walked home in the cold rain, Miranda's portrait under my shirt, against my chest to keep her dry. My heart felt like it was trying to elbow its way out from between my lungs.

I stopped on the corner of Jackson and Magazine to rest and catch my breath. I hunched over a little to keep the rivulets from sneaking under the collar of my shirt.

I caught my reflection in a storefront window: I was scanning the streets like a maniac who'd lost his imaginary friend. I bet stalkers looked like that. Maybe *I'm* a stalker. I seem to have some of the symptoms. I stared at the moles of ancient mashed gum on the sidewalk.

I ran, hugging Miranda.

When I arrived home Mr. Murdoch was on his half of the porch, saturated in contentedness and accomplishment, rocking in an easy chair that had been converted into a rocker by mounting it onto a curved sheet of light blue metal, apparently a hood subtracted from a Volkswagen. He was reading.

"Done with cheese sandwiches?" said Mr. Murdoch.

"For today."

"For me it's twine, rope, and paper all the way down. For you it's cheese sandwiches."

Mr. Murdoch worked at TwiRoPa.

"Aren't you cold?" I said. I hoped he was. Maybe his mother had locked him out.

He made a panoramic gesture. "This is real weather, the nicest a man can hope for. I like to read in nice weather." He waggled his book at me.

"What're you reading?"

"This is about numismatics. It's the *Official Redbook*. Comes out every year and this one is the newest a man can obtain. I got it at Bookstar."

"Tells you what coins are worth?"

"That is *right*!" he said, looking at me with the utmost gravity. "You can never know what you will find in your pocket if you don't know what to look for."

"I didn't know you collected coins."

"Well, I didn't until a short time ago. I'll be an expert before long. Day after tomorrow, I figure."

"You took that up pretty quick," I said innocently. "Must have to do with a woman."

Again he stared openly at me, with even utmoster gravity, for a long, long time. I waited for him to tell me he lusted after my boss.

Finally he slapped his knee.

"God*dammit*, Jerome. I need to take some pointers from you. You must have a big little black book."

He shook his head and laughed to himself, then resumed study.

I went inside. I felt better. If Mr. Murdoch was going to expertize himself in numismatics to seduce Mrs. Hebert, I guess wandering around town in the rain with a police sketch stuck to my chest wasn't really that abnormal. I downgraded my diagnosis from stalker to atypical suitor with hyperromantic ideation.

I went right to bed, the picture of Miranda propped against the lamp on the bedside table, so she'd watch me sleep, like she had at the hostel. Then I positioned my bad hand so that it lay palm up, which was as comfortable as I could make it in the cold and rainy weather. Silence from the Murdoch residence.

I woke up a few hours later to use the bathroom. Miranda, in the buttery light of the bedside table, was so lovely I nearly obeyed an urge to write poetry. I wished I could show my drawing to Carolyn.

Well, why the hell not?

I called her at work.

Machine. I dressed and was at the hostel in twenty minutes.

I rang the buzzer, but it didn't seem to be buzzing inside—you can usually hear it from the porch. No one came to the door. I rang it again. Nothing. A warm light shone through the window onto a septic Barca-lounger on the porch. I went in. No one was at the desk. Batiste, the owner, snored on the couch. I shook him awake and asked him where Carolyn was, and he jabbed a thumb down the hall.

Ecuador, as I suspected, was unstuck by pins of any color. Denmark bristled with them.

Down the hall, something *ussh*ed. I followed the bank of lockers along the wall heading toward the light from a door ajar at the end of the hall. The office.

I stuck my head into the room. There was an old army cot in the corner, and on the cot was Carolyn. She was on her back, her eyes tightly shut and her mouth open, her lips stretched back from her teeth. On top of her was a woman. The woman thrust with her hips, her back arched, chin pointed at the ceiling, eyes delicately closed, tongue out and curving back against her chin. The very end of her tongue curled back up like the end of a play-ground slide. It looked as if she were catching snowflakes.

They were both naked above the waist. Below the waist they were covered with a thin sheet.

The sheet slipped off. The snowflake-catcher had a belt around her hips. I quietly withdrew from the doorway just as the woman pulled a blue tube attached to the belt out of Carolyn. They had not seen me.

I headed back home.

The image of them had burned itself into my retinas, where it radiated in photonegative brilliance for most of the walk. And the high, razoring breaths of Carolyn and her lover, along with the indescribable *tup* of the slick blue tube, played themselves repeatedly in my head.

I was pretty sure that the slick tube was a dildo, as opposed to a vibra-tor. The purple flashlight that Leigh'd had was a vibrator. It had vibrated. So the blue tube was probably a dildo. Although it, too, may have been vibrating, or capable of same; there were probably lots of crossovers and subgeni. In the morning I'd go to the Relationships aisle at Bookstar and do some research.

The lover wasn't exactly as I'd imagined. I'd pictured a delicate, pale sort, a cross between Winona Ryder and Edgar Winter, or maybe like that elongated woman in all the Modigliani paintings who killed herself. But Carolyn had hooked up with a woman that reminded me of a yew-wood longbow—powerful, slender, flexible. Probably dangerous, too, even at a distance.

Back at my apartment, I slipped Miranda into a kitchen drawer, apologizing to her as I shut her away, then climbed into bed and masturbated like I'd just discovered the process.

Afterward, I liberated Miranda and apologized again. I propped her up against her lamp.

I remembered that Carolyn had once asked me—it had been on our drive out to the airport that night—to protect her from bad relationships. She'd meant it—it had seemed as though she was asking me to be godfather to her children. In exchange for my protective services, she'd said she would help me find Miranda. I'd said, "Deal." And I'd meant it.

I'd do it tomorrow, after work.

A cracking sound woke me. It was four a.m., still dark. I wasn't sure if it had been real or a hypnogogic trick. It didn't sound like it had come from next door. Whatever it was, I was wide awake now.

I listened. Presently I did hear something, which I soon recognized as the rhythm of Mr. Murdoch and a fresh conquest, exerting ardor. Maybe it was Mrs. Hebert! Gyaw! I refused to picture that. Mrs. Hebert counted pennies and opened pickle jars; she didn't moan and buck under twine-makers.

But there *was* fire between the two of them. Mrs. Hebert took steps to hide it, but the smoke was everywhere.

The exertions next door accelerated, then leveled off at a canter. Soon they accelerated again. Finally, amid squeaky *fuck*s and clamp-jawed *shit*s and heavy rumbling *gawd*s, they stopped. A few minutes later the whole theater of bawdy collision raised its curtains again.

I was rolling around the idea of masturbating again when another crack, entirely distinct from the metronomic creakings of Mr. Murdoch, made me sit up fast.

It sounded like it was outside. Then another crack, squawky, longer, slower, like someone working a bowie knife out of a block of Styrofoam. No, it was inside.

As a caution, I classified Miranda between the mattresses. I dug my lock-blade pocketknife out of my jeans and tiptoed toward the kitchen. The skin on my backbone contracted. Next door, the cantering had started up again. The hairs on my neck separated and stood. Just before I reached the hall, the cracking accelerated and changed to a high *qwee*, voluminous enough to block out Murdoch and his conquest's orgasmic din.

Then a crash. Like an alpine gondola falling through the roof.

I screeched and ran to the front door, my hand on my heart. Before I could open it, the noise ceased completely, except for gurgles.

I stood motionless, looking down toward the kitchen, ready to flee into the street if aliens or gangsters appeared. But only a cloud of dust billowed out in my direction, illuminated by a streetlamp shining through a window. The shadow of the window's burglar bars wavered on the surface of the opaque dust cloud.

I recognized the voices of Mr. Murdoch and his mother. And another voice, unfamiliar. Cautiously, I made my way to the kitchen. I flipped on the light, bracing myself to see a dozen alpine-cable-car-disaster survivors groaning on my kitchen floor.

Instead there was a wasteland of splintered black planks and powdered drywall. Shattered dishes, exploded boxes of antique Lucky Charms, gallon cans of ancient paint broken open, with chalky, cylindrical rocks of long-hardened lead paint exposed like bones. The handles of blackened pans stuck out of the mess like grave markers. My digital clock had been caught in the avalanche and now lay under an old-fashioned solid-iron iron, split like a cardboard cylinder of biscuits, its green printed circuit board sticking out. An old VCR, paneled in fake wood and as big as a microwave, stood on end by the refrigerator. Pennies, everywhere, many being carried off by the little rivers of thick, dark liquids snaking away and spreading into alluvial fans at the baseboards.

In the wall was a ragged hole where my long bank of kitchen cabinets used to be.

I'd had no idea any of this crap was up there—I had just assumed that if one was going to paint cabinets hopelessly shut, one would choose some empty cabinets, not ones filled with property. Weighty property.

At least there hadn't been a body. Or an assortment of heads, as Carolyn had once proposed.

Through the hole three faces peered into my kitchen. Mr. Murdoch, his mother, and a young woman who seemed familiar but whom I couldn't quite place. Where was Mrs. Hebert? It must have been this tart who was under Mr. Murdoch. She sure looked like she'd just been involved in carnal writhing—her face and neck were plashed with a light sweat. I imagined Mrs. Hebert, at home, tucked in bed, sound asleep in a modest pink nightie, oblivious to her philandering boyfriend.

"What, the motherfuck, *happened*?" said Mr. Murdoch, whose mother immediately clapped him on the back of the head with a cribbage board. Little cribbage pegs rained into my apartment.

"Language," said Mr. Murdoch's mother.

"Aah!" said Mr. Murdoch, holding the back of his head. "Ahh. Ow. That hurt, NiNaw."

"I'm sure it did. This cribbage game's made of ebony, a hard, dense wood, for hard, dense heads."

"Your cabinets pulled off the wall," said the young, tarty woman.

Mr. Murdoch could catch them in their early twenties somehow.

"That's what it looks like happened," said NiNaw. "That's to be preferred over a Sputnik coming down."

"All the Sputniks have come down or been flung into deep space," said Mr. Murdoch. "No more Sputniks, I've told you that, NiNaw."

"There's plenty of space junk out there in decaying orbits, ready to crash red hot from reentry friction into ordinary folks' kitchens. I know—I keep my *Astronomy* subscription current, young man, and they are the authority on space. All you read about is dimes, and why I don't know."

Mr. Murdoch ignored the remark and turned his attention to me.

"What in G… What in moth… How the fu… Mr. Jerome, what in heaven's name did you have up in your kitchen cabinets? Siege cannon?"

"Nothing special! Not mine!"

"Mr. Zique Duplessis will not be pleased about this," he said.

"Zique still owns this place?" said the young woman.

Her robe had fallen open. The dark nipples of her small breasts were erect. She had a muscular abdomen, and a concavity in her chest that gave her an artificial cleavage. There was a little mole in the center of her breastbone.

Before I could turn my attention back to the Murdochs, the young woman closed her robe and stepped back. She had caught me looking. A prairie fire of embarrassment and anger raced across her face.

"Yep. Zique still owns this place," said NiNaw and Mr. Murdoch at the same time.

"Here, boy," said NiNaw to me. "Looks like some of your groceries got squashed."

She handed me something through the hole. I gingerly stepped through the fallout to take it. It was a box of Froot Loops.

"I hope your icebox didn't explode, too," said NiNaw. "Want this?"

She held up a carton of milk.

"Okay. Thank you."

"That's fine. Well, young lady," NiNaw said to the woman, who was tantalizingly familiar now. "Set up the Boggle on my bed. We'll play a quick two-outta-three, then we'll all be ready to try sleeping again."

"Watch out now, NiNaw," said Mr. Murdoch. "She cheats at Boggle."

The young woman tilted her head back and stuck her tongue out at Mr. Murdoch.

Just like she was catching snowflakes.

Now I couldn't sleep. Not at all. I stared at the ceiling fan. Time must have been on the march, but it didn't feel that way. The cloud of dust and flour and cayenne pepper dispersed throughout the apartment. NiNaw snored faintly.

Presently Mr. Murdoch and Carolyn's lover/girlfriend started to fuck again. I heard them through my bedroom wall, but I could also hear them through my kitchen hole, in obscene stereo.

Incomprehensible. Who was that little slut? She was probably fucking Mr. Murdoch up the butt with her slick blue dildo right this minute. And such an *efficient* slut. She'd been fucking Carolyn only a couple of hours before. Imagine the venereal concerns! She must have *run* over here to fuck him. I bet she didn't even get dressed.

I hated Mr. Murdoch.

Cheating on Mrs. Hebert, my Mrs. Hebert, who gave me a job and made me the grilled-cheese champion I was today. I had devoted fans in

France and Bogotá and Sacramento because of her and the training and encouragement she'd given me.

And there was the slut cheating on Carolyn, my Carolyn, who had taken me into her hostel and befriended me when I was but a lost and homeless soul with a gross chopped-up hand!

Murdoch and his little tuck-in friend shuddered and *ohgodohgod*ed one more time and finally called it a night. Mr. Murdoch laughed his deep Geoffrey Holder laugh.

I felt awful. How could I be stuck in a love triangle without getting any of the love? A canted love square, more like. A love parallelogram.

I'd have to tell Mrs. Hebert.

Even more dreadful, I'd have to tell Carolyn. Soon. Immediately. If she was in love and then found out she was getting cheated on, she might get so upset she'd try suicide again. That scar she'd shown me was the real deal—not a timid, so-called cry for help.

If I didn't tell her, she might find out for herself. At least if *I* broke the news, I'd be there to help. *Christ* I hated Murdoch.

The duties that had fallen on me in just a few hours were almost insupportable. I tried to ignore the cabinet metaphor.

I bit off a corner of my pillow.

I woke with the feeling of being in another house, a bigger place. My eyes and nose burned. I smelled bacon and coffee. The pipes under the house burbled and groaned—someone was in the shower at the Murdochs' place.

In the kitchen, the pile of debris was less intimidating than it had been the night before. Everything was lost, except for the iron and an invincible bottle of bacon bits.

NiNaw hollered to me from the kitchen hole.

"Here, son."

She handed me a tin mug of coffee and a plate with bacon and a cinnamon roll. *Don't you know what your son is doing in your own house?*

"Hey, thank you!" I said, far more merrily than I felt, or, I was sure, looked.

"You don't look so good," said NiNaw. "At least you're a dollar or two richer."

She nodded toward my hill of crap. I looked closely.

Oh. I'd forgotten about all the pennies mired in syrup. Some were wheatbacks.

The Murdochs' kitchen shower stall steamed. Through the opaque glass the smooth, dark form of the slut raised a hand so that it was visible over the glass door. She shook her hair and turned off the water.

I went back to bed. I didn't even call in sick to the Luncheonaire. I'd blame my cabinets. I'd say I got pinned under a headache ball that happened to have been up in the spice cabinet.

I stayed in bed all day, under the covers, Miranda there with me.

My eyes burned. The mist of red pepper.

My ancient answering machine suddenly *clkclkk*ed. Capstans squeakily spun.

"Mr. Jerome," crackled Mrs. Hebert's voice, "you are advised to telephone me here at the Luncheonaire by 3:15, or I'll be forced to check with the funeral parlors. It's about seven minutes and nine seconds past three now. That man Dik from the lowlands is here and he looks like somebody beat him with a bag of lemons. And there's a young lady with him who wants a grilled cheese—well, hell, never mind that, I'm no matchmaker, I've told you that, so just forget about that and don't even ask me to matchmake you and this little hotcake here either. My matchmaking days're over. But until I make it big with old coins, my days as an employer of idling short-order cooks are not. So if I have to come down to a funeral parlor and identify your body, you're fired."

I called Mrs. Hebert and said I'd be right down. I begged her not to let Dik leave with Miranda.

"But don't tell them I'm coming. Just don't let them leave."

"I'm no agent of love," said Mrs. Hebert, and hung up.

I ran down the streetcar tracks until one came by and picked me up. I jumped off at Canal and sprinted the rest of the way to Erril's.

I snuck up, sweating, eyes dilated, my tongue a ball of rubber bands. Some tiny part of me was relieved when I saw that the counter was empty. But the relief, lasting only an instant, sublimed into fear. Where did they go? *Why* did they go?

Mrs. Hebert emerged from the back with a brace of empty coffee globes. I paused, trying not to stare.

"What's that look?" she said. "That's a paranormal look. Did you have a paranormal experience? Is that why you're late?"

"No, I, my, the, it, and…"

Before I could shift the conversation to Miranda and Dik she waggled the coffee globes and shook her head.

"Don't ask, don't ask, because I don't know what became of them. All I can say is she eats fast, a couple of hamburgers and candy gone like a conjure."

"She wanted a cheese sandwich?" I asked. "One of my sandwiches?"

"Sure, but Mister Expert wasn't here," she said, pouring bleach into the coffee globes. "He was busy. He was off having a paranormal experience that he could pitch to a movie producer.

"I don't like to worry, young man," Mrs. Hebert added. "I thought you might be dead from a six-car pileup. There are six-car pileups nearly every day now, you know."

"I don't have a car," I said, sitting on a stool, slumped over a dirty plate. "Was this her plate?"

"Well, folks don't walk away unscathed from six-car pileups just because they're not a driver. Innocent folks on the sidewalk die in six-car pileups about once an hour, in this country," said Mrs. Hebert, who was swirling the bleach around and peering into it.

The plate had been licked virtually clean. I picked it up and turned it over: lettuce, stuck just under the rim. Only hamburgers had lettuce. *I* liked hamburgers, too! I took a sip from a sweating plastic cup filled with melting crushed ice next to the plate. Coke! Coke is my favorite drink! *Our* favorite! Her kissy lips had drunk from this very chalice.

"Sorry I worried you," I said. "But…"

"Don't take advantage of your coming-and-going freedom here. You're going to be on time for the next little while, or I'll hand down a penal chore."

"I had a little problem at home. See, my… the kitchen…"

"I heard about your cabinets peeling off the walls."

"You did? How? Mr. Murdoch told you?"

I hated Mr. Murdoch.

Mrs. Hebert stopped swirling the bleach around the coffee globes.

"Murdoch! No, sir. Not that old man. No, no. I just now heard about it, you know. That Lapp told me. He knows everything."

"Dane. How does the whole world know about my cabinets?"

"Well, it was pretty loud. Or so I heard. I wouldn't be surprised if the incident appears in the paper, near the six-car-pileup story. Now enough. Cook a caf and a decaf for me, Mr. Jerome. I'm sorry I got after you. I was just worried. You just come and go as you please."

She gently messed up my hair, then smoothed it out. We had never looked at each other directly in the eyes before—we were both natural eye-averters—but we shared a look. It couldn't have been for more than a half second, but it saddened me.

I opened my mouth to tell her about what I'd seen, but it fell shut, a torn screen door on a rusted spring. Instead I begged her to try and think where Dik and Miranda might have gone.

"I just don't know. All I can say is that they probably didn't go back to see that other, smaller Norseman."

"Knops?"

"Mmm. They are in one serious breakup."

I sighed like Charlie Brown. I needed Carolyn, my Miranda handler, *now*. But *nooo*, she was busy having exotic sex.

"Mr. Jerome, you're going to have to locate that comely Spanish girl on your own."

"Can I use the phone?"

The Danes didn't have a telephone. They used a pay phone located directly beneath their second-floor bedroom window on Bourbon Street that could not take incoming calls. Not officially, anyway. But I happened to know that it had a secret incoming-call number arranged for by Cecil Barger, the phone-company rep who'd come over to break the news to the Danes that, because of zoning laws and an obscure technical obstacle, he would be unable to install ordinary telephone service in their apartment. As a form of consolation, Cecil rigged the Bourbon Street pay phone so it could receive calls, but Knops and/or Dik would have to be on alert for the tinny jangle of the old phone, and race down to Bourbon Street to answer it. Sometimes they might be obliged to steal the handset right out of the hands of some tourist who'd answered just for the hell of it.

I called the secret number.

"Hello?" said a scratchy voice.

"In a moment a large or a small white man is going to run at you from around the corner at your right and take the phone from your hands, and I recommend turning it over to him without contest," I said to whoever it was that answered.

"Well okay then," said the voice.

A moment passed. "Anyone yet?" I asked.

"Plenty of white people," said the man, "but the only ones running are coming from yonder, and the only white ones coming around the corner are not running."

"Wait just a minute more," I said.

"Say, fellah. I need to make a bet against the Saints, so I'm gonna hang up on you. Nice chatting."

I listened to a dial tone for a second, and then hung up the phone Mrs. Hebert had brought from the back room for me and placed on the smooth, worn counter of the Luncheonaire. That had been the only concession she'd made to her embargo on matchmaking.

I made a few sandwiches, bad ones by the standards of a world champion, the whole time giving Mrs. Hebert secret glances that she doubtless would have adjudged paranormal had she caught me. I thought about Miranda, too, and her chances—or mine—of dying in a six-car pileup before we ever met.

I left a sandwich on the grill for so long that it transformed into a kind of blackened cheese cracker.

Mrs. Hebert didn't seem to notice the smoke or the smell at first, but then she came out from the back with a cup of coffee in one hand, grimacing.

"Go on home, Jerome," she said. "I'll watch the grill and make some coffee with no bleach."

I didn't tell her about Murdoch. But I would. I had to find Dik and Miranda first, before Miranda vanished again. And before Carolyn got her heart broken again.

"Oh," said Knops when he opened the door to his and Dik's place. "You."

I looked over his shoulder, but there seemed to be no one else there.

I leaned over and whispered, "Is Mir—"

"No! Gone!"

"Is she with Dik?"

"I do not care."

"You still haven't made up?"

"Ssss."

It turned out that their telephone man, Cecil Barger, who had spent so much time trying to set the Danes up with an indoor phone, had become infatuated with Dik, but had kept it to himself for months.

One afternoon he and Dik were testing a new phone arrangement whereby Cecil had wired a line all the way around the block, stapling it under the eaves of the buildings, running it into his cousin Beauty's apartment, splicing the line with hers, and running it back to Dik and Knops's place through the window. Instead of paying the phone company, they agreed to pay Beauty every month, but they had to hang up when Beauty needed the phone. And if they didn't pay the bill, Knops and Dik wouldn't have to worry about collection notices from AT&T, but *would* have to worry about visits from Fortus, Beauty's boyfriend, who worked three weeks at a time on an offshore oil platform where he ran the tunk games and bare-knuckle fights.

When Cecil had connected his ingenious system, he went down to the pay phone under the Danes' window and called Dik up in the Danes' apartment to test everything out. The phone worked fine.

Then, with Dik on the line, Cecil seized the opportunity to tearfully confess his love.

Dik had had no idea someone had been dreaming of him.

"But I knew," said Knops.

"How long has this been going on?" I asked.

"A number of weeks equaling eight," he said.

He had been watching the developments from the moment Cecil appeared in their lives, and couldn't stand it. Knops, by most standards, was far cuter than Dik, and enjoyed most of the attention from sexually active people, male and female. Generally speaking, only the elderly, and the occasional lonesome dog tied to a parking meter, loved Dik.

Knops knew when Cecil had made his move by Dik's sudden change in behavior. He started to shave every day. He boiled his shoes in salt water.

He delinted his trousers with balls of Silly Putty. He somehow taught himself an aristocratic gesture whereby he threw out his arm to shake his wristwatch from its hiding place under his shirt cuff and then looked at the time while arching one eyebrow. He ate whole boxes of Altoids for the minting of the breath.

A few days after Cecil had confessed his love to Dik, Knops cornered Cecil in the back of a greeting-card shop, where Cecil was shopping for a card with a glib pay phone theme to give to Dik, as they were in the card-giving stage of their secret affair. In the privacy of the naughty-card aisle, Knops told him a great big lie: that Dik would only consent to dating Cecil if they could all three be together for one night.

Cecil, rightly terrified of Knops, agreed.

"And this just happened?"

"'Twas the night before last," said Knops. "I hired a room for all three amigos with a balcony at the scary Cornstalk Hotel. Just before we were all to go to meet there, the telephone down on the street is a ring-ringing and I descend downstairs and take the telephone from the hands of a man drowned in beers. Who do you think it is? On the telephone? Yes, it is Miranda."

"Really!"

"Oh yes. She wants to see her old friends. I inform her that I must rain-check because of—hehhehheh—a big sex appointment. And so she says, Meet me at the spinning bar afterward for a recapitulation and alcoholic refreshing! And I say Yes that will be fine."

So in the room at the Cornstalk, Knops turned on *MacNeil/Lehrer*, stripped naked, then commanded Dik and Cecil to do the same. Cecil shut himself inside a roomy chifforobe for privacy, and Dik locked himself in the bathroom. When they both finally emerged, Knops was already oiling himself up and had lined the end of the bed with insertables. Dik returned to the bathroom to throw up, and Cecil sat down on the edge of the bed and called his cousin Beauty to ask her advice.

Meanwhile Knops danced on the bed, swinging his penis around, bop-ping Cecil on the back of the head with it, and loudly mocking Dik for barfing.

Cecil couldn't get Beauty on the line because she was discussing her rising sign with Alfonz in Saint Kitts at $4.99 a minute.

The evening ended with a catastrophic multipronged estrangement in a rotating bar on top of a building somewhere on Canal Street, where they'd all gone to meet Miranda. Dik, Knops, and Cecil exploded into a physical fight, which even Miranda could not break up without the assistance of a barkeep and a fivesome of barge welders who happened to be there. Dik and Miranda escaped together. Knops chased Cecil down the emergency stairs, but lost him after he ducked onto the seventeenth floor.

"And you haven't seen any of them since?"

"No. I am considering returning to Ydby. I hope I will have time to say good-bye."

"No, don't go!" I said. "Things will work out. Let me help. Dik is staying with Miranda? Where might that be?"

"I do not care I do not know I will never care again!"

Knops began to cry. He sent me away.

It was getting cool, almost cold. When I climbed onto the streetcar, all the windows were closed. I sat next to an old lady who smelled like mentholated popcorn.

She pointed out an obituary to me in the newspaper she'd been examining.

"Played bourré with this man for thirty-one years," she said.

Under DEATHS was a small photo of an intelligent-looking gentleman with a big forehead and a dandyish mustache.

"Played what?"

"Bourré. Two days after I told him I wouldn't marry him he trapped his pinkie finger under the hood of my old Hudson Wasp. They had to pull off that pinkie finger, all of it but a little skin flap that they pulled over the hole where the pinkie finger was and glued it down. He never said another word to me, except 'Deal the cards.'"

The hostel stop was coming. I could tell Carolyn everything right now and get it over with. But what if I walked in on her and the blue-dildo woman playing strip bourré? What if I walked in on them already done playing strip bourré, and going at it on the couch in the foyer, cards and clothes and sopping hard tubes all over the place? What if Carolyn was slicked in emollients and trussed in a leather swing suspended from a scaffold? What if there was an audience? What if they were all in it together? Murdoch, Mrs. Hebert, the Slut, Carolyn, Miranda, the Danes? All seven of them gurgling and clenching under the big world map with the pins stuck in it?

"What happened to *your* pinkie finger?" asked the lady, nodding at my hand. "Looks like it might need attention."

It had never really recovered from my high five with Knops. It trembled and connipted unpredictably, and always ached.

"Well," I started, "it had to do with a girl."

"Of course it did," she said.

"It feels like greasy electricity."

The streetcar passed the stop for the hostel with me still sitting next to the old lady, who had gently taken my hand in hers.

"I missed my stop," I told the lady.

"That stop'll always be there," she said.

At home I easeled Miranda against the lamp on her bedstand. She seemed so disappointed in me, in all my recent failures.

I fried some Steak-umms and ate crackers. There wasn't much else. Someone on the Murdoch side of the kitchen had patched up the hole with election placards. Now T-Don Lopum from Plaquemines stared into my kitchen with an asymmetrical smile and a coffee ring on his chin. He watched me fry Steak-umms.

I climbed into bed. It was cold outside, and I was under two blankets and a sheet. I contemplated bawling, or masturbating, two things reliably tiring, so I could fall asleep.

Instead, I crawled under the bed, without pillows or a blanket or anything else. I lay there, naked, looking up at the rips in the weird material that protects the insides of the box spring from nosy parkers. The armature visible through the tears was dark and complex. It seemed possible that an underworld creature could emerge and bite my face. Let it, by god.

Something shifted in the levee of crap on the floor of my kitchen, bringing down a small landslide of mothballs or brads or something while T-Don Lopum bore witness.

Poor Carolyn. That fucking Murdoch. I hoped he'd perish in a tragic twine mishap. And always on his stupid toilet when I needed mine. Always fucking, always fucking the Slut or some other slut, or else taking musky, strenuous craps, grunting like a backhoe.

All my people were lying fiends, or dead, or alone, or invisible, or missing, or victimized, or completely unknown. So go ahead, box-spring emissary of Hades, bite me.

The next couple of days I went to work on time, exactly, and left on time, exactly. I looked for Miranda and Dik the rest of the time, taking a few hours to sleep naked under the bed. Then, straight back to work in the morning.

I didn't, couldn't, call Carolyn. I didn't, couldn't, stop at the hostel. I always stayed on the streetcar as it passed her stop, carrying me and my tight astronomy of cowardice and confusion on by.

At work I made cheese sandwiches and served them without small talk. I stayed in the back when it was quiet. Mrs. Hebert had become heavily involved in her coin project, and was scarcely ever at the Luncheonaire. And when she was there, Murdoch was always with her—I could never catch her alone so I could tattle on her boyfriend. They would sit on either side of the counter, a pile of coins between them, whispering and giggling.

Just three days after my cabinet failure, the merry couple came into the Luncheonaire during the lunch rush.

"The regular!" shouted Mr. Murdoch.

Then he blew a straw-wrapper missile at Mrs. Hebert's bottom.

"Close as you're gonna get," said Mrs. Hebert, loud enough for all the patrons to hear. He responded with rumbles of mirth.

I stared coldly at him.

"What's the good word, Mr. Jerome," he said.

I stood between him and Mrs. Hebert, who was trying to get a 1928-D Mercury dime to stand on edge in a little dot of dental wax.

"Just nothing," I said.

"Get your old kitchen in order?"

"Mrs. Hebert," I said, loudly. "I need to talk to you."

I glared at Mr. Murdoch and crossed my arms.

"Tell me later, baby," said Mrs. Hebert to me, while showing Mr.

Murdoch the level of the pie rack that held a selection of Indian-head cents, which was just under the meringue level.

I undercooked Mr. Murdoch's grilled cheese and dropped a pickle in his Fresca and ignored them both.

"Be early tomorrow, Jerome Coe," said Mrs. Hebert as Murdoch helped her on with her coat. "I'll be—"

"—at the bank, I know, Tuesday mornings."

She didn't even seem to notice my insolence. Maybe I was being insolent because I knew she wouldn't notice, what with all of her senses dulled by clouds of love butterflies flying around her head.

When I got home late that night, after a fruitless Miranda-search through the bars at the Esplanade end of the Quarter, I set to work mining the couple dollars' worth of wheatbacks stuck in the old syrup. I washed them off. They were all from the forties and fifties. Pretty much worth a penny apiece.

In the morning I went downtown early. I found Mrs. Hebert at the main branch of Hibernia, directing tellers to look for old rolls of coin. She always went there on Tuesday mornings.

Mr. Murdoch was nowhere around.

"What about bags of pennies?" she said loudly to a teller. "Anybody bring in bags to change out? I don't care how they come in, bags, rolls, I don't care if they're wrapped in baloney. I just want coins I haven't seen yet."

A teller slipped a roll of pennies across the counter to Mrs. Hebert.

"No, I know this one here," said Mrs. Hebert, pushing the roll of coin back to the teller, Ms. Ximenes, who was clearly new and not used to this stripe of customer. "None of those pennies even brown yet."

The teller retreated with the roll of pennies and spoke with Bum Perrault, the chief cashier, who smiled and brought a small bag, old and dirty, like a sweat sock recovered from a highway breakdown lane, over to Mrs. Hebert. Her grouchy demeanor instantly improved to one of cheery pessimism.

"Well, I don't know, what is that, a sock?"

"There's $2.50 maybe in old pennies in here, Edna," said Bum, lit up and smiling humbly like he'd rescued the Lindbergh baby. "I didn't look through them myself because I knew you'd be in. Might find something."

Mrs. Hebert slapped three dollars on the counter, took the bag without waiting for change, and went over to a couch area.

There was a coffee depot behind one of the couches, with sugar and powdered coffee white and Styrofoam cups, the kind with flat, lip-scorching plastic razor lids designed to shrink or enlarge in the presence of a coffee cup, so as not to ever fit.

"I'd be suspicious of those lids, Mrs. Hebert," I said, as brightly as I could. "Sharp."

"Why, Jerome Coe, what are you doing at the bank this early? I thought you had no need of banks because you spend all your cash on lady friends. Are you here to rob the place? Because if you are, you're not getting this sock of pennies. I'll knock you down with it and you'll get nabbed by Elvin, that security guard there."

She pointed. Elvin looked like the stump of a redwood tree with a tiny police cap on top.

"No, I'm not a bank robber," I said. "Say, that sock looks promising."

"Never can tell. Might be nary a wheatie here. And I might contract typhus. I could spread typhus without knowing and I'll be remembered in the history books as Typhoid Hebert, and everyone'll forget Mary."

Mrs. Hebert poured out the pennies onto the glass table. Everybody in the bank turned to see what the racket was. The pennies were promisingly brown and worn. Chocolatey.

"Can I talk with you a minute?"

"Well," said Mrs. Hebert, "I need to sift through these old cents right now."

She looked closely at a penny, shifting her body to access a favorable light. Then she introduced the coin to a small pile of presumably like examples. I sat across from her, quiet. I didn't have the energy to move— I'd spent it all on anxiety.

After she sorted a few more coins, she sighed and looked up.

"Okay then. What do you need that can't wait? Just let me say, you can't quit till after Mardi Gras, or I'll have the U.S. Marshals come by your house and bring you in to work. U.S. Marshals can *make* you grill sandwiches. No one can quit a food-service job before Mardi Gras, or U.S. Marshals will betide you."

"No, no, I don't want to quit," I said. "I just wanted to give you these."

I gave her my handful of pennies.

"What's this here?"

"They're coins. They'd been up in my cabinets."

"Why, Jerome. Thank you, baby."

"Sure. I have a feeling they're all spenders, though."

"Hold on now," she said, scrutinizing me and sipping coffee. "I think you have an ulterior motive. I think you want me to matchmake you and that pretty Spanish girl."

"I—"

"I won't do it, even if you cross my palm with these here pennies," she said. "I can't be bought. Besides, I haven't seen her or those subarctic comedians in days. Now don't ask me more. Sit there quietly and we'll look through these coins and see what's here."

"Mr. Murdoch is seeing another lady besides you," I said.

Mrs. Hebert didn't come to work that day, thank god. I stayed my full shift and went right home, without even taking up my nightly search for Miranda.

When I turned the corner onto my street, I discovered police cars and an ambulance out in front of my apartment. The whole block strobed in red and blue and amber. Another cop car came screaming around the corner and stopped in front of the house, skidding a little in the gravel and bumping the ambulance. Someone inside the ambulance shouted *Motherfuck*.

It sounded like Mr. Murdoch.

The doors to the ambulance were open. It *was* Murdoch. There was blood all down his shirt, and one sleeve was torn to limp ribbons, exposing his arm. Two EMTs were wrapping bandages around Mr. Murdoch's head. He saw me and did a double take.

I turned away and ran quickly up the stairs to my apartment.

There were quite a few cops, all standing around on the porch of the duplex fiddling absently with their belts of cop chazzerai. I did not discern any police work in progress. I walked up to them—not many things are as harrowing as walking up to a group of chuckling cops on a break—and asked what had happened. They looked at me for a second.

"Crime scene," said one of the cops. "No admittance."

He was a thin man with a linty cop mustache, wearing white kidskin gloves.

"I live here. There. Next to the Murdochs. Can I go into my apartment?"

"Not advisable at this point in time," said another cop.

"Oh. What happened?" I knew what had happened.

"Be calm. Just a stabbing."

"*Just* a stabbing? Just a *stabbing*?"

"Calm yourself. Remain calm. No one died."

"Who, what…"

"The individual," said Linty, "in the emergency vehicle there was the victim of the stabbing committed by a woman individual. Both parties are free to go their separate ways on their own recognizance.

"Unsworth," continued the cop, addressing a short, eggplant-shaped colleague who had two pistols drawn and a battle-ready look on his face. "Let that lady out the cruiser and send her home. Don't give her that Phillips-head or that sock of pennies back unless she needs them. And help her get her car out from under the duplex."

Our duplex was up on pilings, like most houses in the neighborhood. Under the house a white Chevrolet Impala was stuck up to the windshield.

Unsworth holstered his pistols, picked up a bloody screwdriver and the sock of pennies I recognized from Hibernia—also a bit bloodied—and let Mrs. Hebert out of the back of the cruiser. He asked her if she needed her pennies and/or screwdriver back, and if she didn't he'd have to seize them as evidence.

Mrs. Hebert snatched both seizables out of Unsworth's hand, went to her car, started it up, and shifted it into hard reverse until it finally came free from under the house and screamed backward across the lawn and through the hole in the fence it had made on the way in. Finally Mrs. Hebert got the car out of reverse and pointing down the road. She burned rubber and took off down my street. She turned left on St. Charles, tires faintly squealing.

"Unsworth, let that boy into his home," said the linty cop. "And go tell those EMT bellhops to squirt some Bactine on that man and let him go."

Unsworth produced a machete and hacked away at the yellow scrim of CRIME SCENE tape taped across the door to my apartment. I stepped in.

I leaned Miranda against the leg of the bedstand and got under the bed.

I thought Mr. Murdoch might stomper me for tattling on him to Mrs. Hebert, but I was safe for the moment—there was no sound at all from next door, except NiNaw's dainty snoring. She wouldn't let her son stomper me. She fed me cinnamon rolls and Froot Loops! She'd protect me. I relaxed a little. I fell asleep.

Then: *Boom.*

Bits of my apartment rained down around the bed.

I screamed, but it was pitched too high for human ears.

Yelling. NiNaw's voice, then Mr. Murdoch's.

"Why are you discharging arms in my house, you hardhead string-winder!" shouted NiNaw.

"I'm in my room, NiNaw. You said whatever I do in my room is my business."

"Not with my Franchi twelve-gauge, you puppy. You came into my room and went into my ironing-board closet and took my shotgun, then came in here and shot a hole in the wall."

"My wall. I'm sending a message."

"Message? You know you could have killed that boy."

"Not unless he was hanging from the chandelier, NiNaw."

"And what if he was? You'd go to the penitentiary and you'd have to play Chinese checkers with your Uncle Cowboys every day until your electrocution. How'd you like that?"

I didn't hear anything for a moment, as if Mr. Murdoch was building regret for not considering a future playing Chinese checkers with Uncle Cowboys.

"Now go ask him if he's okay. And apologize," said NiNaw.

"No ma'am."

A dull *thwack*, then a resounding *thwack*.

"Okay! Okay!" said Mr. Murdoch. "But I'm protesting. That boy told Edna I was fooling around."

"Were you?"

"No ma'am. Not too much."

"Go apologize, boy," said NiNaw.

"Sorry."

"No, not through the shotgun hole. Go knock on his door and apologize. And sound like you mean it."

A moment later a knock came at my door. I did not answer the knock at my door. I did not move. The weird, oniony sweat that my body always seemed to produce after a true gaslighting stuck my shirt to my arms and chest.

Then, NiNaw's voice again. "You apologize?"

"Yes, NiNaw," I heard Mr. Murdoch say to his mother.

Big fat liar!

"You lucky *I* don't crown you with a sock of coins," said NiNaw.

"I know it," said Mr. Murdoch.

"Don't you ever touch my guns again, or my throwing stars," said NiNaw.

"I'm going to work."

"Fine. Bye."

I did not move or go to sleep. I was safest where I was: under the bed.

After I heard Mr. Murdoch's car roar off, I emerged to review the shotgun hole up by the ceiling. It was about a foot across, nowhere near the size of the hole in the kitchen. But there was an exit hole in the ceiling, too, and no doubt one in the roof. The pellets had probably landed in Chalmette.

I enjoyed a moment of relief thinking Mr. Murdoch really had just meant to send a message, not cause my death.

But then my old bed-leg temple began to ache, and my pinkie started to itch maddeningly. And I *still* had to go tell Carolyn about the Slut.

As disappointed in me as she was, Miranda was my only comfort. I kept her close.

The phone rang.

"Hello?"

"Fired," said Mrs. Hebert. "Unemployment office on St. Charles across from Lundi Gras King Cakes With And Without Babies."

She hung up. After a moment of dial tone, I hung up, too. The phone rang again immediately.

"Hello?"

"Jerome?"

"Carolyn! You sound... are you okay? Wow am I glad to hear from you! I was—"

"I need to see you. I know you have to go to work, but you can blame me, I need you right now."

"I don't have to work. I got fired. What happened?"

"You got fired?"

"Yeah, dumb story, jeez I really missed—"

"I'll come get you," she said.

She sounded weak. Beaten. Horribly, it made me feel better: she needed *me* for a change. And maybe she'd broken up with the Slut.

Plus, I couldn't wait to show her my drawing!

I folded Miranda up carefully, slipped her into a baggie, and put her in my pocket.

Carolyn was outside my apartment in less than two minutes, honking. It was raining hard.

"Hi!" I said, climbing into the car, almost completely wet from the fifty-foot dash from the porch.

She didn't say anything. She was red from crying and soaked from rain. We didn't talk the whole ride.

Presently we parked in front of a brown house.

"My mother's rental property," said Carolyn. "Nobody ever rents it."

It was one large room—kitchen, bedroom, foyer. Only the bathroom was a separate room, sticking out of the kitchen like a jetway.

"It's dark in here," I said.

"This is as bright as it gets," she said. "Wallpaper eats up all the light."

"I'm going to turn the heater on. You're soaked. You must be freezing."

"Will you see if there's something to eat in there?"

I found a box of animal crackers and a couple of tins of sardines. There was a big can of tomato juice. When I returned, Carolyn was wrapped up in a blanket and sitting in a soft well of pillows. She was leaning against a low, sturdy couch of curved wood and scratchy velvet. Next to her was a pile of wet clothes. Jeans, Grambling sweatshirt, boots. Her bag. A dark bra and white panties.

There was another blanket. I gathered it around myself and lay on the floor.

She ate the crackers. I ate the sardines. We split the tomato juice. I waited.

"Okay?" I said.

"Yeah."

"What happened?"

Tongues and snowflakes in my head. Dark nipples and small breasts and greasy blue pipes. Mr. Murdoch's truffle-hunting cock.

"I started seeing someone," she said. "A few weeks ago. That's why I haven't been around a whole lot."

"Hey, that's great!"

"Acrobat in bed. A real carnival ride."

Carolyn smiled shyly. I'd never seen her shy before.

"Tell me about her," I said, with as much enthusiasm as I could, propping myself up on an elbow.

"You probably figured out who it is. It's Francie. The lighter girl."

That's Francie? Fucking my *neighbor*? A big gold *Quentin* glimmered in my head; a razor parting skin to plumb a deep artery. *Shit!*

"We ran into each other in Monstrelet's. I thought we could just get together for old time's sake, have good sex..."

She looked at the heavily draped windows. The rain, which had been steady and hard, suddenly accelerated, doubling in volume. The house vibrated. The blue flames of the heaters wavered.

"...but it didn't work out like that. I realized I wasn't over her. I'm still in love with her, and she's still in love with me. Nothing changed. Including the crazy jealousy."

I sat all the way up, still wrapped in the blanket. Kippers floated in my guts.

"What happened?"

"We were lying in bed—the backseat of the car, actually—breathless, laughing, talking, and then, like a *total fucking idiot asshole*—"

Carolyn began to slap at her own face. Alarmed, I grabbed her wrists. She started to cry. She'd clearly been crying all day—I wouldn't have thought she'd have anything left, but she did. It was as if she'd merely been practicing for the real thing, and here it was. Finally she calmed down. I let go of her wrists, and she settled back against the wall again. She continued:

"...I told her about me and you and our kiss at the airport in the back-seat."

"Oh no."

"She turned dark red. I'd seen her like that before, when she tried to burn down the hostel after she thought I'd cheated on her with Terence. I told her how sorry I was, that what had happened between you and me had been no big deal, we were full of beer and only friends, but it just made her more and more upset. Then, she starts to laugh. She has a beautiful, sexy laugh."

Carolyn was my friend again. She was suffering terribly, but hey, at least I'd gotten what *I* wanted. I relaxed into a pleasant self-disgust.

"Then she said she hated me. That she wanted to kill me. She wasn't saying, *Gosh I'm so mad I could just kill you.* She *meant* it. Then she just jumped out of the car and ran."

"And that's it? When did all this happen?"

"This morning."

"Maybe," I said, scooting a little closer, "it's a good—"

"I need her. Help me get her back."

"Wait. What? You want her *back*?"

She looked odd, slack but potent, like a tranquilized lion.

"Help me get her."

We were both leaning forward, wrapped in blankets. The blanket drew back from Carolyn's neck the merest bit.

"Help. Me. Get. Her. Back."

"Carolyn, I just really don't think that's the best idea, Francie's kind of unpredictable and dangerous and you know there's the murder threat too and she sort of set that precedent with the lighter and—"

"I don't care. I need her."

She was quiet for a while. She stood up on her knees, pulling the blanket up to keep her breasts covered.

"It's your fault all this happened," she said.

"Mine?"

"You kissed me. If you hadn't this wouldn't have happened. So you have to help me make all this right."

"Carolyn! That's bananas. That was a long time ago and it didn't mean anything. You know it. And you sort of kissed me first."

"It's still your fault."

"It's Francie's fault," I said, lost in a new sea, and a bit seasick. "Or maybe it's... yours. For getting involved again."

"Oh, fuck you," she said. "Just explain to her that the airport thing was all your fault, that you went way overboard even though I kept saying stop..."

"Are you serious? No! She's insane and dangerous and blindly selfish.

You said. That's what I remember about that night—not the kiss, but you telling me about what a nutty bitch she is and how you nearly killed yourself over her."

"Jerome, what's it to you? Just tell her the little fucking lie! She'll buy it—I know deep down she wants to believe I wouldn't have kissed you without being forced to. Or are you mad at me? Because I haven't been quite so *available*...?"

"No, no, not true, and I'm not telling—"

"Nay, I cannot tell a lie!"

I looked at her.

"I don't like you like this."

She laughed. "Thanks for being so helpful and comforting. I thought you'd be there for me. I guess I'll fucking handle it from here."

She made a motion to stand up. She was going to leave. She was leaving. I was not getting her back.

"Carolyn?"

"Fucking *what*?"

"I didn't want to have to tell you this, but—"

"What? You're gay? Tell Francie so I can have her back."

I said nothing, and that got her attention.

"What? Okay, what?"

"She's cheating on you."

"What?"

"Just like she did before."

"I've seen that desperate, Hail Mary look in your eyes before, Jerome."

"You know my neighbor? The man who has the other half of the duplex? He was on his porch rocking-chairing on a Volkswagen hood that time you dropped me off, uh, after the airport?"

"No, I don't know your fucking neighbor."

"Yeah, in the Luncheonaire, the day the photographer came. I told you how much I hated the guy."

"Okay, so?"

"He screws around a lot," I said. "He always has some girl there with him. I can hear it through my wall. *Everything*."

"Get to the fucking point."

"The cabinets in my kitchen fell off the wall in the middle of the night.

Made a big hole, so you can see into the neighbor's place. He came and looked through the hole into my kitchen right after it happened. And the girl he happened to be fucking that night was with him. It was Francie."

"Oh, come on. What're you doing?"

"I'm telling you," I said. "It was Francie."

"You don't even know what she looks like, you lying fuck."

"I do."

"Liar. How?"

I sighed.

"*How!*"

"A few hours before the cabinet thing, I walked over to visit you at the hostel, to show you… something. The door wasn't latched. Batiste was asleep on that couch. I went in. I heard sounds in the back. I saw you, and her. Together. On the cot by the lockers."

"You bastard," she said. "You fucking liar. You know, I knew there was something really wrong with you, you and your dis*gust*ing mystery hand—"

"Carolyn—"

"You're just saying all this *shit* because you don't want us back together because you're a fucking selfish psycho because all I am to you is your fuck-ing PI hunting for your fucking bitch fag-hag drunk Latina cunt *ghost*!"

I waited an instant longer than I would have had what she said not been true, and Carolyn saw it.

"You both had your eyes shut. You want me to describe it? You want me to tell you what the blue snap-on vibrator she was fucking you with looked like? You want me to tell you who was on top? What her breasts look like? The mole on her chest? I *know* it was the same girl fucking my neighbor."

"You fucking sick fuck."

"I didn't come and spy on you on purpose. I came to show you some-thing, and I just accidentally walked in on you."

"This is all your fault, you fuck! If you hadn't come to my city, my hostel—"

Carolyn suddenly sat back down and covered her bare shoulders with the blankets. She cried quietly. The rain leveled off. After a while she looked up.

"Did you really see her with your neighbor?"

"Yeah," I said. "I heard them having sex. I heard everything. The walls are paper. And when they appeared at the hole in the kitchen wall, her robe fell open. She was naked underneath."

"No."

"I'm sorry."

"I don't believe you."

"I know. I don't know what to say. But it'll be all right."

And it would be. I'd take Carolyn to see her mother in a little while. Or maybe we'd go stay with Knops. The magnitude of the Danes' breakup seemed equivalent to Carolyn's, and misery loves company, and all that. Before long, all would be well again. She'd come to her senses; Knops and Dik would get back together, as they always did; Mrs. Hebert would hire me back when she realized her boyfriend was just a two-timing bottom-feeding Casanova mama's boy. And we would find Miranda.

The gas heater hissed. The rain picked up again. We were quiet for a long time.

"Okay?" I said, touching the blanket about where I thought her foot would be. I wished she'd hurry up and be okay. I still wanted to show her my drawing.

She nodded, her forehead on her knees.

"You shouldn't have told me that," she said. "I wish you hadn't told me that. It wasn't necessary."

She stood up. The blankets fell off her. She walked over to her pile of wet clothes. I looked away, into the blue fire of the heater. I heard her empty out her backpack onto the floor. I looked around. She picked up a familiar black object. She looked at it closely for a moment, right at the muzzle, then pointed it at her stomach. I jumped up, and with my bad hand grabbed the barrel. The gun went off, then again and again, the shots going into the wall and floor. I ripped the gun out of her hand. Something inside my palm gave out; a new, warm pop. I squeaked, dropped the gun, and fell back. Carolyn grabbed the steaming weapon and her keys and ran out in the rain. She was in her car and already a block away by the time I got outside.

I stood in the front yard and watched her roar down the street, her car splitting puddle after puddle after puddle.

I ran three blocks down to a Schwegmann's, found a pay phone, dialed 911.

Then I called again and talked to a different person, just in case. I called the hostel, but no one answered. 411 couldn't find a number for Carolyn's mother. Carolyn couldn't have made it home to her apartment yet, but I called there anyway. No answer. I left a message, telling her I was sorry, that I'd tell Francie anything she wanted me to. I asked her to call me at my apartment. Last, I called Ioanna. She wasn't there either.

"Biloxi, Pai Gow tables," said Ioanna's cook. He hung up.

The hostel was too far away to run there. I picked up the pay phone again.

"Cabs," answered the dispatcher, after about a hundred rings.

"I'm at Schwegmann's by Delahoussaye. Need to go to Doyle and Iquem. Youth hostel."

"Hour fifteen."

"It's an emergency."

"Hour fifteen."

I started running.

The rain was still steady. Evergreen leaves and trash formed dams around the drains. The air was acrid. It had a yellow cast, visible only by looking way into the distance, down a cross street leading to the river, or the other direction to Claiborne Avenue. It was late afternoon.

There was nothing I could do but run. I could not think of a time when I'd felt this helpless, this absent of ideas, this friendless, all at once. Even suicide seemed not an option: guilt trumped it.

Nature, like a bounty hunter (you know she's near but still you're always surprised when she Maces you and drags you down to the bail bondsman), called. Fucking sardines. Fucking tomato juice. And my mutilated, disgusting mystery hand ached like a sprain. Good. I hope it rots off. I was tired of it. It was a memory of Tommy, ice, shit, the frozen drops of black blood *tnk-tk-tnk*ing on the hard snow cover.

I ran down the middle of the street, where there were fewer obstacles, fewer puddles.

I got winded. My legs were rubbery. I stopped and listened to a thin, pathetic droning coming from somewhere nearby. I realized I was wailing.

"Get out the street, chief!" hollered a man on the sidewalk.

Over the man's head a bubble ballooned.

Dammit! Not now! Not that!

I shut my eyes and sealed them off with the heels of my hands.

"Fuck off!" I said. I squalled like a child having a tantrum in a grocery store. I didn't have much, but I did have my sanity. I'd held on to it for quite a while this time. Ever since Tommy had slit me in the cold.

But this was the moment. The one, over as it starts, that separates my whole-mindedness from the delusion of it; the one where I'm aware of both but hog-tied from stopping the dissolution of the first or the blooming fission of the second; the one that is so quickly past and so soon forgotten that

I opened my eyes.

You likely too late dummy thought the man. *She bound to be dead by now*

"Shut up!"

A car stopped by me and rolled down the window. The driver's bubble inflated like an airbag.

Me first me first me first, always thinking about yourself

I had to rest. I needed a bathroom. I had to think.

Puddles had formed at the street corners. The air was dark and greenish-yellow and burned. I stepped back onto the sidewalk and walked as quickly as I was able.

A few blocks later a building with long maroon awnings stretching out to the curb appeared. A coffee shop, recently opened.

It was a new place, beautiful. Green library lamps on oaken tables. I would rest, just long enough to use the bathroom and make all my calls again. Maybe all was well. Maybe Carolyn was at the hostel, surrounded by Danes who bring her blanket after blanket after blanket.

The windows looked out on the dangerous world like the shark tank at an aquarium. The place was busy—customers standing at the windows, sitting at all the tables, waiting in line. All were tall and savage and beautiful and forbidding.

And everyone seemed familiar. That eely woman with the muddy yellow go-go boots reminded me of Miriam from the smoking room at the Boll Compound. The hunched-over man sitting across from her talking without pause reminded me of Manny, the manager at Whom House in Reno, who, on the day I aged out at sixteen, gave me a hundred bucks and a bag of peyote and told me to go to Virginia, where the foster laws are more generous. And *she* looked like Marta reading horror, and *he* had gray, pupilless eyes like that ECT anaesthesiologist with peach lipstick, and that thin-lipped, smiley guy toasting and cream-cheesing bagels looked *just like* the cop who'd stepped on my hand down the street from the Boston Public Library whose voice was still ground glass on my ear-drums: *Pissah for you, pal, now shutthefuckup*; that thin girl with lampblack hair sitting cross-legged on a couple of fat yellow pageses and chirping into a phone reminded me of long-ago middle-aged foster mother as she might've looked at twenty; and the girl lying across three chairs near the case of fake books, posing like a 1940s bathing beauty for the benefit of a loose-skinned goth kid pointing an old Kodak Instamatic at her, had a saddle curve to her waist exactly like Leigh's, as I remembered her when she'd been sleeping next to me on the futon the morning of the day Bill beat her to death.

A few clear spots opened in the warm air above the crowd in the cof-fee shop. Some of the spots followed customers around. One or two of the clear spots filled with milk and then sprouted tiny black stalks that swam together to form letters that skimmed here and there through the milk to form words and then sentences.

Dead naked in her car Go now Profunda brachii Oh po thing he tired Fuck it Fuck her Shoulda honed the bed leg guy Ignodome slouch thats a barrette in your lap lil gay man Ooh mama mamas boy Flip over child this wont hurt

"I'm trying!" I yelled.

All the bubbles cut loose and rose quickly to be cut to rags by the ceiling fans.

Objects in the coffee shop began to resolve into faces. Soon they were everywhere—in the designs of the hammered-tin ceiling, the cypress planks of the walls, the peanut-butter cheesecake slices in the glass pastry case. Cartoon faces, just a mouth and two eyes, sometimes a nose, all set in a generally round or oval shape. But they were frozen—they didn't talk or grimace or squint or spit hatred.

I went into the bathroom (a pristine Black; there was likely no other WC of such snowy purity in the whole town) to catch my breath and wait for something to happen with my plumbing. It was the only place to sit anyway. I took out Miranda, but I couldn't bear to look at her.

The faces around me in the bathroom began to appear without me squinting. The rough canvas coffee-bean bag tacked to the wall as a decoration suddenly animated, forming a fat, secretive smile in the shadows of its folds. A soap squirter on the edge of the sink stuck its tongue out at me. The pipes under the sink grinned and puckered. The little rubber-tipped spring sticking out of the wall near the floor to keep the doorknob from punching a hole in the plaster when somebody opened the door too hard looked at me like an asp, weaving slowly and dipping to touch the floor.

Hurry, hurry now, it's time to go.

I came out of the restroom. Bubbles everywhere, like protest signs. I ignored them. I waited for the phone, dancing from foot to foot. I squinted out into the gray of the rain, watching the faces on the parking meters and on the guitars and amps behind the barred window front of the guitar shop across the street.

"I need the phone," I said as politely and calmly as I could to the eely Anti-Miriam, who was chatting with someone about some bar that featured Jägermeister shots issued in test tubes. "Phone phone phone phone. Please."

I looked outside. A maroon Cressida had just parked at a meter in front of the guitar shop. The meter smiled mirthfully, like the sun in an old engraving.

A young woman stepped out of the car. She opened a large, hemispherical umbrella with *Madeline* characters on it. She spent a coin in the meter and turned the knob. The meter winked. I laughed out loud. The young woman put in another coin.

She was familiar, too. She tilted her umbrella back and looked across the street at the coffee shop.

At me.

I ran out the door and stopped under the awning.

"Leigh?"

From under her *Madeline* umbrella, the young woman studied me. It *was* Leigh! Not just *like* her, *her*!

A tremendous bubble, a brilliant, opaque hot-air balloon, swelled over her. The wind pushed it east.

Jerome

"Leigh!" I waved, jumping up and down. "Leigh!"

I started across the street, but was blocked by a slow pickup fording the deep puddles. Leigh jumped back into her Cressida. The pickup finally passed and I ran across the street. She'd started her car and was pulling out of the spot, her door still open. I caught up to the rear passenger door and grabbed the handle, but had to let it go when she picked up speed. She took off, her weather-balloon bubble getting larger and larger as her car diminished in the hazing distance.

I'll guide you said the bubble.

"Leigh! It's me it's me! Jerome! Zits! Accutane! I'm sorry I let you die!"

I'll take you to Carolyn follow me

"Slow down! Stop!"

Just as her car turned at a faraway intersection, her bubble, vast now, like the Superdome, said

Look for the signs Jerome Don't waste time

"Leigh!"

Quick she'll die like I did

Then she was gone.

What signs? Where?

"Who has a sign!" I shouted when I got back to the coffee shop.

I had everyone's full attention. Bubbles, all clear, all void.

"Give me your phone, Anti-Miriam."

She covered the mouthpiece with a copiously ringed hand.

"Nearly done," she said fiercely.

"Emergency," I said.

I looked around. The bubbles were now a silent chorus:

wait

"I can't fucking wait! Carolyn's gonna slit an artery! I need a *sign*! Leigh told me to look for the signs!"

I grabbed the receiver out of Anti-Miriam's hand.

"...made fun of me and my hair but I'm telling you, I don't eat sandwiches anymore, it's just not worth it. Hey, you still there? Cass?"

"I'm sorry but I have to hang up on you," I said. "Anti-Miriam is letting me use the phone to make a quick couple emergency calls. Bye."

I hung up on the guy afraid of sandwiches.

"Anti-foster-mom, please give me one of your phone books," I said. She jumped up and ran over to hide behind the goth kid.

I called all six Marrats in the phone book, even though there were no

Leighs or even *L*s. Half answered, and they told me I had the wrong number. The others were disconnected or had no answering machines.

I called Duke's L-Bo Room, collect. Incredibly, they accepted the charges.

"Dewey there?"

"Hold on."

A voice shouted *Dewey, phone!*

"Yeah?"

"Dewey!" I said. "Jesus I am so glad you're there. Listen, Leigh is alive and—"

"Who is this?"

"Jerome! From Duke's! A few years ago? Bill kicked our asses? Remember?"

"Oh. Yeah. What's up. Got my sixty bucks?"

"Huh? Listen: Leigh's not dead."

"Leigh's not dead," said Dewey. "Okay."

"I mean it. I saw her today, on Magazine."

"You saw Leigh, who's not dead, in a magazine."

"*On* Magazine, it's a street, I'm in New Orleans! I saw her at a parking meter! It winked, it was *her*, Dew. She's here to guide me to Carolyn, my friend who might kill herself because of me, but I need a sign. Do you have it?"

"I don't hear from you for years," said Dewey, "and you call me—at the bar—*not* to tell me you've got the sixty bucks you borrowed to buy acid-washed jeans and hair gel, but to tell me about a resurrection. Listen, Jerome, we're not buddies anymore, but here's some buddy advice: maybe check back into a loony bin and look into a mood stabilizer. New shit on the market, man. Read about it in *Newsweek*. Whole new *classes* of drugs for crazies like you."

"Do you have the sign or not?"

"What?"

"You must have the first sign. Please tell me you have it. Carolyn's gonna die!"

"Jesus. Bye."

"Wait!" I said, tears on the move.

He hung up. I turned to look at the patronage. All transparent bubbles, with words in them in spiky, unreadable languages.

Except one. Anti-Marta's.

Leigh says Maturette Street Go

"Oh thank you, thank you!" I said, then tried to kiss her, but she slapped me with an iced-tea spoon.

I left the coffee shop behind and ran the half mile to the few ugly blocks that made up Maturette.

It grew later, darker. I ran up and down the short street. The caustic air bit harder now. Everything hurt. The relief I'd felt when Anti-Marta told me where to go was caving in to panic. Carolyn might already be dead. I had to stop.

"Leigh, I can't see. Help me."

Set in the ground was a NOPSI manhole cover. It grinned. It formed a bubble, flat and ugly, like a mushroom.

Left at C. P. Horn Street says Leigh

I ran again.

"Hey," said somebody.

I stopped.

"What's the sign?" I said, not seeing anyone. "Where are you? What's the sign!"

"Don't turn around, now. Pop out that billfold."

I didn't move.

"Pop that money wallet, chief."

"No, I can't, this—"

"No? You say *no*?"

"This is an emerg—"

He hit me on the side of the head with something hard. I fell.

"Ow!" I shouted. "That hurt! What happened? I do not understand this sign! Who are you? Why do you need my boots?"

I let the man with the sign have my billfold with my ATM card, but he went through my pockets anyway. He missed my pocketknife, which was stuck way down in my left front pocket. He yanked off my boots, too.

"PIN."

"Huh?"

"Pee. Eye. In."

"Oh," I said. "It's 'Leigh.' 'Leigh!' Okay? You owe me a sign now, pal!"

A terrible *kakt* at the back of my head.

"Ow again! Asshole!"

I stood up slowly.

I tasted blood on my lips. My ear was numb where he'd first hit me. My hearing was a little off. I felt all over my head. There was a new wound, right in the back of my skull, where my old metal plate was. I stuck my finger in the hole, and it went right down to the steel, which had a dent in it. I whacked the side of my head. A little black and crimson cork popped out of my ear.

I stepped on something hot. I picked it up. A little knot of metal. I didn't know anything about bullets, but it didn't look like a *Dirty Harry* kind of bullet.

I dropped it into my Miranda pocket.

Miranda wasn't there.

Someone came down the sidewalk. Two grinning Aleister Crowleys drinking from paper bags and pushing a shopping cart occupied by a brace of squirming puppies.

I didn't have the strength to shout. Miranda was gone. Carolyn was going to die. I just held out my hands, palms up.

Hostel Leigh's squirming puppies thought. *Take off your bloody clothes*

"Oh god, thank you!"

I stripped. Except for my pocketknife, I wrapped everything up in a hobo bindle, and tossed it all into the bed of a broken-down El Camino that positively fluoresced with parking tickets. "I'm on my way!"

Soon I was in the dark channel that was Iquem Street.

Finally, the hostel.

I ran up the porch steps of the hostel and rang the bell. *God I hope she's safe.* I danced from one foot to the other.

The door buzzed open. I ran in. Behind her desk, Carolyn was thumb-wrestling with herself. She had a sexy, vanilla-ice-cream bubble.

Hi Jerome

"Carolyn!" I said, starting to go around the desk to hug her. "Damn, I'm so relieved."

"What the fuck?" said Carolyn. "Get away! Who the fuck are you? Don't hug me!"

"I know you don't want to see me right now, but I thought you killed yourself. I wasn't thinking—I shouldn't have told you, I saw the suicide how-to book in your car, I knew you might, but... God, I had to have help from Leigh to find you. I just love Miranda so much..."

I started crying. It felt good.

"...and I lost her! The fake-sign man took her!"

"I'm not Carolyn, man," she said, "And do not come any motherfucking closer."

"Promise, promise," I said, the tears slowing. "Hey, what happened to your arms?"

She had incongruously large forearms, like Popeye.

"My *arms*?" she said. "What's up with your fucking *hand*?"

"Doesn't hurt. Wow, it does look rough, though. Look, let's both go to the doctor, right now, together. You can get Xanax and I can get my hand looked at. Oh, and my head, too. Look, I got shot. Wish I'd had your gun!"

I looked at my hand. It was gray, and thin red cobwebs stretched up my arm. The original cut had completely torn open again. I touched it, the tarry, cool insides of it. The bone was visible, also gray, but colder and brighter than my skin. What an odd thing, to see your own bone. *Wow, that's mine! Weird.*

Carolyn was starting to look different now, all of her, like how people in dreams morph from, say, your old homeroom teacher into Hirohito. Carolyn wasn't morphing into Hirohito, but into Popeye. She unpacked a fresh bubble, a spermatozoon wriggling toward the ceiling.

How you like me now

She really looked like Popeye.

"Carolyn, you are the spitting," I said, admiring her odd little pipe, sailor's cap, one-eyed squint.

"What the fuck is going on?" she said. "Carolyn's gone, man. Nobody knows where she is."

Right here Safe Relax now Jerome Go use the bathroom if you want

"Haha!"

It's all over. Everyone's okay.

Carolyn eyed me steadily from under her sperm. She did not move at all.

What's the knife for

"You don't remember?" I said. "You gave it to me, silly! To repel highwaymen! I have to carry it in my hand because I threw my pockets that are in my pants into a truck."

She picked up her telephone.

"Who's that? I hope you're not talking to Ef ar ay en cee eye ee."

Of course not That's quite an erection

"And he's standing here with a fucking hard-on."

"I know, I can't help it," I said. "You should've seen the one at the airport! It's Miranda, I love girls with glasses and black hair. You know Dagoberto? What about those thighs?"

"His back is fucking drenched in blood."

I played absently with my open cut. It seemed vaguely sexual. I sniffed at it. Raw chicken, a day or two spoiled.

"Fuck."

Carolyn covered the mouthpiece with her tubby Popeye fist and looked at me.

"Fuck off to Charity, man! Oh, I'm going to fucking throw up."

"You even sound like Popeye, now," I said. "I can't do Popeye. I used to could do a pretty fair Wimpy, though. 'I will gladly pay you Tuesday for a hamburger today.' God, Carolyn, I couldn't have lived with myself if…"

My hand began to itch. And my bullet hole. Then my knees. Then my lower back.

An all-over itch wrapped me.

I dropped the knife and lay down on my back. I pushed myself around with my feet, rubbing the rough carpet against my shoulder blades and the back of my head. I ground my temples into the baseboards. I scratched and rasped all over. My cut itched maddeningly. I rubbed it on the old couch, I scraped it on my stubbly face, I dragged it along the encrusted rim of the standing brass ashtray by Carolyn's desk. My erection itched. Horrible! It hadn't itched this bad since that time I masturbated inside a paper towel tube I'd greased up with Prell.

"Stop that!"

"Help me, Carol-Eye. Scratch it! O, my pocketknife o where are you?"

There it is.

With the dull, nicked blade I scraped at the open bone, I cut at the flesh. I'd take it off at the root.

"It won't come off! Carol-Eye, come back. Help me!"

"Stop it, I'm not Carolyn, you nut! Carolyn's fucking gone!"

She/it came around the desk, phone in hand.

Too dull.

"Corner Doyle and Iquem hurry he's cutting at his hand I'm afraid he'll cut off his—"

Bite it.

"It's *killing*!"

I forced my little finger and as much of the meaty, rotting karate-chop edge of my hand as I could into my mouth, and bit.

V

In the pink room I could not move. I could barely keep my eyes open, which was good because above me was a fairly bright fixture of fluorescent tubes. I'd heard that fluorescent bulbs strobed very fast, producing mini-seizures that manifest as headaches. I certainly had a headache. And I had a bandage on my head. Big surprise.

If I stretched my neck around I could see a window, high up in the wall behind me. It was painted black.

I sat up, or tried to, but I fell back—my elbows were secured with leather belts. They were well worn, soft, and that warm, rich brown obtainable only through years of exposure to acidic, hypermanic sweat. My hand was wrapped up thick and tight.

Great. Another half-mast suicide. I didn't even remember this one. And now I wasn't even enough of a risk for them to restrain my legs. An insult!

A doctor in green scrubs came in. He looked friendly, like he had a genuine bedside manner. He carried a clipboard, a roll of masking tape, its sides gray with stuck dirt, and a thin towel with writing on it, like from a motel chain. I couldn't read it. He had no bubble. This was real.

"Feeling okay?"

"Head hurts. What am I on?"

"Gurney." He laughed at his little joke. "No, just messing with you. Prolixin. Don't worry—you responded pretty fast to it. I doubt you'll need any more. Today, at any rate."

"Good," I said. "What hospital is this?"

"Listen, I need to strap your legs down."

"Okay. What happened to my hand?"

"You don't remember?"

"No. I vaguely remember thought bubbles."

"Whatever. Let's just say you're now officially a step up—or down?— from a cutter."

"What does that mean?"

"Biter. Knees down."

I straightened out my legs. He secured my feet.

"And I need to restrain your waist. Nothing personal, just the rules."

He tied the leather strap across my hips.

"What's your name?" he asked.

"It's not on my chart?"

"Oh, you're a *professional* nut. No, you came in here with nothing, my friend."

"Anton Lyon," I said. It was my regular false name.

"Anton, you need to use the pan?" said the doctor.

"No, not really."

The doctor went to the door, which was open. He reached around and flipped off the fluorescent lights, which was a relief. Then he shut the door.

But he was still in the room with me.

"So I bit my hand?"

He dropped a towel onto the floor and pushed it under the gurney with his foot.

"You sure you don't have to go?" he asked, adjusting the position of the towel with his toe.

"Yeah, what are you doing?"

He peeled off two small pieces of masking tape and stuck them to two adjacent corners of a piece of paper. Then he stuck the paper over the little window in the door.

"Little privacy."

He undid my pajama bottoms. He took out my penis and squeezed and pulled up on it. I yelled and shifted my hips away. He pulled on my penis so hard I stopped shifting and stopped yelling. He leaned in my face and muttered *Shut up I'm a biter too* quietly but with such force that I did as I was told. His breath smelled of overcooked lamb and wood varnish.

He undid his own pants and stroked himself, then took my penis in his mouth, breathing hard through his nose. I didn't cry out. I got hard. I was afraid he was going to tear it off. He had two rings on one finger that pinched my skin. I waited for him. He came quickly, but I didn't, though I thought I surely would. He picked the soiled towel up off the floor and spit into it. My dick collapsed, and he dropped it like a dead bird.

He hit me open-handed, hard across the face. His two rings snuck under my eyelid and dragged across my cornea. My sinuses swelled and my head of stew sloshed. He left, pulling the door shut and leaving the lights off.

I was hungry and I wanted to bathe. I wanted to cut my penis off and die in the translucent madder water.

Later, a nurse came in and woke me up. No bubble either. No question about it now. I shrank from her. She told me to sit still. She had gloves on. My eyeball itched. No, it hurt. And my eyelid was crusted shut.

"What's this bandage on my head for?"

"Sh."

"The back of my head hurts."

"Be still."

"I heard I bit my hand? I don't remember."

"You bit off your finger, and more."

"God."

"I will ask you only one more time to sit still."

"What are you doing?" I said.

"Just giving you medicine," said the nurse.

"A shot? What is it?"

She undid the waist restraint.

"It's a strong tranquilizer. No, it's not a shot. Sit on your hip."

"Sit on my hip? What do you mean? What hip?"

"Your left," she said. "Put your rear end toward me."

She slapped my thigh.

"Mabel!" she shouted.

A nurse came running down to my room, and a doctor. The same doctor. All bubble free.

"What happened to his eye?" said one of the nurses, an older lady, as if I weren't in the room, just my crusty eyeball in a jar.

"John Doe doesn't want his suppository," said the younger nurse.

"That's Anton Lyon," said the doctor, smiling.

"Anton," said my nurse with the gloves. "It's a suppository—works more slowly and with fewer side effects than an injection. And it doesn't hurt."

Okay. I didn't care anymore. I turned over. Maybe it was sodium cyanide, or a bomb.

My eye itched. It seemed all that mattered. If I could have I would've taken a floor sander to it.

I floated for a long time, in a pleasant fog of whatever the suppository was, but soon I developed a dyskinesia in my elbows that compelled me to force them straight, but I couldn't quite. My arms felt airy, like hydrogen zeppelins. I wailed and cried and begged in that peculiar dyskinetic agony. I finally fell asleep.

I woke in what seemed like the middle of the day. The dyskinesia had subsided. I was starving. The bandage on my hand was too tight to move my wrist much at all. The back of my head was squishy. I was so uncomfortable that I started to enjoy myself.

I pretended to sleep, keeping my good eye barely open. I watched the familiar little window of wire-laced glass in the door. Faces appeared at the window every five minutes or so. Nurses mostly, sometimes other patients.

A doctor I hadn't seen before came in.

The doctor came in with two nurses. One was a woman who reminded me a little of how I imagined Ioanna might've looked when she was in her thirties. Jesus, how *long* ago was all that? Carolyn? Miranda? Poor Knops and Dik? I couldn't bring up any of their faces. Even their names seemed distant and fictional, characters in a compendium of fairy tales on a shelf in somebody else's childhood.

"Why's he crying?" said the woman.

The other nurse, a large man with the dense black beard and perfectly bald head of the uncommonly strong, carefully began to unwind the bandage on my hand. The layers grew rustier and more humid as he went deeper. The last layers—intimate, cozy, yellow-black—stuck.

"Okay," said the doctor. "Give him to me."

He pulled off the remains of the bandage. My little finger, its metacarpal, and all the surrounding flesh—gone.

After several weeks of nurses, nurses' aides, the doctor with the two rings, blood-work guys, spoon-feeders, and housekeepers coming in and out of my room, I didn't even bother to open my eyes when the door opened.

More time passed. They never let me up, not once. In Massachusetts at least they hardly ever tied you down for more than a few days.

I had a bedpan here. I stank. I sat up to eat, my legs and waist tied down and sometimes one wrist. They changed my sheets, my pajamas, my bandages, but not as often as I would've liked.

A surgeon who reminded me of a screech owl came in once to work on my hand.

"He really tore the fucking dying rotten gears outta here, huh," he said, but I think he was talking to himself.

The bandage on my head came off one night while I was sleeping. In the morning I saw it on the floor in the corner of the room. It had kept the shape of my skull. It looked like half of a prehistoric egg. It remained in the corner for several days, until a housekeeper caught it in the silent sweep of a wide dust mop.

A girl with cornrows checked on me through the window a few times a day. She couldn't have been more than four foot ten—she had to jump to get a look.

My head had begun to feel better. My itchy eye had mostly healed. My bad hand still hurt, but I didn't get that phantom-limb itch I'd heard about. I did miss my finger, terribly, as though I were its home, channeling its homesickness. I hoped it was all right.

A nurse made a little conversation with me when she came in to check my blood pressure.

"How you doing, Anton?"

"Pretty good."

I'd learned years ago that it was the only thing you could say in situations like this.

"That's fine."

The doctor came to visit me every other morning. His pinching gold rings, his towel, his lambchop breathing. These days he always kept me in his mouth until I ejaculated. On his most recent visit he gave me a shot in my hip and I didn't remember anything after that, but I woke later with a sharp pain that ran from my ear to my shoulder. The back of my head felt gory. My mouth was dry, and I'd thrown up, hours before, apparently—the vomit on my pajamas and on the mattress of the gurney was almost dry.

The doctor came in one morning as usual, but this time he didn't shut the door or turn out the lights. He had a tall stool with him, which he positioned near my head. He left the room and came back with a yellow glass bowl. He set it on the stool, reached into the pocket of his green scrubs, and brought out a blue Bic disposable razor. He shook it in the hot water in the bowl and started to shave my face, which had at least a week's growth.

"Wiry," he said.

"Nurse's job."

"Not today."

My whiskers, sparse but tough, quickly dulled the razor—it pulled them out rather than cutting them off.

He washed the razor in the bowl. The water, mixed with a little blood, ran down my cheeks, and stained the gurney sheets a raw-pork pink.

When he finished, he slapped me lightly on both cheeks.

"See you in the morning, Anton. I'll be bringing a... colleague."

He smiled and left.

I woke early the next morning.

Through the window in the door the girl with the cornrows jumped up to get a look at me. I waved my restrained hands, but she didn't wave back.

It got later. The doctor would be here soon, with his friend.

My legs were unrestrained. I swung my feet as hard as I could to the right, then to the left. The gurney rolled a bit. I swung right and left again. The gurney skidded. Right, left, right.

Then, with one particularly energetic swing to the right, the gurney tipped. We, the gurney and I, fell over.

I was on my side, facing the wall. I extended my legs toward the wall as far as I could, hoping the weight of them would lever me onto my belly. But it didn't work. I felt like I was belted to the side of a van.

I kicked and struggled, unable to tip the gurney. We merely rotated slowly counterclockwise.

I found myself facing the door, looking up at the window. The black cornrows rose and fell.

I extended one leg as far as I could and stuck my big toe under the door. With the extra leverage, I pulled the gurney on top of me.

I pulled my knees up to my chin, shifting all the weight of the gurney onto my neck. I fought my way to my knees, then to my feet, the gurney a huge, awkward backpack.

I stood by the door, just out of range of the window, my legs shuddering from disuse and the surprising weight of the gurney, and waited. On the floor of my room was a rectangle of light from the window. The shadow of the girl's cornrows interrupted it. Then she was gone.

The door opened.

It was a nurse I hadn't seen before. I walked into the middle of the room, the gurney balanced nicely, and then I ran right at her, starting slowly, like a booster rocket. I roared. The nurse jumped out of my way and I ran into the hall, nearly losing my balance on the turn. The hall stretched a hundred yards. Along it were a few people seated in plastic chairs, leaning forward as if asleep or freshly dead. There was a bright spot on one side of the hall about halfway down that must have been the nurses' station. A few nurses milled around in front of it. The doctor was there, too. He was whispering to a tall man in a white velour warm-up suit.

At the end of the hall was a room. Set high in a wall over a flaccid blue couch was an enormous, sunlit window. Beyond it, trees waved.

I leaned forward and began to run, careful to keep my balance while I accelerated. I picked up speed. I roared, continuously, one lungful, basso profundo, running down the hall, leaning forward, unable and not planning to stop.

Some of the people in the chairs looked up. One smiled and waved. Two others didn't move, and one, the girl with the cornrows, pulled her feet up like I was a waiter sweeping under her table. I roared past them all.

Up ahead, one of the nurses was trying to locate the right key to open the nurses' station—their only apparent retreat—while the others yelled at her to hurry. I headed right for them. The nurse found the key, and they all rushed inside just as I blew past them, roaring like a cleaving glacier. I filled the whole hall.

Ten feet from the big window, at the peak of momentum, I leapt up onto the couch and jumped like a springboard diver. My gurney and I shattered the thick glass, but the thin, hard bars behind it stopped us from gaining freedom. We bounced back. The gurney landed on all four wheels, with me on top, still strapped down.

I'd gotten nowhere. But the view was a little better from here—bright sky, trees, and far away, the tip of St. Louis Cathedral.

I enjoyed it for a moment, but soon the clean white thunder of a thousand doctors and nurses and muscular nurses' aides with clipboards and needles and sangfroid rolled down the hall and fucked it all up.

The next few months I spent in a room with a few blinking instruments and a bathroom. I wasn't tied down as often, and soon I wasn't tied down at all except at night.

One morning, a nurse came in.

"What happened to that other doctor I used to have a long time ago?"

"Transferred to a juvie ward. Get up."

"My muscles are a little rubbery."

"Up. Follow me."

The nurse showed me my room, one with four beds. They weren't bunk beds, but they reminded me of those first few days at the hostel, a centillion years ago.

Months went by.

I gradually remembered what had happened. The thought of Carolyn, naked, dead in her car or somewhere else, ran as a red film inside my head all day, all night. I remembered the treacherous bubbles. And Leigh—by far the realest of all the hallucinations—racing away from me, terrified of the crazy man chasing her, hollering about acne. The little bullet, too puny to take me out of this fucking inhuman farce. Miranda. The snap of bit-through bone.

In the dining room I ate with plastic silverware, I watched TV two hours a day, I watched smokers smoke, I watched damaged and forgotten people turn from the ceiling to the floor to the walls to the ceiling trying to avoid some torment or other. I explored the new contours of my pinky-less hand. Tactilely stranger than the missing finger was the missing hand bone—a fifth metacarpal, the bald and bearded superstrong nurse informed me. The skin that had once covered it had been wrapped by the surgeon over the fourth metacarpal and then laced up in order to close the wound. The heart and brain lines of my palm now terminated on the back of my hand. I would consult Mme Creuzault in Treme if I ever got the hell out of here.

The girl with the cornrows watched TV and cussed with perverse virtuosity at the staff and Shannen Doherty and the other patients.

The main door of the unit opened onto a hallway. Through the window of the door I saw mainly doctors and nurses walking up and down the hallway, but also a few patients, and some others who were clearly civilians. The door was securely locked, but there was just the one—no double-door airlock like most places.

They'd long since replaced the window I'd broken, and had installed bars—thicker, I noticed—inside instead of outside. They'd moved my couch springboard under a poster of a trumpet player in silhouette leaning against a Bourbon Street lamppost.

The girl with the cornrows ate peanut-butter sandwiches all day. Anyone could eat what they wanted from a big brushed-steel restaurant-supply refrigerator in the dining room. Little half-pints of milk, chocolate milk, strawberry milk. Loaves of white bread. There was always coffee.

The nurses' jobs were to forbid and demean. They treated people as awkward objects, unmanageable and heavy, like downed livestock or baby pools full of scummy water.

The patients were quite sick. Many were retarded in addition to mentally ill.

One young woman—a girl, really—was blind and deaf, and cried nearly all the time, perfectly silently, except for a deep breath now and then. Her mother came by every morning and dressed her and brushed her hair and put on her makeup. The only time the girl didn't cry was when her mother was there.

When the mother visited, she massaged her daughter's tiny hands and pushed back her cuticles. She messed up her daughter's thinning Afro, really messed it up, putting her back into it, and then combed it all out again, which made the daughter grin.

The mother covered her daughter up to her chin in a big green blanket, then reached under to change her daughter's clothes, removing and replacing each article, one at a time. When she was finished, she removed the blanket and straightened out all the rumples and tucked in the loose ends. Then they played the hair-messing game again.

The mother removed a little paper bag from her purse and put it in her daughter's hands. The daughter leaned forward and started to cry. The mother took the bag and poured the contents out into her daughter's hands, about a dozen clip-on earrings. The daughter felt each one carefully, chose one, and handed it to her mother. The mother found its mate in her purse, then gave the pair to her daughter, who clipped them onto her mother's earlobes. The mother kissed the daughter, stood up, and the nurse let her out. From the moment her mother left, the daughter cried and rocked, her whole being and body deteriorating like a system of entropy, until her mother returned the next morning and combed out her hair again.

One morning the mother came to visit, but the nurse turned her away. It was then that I noticed that her daughter wasn't in her usual place.

I filled up on peanut butter and jelly later that day. I'd made one sandwich too many, so I offered it to the girl with the cornrows. She took it, and made as if to backhand me. I flinched.

She walked down the hall to the isolation rooms, or whatever they called them here. She chewed her sandwich while jumping up and down to see in the window of the same room I'd spent so long in.

I walked down there. She moved to the side while I looked in the window.

The deaf and blind girl was tied to a gurney like I had been.

"Jesus," I said. "What did she do? What could she have done? She's fucking blind!"

"She mean. She go *surprise* a motherfucker sometimes. So, that's what she gets."

"I'm getting the fuck out of this place," I said.

"Let me share something with you," said the girl with cornrows. "Nobody gets out."

"I can get out."

"You do, you better bring me."

"No way."

"Yes way, motherfucker."

"Never."

"Why?"

"I'll get you in worse trouble than you're in now."

She gave me dangerous look, but she didn't argue.

Later, I went into my broken-window room. I sat on the couch and looked at the spire of St. Louis Cathedral through the new bars. It *would* be hard to get out of here.

I lay down, even though it was against the rules. I fell asleep.

I woke up with my hands between the cushions. I felt around for change. I dug deep down inside the couch. I stuck my finger on something, and pulled it out with a gasp. I'd slit the middle finger of my incomplete hand pretty good, and it bled freely and darkly down my arm.

Much more carefully, I slipped my other hand back into the couch and felt around. I pulled out a long piece of thick glass. It was scalpel-sharp along one edge.

I took it to my room and wrapped a few dozen pages from an especially rotten Barbara Cartland novel around one end, as a handle. At the nurses' station I begged for and was granted some masking tape, which I wound tightly around the pages.

I found the girl with the cornrows and told her my idea.

"Fuck you, crazy man," she said. "I'm gonna take *you* hostage. I ain't letting nobody like you put a glass knife at my throat. I ain't going to act scared for *no*body."

"I won't tell anybody."

"Don't talk down to me, racist motherfucker."

"Come on. You told me to take you with me if I tried to get out. Don't you want to get out? Did you see what they did to that girl in there?"

"Like I said, she crazy."

"What're you? Should you be here? Should I leave you here? How old are you?"

"I'm thirteen, and I ain't crazy."

"Jesus. Why aren't you on the juvie unit?"

"For a good reason. Look. If you abduct me, they hunt you down. They shoot you down and piss on you."

The superstrong nurse came into the sitting room.

"Anton, meds," he said. "Window closes in four minutes."

"Okay."

"So get a move on."

"Okay."

"Joy. You can't be in here with a male without a staff member."

"So what the fuck that make you?"

The nurse left.

"They hunt you down," Joy said. "Stick your ass in Angola."

"They don't even know my real name."

"So look, I take *you* hostage. They catch me, where the fuck they gonna put me that's worse than this place?"

"I don't know."

"They just bring me right back. If they catch me, and they won't."

"Maybe they'd send *you* to Angola. I don't want that on my conscience."

"I won't be on your motherfucking conscience. I'll be on a bus to Florida. So let me see your goddamn knife."

I showed it to her.

We waited until the end of the evening shift. The nurses were antsy, distracted, ready to clock out and go party. It was Saturday night, around nine.

Joy and I stood in the dining room.

"What the fuck you doing?" she said.

I was opening up a few notches on the fingers of my bad hand, which I didn't use all that much anyway.

"This is going to make it look more authentic. People obey blood. Let me put some on your pajamas."

"You better not have no fucking AIDS."

I dripped blood down my face and wiped a little on the knife. I smeared a little on my pajamas. I squeezed my finger and dribbled some on the neck of her pajamas.

"You one disturbed individual. Maybe I go by myself."

"Ready?"

"Come on," she said.

I gave her the knife. She reached up from behind and wrapped her arm around my throat, her forearm under my larynx. She was gentle. She was shaking.

She walked me down the hall toward the door, stepping on my heels.

A nurse appeared. She was no longer dressed in her nurse's uniform, but in a corseted wedding gown. Her face was powdered eggshell china white, except for her forehead, which she hadn't gotten to yet—it was still her normal flushed and mottled complexion. A toy axe stuck out of her neck.

"I will stab this motherfucker in the eye till it break off on the inside of his skull you don't open that motherfucking door right now."

I dug my nails into Joy's forearm. I should have gone to the bathroom first. I yelled.

No one even looked out of their rooms. A few of the people in the chairs down the hall looked up, and one of them smiled and waved.

The nurse, who seemed more inconvenienced than concerned or frightened, reached inside the nurses' station, found a ring of keys, and opened the heavy steel door.

Joy and I went out into the hall and pulled the door shut. There were a few people in the hall, but no one paid us any mind.

"That was easy," she said.

She was sweating, and breathing hard. Her eyes were circles and the hand with the knife jittered.

"Okay?" I said.

"Take this fucking glass knife away."

"Turn your pajama top inside out to hide the blood," I said, taking the knife. "And don't run. Don't run until you get to your neighborhood."

We stopped. I pointed down a hallway, which had a red EXIT sign at the end. "Go that way. And don't run."

Then Joy, the girl with the cornrows, was gone.

Costumed drunks clotted the streets. People dressed like pineapples and easy chairs and the undead. O.J. Simpson everywhere. The ground was a pale orange refrigerated jelly of vomit, stomped pumpkins, and piss that soaked through my paper shoes. Brass bands honked in the distance, and sirens wailed in every emergency melody.

I was spattered with blood and holding a glass knife. No one paid me any mind at all—even if it hadn't been Halloween, somebody wandering around with a blood-slicked knife was hardly a double-take-worthy sight.

I didn't know exactly where I was, but soon I emerged onto Canal Street from a direction I'd never come before. I was only a few blocks from the site of my last memory, where I'd hallucinated Carolyn and a few others and then bitten off a fifth of my hand. Must have been close to a year ago.

On Canal, a few blocks from Erril's, a bum was sitting in a wheelchair parked by a FedEx box. He was bent over and hammering with a ketchup bottle at something stuck to the arm of his chair. He was about my size. I went up to him and asked if he had a clean change of clothes he wouldn't mind trading for my glass knife. I explained how sharp the knife was, and suggested he fashion a little sheath out of cardboard or something.

He was very helpful, and immediately gave me some brown pants and a green polyester guayabera shirt and a pair of flip-flops with thumbtacks and mule shit stuck to the bottom.

I took off my bloody pajamas and changed. I'd seen people naked on Canal before—there was nothing to it.

My new clothes were a little loose, and they smelled pretty bad. The pants were not of a known style or standard make, but there was a dollar in the watch pocket.

The Danes' place was dark, which was a relief—I didn't want to see the Danes, or pretty much anybody from the year before. I wouldn't have even gone near their place if I hadn't needed to use the pay phone.

"Erril's. Payroll. Darla."

"Darla? This is Jerome Coe, I used to work for your mom at the Luncheonaire? I think I have an old paycheck waiting for me. Can I come by and get it?"

"Jerome Coe? Where you been?" said Darla. "Your check been here forever. You gotta cash them in ninety days or they void. Your check void."

"Can you pay me cash out of petty cash?"

"Sure, what the hell. Come on by tomorrow morning."

I didn't ask about her mother.

Then I called Bay Bank in Boston to make sure my account was still active.

Then I called the hostel.

"Carolyn there?"

The guy on the end of the line asked me to hold on. I waited.

Then a voice said hello. Carolyn.

I hung up. I was so relieved she was alive that the ginger-ale fizz of an approaching faint nearly got me—I had to sit down and lower my head between my legs.

It was cold and raining, so I spent that night under the banana trees and elephant ears in Jackson Square with the bums and crust punks and blacked-out Halloweeners.

I was still wet when I went into Erril's in the morning to get my back pay.

Before going upstairs to payroll I paused at the dark theater of the Luncheonaire. On the counter were two racks of high-heel shoes, furry with dust, a spool of zip cord, and roach droppings as big as cloves. The old cash register was gone, leaving uncovered a square of counter so sticky from spilled fluids it proved the final resting place for thousands of bugs, assorted change, a few S&H green stamps, and somebody's medical ID bracelet. The stools had been uprooted and left lying about the floor.

The doorway to the back room where Mrs. Hebert used to search pennies was closed. On the doorknob hung the SORRY WE'RE CLOSED sign Mrs. Hebert had stolen from Popski's Pawn.

Darla wasn't in the payroll office, but her assistant, an old man with bronze bangs and teeth like little corks, gave me a distasteful look and an envelope with my name on it. It had $20.35 in it. On the back of the envelope I wrote a note to Darla saying I was expecting a FedEx letter, in care of her, and that I'd call now and then to see if it'd arrived.

Downstairs I paid for a four-dollar robe and a pair of socks. Up the street at Jam's Drugs I picked up a few cheap store-brand essentials like Jambuprofen, SlimJams, a sample bottle of Jam's Apricot-Chypre Hair Soap, and a disposable razor. At the register I impulse-bought a cold can of JamItDown. As I made my way up St. Charles, dodging the massive humming crowds assembling for some parade or other, I tried the JamItDown. It was like a blendered cabbage in many ways. But it was generously caffeinated, so I drank it all.

At Duds & Buds, I bought a Lite at the bar then went into the back where the pool table and washing machines were. I loaded my dirty clothes and dressed in my new robe and socks. While everything was in the wash I drank my beer and played pool with the proprietor, Oily, who fancied my robe and nearly convinced me to wager it against his softball lighter in a game of nine ball.

A whole suit of clean clothes later I called the hostel again. The same guy answered.

"Carolyn there?"

"Gone."

"Gone? What does that mean, 'gone'?"

"It means 'not here,' just like it has since the dawn of English. She's never here on Mondays."

"When does she work next?"

"Wednesday. In English, that means 'Wednesday.'"

"We are talking about Carolyn, tall, with the little dimple in the end of her nose? Messy hair?"

"That sounds like the only Carolyn who works here."

I hung up.

With my robe still on and my clean clothes rolled up under my arm, I walked down to the hostel.

I rang the bell. Batiste let me in. He didn't seem to remember me. Some kid I'd never seen before was at Carolyn's desk. The place had been remodeled. The soot had been cleaned off the walls. There was new carpeting. Reflexively, I looked around for my metacarpal and my finger. I'd always wondered where they'd gone. I sometimes pictured them as a couple, stretched out on tiny chaise longues on a black-sand beach, sipping B-52s.

I went to the floor my old room was on and showered and shaved in the communal bathroom. I shaved every hair off my body—while in the hospital, I had been a metropolis of lice.

In the steamed mirror of the shower room I took stock of my old cuts and dents. My missing-finger hand was getting pink and didn't hurt too much. My head didn't hurt either, even when I shook it. That was something. But it *looked* like it must hurt, mapped as it was with gullies and craters and wandering railroads of old suture scars. I'd need a hat.

I pulled on my clean clothes. I snuck into my old room. All four bunks were taken, but there was no one in the room. I climbed up to Miranda's old bunk and lay down. I looked at the things in the room she must have looked at. Across the room was my old bunk. I imagined myself as Miranda, watching me masturbate like a lonesome gibbon.

I climbed off Miranda's bunk and crawled under what had been Dik's lower bunk. I spied my old sock in the corner.

I slept for twenty hours.

I wrote Carolyn a note of apology, appended with a promise that I'd never bother her again. I left it with the smart-ass etymologist who'd answered the phone earlier.

I visited Darla the next day. She wasn't in, but my FedEx was there, according to the odd guy with the cork teeth I'd seen the day before. He had warmed toward me a bit during the night. Maybe because I'd cleaned myself up and was wearing a sharp *Miami Vice* cap I'd removed from the head of a little kid passed out on the neutral ground, surrounded by empty chardonnay wine coolers.

In the envelope was my replacement ATM card. Maybe my mugger had thought I'd said "Lee" when he demanded my PIN, because there was nearly a grand in untouched accumulated disability payments. I withdrew half of it, and by the end of the day I had a change of clothes, a pair of new Stan Smiths, and an apartment on the other side of town.

VI

I studied on avoiding my last life. I studied on its opposite, sheer hermit-age. I avoided newspapers, the hostel side of town, the French Quarter. I dodged neighbors, locals, chatty busfellows. Diners. I didn't masturbate, or even allow myself to think about sex very often, partly as a penance, partly as observation of the hermit's rules, but mostly because that doctor, with his masking tape and towel and clipboard of typing paper, always dropped by and wrecked the show. I didn't think about love.

I did think a fair bit about love's well-removed relative, romance. Or at least I read about it—much of my free time I spent buying, reading, and then donating romance novels.

I thought about passivity, submission, being chosen. Old bus transfers and crepe myrtle petals blowing down deserted streets, falling bodies, butlers, oarless boats, infantry. Me, so far. And I thought about action, about doing. Choosing. Me, from now on. I'd *pick* what to do. I wouldn't wait for things to happen. Maybe contentment would come eventually; maybe the ignodomic shudderings would someday leave. But I wasn't going to sit and wait for either of them.

I took a job working in a barren padlocked shack near the Pauline Street

Wharf with two other nameless men, sitting at a picnic bench, dipping wire into hot crucibles of lead-tin solder and then sticking the wires to little devices of some kind that measured something and registered the result on an LED screen. I didn't know or care what.

I got paid in cash. A stack of fives, anonymously tucked under my crucible like a big tip, waited for me every Thursday morning.

After work, I'd walk home, which was the third floor of a grumpy, uneven house surrounded by a tall brick wall with glass shards on top that had been rounded like pebbles in a stream from time and the elements. I'd eat a steak sandwich, listen to the Astros games, maybe read, and then fall asleep without any trouble—I had few worries to toss and turn me.

The present landlord didn't like me much, even though I was quiet and pleasant and had no visitors and ran no drugs and paid the rent on time, in cash, on the third of every month when he came by with his son, a six-foot-nine colossus of dudgeon who carried a length of PVC pipe with a brass elbow joint at one end. It had dried blood on it.

Just down the street was a deserted gas station surrounded by a hurricane fence. Inside the fence, chickens wandered around the old pumps, clucking and pecking at promising bits of gravel. I thought of the chickens as pals, and as an audience: on the walk home from work I sometimes stopped in front of the fence to try out voices on the chickens. They seemed to like Mr. T. I never saw the chicken herder or whatever he was called.

I arranged a chair by a window near my bed so I could watch the sparse traffic and the thunderstorms and the occasional gang walking down the middle of the street. At eye level the phone and power lines crisscrossed above the street from houses to capacitors to poles to houses. For a couple of months I watched umbrella wasps build a nest under one of the capacitors. The hive grew from a little inverted mushroom to a newsprint-gray, fruitcake-size hexagon, until one day I came home from work and it was on the street, crushed flat, its gray stained black and yellow from the smashed bodies inside.

When the cooler weather came, smoke from the jungle fires in Mexico came too, as if they were their own subseason. The city air became acidic and yellow, and the rains couldn't wash the chemicals away. The smoke reminded me of the hissing wisps of cigarettes put out in dirty snow.

Just like they say, old wounds ache more in the rain. My hand whined with especial vigor during the cold, acidic rainstorms. I took a lot of ibuprofen and acetaminophen and ordinary headache powders, but they didn't do much except twine the guts and eat money. The only thing that really helped was to lie in bed and imagine my hand as whole and flexible, gripping a subway balance bar—an act I considered the most demanding of the full range of a hand's sensitivity and motion. I rode this subway all over, up and down and crosstown on every line, all day and night, in every season, squeezing the bar, anchoring myself during the hard turns and starts and stops, the muscles in my hand constantly adjusting to the minute changes in velocity and position that an old subway car on fifty-year-old pitted-steel tracks can deliver to a healthy, powerful grip in unconscious but full surety of its purpose. It was the closest I'd ever come to meditation. But even that didn't help much.

Six months into my monastic and unsexy yet semi-comfortable life, I had succeeded in having regular contact with only five people: my land-lord and his son, my two colleagues on the soldering bench, and Nyelle, a K & B clerk with an outstanding gilt rococo pineapple-stack do who rang up my Slim Jims and paperback romances and analgesics.

"Are there any other pain pills on the market?" I asked Nyelle one raining-like-hell day when the ache in my hand was not responding to chemicals or deep thought. "None of that regular stuff is working."

I was shocked by how corroded and fractured my voice sounded— I realized I hadn't said a word in weeks.

"Hm. You try Nuping it?"

"Yeah. Nothing."

"You outta luck then, unless you got a script."

"No," I said, and then ahemed mightily to shake the rust off my vocal cords.

"Well," she said, "I know this lady out by Satsuma who live in a church. She can cure pain with a bamboo back-scratcher. Cheap, too."

"Where's that?"

"West. A ways. A drive."

"Oh. Damn. No car."

"What, you crash it?"

"No, never had one."

"Oh. You look like you maybe been in a crash."

"That's just my look."

"I ain't got no car either. Got to ride the loser cruiser. I got to take three buses to get home."

"Where that?"

"By Tchoup. Down from the Bridge Club. You know where I mean?"

"Kind of," I said. "I know it's a long way."

"You know *that*."

I paid for my Slim Jims, a cheap umbrella, and a copy of *Rising Bosom, Falling Bosom*, by Kassandra LeeAnna Forsythe. I walked home, squeezing the hilt of the umbrella, my subway balance bar.

○

On an unnaturally hot day near Halloween, almost a year after my bolt from the hospital, I filled a couple of paper bags with a bunch of K. L. Forsythe books and other twice- and thrice-read romances, and then hiked over to a thrift store a few blocks down from my apartment, in order to leave the books as a donation, and to do a little shopping.

The Poke Round Thrift Acre had clearly acquired a first-rate lot—the place was in high entropy. But the initial wave of thrift hawks was long gone, and the only ones left were treasureless zombies crawling through the paperbacks and dirty sneakers and bags of AC adaptors and Beta workout tapes scattered everywhere. Fussbudget toddlers imprisoned in shopping carts wailed in torment while mothers and big sisters scavenged the fallout. There was the occasional exclamation of victory when someone found an overlooked *Marmaduke* mug or a retro T-shirt without sweat stains or blood on it. There appeared to be zero Halloween-related objects remaining.

But I wasn't there for a costume. I was there for pants—I'd scorched the lap of my work jeans with spilled solder—and a Crock-Pot. I'd decided that it would be nice, for a change, to come home to stew or whatever Crock-Pots made during the day while you were at work, instead of steak sandwiches.

The selection of pants available at the Poke Round for an individual of my size (32–32) was exactly the same as it had always been; viz. meager. If any fresh, exciting pants had come in earlier in the day, they were walking around on new owners now.

On the bottom shelf of the Crock-Pot display was an especially antique example with wood paneling and dials like a prewar radio. It had a film of antique stew inside, but it was reasonably priced (fifteen cents) and came with its original box. I claimed the pot and its packaging, and went up to the register.

The Poke Round clerk, a small, elderly woman with a taut forehead, had never liked me for some reason (maybe she saw me eyeing her enviably meaty metacarpals), and to prove that today was no different, she snarled at me like a miniature tapir. Then she rang me up.

I became aware of a presence behind me. It was a warm and protective presence; a heavy wool blanket. It was quiet and near. I got lost in it for a moment. Then I realized the tapir lady was malocchioing me.

"Some. Thing. *Else?*" she said.

I stepped to the side to make room for the warm, protective customer. It was a she, and she was wearing large, lozenge-shaped sunglasses. A fluorescent orange price tag was stuck to one lens. She placed a paperback—something called *The Pnume*—on the glass counter. She smiled at me. Weird, goosey embarrassment, obviously a cousin to shame, billowed around me. I delivered a word I intended to be heard as *Hi*, but for some reason it came out as a creepy, barely audible *iyee*. It had probably looked to her like I'd simply opened and closed my mouth, like a lungfish.

Then, from above her mouth a wide red ribbon began to unroll. It followed the contours of her lips, and of her tongue, which had reflexively darted out to taste it. A thick, lush ribbon; shiny, without a trace of weave. The ribbon paused at her chin, then fell heavily. I rushed forward with my hands cupped and caught the ribbon in midstream. She jumped back and some of the blood splashed onto her white T-shirt. It continued to pour from both nostrils, bright cadmium red. In an instant my cupped hands filled with several ounces of her blood. On the glass counter streaks and pools and spatters glowed around their edges from the fluorescent light below. A fan of blood spread out onto the cover of *The Pnume*. Another soaked a knee of my solder-scorched jeans.

The tapir lady sprang into action. Almost instantly, she had an entire roll of paper towels tucked under the girl's nose, and was leading her away to the back of the store.

I left, backing out through the glass door, careful not to drop her blood.

I stood on the corner. Sleepy locals paused to grimace. A tourist mule-cart squiring twin girls and an elderly couple also stopped. The mule-cart driver pointed me out as an example of the colorful surprises in wait around every corner in the city. The day was still hot.

Her blood darkened. It began to leak through the gap where my pinkie would have been. A green, metallic fly landed on my thumb. I started to run, carrying her blood like an egg on a spoon. I ran through a parking lot, down a long street with a cat under every parked car, then up old stone steps and over the levee, and down to the mud and trash that was the bank of the Mississippi. I stood in the water for a moment, then carefully let her blood run into the divine river.

Who was that woman? I couldn't even remember what she looked like—the only visual I could bring up was an edgeless field of red, a bright carmine abstract of that bizarre, erotic cataract.

I took my jeans off when I got home. Her blood had soaked through the denim—the skin of my knee had accepted a kind of a smeared transfer, which after a moment's audit I realized resembled a kind of rust-toned photonegative of a famous police sketch: a mustachioed, curly-haired man wearing sunglasses and a hooded sweatshirt. The Unabomber.

I did not resist a sudden urge to lick my knee; to lick him; lick *her*. The blood silhouette seemed vital and confident. Or it at least *represented* vitality and confidence—two of the principal groceries, I realized, of sex appeal. There had always been something sexy about the Unabomber. There had always been something sexy about blood.

I occurred to me that this was the first time since I'd begun my new, other-side-of-town life that I felt safely, permissibly lustful. Alive. Maybe *live* was a better word, as in *Live Nude Girls*. As perilous as it might be, I wanted it. What *it*? Actual sex? No—it had been years; I wouldn't know how to properly comport. It was the *taste* I wanted, the proof that it was still there. A briny, motile, riskless, doctor-free, up-close look. I wanted to be in the lap of the redding heat of it.

I'd just poke a periscope out of the tumulus and take a look around. I'd be careful.

"I'll be careful," I told the dried black blood of my nosebleed ghost.

The next day I headed back to the Poke Round.

I peered in the store window before I went in to make sure the nosebleed ghost wasn't there. A meeting now would have been weird for both of us.

And the tapir lady wasn't there either. Another woman, dressed as Pippi Longstocking, appeared to be in charge.

It was still barren of ordinary Halloween costumes, but I found everything I needed. On a high shelf over the broken picture frames was a curly blond wig crookedly perched on a faceless styrofoam head; the plain gray hooded sweatshirt was on the floor where I'd seen a man leave it after sneaking under a clothes rack and trading it out for a purple one with racing stripes; and the peculiar sunglasses, exactly the kind I needed, were inside the glass case next to the register wherein dwelled exceptionally valuable merchandise. They were eight dollars.

"I'll take those, please," I said to Pippi, while looking around the counter for signs of blood. There were none. "Say, would you mind if I take a shoe box with me?"

"You may select a shoe box which I may then sell to you," she said.

I left my stuff at the register and went to the cardboard-box aisle. I dug around for a while until I found a good one—plain, cheap, not too big.

Next to it was a much larger box full of shoes. Homely Birkenstock singletons, a pair of cross-country skiing shoes, one with a dirty wool sock stuck in it, a pair of bleached sneakers tied together by the laces, apparently freshly rescued from a decade hanging on a power line.

But at the bottom of the box, under a galosh, was a pair of old black work boots. Mine. The ones that had been stolen along with Miranda and my ATM card.

I ran up to the cash register.

Trembling, I asked Pippi if anyone had brought in a charcoal portrait, folded in ninths, of a South American girl with Henry Kissinger glasses and a beauty mark.

"Ninths?" said Pippi.

"Like this," I said.

I took a cocktail napkin from a small stack of cocktail napkins sitting there by the register, and folded it like I'd folded Miranda's picture. My heart flopped. My hands shook.

"No, nothing like that," said Pippi. "But you going to have to pay for that napkin."

I laughed, but I stopped when I realized she wasn't kidding.

"That's a much-sought-after *Love, American Style* cocktail napkin that the young with-it people collect that you just ruined," she said. "I'll add it to your total."

I bought everything, including—after a moment of hollowing anxiety about inviting back relics of a much darker age—the boots. I took home the Crock-Pot, which I'd left behind the day before.

At home I wrapped the shoe box in grocery-bag paper and tied it with twine. I glued a broken digital watch to it. I stripped the insulation off the cord to my Crock-Pot (which turned out to have been broken—fifteen cents down the toilet), and inserted the bare copper wires here and there into the box. I stuck a bunch of stamps on one corner and addressed the box, in the studied block letters of your garden-variety parcel-bomb serial killer, to IBM.

I polished the sunglasses on my shirt. I snipped off a lock of blond from my wig and fashioned it into a mustache, which I stuck to my upper lip with wet sugar.

I reviewed my getup in the bathroom mirror. I'd be safe. No one from my past would see me. The past itself would not see me. *I* wouldn't see me—the barroom mirrors and security monitors of Halloween night would reflect and record only my costume. I would be simply... touring. A garden tourist, sniffing phlox. I'd go home right after.

As I was shutting the door on my way out, I noticed, in the corner by the window, my black boots. They were a yard apart, pointing away from me, as if trying to run off. The anxiety I'd felt when I bought them blew back like a zephyr. I quickly locked the door and ran down to the bus stop.

There were a lot of other Halloweeners on the bus, but they were your ordinary devils and Baron Samedis and drunk sailors. No one else on the bus was a Unabomber. And no one congratulated me on my originality, or even seemed to recognize who I was supposed to be.

I got off at North Rampart and slowly edged into the Quarter carrying my shoe-box bomb. I felt powerful. Thrilled. As nimbly free as I'd felt since I'd first moved to New Orleans and found the sidewalks on the walk to Monstrelet's lined with whoring flowers, syrupy with carnal promise.

It was just dark, and getting crowded. I passed Knops and Dik's old place over the Gumbeaux. Their apartment appeared as dark and lifeless as it had the night I'd called Darla for my back pay.

I could see perfectly well through my sunglasses, even in the dark. I walked around, looking fugitive.

Even though I was excited about the evening, whatever it was to be, I became a little depressed when I realized that I wasn't the only Unabomber after all. There were lots. The other Unabombers, behind their sunglasses and wigs, seemed as disheartened as me. Some carried their bombs at their sides like baseball fans toting the felt pennants of a team that had just suffered an especially smothering loss.

I felt particularly deflated, as my ensemble was quite precise. My bomb was the only one with wires, an address label, and the correct postage. My hood had little drawstrings, and my blond locks had the proper density and curliness. Some Unabombers didn't even have wigs. Others didn't even have *bombs*.

I found a bar that was just barely less crowded than the others. Incredibly, a barstool became available the instant I came in—a man outfitted as a convincing Olive Oyl had just vacated it.

The bartender was Malibu Barbie in a bikini. Every twenty minutes or so she'd climb up on the bar and lie down, then encourage the patrons to do body shots, charging in accordance with the erotic potential of the part of the body from which the shot was to be consumed. The final body shot was the highlight of each performance. Leaning on her elbows, Malibu Barbie would produce a valley of airtight cleavage that would hold a few jiggers of liquid. An assistant then filled the valley with liquor from a costly-looking bottle. Then an auction was held. The high bidder won a cleavage body shot, a privilege often valued at eighty or ninety dollars.

I declined to bid, but drank beer and tipped grossly. Every time the bartender brought me a fresh beer, she reached over and took the two strings of my hooded sweatshirt under my chin and pulled them one after the other, like milking. While she did that she puckered her lips and mumbled syllables that girls will sometimes mumble when presented with something cute or helpless or both.

On my right was a dejected Grim Reaper drinking ice water. He had been outbid in the last four body-shot auctions, maxing out at $62 every time, and was apparently determined not to spend any of his $62 on beer or the jukebox, in case it was just enough to win a coveted slurp of garbanzo schnapps or whatever it was in a future auction. The Grim Reaper also seemed to resent the occasional milking that I received from the bartender, and so beamed mortal looks at me and my shoe-box bomb on the bar.

On my left was a mad scientist in a lab coat, carrying some dry ice in a beaker. He casually smoked Camels and drank modest domestic beers, as though on a break from madness.

The jukebox was loud, and there was plenty of shouting. Between songs, the shouting would cease and for a moment the din of the Quarter outside could be heard.

During a lull between some French ballad with bells and a song about martinis, there was the sound of breaking glass outside.

People in the bar crowded around the door to watch the fight. The mad scientist followed, grabbing his beer and beaker. He left an empty barstool.

In an instant the barstool was reoccupied. To my horror it was another Unabomber, a bombless one, with totally the wrong kind of sunglasses.

The fight outside had apparently broken up, or perhaps had ended in a knockdown or a death. The patrons were coming back in, trapping me and my Unabomber pal at the bar. Before long, the room was again so densely packed that I was squeezed up against my barmate. Close enough to smell perfume.

Whatever was on the jukebox was deafening—it completely obscured the sound of the bartender chortling at the two of us in our not-quite-identical garb. She milked both of our sweatshirt strings and brought us both beer after beer, pushing our tips back toward us. However, as much as Malibu Barbie considered us a droll spectacle, my companion and I did not play along. We ignored each other. I told myself I was content with my proximity to her, that this what I'd come down to the Quarter for: little squalls of perfume, looks, radiation. No more, though. No *talk*.

A few auctions later, my barmate tapped on my shoulder. I leaned into her, but I couldn't hear a word. I could only feel her breath on my ear. I looked at her. She pointed to my bomb. I just nodded. She tapped on my bomb, then did a thumbs-up. I responded with a thumbs-up. Then we pretended to ignore each other again for a while.

She tapped on my parcel bomb again and held up her whole hand and grinned brightly.

She had painted tiny black bombs on her nails, complete with infinitesimal yellow sparks.

She stuck her finger under the twine of my box. Then she smiled slyly and made as if to pull the shoelace knot open. I smiled, but had to turn away to grandly belch. When I turned back, her attention had been snared by somebody dressed as Charlie Chaplin who had snuck behind the bar and was trying to gaff Malibu Barbie's bikini bottoms with the crook of his walking stick.

My Unabomber and I resumed ignoring each other.

Then she stood up. She tapped me on the shoulder again, and pointed to her seat. Then she squeezed through the crowd toward the bathroom.

I defended her barstool. I gave no quarter. Aggressive Green Lanterns and Divines and giant Slurpees tried to invade, but I fought them off as well as I could without straying too far from my own barstool.

An Underdog took off his papier-mâché Underdog head and came at me with it. I didn't think the real Unabomber would have flinched, so I didn't flinch. The Underdog head came down on my own with none of the pillowy crumpling that I'd been expecting—in fact, it felt like he'd hit me with a hamster cage. The blow to the head was enough to distract me from my sentinel, allowing an icy Xena to sidle in and gain my Unabomber barmate's barstool.

It was soon clear that Underdog had been accompliced to Xena. They were both eying my own barstool now.

Doomed. I'd failed in a simple seat-saving task. And instead of a flirty anonym playing with my shoe-box strings, I was sitting next to a leather-torsoletted warlord from TV.

I was drunk, too, but not drunk enough not to notice that the evening in the bar had so far been a loose allegory of my whole life: try, fail, flee. It was my pattern. And as befit my pattern, the next step was to run away and start my life over in another city. Or at least another bar.

But my Unabomber came back before I could act. She looked at Xena on her stool, then at me. I shrugged helplessly.

She squeezed between me and Xena, right up to the bar. I thought there was going to be a knifing. But instead of starting a fight, my Unabomber placed one hand on my shoulder and the other on Xena's, then hoisted herself in the air like a gymnast on parallel bars, did a half turn, dropped into my lap, and draped her arms around my neck. She glowered at Xena, who stuck out her tongue in a very unwarriorlike way.

The memory of Marta sitting on my lap after the Twister bacchanal at the Boll Compound returned with such bright shock that I would have swooned had I not been buttressed on all sides by superheroes. With a lurch of the insides I thought my Unabomber was going to kiss me, but instead she turned to the bar and bought more beer.

I put my arms around her waist—there was really no other place to put them. She leaned into me. I rested my head against the soft sweatshirt material. Under my cheekbone I felt an irregular surface, which I soon realized was the central fantasia of the bra and indeed the whole system of underthings: the clasp.

By now I was a high tide of beer. I gently held my Unabomber still, to keep the pressure on my bladder to a minimum. Before long, though, I had to slide out from under her and make my way to the men's room. She pointed at our seat and nodded.

The room was outhouse-rank, and dense with impatient, beer-crammed imposters. The floor was an inch or two deep in water. To prevent footwear from becoming logged, a few planks had been laid down, like a path through a bayou. The path led to the only toilet; in fact, the only relief station of any kind.

The stall's tenant was taking his time. The crowd began to agitate. Some members threw little temper tantrums; others hollered commentary about the stall occupant's performance. Still others bargained, offering beers or cigarettes or drugs underneath the stall door. The rest of the crowd resorted to open begging, or simply urinated off the planks into the sinister bog below.

Ten minutes passed. The slowpoke tenant was still inside. The crowd was becoming a desperate hivemind of clenched excretory ports. If I had to wait much longer, I would be trapped in the inevitable riot, and the Unabomber would leave.

I pissed in the bog.

But when I went back out she was already gone.

Our barstool had been annexed by Underdog, who was pawing at Xena's armored bosom in such a manner that I would never, ever think of Underdog in the same way again.

I tried to ask the bartender where my companion went, but she just puckered and milked my strings.

I went over to the ladies' room. It seemed that many of the unrelieved men from the men's room had tried to invade the ladies' demesne, and a battle, still in progress, had followed. Meanwhile, the men's-room riot had begun and was already spilling out into the bar. Somebody hurled a shot glass, hitting the jukebox. The song skipped. Then a guy dressed as a buoy threw a punch, flooring Xena.

That was it. The chum was in the water. The frenzy was on.

I escaped by crawling on my knees between the bar and the barstools.

Outside, I jittered with indecision: wait to see if my barmate comes out, or start searching the Quarter in case she was already out?

Search. I walked quickly up and down the streets, crossing and recrossing Bourbon Street. I went up to every Unabomber I saw and took them by the hands. There were a few females, but no one had white polish with little bombs with fuses and tiny yellow sparking dots on them.

I jogged the twelve-block length of the French Quarter six times. I went to the Griz Lounge, where I could watch the melée of Jackson Square from the balcony. I was sweating despite the chill and rain, and I would have loved to have taken off my costume. But I was afraid my Unabomber wouldn't know me if I did.

The buses ran late on Halloween, but I headed home on foot.

The farther from the French Quarter I got, the fewer Halloweeners I saw. My street was deserted as usual.

My shower stall was on the small side, but if I curled into a fetal position and took care not to occlude the drain with my head, I could still lie down fairly comfortably.

I stripped off the wig and hooded sweatshirt, but I'd grown accustomed to the shades, so I left them on. I curled up on the shower floor.

The evening was over. What had happened, I didn't know. But something had been disturbed or busted open, or had had its halves prized apart. It frightened me. I would not do anything like that again. No more safaris. No more tastings or garden tours or window shopping.

The water ran cold. I dried off. I ate a few ibuprofens. I rearranged my old boots so they didn't seem quite so animated. I fell asleep.

In a dream that night, the bad doctor appeared.

He gets under the covers with me. From a paperback he reads me a story about a boy who dresses in rain on sunny days. The boy becomes the doctor, and with a strange plastic tool he planes the skin off my thighs. Resurrection ferns grow out of the discovered muscle. The doctor combs the plants out straight with his fingers. In the corner of the room a noisy computer printer prints out some information on the ferns. The doctor reads it and laughs, and then gives me a prescription bottle filled with perfectly spherical white pills. There's no label on the bottle, so I don't know how many to take. Later, I'm flying over Lake Pontchartrain in a tiny, one-seat single-engine airplane, smoking a cigarette, when I suddenly remember I've swallowed them all.

o

In view of the psychosexual fog that the Halloween siren had wildered me into, I decided to renew my hermit vows. To this end, I began riding buses more frequently, figuring the faster I got from place to place, the more time I would have to spend at home in monasterial service.

The buses were always piloted by either jittery thrill-seekers or pokey yawners. They were never on time. Even though I went to and from work at exactly the same time every day, I always had different drivers, who came at different times, who always had different passengers, and who occasionally took different routes to our destination, and more than once whimsically chose a new destination without advance warning.

On Christmas Eve, as I rode home from work (solder-dipping is a seasonless industry), a sixty-hour week's worth of payday cash in my pocket, a storm began to gather way in the west. The bus driver, a member of an especially laid-back pokey-yawner tribe, departed from the semi-established route and presently came to rest in front of the Lucki Granni Bingo Hangar. Everyone on the bus debussed and went inside, presumably to ride out the storm playing or spectating bingo.

I hated bingo. I wasn't fast enough, or I blotted out the wrong alphanumeric, or I missed post time trying to tear open a plastic mustard pustule for my hot dog. So I sat on the bus for a while, in hopes that the storm would come and go speedily and the driver would emerge from the bingo hall and drive me to my stop. I waited and waited. An occasional wind rocked the bus. Some mechanical part ticked as it cooled.

The late afternoon, lit with slanting sunlight from the west, was growing slowly dark from the pregnant storm clouds. This kind of weather made me feel logy and pleasantly helpless. The barometric pressure dropped, and I fell asleep.

I don't know how long I was out, but when I woke the houses and buildings racing by were not ones I remembered having ever seen.

I watched out the window, waiting tensely for some house or storefront I recognized. It was darker out now, and raining harder. We crossed a rickety bridge over a cement canal filled with racing water.

There were a dozen people on the bus, all nodding off. Every head wobbled in time with every other as the bus rocketed down the road.

An especially harsh jolt woke everybody up. Some people rubbed their jaws. A few of the women dug compacts out of their purses and examined their teeth for chips and cracks.

I leaned over to a woman across the aisle.

"Excuse me," I said. "I fell asleep. Where are we?"

"We in the East. By Chef."

"Oh. I got on the wrong bus again."

"Probably you on the right bus. The driver today's Mrs. Dauvie. She wander this way and the other, looking for her cat, Aug. Sooner later she get back on the route."

"I don't think I could see a cat if I was traveling this fast in the rain on a bus with foggy yellow windows."

"It don't really matter what anybody think," said the woman. "She won't listen to reason. You know why? Because anybody looking for a cat who died of the worms in 1961 ain't going to listen to reason."

Something caught my eye out of the window. We raced by so fast that I couldn't be sure of what I saw.

"Did you see that?"

"Don't fool with me, young man. Aug dead more than thirty years."

"No, not Aug. That store we passed. Did that say Penny Barn?"

"It likely did," she said. "A lady opened a business in old pennies by here someplace, I heard."

"Mrs. Hebert?"

"I don't know, but they so many Mrs. Heberts in this town, odds say two, three operate old-penny joints."

"Do you think Mrs. Dauvie would stop the bus for me?"

"Certainly. You just got to tell her you thought you seen Aug just now. Hold on though, she stomp the brake hard."

I went to the front of the bus, held on tight to a bar along the ceiling, then mentioned to Mrs. Dauvie I'd seen Aug peeking out from under a mailbox a few blocks back. She stomped on the brake with both feet. I held on tight, but the other passengers got caught unprepared and were tossed around the interior of the bus like hacky sacks.

Leaving the passengers moaning and crawling around the bus, I jumped off and started jogging through the solid block of rain, back the way we'd come.

I don't know why I wanted to see her again—the shrinks would have said I was following my naturally codependent programming, and the social workers would've said I wanted "closure," a monstrous word I associated with capital punishment. Maybe I was testing the armor of my renewed vows. Maybe I just wanted to see what penny she'd found that was valuable enough for her to open a business. If she still blamed me for wrecking her relationship with Mr. Murdoch, well, to hell with her. I would've wanted her to warn me if my girlfriend was having sex with somebody else, and I'd tell her so.

I was soaked to my socks when I finally came upon the Penny Barn.

The shopwindows were covered corner to corner in tempera colors advertising the Grand Opening. Someone had painted a pretty good likeness of Lincoln on one window, and a fine Indian on the other. They'd messed up the buffalo nickel, though—it just looked like a cookie.

Somebody moved inside, but I couldn't tell who. I took a step closer.

Mr. Murdoch!

It looked like the Barn was about to close up for the night—there were accordion bars drawn almost up to the door. I slipped into the gap, and stood dripping just inside the door until Mr. Murdoch, who stood behind a low glass display case with slowly revolving Ferris wheels of coins inside, took notice.

"Well, well, well!" said Mr. Murdoch. "Look what the cat drug in! It's Mr. Jerome Coe, lately of the Luncheonaire Cheese Sandwich and Flat Cold-Drink Concern. Mr. Jerome, where *have* you been? I didn't think I could scare you off for more than a year with a little birdshot to the rafters."

He was grinning. Mr. Murdoch seemed genuinely pleased to see me.

"Hi," I said.

"Mrs. Murdoch," he hollered to his left. "Come on out and see who came by!"

NiNaw?

No, not NiNaw: it was Mrs. Hebert.

They'd gotten married, not too long after Mrs. Hebert had morning-starred Mr. Murdoch with the sock of pennies and stuck him in the biceps with a Phillips head.

"So you two made up," I said, glaring.

"Yes, we did," said Mrs. Hebert. "Found a 1955 double-die in that old handful of pennies you gave me that day at the Hibernia Bank. A *key* error cent. Auctioned it off at Heritage galleries for five figures. You disappeared so I couldn't find you to thank you, baby."

Mr. Murdoch grinned and reached for Mrs. Hebert's bottom, but she racketed him on the ear with a flyswatter, one of the old kind made of a coat hanger with a rusted screen sewn on one end, ex-flies divided among the tiny squares.

"Well, I'm really happy for both of you."

I stood there, dripping, waiting for one of them to at least mention that they'd been worried sick about me. Or at least wonder what I was doing soaked to the bone. But they just stood there and grinned. On the glass counter was a little fake Christmas tree hung with war nickels.

Mrs. Hebert looked happy. She clearly *had* forgiven him for his tom-catting.

I pointed to Mr. Murdoch. "You should consider yourself very lucky. I wouldn't have taken you back."

"Ho! Ho, you overreacting there, Mr. Jerome," said Mr. Murdoch. "Look what all it cost me."

He pointed to a low pink knot on his forehead.

"Jerome, babe," said Mrs. Hebert, "we got it straightened out. You had just made a mistake someplace. I forgave you. A long time ago."

"Forgave? You forgave *me*? I was trying to help!"

"I know you thought you were doing the right thing when you thought he philandered," she said. "And I know I went a little too far when I fired you and sent you to the unemployment office, but somewhere you got that mistress idea in your head, and it confused the facts and made a mess of things."

"I didn't confuse facts," I said, getting madder. "I merely related non-confused facts to the proper parties."

I had my arms out away from my sides, like a quick-draw gunfighter.

Mr. Murdoch crossed his arms over his chest and looked down at me fiercely. I wished I did have a brace of six-guns to empty into him.

"Just what made you think Mr. Murdoch here had been fooling around with anybody anyway?" said Mrs. Hebert, whacking Mr. Murdoch on the belly with her flyswatter.

"Because I *saw* him," I said. "What makes you think he *didn't?!*"

"You were mistaken," said Mrs. Hebert, waggling her flyswatter at me. Bits of fly were thrown from their tiny squares.

Mr. Murdoch had abandoned his fierce look and adopted merriment; he rocked smugly on his heels behind the glass case, enjoying the whole exchange.

My old faithful biting urge returned. My mouth filled with spit and my gums tingled.

"No I wasn't! He was sleeping with a young lady! Too young! Like low twenties, with lots of sexy know-how, too. I *saw* him! Them! Brother, does he have you fooled. And you *married* him!"

Mr. Murdoch stopped rocking. Nobody moved. My gums dried out. A bus roared past in the rain. I begged the gods to put me back on it, right now, but the gods frowned.

"Plus," I said, with a lot more cow, "she was living with him and NiNaw. I saw her kitchen cot through my cabinet hole."

Mr. Murdoch leaned his fists on the glass countertop.

"What?" he said.

He's scary.

"Plus plus, she was my best friend's girlfriend. So there's that."

"Are you crazy? Is that why you've been scarce?" said Mrs. Hebert. She said it in a gentle, maternal way that made me suddenly feel a part of a very large tragedy.

"No, I am not crazy," I said. "I was—partly because of you, Murdoch—but I'm sane right now."

My voice rattled dully, like the ball in a can of spray paint. Why had I come in here? Could I not keep my word to stay away from my past? *What lies were as whole as those you tell to yourself?*

"I want to know what is happening here," she said. But she was looking at Mr. Murdoch, not at me.

He pushed a buzzer under the glass counter and the door locked.

"Don't believe me? Her name's Francie. Ask him about the big blue pipe Francie uses on people's bottoms."

Mrs. Hebert looked at me with an expression I'd never ever seen on her or anyone else. Mr. Murdoch disappeared into the back room.

"You really don't know, do you," I said. "You know, my friend Carolyn nearly died because of him and his wandering johnson."

Mrs. Hebert said nothing. Her eyes were wide but somehow squinting, too, as though she were focused on a bright object at the edge of the universe. There was some rustling and crashing of boxes in the back room.

"Tell me why you think he interfered with a woman called Francie," she said with alien calm.

More rustling and some low cursing from the back room.

"I lived next door, I could hear everything that went on in his room, like the walls were made of lettuce, you know?"

"I know," she nodded, eyes closed. Her flyswatter bounced on her hip.

"And the night my cabinets were about to come off the wall I heard him having sex with someone, and then my cabinets came off the wall, and then there was a big hole in the wall, and Francie and him were standing on the other side of it, both with their robes barely on, and I could see Francie's, you know, the bosoms. Murdoch and her looked like they'd been at it for a while, all sweaty and puffy-looking, with crooked hair. At the time, I didn't know it was Francie, until Carolyn told me."

"Hum," said Mrs. Hebert.

"Carolyn tried to kill herself when I told her she was getting cheated on. Then I got sick, too, I was so disgusted with myself. I should never have said anything."

There was no more rustling or low oaths from the back room. My digestive muscles slackened.

Mrs. Hebert's focus returned to the room, and her expression resolved into one of contemplation. She looked down at the glass counter, still holding the flyswatter, now motionless, at her hip.

Mr. Murdoch emerged from the back with a shiny black shotgun which he had broken and was stuffing two blue shells into.

Sometimes it happens after filling up on certain combinations, like beer and coffee, or chowder and Twizzlers, or tacos and sherbet, or V8 and any legume; sometimes it happens when I'm guaranteed not to be near a toilet for many hours; and sometimes it happens in a period of extreme stress. And there was no stress with as much extremity as Fear. And I was verily pickled in Fear when I saw that oily shotgun.

So it happened: I lost control of my bowels.

Even so, I wasn't transfixed by Fear. I turned to Run. I didn't get Far. The door was Locked. I shook the Handle and Whimpered.

Every store in New Orleans has a gum-ball machine. I picked up the Penny Barn's and tried to run it through the glass door, but only the gum-ball globe broke, spilling marble-size primary-colored balls that bounced and rolled in every direction.

"Put that shotgun down, Murdoch," said Mrs. Hebert. "Put that down or I'll slap the steaks off your bones. Put it down. It's all a misunderstanding."

Mr. Murdoch did not lower the big greasy cannon pointed at my head. There was a dead silence in the room, except for the pinball-parlor sound of caroming gum balls.

"Put it down."

Mr. Murdoch lowered the barrel. The gum balls came to rest, and Mrs. Hebert explained the finer points of the misunderstanding, which, of course, had been my fault.

At least Mrs. Hebert had kept her head. Mr. Murdoch and I had nearly lost ours.

"That was me you heard through your wall, Mr. Jerome Coe," she said. "I was with Murdoch all night when your cabinets pulled off the kitchen wall. Francie—Mr. Murdoch's *daughter*—stays in the hall on a cot when she stays there. She stayed there all year after she got into that mix-it-up with the Cricket lighter some time ago. That night with the cabinets she'd just come in from someplace, and had gone to bed.

Then when the cabinets came down I hung back in the bedroom because I didn't want you to see me in my housecoat. It wouldn't do to have my cheese-sandwiches man catch me in a social setting."

We were all still pretty jittery. Mr. Murdoch because he'd been accused of sleeping with his daughter; Mrs. Hebert because she'd thought, for a few moments, that she'd married badly; and I because I'd been a trigger away from a closed-casket death. Not to mention I'd fouled another set of clothes. And, especially, because I'd been so wrong. Wrong enough that Carolyn nearly killed herself. It was as if I'd pushed the revolver barrel into her stomach myself.

Mr. Murdoch was pouring Heinz vinegar into a Dixie cup full of head-ache powders.

"My word, babe, what have you been eating?" said Mrs. Hebert, who was helping me clean myself up. The situation was mortifying enough as it was, so I didn't reveal that I'd lunched on nutria jerky and two liters of flat Bubble Up.

"I can't believe you thought I was molesting my baby, Jerome," said Mr. Murdoch. "I can't believe you believed that for so long. Oh, me."

"I didn't know she was your daughter till just now! I never thought you were a molester. Just a seed-spreader. Where is Francie?" I added, shivering, not yet able to believe the mistake I'd made. This had cost so much.

Mr. Murdoch started to laugh, his body shaking. It was only after a moment that I realized he was crying.

"She's in a jail-hospital," said Mrs. Hebert. "They found her at that hostel she tried to burn down, where she wasn't allowed to be, so they took her in. That was some time ago, after you disappeared. Murdoch and I go visit her every week, but she'll be there awhile yet."

Mrs. Hebert dragged a canvas bank bag of pennies across the room, untied its drawstrings, then poured the coins out onto the floor. There must have been twenty thousand, some of which vanished into the gaps between the floorboards.

Mrs. Hebert cut two holes in the bottom of the empty bag.

"Here," she said. "Just slip these on and pull on the string."

I holstered myself into the big canvas diaper, on which was stenciled a green dollar sign. I tied the drawstring about waist-high. I looked, and smelled, like a huge, wealthy infant.

"Want me to make you a shirt? I can fashion it out of manila folders and a stapler."

"I just need my own toilet and my own shower," I said.

"I think we'd better get shut of these dungarees."

Mrs. Hebert pointed to the item in question, which was in a far corner, wadded darkly.

"I'd really like to keep them," I said. I'd committed worse gastric crimes on jeans, and they always cleaned up nicely.

"I'll wrap them in tinfoil," she said, "but they're going to have to go in the trunk."

"I think he ought to ride in the trunk along with those dungarees," said Mr. Murdoch, who'd stopped crying and was sealing off his nostrils with first-aid tape.

"Fetch me my car keys, old man," said Mrs. Hebert.

We all climbed in Mrs. Hebert's old Impala, the same one that she'd shimmed under Murdoch's duplex the night she'd stabbed him with a screwdriver.

"By the way," said Murdoch as he stopped in front of my apartment. "What was that nonsense about big blue bottom pipes?"

"Oh," I said, scrambling to get out of the car. "Never mind."

In my apartment I rescued my billfold and pocket junk from my night-soiled jeans before I stuffed the odious article in a triple-bagged Hefty bag. I dropped the bag next to my boots, opened a window, washed up, and put on clean clothes. I lay down on the floor, ate Slim Jims, and drank Kaopectate—comfort food if ever there was—and, while waiting for Christmas, meditated on my short-term past.

The boots. Buying those back was what started this sucking visit to the Carolynian era. Or at least that was *when* it started.

Then, the same day (fittingly seduced a day earlier by a stranger's splashing blood): Halloween. And that Unabomber. She smelled nice. She sat in my lap and played with the string on my box. The End.

I could still get out of all this. I could send Carolyn a letter confessing to and apologizing for my unforgivable mistake. Then stuff the boots in the trash bag with my jeans and pitch it all into a dumpster. Then move

again. Maybe Austin. I heard they manufactured computers and other gad-
gets there—no doubt good solder-dippers were in demand.

I sat up. I gave the Kaopectate a good shake and took a slug. A resigned,
depressed slug: I knew I wouldn't go anywhere. I knew I wouldn't do anything. I'd just sit here in the faintly stinky gloam and wait for my come-
uppance. What form would it take? I didn't have kitchen cabinets. Maybe
a space-time wormhole would yawn open and suck me out to the Horse-
head Nebula.

A tap on the door. I froze.

For fucksake. *This* is how? A knock, like the Grim Reaper in a *Ziggy*
cartoon? How trite.

The someone tapped again.

Giggling, female. She tapped one more time.

"Jerome, it's just me!" stage-whispered the voice. "Open up! I know
you're there. I smell meat jerky. And something else."

Holy shit. Carolyn? No. No!

Then more giggling, plural. Loud knocks now, demanding hushing.

I scrambled up in order to jump out the window, but I did not. I did
what I always did. I let it all back in.

"Carolyn?!"

Carolyn and two others, a short one and one my height, both in the
anonymity of silhouette. Before I could turn on my light, they tackled
me. I went right down. Mercenary tickling began. Rib pulvers, neck jabs,
fists lodged and rotating in my armpits. I yowled. It ended with all three
sitting on me.

"Carolyn, my god!"

"Merry Christmas, Jerome!" she shouted. "Get me a Christmas beer!"

She was sitting cross-legged on my thighs. The small person was sitting
sidesaddle on my head, tugging at my hair and stabbing at my floating
ribs with her tiny, hard hands, sharp as cement trowels. The third party,
whom I could hardly see because of the party on my head, sat Western style
on my belly—lightly, though—with her arms crossed and her head tilted
toward the window. The light from the streetlamp came in from behind
her, illuminating long strands of thick, flyaway hair.

"Jerome, please get Carolyn a beer," said the dark shape on my belly.
"And please get yourself one while you're up."

Her knees pinned my biceps. My renal arteries thumped between her thighs. Her femorals thumped back.

"And get Julie two beers," shouted Carolyn. "And get my little bitch four!"

"Shit," I said. "Carolyn, is that really you? Jesus, I'm so sorr—"

"Forget it, man. Forget it. I forgive you. We'll talk about it later. Now is the time for Christmas cheer beer."

Carolyn segued into a booming version of "The Little Drummer Beer."

The small person took a fistful of my hair, climbed off my head and bent down low to my ear.

I realized who it was before she even uttered a word.

"We don't know each other," whispered Tommy. "We've... never... *met*."

"Oh lord." What a hard, spiny frost it was, that of sudden despair.

"Ra-pompa-pom-pom! Shall I play for you!"

"You don't want to hurt Carolyn again, do you. *Do* you. She nearly *died* because of you. *I* saved her."

"Where..."

"Ra-pompa-pom-pom!"

"You keep your mouth shut about me and everything'll be cool."

My neck thrummed. She'd found me, and now she was going to take my head off at the clavicle with her Sweeney Todd.

"On my beer drum! Pom! Pom!" sang Carolyn, squeezing the tendons above my knees.

"Swear you won't tell," hissed Tommy.

"Swear," I hissed back.

"Shit," shouted Tommy, letting go of my hair and jumping up. "Smells like shit here. Shit!"

The dark shape on my belly, Carolyn's friend Julie, I guess, the one whose blood bumped against my own, leaned over, her hair falling in my face.

"Okay then," said Carolyn, rolling off my legs. "Let's go to Hy's."

"Come out and have another beer with me, Jerome," said the Julie-shape.

The shock of the coincidence of so many people from my past renewing themselves in the present—on the same damn *day*—hurt much more than the brutal tickling, and that had hurt a lot. It rendered me passive and malleable, so in spite of my earnest declinations, my visitors easily hustled me out of the still-dark apartment to go drink beer with them.

In the street I caught an instant of an image of Julie from behind, her dark hair, shoulder-blade long and falling in illogical waves, before the moody streetlight blinked out.

"Fucking dark!" said Carolyn.

I should've been running as fast as I could. Why I sometimes didn't— or sometimes did but never far enough—just might have been my core tragedy.

The three of them wobbled, dark forms in the road, toward a Ford F-150 parked up on the curb.

"C'mon, let's go for a ride," said Tommy, in a chillingly convincing mobster voice. More than a year after my rebirth into a crosstown witness-protection program, they catch me. Now, the ride. I glanced in the bed of the pickup—at least there were no shovels or sacks of quicklime.

Tommy was the same, except her hair, which she had grown to neck-length, dyed blue, and tied up in random knots with little-girl hair baubles. She drove. Julie and I sat in the narrow backseat of the extended cab. Our knees did not touch. I could still feel the hot, two-part movement of her blood against my belly.

"So, Jerome," said Carolyn, turning to look at me. "You might be wondering about our little surprise visit."

Why, yes, I certainly am.

"I'm sure happy to see you," I said, a robot simpleton. "How've you been doing? Since, you know, since..."

"Julie—the sweet young thing to your left there—and I got to talking one day and the old Luncheonaire came up. I got pangs of nostalgia about you and me's beer-sucking days. I told her about you and the big mess you made, but she saw it another way, and convinced me you had just been doing your best, you know, that your heart was in the right place in telling me about, you know, that whole thing with your neighbor. So I forgave you. And I also beggeth of thee thine absolution. As an emblem of our mutual forgiveness, I bring you Julie here, who has graciously agreed to act as this evening's emblem. What do you think about that?"

"How did you find me?" I said, so frantically confused I thought my hair would fall out. "I was kind of in hiding."

"Tax returns," said Julie. "Public record."

Tommy ran over something. Julie's knee bumped mine.

"Sorry."

"Sorry."

My voice sounded oddly frothy. Boggling terror, with temptation mixed in, I supposed.

Hy's was as dark inside as out. The bartender was barely visible behind the bar, which appeared to have been made of three old wooden doors, still with crystal doorknobs on them, lying across a few stacks of cinder blocks.

At the bar was a woman with a bottle of Lite in front of her. She had a neat stack of money, on top of which were two cockroaches trapped under an overturned shot glass. The woman drank down her beer just as the bartender brought her another. She expertly pulled a five out from under the shot glass, like a magician pulling a tablecloth out from under a fully set table. The bartender brought her four dollars, which she carefully worked under the shot glass without letting the cockroaches out.

I bought four Millers. I carried them to our booth with my good hand, a finger down the neck of one of the bottles. My bad hand I kept hidden. No one had asked about it. No one had inquired of me at all, thank god. There had only been shouting about beer. And a "Please" from the Julie person.

I skidded the bottles onto the table, giving Tommy the one I'd had my finger in.

The time, which was being projected large onto the ceiling by some kind of digital clock designed for the purpose, surprised me: barely eight in the evening. It felt like three in the morning.

Julie sat next to me. I still couldn't really see, but Tommy lit the little candle on the table and pinched out the match. Julie was just barely illuminated by the green, knotty glass of the candle, and by the dim auroral blue from a jukebox.

"Country-Western time," said Carolyn.

Armed with their beers, she and Tommy slid out of the booth together and headed toward the light of the jukebox.

Julie tapped me on the shoulder with her bottle.

"See that bartender? Hy? He's killed more people than some serial killers. He's shotgunned four people that have come in here to rob him. They're dead. One guy's head disappeared completely. It's probably a vapor still floating around this place."

Her breath smelled like unfired clay and carrot cake. I breathed in her plosives. *people people probably vapor place*

"How do you kill four people and still wander around free to run a beer joint?"

"Are you kidding? He's a hero, at least to the cops. I feel safe in here." I studied Hy.

"Me too," I said.

It was even sort of true. Hy would protect us from bandits, and Julie— why or how I could not say—threw off beneficent rays of some kind. Comfort waves.

"The really dangerous, the really sociopathic bartender, she's in the Quarter. Mama. She has a bar on my rounds."

"Rounds? Are you a kind of French Quarter medic?"

"Cigarette girl. You know, with the little pillbox hat and short skirt and big tray of cigarettes? I look very silly. Anyway, Mama once shot this guy in her bar, some wasted LSU ballplayer, because he made fun of her glasses. The cops came by and told her not to do it again, closed her bar for the night, then sent in a deep-cleaning crew to address the blood."

Pillbox. A breathy word. Maybe she'd say it again.

"You mean she didn't get arrested? Why?"

"Cops were Tulane fans. They gave her her shotgun back and let her reopen the bar. It has a name."

"The bar?"

"The shotgun. Can't think of what it is, though. Something like Samantha."

I wondered if NiNaw's and Mr. Murdoch's guns had names.

"Sounds like a good barroom to skip."

"I usually do. The place is creepy as all get out. You get the feeling that CIA interrogations are going on in the back rooms. Or like that's where sex offenders meet to trade videotapes."

A whole sentence of exhale, clay and carrot cake.

We stared at the candle for a while. She dropped napkin shreds into the little puddles of beer-bottle condensation on the table. She had short nails, and a big scarab ring on her left ring finger.

Carolyn had come from nowhere with a bury-the-hatchet gift of a human being. I did not know what "gift" meant, but I couldn't help but think of wrapping and unwrapping.

"Don't go in there," she said. "We can't let anything happen to you."

I blushed great pulsing hives. What was happening here?

"I'll buy if you order," she said, handing me a five.

The lady at the bar's shot-glass roach prison was empty, now. Maybe she ate them, special Christmas beer nuts. It was nearly nine, according to the ceiling.

Tommy (my attempted murderess! The coincidences of the day were still, literally, incredible) and Carolyn had abandoned the jukebox and apparently disappeared into the black of the back of the bar.

As I grew used to the low light, Julie brightened. She had shiny lips, and an X of Band-Aids on her cheek, like a comic-book character who'd gotten roughed up.

"What happened?" I asked.

"Spider bite. What happened to your finger?"

I couldn't imagine how she'd noticed it. I was well conditioned to keep it hidden. And it'd been nothing but dark or darker since we met.

Jesus, what am I doing? Hermits don't sit in bars with erotically magnetic hypnotists talking about scar provenance! She must be a darkling siren! Run, hermit, run! Be true to yourself!

"Carolyn used to call it the disgusting mystery hand," I said. "That was before my pinkie... went missing. She didn't tell you about it, I guess."

"No. But we haven't known each other that long. We met at the hostel she works at a while back. She's cool. That little wood rat Tommy, though, I don't know. She's quite the bitch to me."

"She's just a general bitch. I mean, she seems to be. Tommy. But I shouldn't judge."

"Judge away," she said, and then drank two thirds of her beer in one swallow.

"She sat on my neck too hard."

Julie reached across the table and poured the rest of her beer onto Tommy's seat. I snuck a look at Julie's plump, live metacarpal, flushing red against the bottle.

The song on the jukebox ended.

"I wonder where they went?" I said.

I don't see Carolyn for ages, then, moments after she recurs, she vanishes again, leaving me in a fresh state of worry. If there was a quality that the hours following my Penny Barn visit owned but that the months before did not, it was worry. I didn't like to worry. Hermits didn't *worry*.

"Just so you know," said Julie, "Carolyn told me about your unpredictable tubing. Your fluxes."

"Ak."

"Don't be embarrassed. Everyone has something like that. I'll never make fun of you."

The distressing voice of Tennessee Ernie Ford came to cover the silence. When he was gone, I said:

"Did you really tell Carolyn to forgive me?"

"Sure. You didn't do anything wrong."

"But I think I did, after all."

"What do you mean?

"I'd always had a certain idea about what had happened with Carolyn's whole sociopathic girlfriend thing, but I found out that I had been wrong, that I'd misinterpreted one little bitty piece of information in a very, very big way. If I hadn't read it wrong, none of what happened would've happened. It was a big, giant, huge misunderstanding. Imagine a season finale of *Three's Company*."

"So she doesn't know you fucked up?"

"No. I just found out. Like, two hours before you guys's surprise party. The weird coincidence of it all is... well, a weird coincidence. I kind of feel numb, like from an electric shock. I got a shock once, from taking apart a plugged-in electric eraser when I was seven. I feel like that."

"What was it? What was the misunderstanding?"

I tried to focus on something, anything luminous in the back of the bar, but it was spinel black. The skin over my missing bones felt like a leather glove, so tight that it hurt to make a fist.

Julie speed-bagged me lightly on the shoulder. "Couldn't have been that bad, Jerome. You don't have to tell me if you don't want. But keep in mind it's easier to tell a stranger your dark secrets. I used to drive a cab—who's more a stranger than a cab driver?—so I heard a lot of confessions. Some notably unwholesome."

"Oh, shit, I don't know..."

"So tell me about your pinkie then."

I told her I lost my finger in a sawmill accident, that it had happened so fast it didn't even bleed much, and that I'd gotten a week off from work and all the other millers gave me a big party at the VFW.

"They served chicken fingers and chocolate fingers and everyone taped their pinkies to the palms of their hands and made like they were missing their pinkies. In solidarity, like. All in good fun."

I hated Tommy. I had just lied to keep a promise to her. I hated the demon. Why had I thought I'd never encounter her again? I'd been doomed to see her return—and doomed not to see it coming. She comes back, she brings Carolyn for a puppet, who in turn brings this extraordinary Julie as a razor-bladed apple, an irresistible lure.

I should run for it. To hell with Texas—go to Death Valley. Never open my door to anyone again. Don't file taxes either.

Julie took up my hand in hers.

"Doesn't hurt a whole lot anymore," I said. "Except when it rains. And when I get an urge to crack my pinkie knuckles but they're not there. Hey, you need another Miller, don't you?"

"When I'm rich I'll buy you a bionic pinkie," she said, holding on to my hand and making no sign she was going to let me out of the booth to buy more beer. "We'll get you one with a crackable-knuckle option."

"How are you going to get rich?"

"I'm working on a new kind of tea bag," she said, still holding my hand between hers. One was warm, the other cool and moist from beer-bottle dew. "When it's perfected and I'm granted a patent, I'm gonna foment a bidding war between Salada and Lipton for the rights."

"Don't forget Nestea."

"Look, gotta tinkle," said Julie, sliding out of the booth. "Don't go anywhere. Promise?"

"Okay," I said.

"Promise."

"I promise."

The dark ate her. The candle spit. I counted. I slid out of the booth and looked at the door. I thought of the robber's head, a ghost of scattered cells in the dark of Hy's. I'd had a shotgun pointed at me today. I wished he'd done it. I would be happy as a ghost.

Run! Death Valley! Pahrump!

Julie came back.

"Hey, sit down, you," she said, her dark form pointing at the booth. "No one can escape me."

"Oh, I was just getting more beer."

"Want me to tell you what I think?"

"Okay."

"I think you have a little bashful crush on me and decided to decamp in case I made a pass at you and you were not able to compute your feelings. I'll have you know that I'm very hard to get. I have many suitors and stalkers. And I do not bestow kisses upon just anyone. And I am, sir, unavailable. Sit."

I sat.

"Now," she said, digging into a pocket of her skirt. "I am going to program some songs into the jukebox. Don't try to flee, because I will catch you and pin you, like I did earlier."

"Wait."

"A request?"

I drew a breath.

"She's the one who cut my pinkie," I said. "Later it got infected, and then I... it had to come off."

"What? Who?"

She sat back down, dropping her handful of jukebox dimes onto the table.

"Tommy," I said, my jaws unmoving, as if a hard whisper would allow both the telling and the keeping of a sworn secret.

I checked my heart.

"I thought you didn't know her."

"I do. From a few years ago, before New Orleans. She didn't cut it off, but she cut me pretty badly. With a straight razor. She said it was an accident, and maybe it was, but a couple days later, she hit it as hard as she could with a big metal drill bit, then tried to kill me because she thought I'd been responsible for the death of someone we both knew. My finger never healed. It was a few months later that it... came off."

"Back in a second," said Julie. "Move, please."

"Where are you going?"

There was enough light to see that Julie's teeth were bared. The cross of her Band-Aids buckled.

"I'm just gonna tell Hy I have to kill someone. He'll loan me his shotgun."

"No, no, don't, don't, please!"

I held Julie back by the shoulder. She was strong. I curled my hand into the warm depression between her collarbone and the muscle across her shoulder. Finally she sat back down. She was trembling.

I'd been alarmed enough that my pupils had dilated, so the room was brighter. In this glitter of fear, I saw her, I really *looked*, for the first time. She had a silver clip in her hair. She was nakedly beautiful. That she was unavailable made her, ironically, permissible to be close to, to confide in.

"I *hate* that chick."

"Carolyn doesn't know Tommy and I know each other—Tommy made me promise not to say anything, just a little while ago, when you guys had me pinned. I can't believe I'm telling you all this. Tommy said I'd just ruin things for Carolyn again."

"So you have to be sweet to the little monster? That's almost blackmail. Or extortion. I was never sure what the difference is."

"It's a long story."

"You want me to tell you something I figured out? Whenever anyone says that, it means they want you to listen."

My fear subsided a little, my pupils contracted. Julie receded into the dark; the highlights of her beer bottle and her mouth and the Band-Aids on the apple of her cheek were all that I could see. Where had this woman come from? It was as if I'd just popped up on the radar of some minor god whose prime directive was to reduce the world's hermit population, and who had spent the day concentrating on me.

I wondered if the demigod was finished with me, or if he/she had other ambushes set up around town.

Julie and I were quiet for a while. It was 9:19 p.m.

"Want me to just break her arm?"

"Oh, that's okay."

"I will."

Her silhouette suggested she was looking directly at me.

"I believe you."

"Tell me everything."

A shadow obscured the light of the jukebox. A moment later Carolyn and Tommy slid into the booth across from us.

"What've you two been up to," said Julie, friendly, teasing.

"Same thing as you," said Tommy. "I bet you had her under the table ten seconds after we were gone, Big Coe. Or maybe she had *you*."

"Fuck you, Tommy," I said politely.

"Ho!" said Tommy. "I think I just sat in the wet spot."

The jukebox paused between songs. The flame of the candle burned without movement, a neon bullet in a wax pond.

"Jerome," said Tommy, "Carolyn tells me you're a gentleman. Kind sir, bring me more beer. Please."

Carolyn didn't seem to notice the exchange, or the mood at the table. She was drunk, sleepy, warmly mellow. Unkempt.

I got up again for more beer.

There was a single roach under the woman's shot glass now, a big one, with one leg caught under the rim. From somewhere she had produced and donned a Santa cap. I stared at one of the doorknobs on the bar, while Hy uncapped the bottles. Presently I felt arms around me.

"Hy, pour two of these in go cups, *vous plaît*," said Carolyn.

She turned to me and cupped her hand around my ear.

"Hey," she said. "It's good to see you. Glad you came out with us, even though we really gave you no choice."

"I'm so glad you didn't... you know, hurt yourself. Hell, kill yourself."

"We'll talk about that some other time. Don't worry about it, though."

I smiled and said okay, but I was so filled with fresh guilt that she surely would've been able to see its steep black waves cresting behind my eyeballs had the bar not been so dark.

"So what do you think of Julie?"

"She's cool."

"You can't see it because of her long coat, but she has a spec*tac*ular ass. Aren't you glad we flushed you out of seclusion? Enjoy her. Although I think she has some giant Indian scholar for a boyfriend. I suspect she might have a bargeload of boyfriends, so be careful you don't get your ass kicked.

"Annnd," she added, "what do you think of *my* new chicken?"

"She's pretty great, yeah, I really like her. Cute. Nice hair."

"Yesss. I won't let her go. No fucking way am I letting her get away." Carolyn kissed me on the ear and weaved off.

Tommy appeared. She drew her face close to mine.

"Go get that Julie. She's hot. Best you'll ever, *ever* get. And you're smart to be cool. We'll catch up later. Until then, don't fucking fuck it up."

Tommy grabbed my remaining pinkie and held it between her thumb and forefinger. She lifted my arm up by it, like a dead hare, then let it drop.

Carolyn and Tommy took the plastic beer cups and left.

Julie came up behind me. "Where was I? Oh yeah—tell me everything."

"Now?"

I'd assumed the three of them would leave together. Alone with Julie? I panicked. A chill scuttled around on my back.

"*Sure* now. Let's walk."

We poured our beers in go cups and left. Like moths, we headed toward the low dome of warm light over the French Quarter. The city glowed faintly red-green: Christmas was less than two hours away.

On the walk I told Julie about Marta, Boll, Carolyn, the cabinets, the glass knife. I told her I'd stolen Tommy's money and her car after she crushed my hand with an auger bit. I told her about my weird quasineuropsychophysiological complexion—thought bubbles and faces, and the black tadpoles in my vitreous humor, always ready to rush my visual field in times of bale.

"Plus I'm worried my heart will stop," I said, just as we crossed Esplanade into the Quarter.

Somehow, we had reached an unspoken accord about our walking itinerary: up a northwest street, down a southeast. I was growing more and more anxious about the moment we would reach the end. What then? See ya round? I felt sure she'd never want to see me again; that she really was just doing Carolyn this social favor. I'd have walked to Atlanta if Julie'd wanted to. I could think of nothing to delay the end of the night; nothing to delay the end of *us*.

Then, a nice light bulb from a benevolent spirit.

"Do you mind if I stop at the Western Union?"

"Okay by me," she said.

"It's kind of a hike. Sure you don't mind?"

"Nope. Scoring or sending?"

"Sending."

At the Western Union Julie leaned over my shoulder as I filled out a send-money form for a hundred dollars.

"Who's Dewey Martin? And who's Leigh?"

"I owe Dewey sixty bucks from a long time ago. And Leigh was some-one we both knew. She's dead now."

"This Leigh," said Julie. "I will bet that you and Mister Dewey were competing for her favors."

"Another long story," I said, and glanced up at her.

She was smiling, the corners of her mouth arcing south the merest bit. I didn't deserve this.

"Bet I can make you tell me," she said.

I'll tell you anything.

"The money's in the ether," I said. "Now I have to go find a pay phone and tell Dewey it's on the way. As far as I know, there's only one phone in the Quarter."

It seemed like we couldn't walk ten yards without someone recognizing Julie and asking where her smokes tray was. They came up to her, impris-oned her with hugs, then hovered nearby, watching her, calling out.

"I'd start smoking for you, Miss Julie!"

"Julie-boo, where they Player Navy Cuts? Where you cheerlead uni-form, bay?"

"You ever gonna let me paint you or what? I got oils and canvas in the van right now, bay!"

"Where you hiding my Cohibas?"

"One kiss I die happy, bay!"

Jealousy, wholly uninvited, rippled through my guts like gamma waves.

It was nearly midnight when we arrived at the pay phone. I looked up at the Danes' place.

"What?" said Julie, following my gaze and shielding her eyes against the glare of the Quarter. "You see Spidey up there?"

"I used to know some guys that lived up there. Looks deserted now."

"The Danes? You know them?"

"Yeah!"

"I love them. They still live there. I saw them just a couple of days ago. They holler out their window for Nobel Petits all the time. Hey! Knops! Dik!"

I cringed—I wasn't ready for the reoccurrence of every single cast member of the silly masque that was my pre-hospital New Orleans life. Next thing you knew, from around the corner, Ioanna would appear with a globe of coffee and a dressing-down.

But Ioanna did not appear, and the Danes did not respond.

I fed a bunch of quarters into the slot and called Duke's. It was easy to picture the bartender passing the old black telephone receiver across the walnut bar to Dewey. It was hard not to imagine that bartender as Leigh.

"Yeah?"

"Dewey? Jerome Coe."

"Oh for—"

"Wait! Don't hang up—I just wanted to tell you I put your money back in Western Union. Plus forty. Password's 'Leigh.' Thank you for the loan."

"Oh. Shit. You didn't have to do that."

"I should've done it a long time ago."

"Yeah. Look, I'll tell her the flowers are from both of us."

"Flowers? Who? What flowers?"

"Tomorrow's Leigh's birthday, man. I'm gonna buy some pink roses and some of those yellow flowers that look like Victrolas and bring them down to St. Benedict Cemetery. I'll tell her you sponsored the pink ones."

"You make her sound alive."

"Yeah. Keeps me sane. When I first heard that fucker got out, I thought about how fucked up and unjust the world really is, and that I wouldn't mind so much being dead myself, and—"

"Out? What? Who?"

Some member of the French Quarter crowd started screaming *Merry Jesus's Birthday* in any available ear.

"Oh. Fuck *me*. Coe, please don't tell me you don't know, man. Bill, man. He escaped. During a medical exam. Killed a fucking doctor."

"Jesus! When!"

Now the whole Quarter was wishing the whole Quarter *Merry*

Christmas. Julie grabbed me playfully by the neck and mock-throttled me while mouthing *Merry Christmas Jerome Merry Christmas.*

"Few days ago," said Dewey. "He's likely on his way down there to discuss things with Dee."

"Dee? Leigh's sister? Here? In New Orleans?"

"Yeah. Moved there a couple of years ago. Around when you called me the last time, all lathered up and broke and psycho."

"I wasn't feeling my best then."

I wasn't feeling my best now.

"Collect, too, you ballsy lunatic. Cost me $4.75. But look, maybe you're not so psycho as you'd like to think—you're not the first to confuse those two Marrats. Hey, what's all that fucking racket?"

"It just turned Christmas," I yelled into the phone. "What do you mean Bill's going to *discuss things* with her?"

"Just any old reason's good enough to start screaming like a loon down there, huh? You're finally with your people, Coe."

The nearby celebrations were growing more frantic. Julie lightly stamped on my foot and composed a what's-wrong face.

"Dewey!" I yelled. "Please shut up and tell me what 'discuss' means!"

"Coe. Awaken. He got caught because of her. She called him up where he was hiding out and the cops had her phone tapped. Armed with this data, what do you think 'discuss' might mean?"

"I don't believe this. I don't believe it. Do the cops know he's out?"

"Are you shitting me? I'm not even gonna answer that. Of course they fucking know. His picture's already in the fucking post office. I saw it when I went in to get a sheet of the new weed commemoratives. Seen those? Knotgrass, spurge... pretty sweet. Gonna septuple in val—"

"Oh no," I said.

Tadpoles.

"Watch yourself, Coe."

"Does he know," I screamed—a gargle, as though the tadpoles were diving down my throat—"that *I'm* here?"

"How the hell would I know? But I wouldn't leave Dee any *notes.* You'd hate yourself even more than you probably do now. Thanks for the money, Mr. Zits."

He hung up. I watched the zesty amphibians crowd out my peripheral vision. I heard Julie, far away, asking me if I had a bad cold, bad cold, bad cold?

Bad cold?

"What?"

"Tadpoles?" said Julie.

The violent Quarter merriment suddenly dropped to its ordinary levels.

"Yeah."

"Jesus, Jerome. What was that? You went white, your pupils dilated, you grabbed your chest..."

I took a deep breath and squinted at the street.

"Tell me what that was all about," she said, grabbing my jacket, which was filled with the slackest, slightest of people.

I didn't feel good.

"I don't feel good."

"You don't look good," said Julie. "Do you have bubbles? How's the ticker?"

She placed her hand on my chest under my coat and looked at the sky. The gesture caused her own coat, a black pea jacket, to open up, revealing a yellow T-shirt signified with black iron-on block letters: TCHOUP BRIDGE CLUB.

"Sounds okay," she said after a moment. "A little rapid. Sit."

She took her hand away. Her coat fell closed.

We sat on the stoop of a shuttered door. I told her what Dewey said, and filled in many blank spots in my long story.

"Shit, Jerome. Your past really is on to you. Anybody else from the olden days we should be watching for?"

I thought about it.

"Plenty," I said. "A lot of them would have to rise from the dead, though."

"Okay, no problem," said Julie. "One thing at a time. Cop station's over by Royal. Let's go."

I felt calmer, but despair was often a calm thing.

Just inside the heavy brass and glass doors of the police station I found a certain Officer Blount.

Officer Blount was evidently charged with the responsibility of building security, using what was possibly the original metal-detector prototype. It looked like somebody had built the thing from a dismantled Roaring Twenties electric chair. Its long cord, all knotty and wrapped in woven, fraying fabric, was comically unplugged.

Officer Blount stood up, came through the metal detector, and frisked me. Then he waved me through. My pocketknife and telephone quarters were discovered by neither the powerless metal detector nor Officer Blount's artless frisking.

"I need to report a potential murder," I said.

"A potential murder," he said, sitting back down. "Why, that'd be the last door on the left. And across the hall you can report potential burglaries. On the second floor—take the potential stairs yonder—reports of potential carjackings are taken. If you think a potential drug deal is afoot, you fill out the report right here."

Officer Blount farted, an oily blare. He kept a straight face.

I opened the last door on the left. Just inside the door was a counter, protected by thick plastic, a little like at the Western Union, except I could see through it. An officer behind the glass was spraying it with Windex and squeegeeing it with a Texaco card. He was smoking a cigar. Beyond him, in the back of the room, was another cop bent over a little family of houseplants on a windowsill.

"Sir, yes, sir, a Merry Christmas to you," said the window-washing officer, who paused in his squeegeeing to adjust a small plaque on his desk that read TONY UCILLE. Embedded in the plaque was a small clock, which recorded the present moment as 2:30 a.m.

I quickly explained that a certain Bill Izzoli, an escaped prisoner, was on his way to New Orleans from Boston to cause harm to a person. I was careful to leave the word *potential* out.

"Well, we ain't heard nothing about a Mediterranean Yankee killer at large," said Officer Tony Ucille, who stubbed out his cigar in some bean dip. "You heard about a killer like that, de Trie?"

His colleague in the back of the room, who was busy brushing a salve of some kind on a sickly bonsai tree, appeared not to have heard.

"De Trie!"

De Trie continued to ignore Ucille. A moment passed. I was anxious to get on with things. Julie was waiting on the steps outside, and she might just get up and go find some other helpless, pitiable boy to save, instead of me.

I said: "And he's going to kill the sister of someone he's already killed. Can you help me here?"

"All right," said Ucille. "Let's fill out a form. De Trie! Bring me a ink pen!"

De Trie was now threading a patient cat through a legwarmer.

"I'm putting this Flashdance sock on Ivy right now," he said. "She cold."

"Well, I can't fill out this form right this minute," Officer Ucille said testily, "because Mister Eugene de Trie *busy* playing dress-up with a cat."

Officer Ucille rolled a dark look at Officer de Trie, who ignored it.

"I'll go find a pen!" I said, hopping from foot to foot in a state of effervescent impatience. "If I find a pen, will you help me out?"

"Why don't you tell me about the young lady in the path of a killer, and I'll commit everything to memory."

Officer Ucille closed his eyes, pinched the bridge of his nose, and cupped a hand behind one ear.

As concisely as possible, I explained what I knew.

"What Dee last name?" He pinched hard, squeezed his eyes shut, and leaned forward.

"Marrat. I—"

"She white?"

"She's white. I don't know her. I've seen her once, at a coffee shop on Magazine, but not since. She's not in the phone book."

"She my shade of white? Or white like de Trie yonder."

"In between, I'd say."

"We find her. We have information the general civilian population is not privy to, and it the job of us the police to use it."

"When can you start?" I asked. "Can you start tonight?"

Officer Ucille turned and bellowed at his colleague.

"De Trie, when can you find Dee Marrat and get her into a safe house?"

De Trie was petting Ivy, who did indeed look warm inside of her legwarmer.

"Not now. I'm still busy," he said. He didn't look busy.

"Ivy look plenty cozy," said Officer Ucille.

"Ivy fine," said de Trie. "Stephen battling aphidius colemani, though.

Need to keep watch on him. I go start hunting Miss Marrat tomorrow. She white?"

"Yes she is, de Trie," said Ucille. "You start tonight."

"Maybe I will maybe I will not."

They started to argue. It escalated quickly. I left after Ucille antiqued de Trie with a beignet.

Julie was still outside when I came out, thank god.

"I see you weren't held for questioning," said Julie, looking happy.

"They couldn't even find a pen to write anything down," I said, sitting heavily next to her on the stoop. "They'll never be able to help. Never. I don't even want them to try."

"I was afraid you'd say that," said Julie. "So: we'll catch him. I was trying to figure out what to do on our next date, anyway, so we'll just start hunting murderers."

It was noticeably colder than when I'd gone into the police station. The wind had picked up and the relative humidity had dropped several percentage points. And I was all the colder for burning up so much energy trying to divine her meaning behind words like *our* and *we* and *date*. Carolyn may have brought her along as a kind of gift/peace-pipe, but I could find no reason why Julie, this sudden, vivid, ambient, unavailable creature, had remained alongside me for as long as she had. A needy, yellow, luckless, less-than-reliable mutilatee who comes with fallible shutoff valves, connections to devoted murderers, and a guarantee that he'll fall hard in love? Come on.

Despair came as a flood. Little whorls of panic and incredulity deepened and spread as I considered the irony of being allowed Julie for a few hours, then given a chance to atone for Leigh. The gods, likely amused, challenged me to reconcile the two; to twine them together; to have both.

But there wasn't a way. Bill was no one to monkey with—if he realized I was after him, he surely would stomper me to death before I could stop him—and, maybe, just by virtue of association, stomper Julie, too.

And I couldn't just ignore the fact of Bill; couldn't just steer well clear of him in order to be with Julie. Who would stop him from killing Dee? I would have let both Leigh *and* her sister be murdered by him. That could not happen.

The choice was so obvious, it wasn't even really a choice.

I hated the gods. I hated, *hated* Bill.

I stood up.

"You're going to have to get as far from me as you can, Julie," I said, with a one-corner-of-the-mouth smile.

"Har. Funny. Now sit and let us brainstorm. First, I think we oughta—"

"I—uh, you're pretty neat, and I really appreciate you hanging out with me, but I have to do this Bill thing on my own."

She stood up and put her hands on her hips.

"You're dumping me?" she said, completing my half-smile with one of her own, along with a smoothly arched eyebrow. "Tell you what: you can dump me after we catch Bill."

"I'll take her!" hollered one of Julie's pawing fans who'd been brushed off a while ago but had been hovering within pawing range. He had barf or perhaps polenta on his knuckles. Julie ignored him.

"Maybe after Dee's safe we can hang—"

"If you dump me now, I'll cry," she said, still smiling.

"This Bill... I have to... Oh, shit. I'm bad, bad luck. I'm dangerously bad luck. I'm not right. I'm poisonous. Lethal! Like raw-bacon eating! I'm trichinella spiralis in everybody's brains! Ignodomic worms! He'll kill me too, if he finds out I'm here! What a bonus that would be for him! I think he thinks I was with Leigh when I wrote 'Love, Zits'! And he'll kill you, too! Get away! Get away!"

I turned to run, but Julie grabbed me by the wrist.

"Whoa. You're not making any sense. Stay put."

"Go!"

"Nope. See how strong my grip is? I'll use it to squash Bill's head. He'll never be able to hurt us. Our budding friendship will become so keen and powerful no murderer can elude us."

"Wah!"

"You don't want to be responsible for making a girl cry, do you? You haven't had crying until you've had *me* cry. Especially late at night. Especially when I want to help and my assistance is shunned."

"It was the damn boots," I said to myself. "That's what started this."

"Boots? What boots? Look, I'm gonna help whether you like it or not, even if you do make me cry. So get used to it, mister."

A play-along smile still lingered on her lips, but there was no frisk in her voice anymore. Little whitecaps of a genuine tidal sob were silently gathering.

A few people had stopped to watch us.

"She love you, bra."

"Let her go help you, bra."

"He need help. Look at this man."

"He ought be begging for help."

"Somebody go buy a throwaway," said someone else to someone else. "I want a picture of this motherfucker before he dies of helplessness."

"This Bill is a crazy man!" I said, addressing Julie and the gawkers. "He robbed millions of liquor stores and made a boot dent in my head and killed Leigh and he killed her little Shelton cat, too! Oh, I need to be a hermit again!"

I tried to bolt again, but Julie held me fast. She did have a mangle for a grip.

"You need me," said Julie. "Let me help. Let me help. I'm gonna *help*."

She stomped and jumped.

Somebody took a picture.

"Wait," said somebody. "He about to faint."

"Yeah. Don't go waste that film. Wait'll he in motion. Then get a action shot."

"I'm not gonna faint!" I yelled. "I'm gonna go live in solitude!"

"Hermits always come back out."

"Yeah, look at Obi-Wan."

"And crabs."

I slouched grandly.

"He going down! Don't miss that shot!"

"You can't catch him by yourself," said Julie. "So get used to me."

I sat heavily on the ground. Flashbulbs.

She sat next to me and gave me a merry little punch on the shoulder.

"I can help," she said.

The chorus dispersed.

We'd known each other for less than eight hours, and now we were planning to prevent a murder.

On the stoop Julie and I discussed the plan, which would be simply this: we would find Dee and save her from Bill. Or, if it so happened, simply catch Bill. It would be easy, she said. We'd do it together.

"I already have some ideas," said Julie, sitting next to me and hugging her knees.

It was at least three in the morning now, and the temperature was still dropping.

"Aren't you cold?" I said. It was as if Tommy had brought back not just a raft of cancerous New England memories but its weather, too.

Julie had on a black skirt made of some kind of thin, unwarm material. The scalloped hem, lightly wrinkled, just covered her knees.

"A little. Look, can you draw?"

"No. Well, X-wing Fighters. And Don Martin tongue-flapping guys. From *MAD*."

"Can you draw a picture of Bill?" Julie asked.

"I suck at that kind of drawing. I can describe him, though."

I told Julie about Bill's balding head and his general tininess. About his black jeans with a threadbare rectangle on the back pocket from his billfold. About his combat boots. About his weird facial hair.

"He has a little black goatee, kind of shaped like a Frito," I said. "You know the little bit of beard just under the lip? He licks that all the time. His tongue has a white scum on it, like a symptom of some medieval disease."

"I bet he's in disguise," said Julie, kicking at a bit of crud stuck to the French Quarter. She had on black shoes, shiny, with buckled straps. No socks underneath. As she kicked, her calf tensed, then slacked, then tensed.

It was a resilient piece of crud, but it finally came loose and bounced off, coming to rest in a puddle on Royal Street, where it began to dissolve.

"He probably is," I said, resting my head in my hand.

She clapped her knees, and her calves slapped against each other. She stopped, and then kicked at the remains of the crud.

There were little crescents of dirt below her kneecaps. Faint bruises rose yellowish green on her shins.

Slap went her calves.

"I bet he grows his hair out and dyes it," Julie said. "It's what I'd do. What about Dee? What's she look like?"

As I described her, Julie drew her knees up to her chin and covered her legs with the tail of her coat. She looked at me.

"Cold," she said, smiling.

The *slap* was audible under her coat. She leaned into me the tiniest bit, a thousandth of a degree off the vertical.

"Bill'll probably go to the hostel," she said. "The cheapest and most anonymous place to stay. You don't even need ID to get a bed there."

"Should we tell Carolyn?"

"I think we should keep it to ourselves. No need to drag innocents into this."

"That's good thinking," I said. "Maybe we'll just stake out the hostel a lot. I'll need a disguise."

"Are you sure he'd remember you?"

"Yeah. I'm sure. At least I'm sure I don't want to take that chance."

"Can you grow a beard?"

"I can grow a kind-of beard," I said. "Sparse. Like Fidel Castro. I'll wear some sunglasses I have left over from a Halloween costume. And a hat."

"You'll look like a depressed celebrity," said Julie. "I love depressed celebrities."

"Okay, then," I said.

"Okay, then," said Julie, stretching out her legs again, then standing up. "We have to find your Dee first."

I stood, too. But not all the way—a big new boner as hard as a shillelagh kept me from straightening up.

"Ow," I said, reaching for my lower back, as if some small infirmity there had been what hunched me.

"Stiff?" she said, turning me around and vigorously rubbing my back. "Okay, here's what we do next: go to that fancy coffee shop where you saw her park her car that time you were nuts and thought she was Leigh. They're open all night. While we're waiting to see if she turns up, we'll plot and drink coffee. Your back gonna be okay? You've been through a lot today."

"Ah, yes, getting better."

"Right on, then. March."

Unlike two years ago, the fancy coffee shop was not vacuum-packed with hipsters in sly imposture as folks from my past; rudimentary faces did not resolve from the decor; thought bubbles full of vituperation and mockery did not inflate above the heads of the patrons. Now it was just an ordinary, mirage-free fancy coffee shop, with advanced coffee mixtures and valuable tortes and charlotte russes in the dessert cases and powdered nutmeg at the beverage-additives station. Frosty baristas of great height and eroticism paced dangerously behind the hiss and steam of the espresso machines.

"Two bottomless drips, please," said Julie, addressing the wintriest barista. "Hey, do you know a chick who used to come in here called Dee Marrat? Cute, perfect ski-jump nose, black hair, my height? Busty, busty, busty? Big umbrella with Ludwig Bemelmans characters on it? *Madeline?*"

"Nup."

"Mind if I use your phone?"

With her chin the barista pointed to a pay phone on the wall. I remembered it well. This time, at least, it was available.

"This is gonna be easy," said Julie, putting our coffee cups on a table by the big picture window. "You sit here while I make calls. We'll find Dee and have her in a safe house by sunrise, you watch."

While she dialed, the picture-window reflection allowed me to stare at her calves with the freedom of a voyeur.

Presently she returned.

"Six Marrats in Orleans Parish, just like you said. And none named Dee, and none that liked being disturbed at four in the a.m."

"That was fast," I said. "Your coffee didn't even get cold."

"I'm very skilled at research, surveillance, and pursuit. My mom was the same. She would've made an excellent stalker. Got anything to write with?"

"Ah, no," I said, patting down all my pockets. "Would've?"

"Yeah. She's dead now."

I'd been staring at a motherless daughter's calves, thinking about nibbling at them like a koi. Jesus. Does reprobation grow any quicker?

"When—"

"Long time ago."

Julie'd come from Albuquerque more than twenty years before with her mother, a veterinarian who specialized in geriatric cats.

"My mom was also a contract and duplicate bridge champion," said Julie, as she searched for something among some board games and newspapers and other crap on the windowsill next to our table. "She loved old cats as much as she hated bridge players, which was a lot.

"Aha!" she said, pulling a crayon out of the mess on the windowsill. "This'll have to do. Asparagus? Is that a new color?"

"Yeah, came out in 1993," I said. "She *hated* bridge players? Why did she play?"

Julie began writing something in the margin of the front page of the *Gambit*.

"Bridge was—is—a male-dominated sport. She was one of the only world-class women players, and she constantly made the Race of Men feel threatened. Mom came to enjoy toppling lofty male bridge egos."

Julie's mom had once thrown down a trump with such force that it skidded off the table, sailed halfway across a bridge club, and stuck into Omar Sharif's chin like a Chinese throwing star.

"My mom didn't play bridge much after that. Not professionally, anyway. Omar Sharif has some pull. She just devoted all her time to her vet practice over on Freret."

"Do you know how to play?"

"Sure!" She smiled, sat up straight, and opened up her peacoat like Superman tearing off Clark Kent's shirt, revealing her faded yellow TCHOUP BRIDGE CLUB shirt. Then she curtained it shut again.

"I bet you're as good as your mom," I said as evenly as I could—the sudden and unexpected view of Julie uncloaked had shaken me. My vocal cords loosened. Gland systems secreted. Lust slid like a pat of butter in a cast-iron skillet. The fresh-blood threat of Bill seemed to be receding further and further.

"No way," said Julie. "Mom never talked about it, but I think she mourned bridge. The mourning turned into a depression, then a psychotic depression. The regular clients stopped coming, because my mom had started behaving strangely and the office was getting dirty and it was understaffed and falling apart. Eventually the business collapsed."

Slap went her calves. Tiny spankings. Moist, polite applause. *Sap. Slap.*

Julie stopped writing in the margin of the tabloid, then looked up at me.

"Here are my ideas so far," she said, neatly tearing off the margin of the *Gambit* with all her asparagus writing. "How are you with libraries?"

"I like them. And I like librarians."

"Okay, you do the library microform work, then. You never know what you'll find in out-of-town newspaper archives. And you better start working on your beard. Any way you can you speed the process?"

"What, you mean, like... pushing?"

"Yeah."

I shut my eyes and bore down.

"Okay, at ease, never mind," said Julie, patting my hand. "Me, my job will be to conduct a discreet local enquiry. I'll drop by the other two hostels and all the flophouses and bedbug motels. And naturally I'll watch for him on my rounds. I stop by more than seventy-five different bars a shift. Jesus, I'd like to get my hands on this guy. Did he really kill Leigh's *cat*, too?"

"Yeah. He did."

"I can't *tell* you how much that would've disturbed my mother. She thought cats ought to live twenty-five lazy, plump, and pleasant indoor years, and it was her professional goal to ease as many cats as she could into such a life. When her depression started to get in the way of work, she got even more depressed. It wasn't too long before she was positively inert. She was on an army cot near the bathroom for months. She wouldn't go to a hospital. She expelled EMTs. I called the police a bunch of times, but they either never came or Mom expelled them, too. Finally, I called Omar Sharif."

"Really? You *know* him?"

"Sure. He was always at the same tournaments."

"Still, I'd've thought Omar would be the last person you'd call. How old were you?"

"Like, thirteen, maybe. He came, all the way from Syria. My mom was dead by the time he got here."

Omar stayed with Julie for several weeks, making tuna-mac, upbraiding bill collectors in Greek, speaking to Julie's teachers, shaming her aunt Corina into moving to New Orleans from Tucson so Julie wouldn't have to leave school.

Julie asked about my mother. I told her I didn't remember anything about her.

"Well, then," said Julie. "I'll be your mommy. And we can share Omar for our daddy. He visits once a year or so, and I get letters, but not so many as in the past. He'll be here after Mardi Gras for a couple of days. He'll probably play with old friends at the Tchoup and maybe drive out to Bally's and toss some chips at a roulette table. You'll like him. He'll have us up to his room to drink Oban and tell stories."

"I can meet him?"

"Of course! He stays at the Saint Louis on Bienville. Know that place?"

"Great bathroom. A clear Black in every category."

"He gets me my own room so I can hide from everything and everybody and watch TV and order room-service T-bones and read sci-fi."

"I can't believe you know Omar Sharif. I don't know any famous people. I saw Don Ho at an Abdow's Big Boy in New Hampshire once. He had two lecherous henchboys."

Sap. Slap. Lap. Sip. I was the lech here. Julie hooked a finger over the edge of my coffee cup and tilted it toward her. She peered down into it, as if she could read from the gyres of steam just how blinkered and one-dimensional a perv I really was.

"You drink fast," she said. "I like that in a crime fighter. Okay, back to bidness. Do you remember what kind of car Dee was driving?"

"I think it was a Toyota," I said, turning my cup 180 degrees and taking a sip from right where she'd touched the rim. Salty sweet, like caramel popcorn! "A Cressida, maroon. Four doors. Probably 1990."

"Right on. Let's watch for it. Okay, what'd she do in Boston? Was she a barkeep like Leigh?"

"Jeez, I don't have any—wait, I think she worked at a Lechmere in the Washing Machines and Dryers department."

"What the hell's a Lechmere?"

"Big store. Appliances and stereos and stuff. I only went in once, to buy a Cheap Trick record."

"I won't judge you," said Julie, writing down *dryers n shit* in asparagus. I licked the inside of my cup. "Okay, so I'll borrow a car and drive out to the burbs to canvass likely stores. I wish I still had my job at Devlin's Pipe-Threading Concern—they had a company car, an old orange Peugeot. It smelled like wolverine piss, but I could drive it whenever I wanted."

"What happened?"

"I got fired for trying to get a Coke out of the break-room machine for free. They caught me with my arm stuck up to the triceps in the chute. This forearm isn't quite straight. See?"

Julie rolled up her jacket sleeve. Her forearm was in fact noticeably arced, like a Japanese sword.

"It's perfect for getting cans out of machines," she said. "I can even pull beers out of that machine at the Hummingbird."

Julie held her arm out to me, then let it go limp. I caught it with both hands. Her arm was heavy and warm but covered in goose bumps. *Lap* went her calves.

"How'd you do that?" I said, not holding on but not letting go either. I arrested an urge to check her pulse.

"Busted it arm-wrestling with an old boyfriend. It didn't set right, and now I have this useful can-getting arm."

Old boyfriend. Julie took back her arm.

"You took up cigarette girling right after the pipe-cleaning job?"

"Threading. No, I went straight to unemployment first, but they said I didn't qualify—I needed one more day on the job to get it. So I went back to Devlin's and asked the boss, Brad, if he'd fire me tomorrow instead. He said okay, he'd write up the paperwork and say I'd been laid off due to budget cuts."

"That was cool of him," I said.

"He wanted a blow job."

"Oh."

Sap. Sop. Slap.

"I felt disgusting afterward. My mouth tasted like leeks. I didn't want to go home and tell my boyfriend anything—that I'd lost my job, or… any of it. Omar was visiting at the time, too. I always like to show him when he visits that I'm doing okay, I have a good job, that he doesn't have to worry. I was going to lie and tell him everything was super, but when I met him at the Saint Louis that night, I started crying like a wet kitten, right in the lobby. I told him what happened. He took a cab to Devlin's. He found Brad, kicked him in the nuts, punched him on the top of the head, then took a throwaway snapshot of him wincing and clutching on the floor. Then he stole fifty-five cents out of Brad's pocket, bought me a Coke out of the machine, came back to the hotel, gave me five hundred bucks and the keys to his rental, and told me to go have fun.

"And you know what I realized from all that?" said Julie.

"What?"

She covered her coffee cup with both hands to keep the steam in.

"That he'd been in love with my mother. And she with him. And that he felt somehow responsible for her death. I don't know how to explain how I knew all of that, all at once in a single instant, but it had something to do with the angles of the creases in Omar's face when he came back from Devlin's. It was, like they say, writ large. Love has a lousy poker face."

Julie drank her coffee down, picked up both our cups with one finger, and went up to Miss Frosty for refills. When she came back, she had coffee and two Millers.

"If you alternate beverages, wait a few secs between sips," she said, "or else the hot-cold shock is liable to crack a molar. Now, enough: we have sleuthing to do. Your job, in addition to library work, will be to see if you can get in contact with Dee's family. She's gotta have some somewhere."

"So," I said, not yet ready to sleuth, "did you ever wind up telling your boyfriend about the, you know, the..."

"Hummer? Yeah. Vishy didn't take it too well."

"Oh. Broke up, huh."

"Almost. Funny, it wasn't hearing about the humming part that upset him, but the swallowing part. That detail wrecked him. But things are pretty good between us right now."

"That's great!"

"Mmhmm."

Sap. Lap. Op.

"So do you think, uh, Vishy will mind that we're hanging out? I mean, not that we..."

"Nah. He's cool. You and me, we're partners in murder prevention. We're McGruff the Crime Dog. I'm your *mommy*, for chrissake. Vishy'll appreciate that. As long as I don't start blowing you! Ha!"

"Ha ha!"

I hated Vishy.

"Shit," said Julie, looking at the clock over the granita machine. "We've been sitting here for hours. I gotta go labor."

"Really?" I said, alarmed. "Now? Dawn? On Christmas? Don't you work at night?"

"Yeah, but I'm covering for a colleague who got an infection trimming her corns with some twig loppers. Tobacco demand in the French Quarter knoweth not abeyance."

"Ah, well, let's see, hmm, I guess, geh, hmm..."

I thought I might cry, but at the last instant the gods in their infinite magnanimity granted me a way to be with Julie for another hour.

"Hey!" I said. "I'll walk down to the Quarter with you. I can get this guy Coryate in Jackson Square to draw pictures of Bill and Dee."

"Coryate? The caricature guy? Can he make a drawing from just a description?"

"He's a police sketch artist," I said. "He did a sketch for me once."

"Who of?"

"Uh. Somebody. Person. A Miranda."

"Ohh. That was the one you chased for so long without knowing what she looked like. Still have her picture?"

"No, it's gone. My mugger took it."

"She must have been something."

"Oh, I don't know," I said, a yawny dismissal.

"Wow, she *was* something! You fake-yawned!"

Coryate's regular spot, across from the old perfumer's, was occupied not by Coryate but by a puzzle-ring vendor, who had a dragon of some kind on an insubstantial leash.

The dragon had puzzle rings on his toes or claws or phalanges or whatever those were, and was eating popcorn out of a Bundt pan.

"He's an artist," Julie said to the puzzle-ring vendor. "He sits on a red Igloo cooler and draws humorous distortions of tourists all day."

"He's kind of grouchy," I added. "He used to be right here, where you are."

"I know," said the vendor, slipping a ring onto the end of the dragon's tail. "He sold me this spot. He's retired. He moved to Browerville, Alaska. He said coffee's much better when the weather's very, very cold."

"Oh," said Julie and I at the same time. "Jinx," she added.

So that was it then. My time with Julie had come to an end. She had to go work. Maybe she'd let me come along on her rounds! Maybe I'd just follow her. No. If she caught me, she'd think I was a stalker and never, ever allow me near her again. I had no choice but to go home and lie on the floor by the phone for hours and hours, while the jaws of lust and uncertainty ground me to a digestible paste.

I opened my mouth to say something.

"Silence!" she said. "You're under jinx. Now, go home and do this additional homework I just thought up: compose a letter to the FBI requesting a mug shot of Bill."

She hugged me. Her cheek touched mine.

"Include an SASE," she whispered in my ear.

Then she let go, and was gone.

Over the next few weeks Julie's crime-fighting enthusiasm remained at a rolling boil. Mine diminished. Instead, my psyche grew two spring branches of incredulity: One, that Julie had not yet gotten bored or disgusted or weirded out and thus moved on; and the Other, that an awful lot of details of my pre-hospital life, in ugly and arrant spite of all my work at isolation, had returned and settled in my head and chest, and were now mutating and metastasizing. They'd be lethal, too, these congesting details. Bill might kill me. Or Bill might kill Dee, and that would kill me. Or Bill might realize Julie was on to him, and he'd kill her, and that would kill me, easy. Or maybe Dee would be saved, and Julie would then be done with me, and that would kill me. The only way to arrest the spreading disease was for Bill to remain a threat. For things to stay the same. Unrequited. And that might kill me. I'd never read *Catch-22*, but I was pretty sure that's what all this was.

So, for Julie, I pretended crime-fighting enthusiasm.

After I proved dim as a library researcher, Julie took over, spending hours at the libraries going through microfilm. She read several papers every day, including the *Globe* and the *Herald* in Boston, and all the big-city newspapers between here and there. She went to the Vital Records Registry once a week and, always under the pretense of seeing her mother's death certificate, surreptitiously thumbed through all the recent deaths. She never found anything.

Me she sent to the Danes' place, to watch out their windows for Bill.

"The view of the Quarter's perfect for several blocks in four directions," Julie said. "And such a task suits your leisurely nature."

"A close cognate of *leisure* is *lazy*."

"But don't tell them what you're there for. Just say you're lonesome and soul-searchy and you missed them while you were pent up in the loony bin."

That was all pretty damn close to the truth.

The Danes did not seem unhappy to see me.

"Jerome, my great friend!" said Knops, swinging his door wide open and ushering me inside. "Come in, I am so happy to see you!"

"Hallo, my bra!" said Dik. "Where is hand element?"

They looked exactly the same as always.

"It's gone," I said, looking down at the finger-shaped bit of carpet that I wouldn't have been able to see if I'd still had my whole hand.

"Dik, that is rude," said Knops. "Well, Jerome, long time no see. Two years plus some months! But I know that you have been busy with love and cigar woman and did not have time for poor us. Okay, we understand love."

"I'm sorry I didn't come to see you guys," I said. "Hey, how did you know about Julie? And me?"

Julie and me.

"Oh, we are watching through our windows always for sights and crimes and personalities, and we saw you on the street together."

"Yes," said Dik. "Cute!"

"We are also cute," said Knops, pinching Dik's earlobe. "Now that the evil Wichita lineman Cecil Barger is no more."

Dik jerked his head away.

I asked if I could sit in the window nook.

"Of course, my friend. You may sit in any nook forever. But you must tell us your pinkie-finger story."

I told them the story as best I could—it was hard to keep it straight now that there were so many versions. Julie's, Tommy's, Carolyn's. Mine.

But the larger distraction was the view from the window nook. Four ordinal directions of bobbing tourist heads.

Please, ye gods, do not let Bill be among them.

I was getting used to constantly wearing my Unabomber sunglasses, even at home and at the Danes'. The silvered lenses conferred a pleasant invisibility. To a ranking degree, so did my growing beard.

Most of my face was for some reason not arable to whiskers—I only had about seventy-five, all in ordinary browns and ochers, except for a scattering that were fiber-optic colored. But they made up for their paucity with tensile strength: each one was hard, sharp, and inflexible. Some grew straight out; others curled back and lanced my cheeks. They'd be a project to shave off. Just for regular shaving, I had to go to K & B every couple of months to order specialized disposable razors from Tübingen. But for these tiny ironwood saplings I'd have to get Nyelle to order some kind of miniature thresher. The worry I had the least claim to was the one that preoccupied me the most: no one would kiss a person with such a growth. I hated this beard.

I scarcely ever saw Julie for more than a few hours—our work schedules did not coincide—and even when we did find a little time, it seemed all we ever did was compare notes on the caper. She told me no more about her life, about her mother, Omar, Vishy. Because of this, my subconscious invented inane truths, especially about Vishy—he starred in my dreams as a three-story sword-swinging male Kali with prehensile erections for arms. I had no idea where Julie lived, except that it was somewhere near. She had no phone.

But when we did meet, Julie seemed happy to see me, sat close, and hugged hard and long when she left.

The only non-caper thing we discussed in any detail was my complicated guilt surrounding Carolyn.

"Can't I help *you* with something?" I asked her late one night while we sat in the fancy coffee shop, reconnoitering and watching the door for Dee. Julie was going through the police blotters in a week's worth of Baton Rouge papers while I listened to her calves. "All you do is help me redeem the great fuckups of my past. I feel selfish and guilty and like a bad friend."

"Aiding in your redemption is one of the things that makes my life peachy and in no need of up-perking. At the moment. Stand by, though, just in case."

"How about a refill? Do you need that?"

"No, I've had fourteen," said Julie.

Julie's unconscious calf-slapping generally picked up speed after ten or so cups, and was now apace with a bounteous oil-patch pumpjack. *Lap, slap, lap, lip.*

"Ah!" she said suddenly. "I know what you can do for me."

"What?"

"Go tell Carolyn about Francie."

"I knew it."

"You've been putting it off for as long as we've been hunting Dee and Bill, and I'd say it's just as important to your future mental health and personal esteem."

"If I do, I'll never see her again, you know. Tommy'll make sure of it. It's just the sort of data Tommy'll manipulate to persuade Carolyn to write me off forever. I think I should just keep it a secret."

"Secrets are just little black resentment acorns that grow into big black resentment oaks that tip over in stormy weather and crush babes and innocents. Just get together with Carolyn one night and say: (1) I was inexact about something with Francie, and (2) I happen to know Tommy and she's Beelzebub."

"But what if she tries to shoot herself again!"

"She won't. Just be gentle. Tell her you only ever mean well. I'll help, of course. I'm a helper."

"I don't know... I think I should just—"

"I'll prep you," said Julie. "We'll write a script."

"Maybe Tommy will get hit by a stray bullet or fall off a riverboat."

"Look. Tommy's a dwarfin, soulless narcissist. Carolyn just can't see it because of the big foggy sex cloud she's always lost in. Tommy can, and will, do so much more damage than you ever could. It's better you tell Carolyn now."

"I know. She'll hate me though."

"But that's the only con!" said Julie. "The pros: first, it's the right thing to do, etc. etc., Spike Lee and all that. Second, it'll relieve your guilt. Third, it might even make Carolyn dump Tommy. Then we can concentrate more on Bill and Dee, which will—most important—please me."

"I'm bad at being hated. It hurts a lot."

"She'll forgive you. Just like she did before. You didn't do anything wrong. Don't forget that."

"There's another con," I said. "Tommy may try to retaliate against us.

Like, against you and me. And Carolyn."

"Hmm," said Julie, standing up and grabbing our empty cups. "Just let her mother*fucking* try."

She went to the counter and refilled us and bought two more beers. I did not watch her calves. Instead I stared out the window at the mirthful parking meter Dee had fed quarters to so long ago. It was blank and inanimate, now. By the time Julie returned, I'd decided, though my motive was the most selfish of all of them: Julie's approval.

"Okay, I'll go confess to Carolyn tonight," I said.

"Good," said Julie, smiling large and depositing her unfinished Budweiser carefully in her backpack. "You'll feel better."

"I don't know."

"Come over after."

"Where? Here?"

"My place. I have to show you something."

Surely Julie saw the fat poppies of lust—of *need*—flowering all over my body. Love certainly had a rotten poker face, but lust? It was like having your cards face-up on the felt.

"Vishy'll be there, too," she added. "He wants to meet you."

"Your new girlfriend wouldn't like this," said Carolyn.

"What?"

"You and me snuggling on the levee in the dark."

"We're not snuggling," I said. "And she's not my girlfriend. And she wouldn't mind if she was."

Carolyn snorted.

"What?" I said.

"Oh nothing. She fuck you yet?"

"Uh, she has a big boyfr—"

"Kiss?"

"Well, we're—"

"What's wrong with you, Jerome? I see the way you look at her. I've seen you stare at her ass and her legs. Legs and ass worth staring at and risking boyfriend reprisals, too. Make a moooove, Jerome!"

Carolyn and I were sitting on the levee under a blanket she'd found in

Tommy's F-150. A lukewarm six-pack of Pabst sat between us.

"Whatever happened to your old car?" I said, artlessly changing the subject.

"It's in some impound lot under the I-10," said Carolyn, allowing the change of subject—she knew I wasn't here to impart nonexistent salacities about Julie. "It'd probably cost me a thousand bucks in storage fees to get it out."

"What happened that day?"

Carolyn shrugged. She dug up a divot of turf and tossed it at the pickup.

"I missed," she said. "All three shots. Those were all the bullets. Then I drove off naked in the rain."

"I remember all that. I didn't know you were out of ammo, though."

Carolyn had then driven all over New Orleans, in shock, not knowing what to do, until her car stalled somewhere not too far from the airport. She fell asleep in the front seat and woke the next day to the sound of a man tapping on her window with a nickel.

She had been past the shivering stage of hypothermia. The man placed her in the bed of his pick-em-up truck, which was filled with the Attorneys. The Attorneys were the man's eight wolfhound-corgi-malamutes, who he reasoned would keep Carolyn warm for the trip to Touro Infirmary. The man arranged all the dogs around and over Carolyn, in a scheme to provide her the maximum warmth and comfort.

"Now, nobody move!" the man had said.

After a few days in intensive care, Carolyn was moved to a semiprivate room where she confided to her roommate the story of Francie, Francie's threat to kill her, and my revelation. The roommate was immediately familiar with that ilk of story, and soon after called a women's shelter she knew, a representative of which was by Carolyn's side in less than an hour. The woman persuaded Carolyn that she was a battered woman and that it was best to stay at the shelter.

A couple of weeks into her stay, Carolyn was handed a little item in the *Times-Picayune* that mentioned that a Frances W. Murdoch had been jailed in connection with an assault.

"Terence," said Carolyn, shivering. "The guy at the hostel whose dreads she half burned off a long time ago? You rented his apartment? Well, he'd moved back from Canada and had started working at the hostel again. Francie went there digging for information on my whereabouts, and Terence happened to be there. He offered her no useful data, so she pulled off one of his ears. He went back to Canada. She's still in jail. A jail-hospital. You know the kind of place I'm talking about."

"Yeah. I do."

My bottom was damp from the dewy grass. I tried to roll my empty can down the levee but it simply stalled in the wet grass at the edge of the blanket.

"Did you really see Francie and me?" she said, opening her second can.

"I didn't mean to," I said.

"You heard groans of ecstasy and decided you'd go investigate."

"I didn't know it was ecstatic groaning," I said, feeling defensive.

"Did it turn you on?"

"Come on."

"Don't be coy. Men love it when girls get together. Every porn mag in the world is half girl-girl. Did it give you a kangaroo tail? Jerome?"

"Just talking about it turns me on, so quit," I said.

"So did you go home and shake the flashlight?"

She poked me in the ribs and giggled.

"I was freaked out," I said.

"What'd you use, a dress sock?" said Carolyn, poking me in the ribs again, fingers stiff as bamboo. "Knee socks, a scratchy woolen foot mitten? A fancy royal buskin with colorful embroidery?"

"If you must know, I don't employ socks anymore. I squeezed a banana out of its peel and replaced it with my thing. You know."

"Thing!" howled Carolyn. "Thing!"

"Well, what? What do you want me to call it?"

"Dick! Boner! Cock! Muffin-finder! Anything but *thing*, Jerome!"

She ran off a few more priapic synonyms, many I'd never heard.

"So, what was that like, Jerome? The bananagina?"

Carolyn squealed and slapped the soles of her shoes on the grass. She made *boys-are-repulsive* sounds.

"Where's the beer," I said, partly to change the subject and partly because I wanted a beer.

"We're on the outside of it."

I counted six cans in the grass.

"We need more," I said.

Maybe I was making a big deal out of nothing. After all, it was a long time ago, Francie was in jail, Carolyn had another girlfriend, who'd maybe gotten over being a psychopath. Why tell Carolyn at all?

"That," she said, breathless from giggling, "is just what I was thinking."

"At home I have Busch."

"Fuck *that*," said Carolyn, standing up and doing a *fuck that* calisthenic. "We need Lite."

The truck wouldn't start.

"Come on—we'll walk."

By then it was after midnight.

On the walk to K & B Drug, Carolyn told me she didn't know when Francie was going to be out of the jail-hospital.

"The shelter promised me that Francie wouldn't be turned loose without them knowing. They'll get a letter from the parish with her release date, then they'll call me."

"Do you believe them?" I asked.

"They said it was their job."

"I went to the hostel a couple Halloweens ago to find you. You weren't working that day, but I was so happy you were alive. I told myself I'd never bug you again."

"Yeah. I got the note."

We walked past the gas station with the chickens, but there were no chickens in evidence. The last time I'd been here, I hadn't yet lied about a dead cat to get off a bus so I could have a shotgun pointed at me and ruin another pair of pants. Tommy was still just a shrieking memory, a psycho tangled up in a pair of bell-bottoms and rolling around in a gravel parking lot, bathed in the red wash of her own car's taillights.

I hadn't met Julie.

My head hurt. Here I was again, in the late-night dark, stinking with guilt, on my way to get beer.

In silence we walked toward the K & B's purple glow.

We picked up four six-packs and a can of starter fluid.

"Hi, Nyelle," I said.

"Hey, bay, how you doing?" she said, walking up behind the register. "Case cheaper, y'all."

"No car," said Carolyn. "Easier to carry two sixes apiece if you're walking."

"Ain't neither *one* of y'all got a car?"

"I still don't," I said. "Carolyn here has one, but it broke down by the levee."

"Mmm. Look, y'all, we can't sell no beer wine spirits after one a.m."

"You're shitting me," said Carolyn. "What time is it?"

"One oh one," said Nyelle immediately, without even looking at a clock. "What time do you start selling?"

"For six," she said, resting a palm on her hip and tilting her head off to one side.

"That is fucked up, in this fucking city," said Carolyn, turning around to address the rest of the store. "The bars are open all night, you can get a daiquiri without getting out of your car, you can get whiskey sours for *free* playing nickel slots at Bally's, and we can't buy beer?"

"City ordinance," said Nyelle, who then proceeded to ring up the beer. "That's twelve eighty, baby."

"What's going on?"

"We can't *sell* booze, but anybody allowed to *buy* booze. City ordinance loophole."

"Nyelle," said Carolyn. "I'm going to light a candle in your honor at the shrine of the great clerk."

"Thank you, bay. You be good now, Jerome bay."

We got the car started.

She didn't need to know about Francie. She didn't need to know about Tommy.

"I couldn't tell her."

"Oh Jerome," said Julie. "Pull up a crate and sit down."

Julie lived on a shelf. A kind of shelf, anyway, a hundred square feet of tarry cypress planks laid across three cantilevered I-beams high up near the ceiling of a four-story Quonset hut off Annunciation Street that was being used as storage for hundreds of thousands of empty plastic milk crates.

"She was acting like good old Carolyn again," I said. "I didn't want to ruin it."

"Jerome. You know I'm gonna make you try again."

"I know. Hey, where's Vishy?"

"Couldn't make it. Test. Brauer trees. Cramming."

"Oh. Maybe he'll be here later?"

"Nope."

"Darn, that's too bad. I was really looking forward to meeting him."

"Hey, watch out."

I'd been sitting too close to the edge of Julie's shelf, which had only a few two-by-four stanchions strung with blown Christmas lights to separate shelf-dwellers from sixty-foot plunges into shallow piles of broken milk crates.

I scooted inward to safety, closer to Julie, who was using a wooden clothespin to twist a couple of wires around the prongs of the Christmas-lights plug. The lights went on.

She was in full cigarette-girl uniform.

"Hey, you were working those wires hot?"

"I've got four appliances but only three leads. I leave the refrigerator and the stereo on all the time, but I switch back and forth between the hot plate and the lights. This is the easiest way to do it."

The little white lights illuminated a small part of the huge building. I looked down at the staircase we'd climbed in near dark to get up here. Julie'd made it from crates.

"I feel like I'm on a ten-meter high dive."

"Dinner," she said, opening a tiny college-student-size refrigerator and taking out two bottles of Budweiser. She also removed a fat blue cylinder: Cheez Balls. "And I'll show you what I've got to show you.

"But first, I know you'd like to know that directly beneath us is my bathroom," said Julie, tossing the plastic Cheez Balls lid into space. "I don't have to pay for water, either. And I use a lot. I'm very hydrophilic."

She pointed at her crate staircase.

"But that's the only way to get there, I'm afraid. I'm thinking about getting a shiny pole put in, just to go down on. Fireman-style."

"What's the rent?"

"Seventeen bucks a month. Lights're an extra six."

"For that kind of money the landlord ought to just install a pole. That way you can escape the building in a flash if brigands get in."

"No one ever comes into this building. And I have a surprise for them if they do."

She was suddenly aiming a crossbow at an especially high stack of milk crates. She shot at it, but the bolt flew only thirty or so wobbly feet before dropping into the mess of crates below.

"I need to get it restrung, or whatever," she said, squinting and sighting down the stock. "And my bolts need fletching."

All the women I knew were armed. "Did you carry all this stuff up here by yourself? That mattress, too?"

"I had a little help," she said, jumping on it a couple of times. "But this is not a mattress. It is a very tall stack of blankets. I slip in at different levels depending on the temperature."

It was warm for this time of the winter—Mardi Gras was less than a month away. I was more than curious what her blanket level would be tonight. I wondered if the level changed when she had Vishy under there with her.

"In fact, this is exactly what I wanted to show you."

Julie reached down, took hold of a corner of the mattress stack, and flipped it. The stack folded along the diagonal like a quesadilla, in the process uncovering a triangle of creosoted cypress floor illustrated with a map that had been cartographed directly on the planking with a white paint pen.

"It was the only place to draw it."

"What's—wait, is that East Coast coastline?"

"Yep. Know what that green jagged line is?"

"A road? I-95?"

"Yep. All the way down to South Carolina, and then I-20 to Meridian, Mississippi. Know what the little red dots are?" she said, indicating said dots, which looked like berries on the big twig of the interstates.

"Uh, bad bathrooms?"

"Recent, unsolved liquor-store holdups."

"You mean—"

"Bill's on his way. He might even be here already."

"Shit!" *Shit!* "What now?"

Julie sat back on her blankets and told me I'd better come with her tomorrow on her morning rounds.

"Even though cigarette girls are not supposed to have hanger-onners, I'll risk it—we'll need two sets of peepers in the Quarter tomorrow," she said. "So you might as well stay here tonight."

"But—"

"Old Vishy won't mind a bit," she said, finishing both her beer and the rest of the Cheez Balls all at once. "Jerome, another thing, before I forget. While you were out with Carolyn, I ran over to the pay phone at the Twinkletone Lounge and called Dewey at Duke's to ask him for more details about Dee and Bill. But the number had been disconnected. I tried 411 and 555-1212: no listings. He's gone."

All night and all day. With Julie. I listened carefully for the cracks and screams and hisses and booms that might signal the collapse of the building or the streaking meteor of the apocalypse or the gas leak or the nuclear ordnance from a surprise Cuban invasion or whatever it was the gods had in mind to destroy my magnificent luck.

"Out of business, I guess," I said, casually. "Duke's was always on the brink of it. Dewey'll turn up again, somewhere."

"Maybe, but for the moment, we're out a source."

"You do a hell of a lot more investigating and sleuthing than me."

"People often like, and do, the things they're aces at. That's a fairly hearty motive." She smiled. Then, in a maddening and inscrutable non sequitur, she added: "And you amuse me."

Julie crawled across the floor to her stereo. She dropped the needle on a record. Lullabies. She crawled back, remade her bed, tucked herself in, fully dressed, about five blankets deep, then patted the spot next to her. Vishy's spot.

"Sleep," she said. "We're getting up early."

I got in at her level, fully dressed, lay down at the very edge of the blankets, and let my head down on a wide-wale corduroy cushion that smelled of Head & Shoulders and unfired clay. Julie turned away, set an alarm clock, and laid her head on a couple of little throw pillows. She didn't say anything, but after a moment, she lifted the hand that was resting along one hip, and waved.

The second lullaby started. It ended. Neither of us had moved. The third lullaby. The fourth. Then the fifth lullaby started. It was quieter than the others, and for some reason scratchless, pure, and clear, a melancholic a cappella that seemed genuinely innocent, as though it was never meant to be heard at all. It ended, and the needle traveled to the edge of the record label and remained there, playing a two-second crackle over and over and over. I looked over at Julie. She was still facing away. She drew full, deep breaths every ten seconds. I counted one hundred of them, then rolled over and tossed my arm gently across her wool-blanketed waist as if it were the perfectly innocent change-of-position arm-toss of a perfectly innocent sleepover pal. I bent my leg so my knee touched the back of her thigh. It was muscular and warm. I began to count again. The periods after she exhaled seemed to last forever, but eventually her chest would swell and the creases in the blankets across her shoulder blades would smooth themselves out, until she exhaled again and the rough wool wrinkled up as before.

She rolled onto her back and drew up one knee. I counted to one hundred again, and then told myself to go to three. At three hundred I promised myself I would at five. At seven hundred and fourteen I laid my arm across her hips, just below her belly. I rested my forehead on a taut muscle in her shoulder. She didn't move. Her breathing stayed the same. Her belly pushed against the inside of my forearm. My own breathing shallowed out. She straightened out her leg, and my arm resting just below her navel fell flush against the surprisingly solid arc of her pubic bone. Through the blankets, the calm, sleepy bounce of a femoral artery.

Without warning she turned her head my way. Her breathing sped up, then settled. I looked up at her. She was still asleep. Her mouth was open.

I held my breath and counted and counted. Finally I let my entire body go slack, allowing the weight of my arm and shoulder and hand to rest against her. I looked at her lips, her open mouth. My erection was raw and hot in my jeans. I moved my hips a hundredth of an inch and the world flared. I stretched to reach her mouth with mine. There was a pearl of saliva at the corner of her lips. I stretched more. Under the blanket my erection— through my jeans, through the polyester of her skirt—was stone along the blood and muscle of her thigh. I stretched farther. The pearl began to slowly fall. I strained another inch, another half. The skin across my throat felt as if it would tear like gold leaf. I opened my mouth, curved my tongue out and back against my chin. I stretched again, asphyxiating. I caught the pearl and drank it. I bit hard on the pillow below her lips, and came with the silent violence of a fall.

○

Over the next few weeks, neither Bill nor Dee occurred, either in person, as a rumor, or in the news. There wasn't a single Dee Marrat, one *r* or two, one *t* or two, dead or alive, in the whole country. The series of liquor-store holdups that appeared to have had New Orleans as its target had stalled; following our night together, Julie had discovered no other unsolved heists to plot on her map. It seemed that Bill had been delayed.

As Bill grew less ominous and Dee consequently safer, Julie and I settled into a stasis: she was always confident and virtually pregnant with schemes and vigor; I pretended the same, but was in truth just a jammed-up sluice-gate of wicked lust and longing. Add to that guilt and shame: I'd probably committed a sexual felony the night she let me stay with her. I'd certainly stolen something of hers. From her body—an essence of a kind. And I'd *drunk* it. Pervo! Deviant! Trespasser!

We hadn't spent the night together since. And the closer it got to Mardi Gras, the less likely we would. I spent hours and hours lying on the floor of my apartment, either dreading work or waiting for Julie to come by with progress reports on Bill and Dee. The former had lately outpaced the latter.

I was lying on the carpet by my bed watching sugar ants debouch from a crack in the flooring and march off toward the kitchen when Julie came by and banged on the door and shouted through the gap underneath that Omar would be here in the next few days so I'd better find some time for a visit.

"Steaks and cable!" she said, her nose and lips and one eye and a drape of black hair visible under the door.

"Hi!" I said, struggling briefly to get up—my beard had Velcroed my head to the rug. "It's been a while!"

"So you better let me in. For just a minute, though, I gotta go to work."

She was in full dress. Little red pleated skirt, white blouse, lots of Betty Grable–style matte makeup: perfectly defined vermilion lips, kohl-lined eyes, Raggedy Ann circles of blush. The black patent-leather brass-buckled

Mary Janes that she wore on duty and off.

I couldn't stand this much longer. The partnership; the friendship; the platonic *cosa nostra*—all so mere.

"He doesn't strike me as the Mardi Gras type," I said.

"He's not," she said, sitting down on the floor. "He hates it. But that's when he'll be here. He's mysterious, at least when it comes to itineraries."

"Hey," she added, pointing under the bureau, "are those your old stolen-and-then-recovered boots?"

"Yeah," I said, sitting down across from her.

Julie kicked off her Mary Janes, and was now shoeing herself in my old boots without using her hands.

"I've never seen you wear these," she said, finally getting the second boot on with the help of the dresser leg. "Since they fit, I'm commandeering them. Lace 'em up."

She lifted her legs in the air and spun on her bottom, construction-crane-style, until her booted feet were in my lap. I laced them up. Slowly; these moments with her—out from under the shadows of Bill and Dee and Carolyn and Tommy and Vishy—were terribly rare. Especially infrequent were the ones where we touched. Even though I was just tying her laces, down the black nylon fibers came her merrymade arc.

"Here," said Julie, using her freshly shod feet to grab her Mary Janes and drop them into my lap.

"You might get blisters," she added. "And don't stretch them."

They smelled sweet and dirty and rowdy, like an oily old revolver holster I'd found in a dumpster once. The stamps of the manufacturer on the insoles were almost completely worn away; the heels, a couple of inches high, were rounded at the edges; the leather of one shoe was shallowly slit from the toe to the strap; the brassy silver buckles were rubbed and pitted and shiny like old padlocks.

A salivary urge to chew on them popped up. I erected an erection. Not only did I obsess and prevaricate and cower and molest motherless daughters in their sleep, I had come out to myself as a helpless fetishist.

She stood up.

"What if *you* get blisters?" I said. "That'd be bad news for a cigarette girl in the middle of a shift, wouldn't it?"

"My feet are as callused as a Masai warrior's," she said, standing up and then bending over to drily buss my forehead. "Look, I also came by to order you around some more."

"Anything!"

"Hang out at the hostel. Watch for him there."

"Will you come by while I'm on duty? We don't hang out much lately. You know, to connive."

"I have to toil every day these days. But I'll drop by. And, incredibly, I have Mardi Gras Day off."

Julie stomped and jumped and waggled her new boots.

"Perfect!"

Then, again, like that, she was gone.

I ran to the mirror to see if any vermilion remained on my forehead. There was nothing.

Julie and I sat on the porch of the hostel drinking beer. It was a cold, windy Mardi Gras Day. All around us were staggering persons heavily necklaced with beads and barf. On every gust of wind came either the bare yet complex but otherwise indescribable stench unique to Carnival, or various strains of any or all of the five or so standard Mardi Gras songs blaring through giant speakers propped up on every veranda, with the vocal accompaniments of thousands of wandering sots.

It was the first time since I'd found my old boots at the Poke Round— barely five months ago!—that my past seemed to have paused in its stealthy gathering, and in the moment I found myself enjoying the spectacle of the strident Catholic melee around us. Even the sight of my boots on Julie's feet didn't bear murky omens—instead, a quiet, circumspect, sleepy-eyed peace anchored itself. I scooted one Planck length closer to Julie. She met me halfway. We slugged our beers at precisely the same moment.

Tommy and Carolyn came up the walk. Tommy had somehow finagled a job as Carolyn's aide-de-camp. They were never apart. They had scarves and coats and hats, in dark greens and reds. They looked happy.

"Jerome, you look like a B-movie star in disguise," said Carolyn.

Tommy reached out and rubbed my whiskers.

"Wow," she said. "We better just kiss him on the nose, Carolyn. And be careful where he kisses you, Julie-Jule."

"You're here a lot lately, Coe," said Carolyn. "I mean, we love to see you, but shit. And you both always have top-secret looks."

Carolyn was starting to sound like Tommy, in tone and temper. She had developed an impatient nasal chirp, and her address was like a brushback pitch. Tommy, on the other hand, seemed to have mellowed.

"We're on a mission," said Julie. "It's an important part of the day's mission to be on this porch drinking beer."

"What's your mission at night?" said Carolyn.

"Classified," said Julie.

"I bet," said Carolyn. "My mission? The sweet pussy here to my left. And taking care of all the new people that came in this morning. Goddam Danes, most of them."

They went inside.

"They look like they're doing okay," said Julie.

"I think I've been overreacting," I said. "About Tommy."

"Maybe she was just crazy when she cut you," said Julie. "Not bad, just crazy."

"Maybe we were both crazy and it was a crazy time. It *was* a crazy time."

"Maybe love has killed off her badness."

"Maybe because Tommy and Carolyn found each other, they both escaped the jaws of doom."

"We really ought to just quit worrying about other people," said Julie. "Let other people take care of themselves."

"Yeah."

"Yeah. Bill and Dee, too. If anything was gonna happen with them, it would've. Don't you think?"

What was happening here? Was I getting broken up with?

"So that's it?" I said. "No longer our problem?"

Panic rushed at me. It's done. She's going back to Vishy.

"The investigation is officially closed."

"You mean—"

"Unless we get new intelligence."

"We'll burn that bridge when we get to it," I said, all hivey, like I was slipping into anaphylactic shock.

"So what do we do now?" said Julie, finishing her beer. "We're out of a job."

Declare your love, fool! Now! Get a place together in the Marigny! A felt bridge table! Collect rare books and antique cats! Close moments under layers of blankets! Be a force, permanent, invulnerable! Start taking vitamins, for the health! Nibble her calves!

"I have a little bad news," said Julie.

My testicles shrank and ascended into my body.

"It's not working out with me and Vishy."

"Oh. Shit. Julie, I'm really sorry to hear that."

My head began to feel heavy and warm. Gold-bar heavy. My lips buzzed. Little grinning gnomes of joy, each armed with nunchaku to fight off panic ninjas, started running circles around me.

"Yeah. Still in shock."

"What happened?"

"It's ugly. I'll need a shoulder."

"Okay. I'm so sorry."

"Bill/Dee/Vishy. All gone."

"All pretty sudden."

We tugged on our beers and watched wayward Carnival revelers try to find their way back to St. Charles. I watched the airspace just above their heads, expecting the *floomp floom floopf* of hundreds of simultaneously inflating thought bubbles, each laden with a different perspective on the same theme: that the present developments were too good to be true.

Not your *shoulder dummy*

Those aren't gnomes of joy those are bogies of desolation

Wave bye-bye to the pretty girl Jerome

But there were no bubbles.

"I think," said Julie, "that we should at least shave off your beard. I want to do it. What do you do, squirt Barbasol into your hand and smear it on? Then scrape it off with a Bic? Just like my legs?"

"Yeah," I said, the word poking along in the hot, narcotic drawl peculiar to the speech of prisoners of love who've suddenly awakened to find their cell door open. "Except since my whiskers are so tough, I have to use these special blades. I order them through K & B."

"I'm skipping work tomorrow. Too depressed about Vishy. How about then?"

"Mmm... okay."

This was imaginary. I scanned the crowds. There must be a bubble of truth out there somewhere.

"I'll be very careful not to give you any new scars," said Julie.

The melted-gold warmth in my head had begun to lava through the rest of my body, and was now settling pleasantly amidships. I had to propose before I fainted.

"Are you sure shaving's the thing that'll help you deal with your Vishy feelings?"

"Feels right."

I was about to turn and say *I love you Julie I love you Julie I love you Julie* and just go ahead and start bawling and supplicating, when behind us the door to the hostel opened.

Scores of Danes came out and walked past us. The recent admissions, I guess, chortling and jostling. The last one that came out was a small man whose puffy blond hair was creepily motionless in the stiff wind. Except for the weird do, he resembled Knops from behind. Julie evidently thought the same.

"Knopsy!" she shouted. "What're you doing here? How'd you grow those curly locks so quick? Where's Dik? Knops!"

Some of the Danes turned around. The tiny man at the back of the bunch turned around, too.

My warm gold confession froze and shattered to flakes and vanished on an updraft.

He wore sunglasses, aerodynamic and mirrored, with a green plastic lanyard running behind his ears and lying like a yoke across the back of his neck. He was wearing the tiniest pair of tiger-striped body-builder-style parachute pants I'd ever seen, and a brown leather coat. Gray Adidas running shoes. He'd bleached his goatee so drastically it appeared translucent. His bald head was now fledged with a feathery periwig styled after Harpo Marx.

He turned around and walked backward, smiling broadly at Julie. He stuck out his tongue and licked the glassy soul patch under his lower lip. He turned back full circle without missing a step.

"Fuck, that hayseed looked a combo of Knops and the Golden Girls from behind," said Julie.

I held my heart. I kept my cool. I held my heart.

"Keep your eyes in your head or I'll send my boyfriend here to suck them out!" shouted Julie.

Bill hitched up his tiger pants and stuck his middle finger in the air without turning around.

I bent over and pushed my heart against my knees.

How silly and cloak-and-dagger it had seemed, before, to wear a disguise. But what if I'd been me just then? I might be a pulped mess, dying on the sidewalk. Julie, too.

"That freaked me out," I said. "Do *not* do that again."

That was the first harsh word I'd said to her, ever.

"Sorry," she said. "I wouldn't really send you into battle. Come on, let's go to your place and smooth you up. Can I shave your ankles, too?"

"I have to go someplace. I forgot."

"Where?" she said, a child.

A lie didn't come easily.

"Just someplace I forgot I said I'd be."

I knew my tone was mean—I'd meant to be casual and no-big-deal, but it came out wrong.

"I'm sorry about that guy," said Julie. "I really didn't mean to freak you."

"It's okay," I said, standing up. "I just need to go."

"Can I come?"

"No, I'm cool," I said, backing down the steps.

"Why?"

Because

"I'm cool."

if Bill figures out

"Are you? Do you have tadpoles?"

what you're up to

"No. No tadpoles."

he

"Not bubbles!"

will

I shook my head.

murder you.

"Okay," she said. "You want me to go to your place and wait for you? I'll strop and steam towels."

"Sure."

"Jerome, what's up with you?"

"Nothing," I said, turning around to see where Bill had gone.

"Come on, what?"

"I'll see you later on tonight," I said, praying I would.

"Did you find Miranda?" she asked, shifting her weight to the other hip. "Are you going down to... see her?"

"No."

"Is it... Ohh. Look, Vishy's history, really. It's like the guy never existed. See, I'm already forgetting his name. Mmm... what was it? Boshi? No... Wishy? Banjo? No, that's not—"

"No, it's not Vishy. I just have to—"

"Are you dumping me again?" The line she used so often in jest but that so often gave me hope. "Just because we decided to let everybody take care of themselves, to quit worrying about everyone? I didn't mean *us*."

Bill was just turning the corner onto St. Charles.

"No."

"You're not gonna faint?"

"Not going to faint." I pulled a smile out of somewhere and backed down the walk. "See you later."

"Maybe maybe not."

She didn't smile. She stood up and went into the hostel.

I went in the direction Bill and the Danes had gone, trying not to run, trying not to walk.

VII

They all boarded a streetcar, Bill and the gaggle of Danes, two blocks up. I chased it down the tracks, falling farther and farther behind.

It was midday. The cold wind blew. There was no parade on St. Charles at the moment, but the evidence from the last one was everywhere—beads on the wires, vomit in the brown grass, scarred doubloons everywhere, plastic cups, and tons of colorful dough ground into the pavement. I ran through it all.

In the distance Bill's car stopped. I raced through the green-purple-gold peatlands. I caught up just as the last member of an especially fit-looking sorority added herself to the critically stuffed car. I pushed open the rear door and grafted myself between an old man and a tall sorority girl, as thin and whippy as a birch sapling. The old man had the better breath, so I faced him. He didn't look like he felt well at all.

I craned my neck. There, way up front. Bill. Standing on a seat, still shorter than everybody. He was facing the front of the car. I struggled to get closer, but the old man and the twiggy soror held me fast. I could barely breathe. My heart chugged, as though it had thrown a rod.

"You look like you got a little heartburn, too," said the old man to me, gesturing to my hand on my heart. "Help yourself."

He handed me a big plastic bottle of Tums with a flip-top lid.

"You don't have to take just two, like it says under Dosage," he advised. "Why, you can have up to sixteen if you're really hurting. Same with aspirin and Advil. Not true of Tylenol though, or Excedrin. Bear that in mind when you're shopping for OTC analgesics next time."

"I will," I said, watching Bill. "I think I'm a twelve."

"Well, go ahead and take yourself a dozen Tums."

We crunched Tums. The mashing ruck of the streetcar had entirely deactivated me—all I was able to do was keep an eye on Bill, listen to Twiggy occasionally squeal at some or other private delight, and bear witness to the old man as he talked about New Orleans during the Second World War.

He said he'd walked around, drunk beer, whored, gambled, drunk beer, all while waiting to be sent someplace icy to get pulped by a mine.

"It was quite a time at first, especially all the girls. I see that hasn't changed much," he said, nodding toward the front of the streetcar, where most of the sorority was sardined.

"But," he continued, "everything started to fall apart after a few days. Two of our boys, Nick and Weedy, got into a scuffle over who got to sit on the loveseat with Agnes at the whorehouse. Nick lost. A couple hours later he died in bed with Stretchy Marie of what they'd today call a blood clot. The MPs came and rousted Weedy out of bed with Agnes and court-martialed him. He died in prison just ten years ago. And another fellow in our company disappeared and ended up in the river, right behind the Café du Monde. And Benny Chow Mein, he loved chow mein, went AWOL home to Kokomo and hanged himself in the head of a griddle-cake joint. The ones that left here okay went to war and were largely massacred by mud and Germans."

"I don't understand anything," I said, mostly to myself.

"Just before I left," he said, "I met a nice lady. A nice lady."

"A nice girl," I said, thinking about nice girls I'd known.

"Yes. A nice girl."

"What happened to her?"

"New Orleans is a greasetrap," he said. "It catches all the lumps and twigs and shards and torn flesh. The clean water goes into the Gulf, everything else is trapped here, where it rots."

"What are you doing here?"

"This is the only place where anything ever happened that made me want to die, or to live," he said after a moment.

"I might have to kill somebody to save somebody else."

"I know what you mean," he said, as if he really did.

"But just so I can live with myself, and have what I want."

"Folks can live with an awful lot," he said.

"I get black tadpoles under my retinas."

"Have some more Tums."

The streetcar stopped. We were a couple blocks away from Canal. Our carriage's great interior pressure squirted a score of passengers onto the sidewalk, Bill among them. He picked himself up and began to walk briskly toward the French Quarter.

I struggled, torqued, elbowed, shouldered, kneed, and finally found my way off the car. I ran after Bill, but it was too late—he'd vanished in the French Quarter crowds.

I found myself on Bourbon Street during Mardi Gras, something I'd sworn I'd never allow to happen. In every direction, hairy heads, dreadlocked heads, shaved heads, heads with knobs and clamps, heads with hats and hair spray. In a crowd like this Bill's lowly presence would manifest as a void among the heads, but I saw no void. There was a T-shirt shop on one corner, a fake jazz club on another, a spooky strip club called the MoneyMaker on another. On the fourth corner—Gumbeaux. And above Gumbeaux, the lights were on in Knops and Dik's apartment.

"Happy Mardi Gras!" shouted the Danes as they ushered me inside their place. "You have come to be in our window?"

"Yeah. Just got the urge to people-watch and soul-search. Again."

"Hmm, you have advanced whiskers now," said Knops, reaching to test one with a fingertip. He promptly lacerated himself. "Ow! Sharp! Ow!"

Knops sent Dik away to fetch ice cubes and first aid.

I noticed there was a gray shoe box standing on end in my window nook. The shoe box had a telescoping antenna.

"Hey, is that a cellular phone?"

"Yef," said Knops, sucking on his injured finger.

Dik returned with a bandage and a ten-pound bag of ice.

"You can call anywhere?" I said.

"Oh no," said Knops, peeling a Curad with his pinkies. "Also is costly, and heats the ear."

"Better than not phone," said Dik, a little testily. He dropped the bag of ice on the floor and attacked it with an ice pick. A big chunk cleaved off, and Dik handed it to Knops.

"Call your Julie and ask for her hands in marriage," said Knops.

"I just need to sit and look out your window."

"All right, dog. Dik, present Jerome Fresca. We will propose to your Julie later."

"High time," said Dik.

Dik and I went into the kitchen while Knops dug around in a chest of some kind looking for a game he and Dik could play while I stared out into the crowd.

While Dik was pouring my Fresca, he leaned over to me and whispered.

"Bra," he said. "Cecil give me phone. Secret. Knops in dark."

Dik giggled in a peculiar way, and then garnished my Fresca with an olive.

"Bom Tee Bom bombombom Bom Tee Bom," sang Knops, when Dik and I returned. "Game time! Hooray! BomBomBom Tee Bom!"

Dik and Knops sat on the floor and immediately started to argue over how to set up the Danish *Jeopardy!* board.

I sat in the window and watched the people below. I monitored the MoneyMaker strip club across the street. The squirming, undulating crowd below was packed together so tightly that from my second-floor vantage point it looked like the street was six feet deep in boiling lamb stew. But no voids. No Bill.

Knops and Dik left me to my sentinel. Now and then I caught a word. *Pontopiddan, Hammarskjöld, Aksel Schiøtz.*

Late afternoon snuck in the room. I was lightheaded, but not faint. *Hurry.*

"Jerome, you look wiped," said Knops. "Why don't you crash into this divan. Boocoo comfy."

"I have to watch for somebody," I said.

"Then I shall watch window with you," said Dik.

"Well, okay. I'm looking for a guy—about your size, Knops—with blond curly hair and sunglasses with a green strap. And a goatee."

"Goatee?" asked Dik.

"Baseball beard," said Knops. "Like the Rocket."

"Ah," said Dik. "Kayo. But what color goatee?"

"White. I have to kill him."

We all had a good laugh over that.

Hours passed. Night came. Boredom had transformed Dik into a bellows of vast Danish yawns.

"No blond-headed men growing goatees," he said, for about the hundredth time. Then: "Wait! There!"

It was Bill, his tiny, furry head wedged between the breasts of an elderly woman in a leotard. Both Bill and the leotard lady were trapped motionless in the crowd.

"Thanks, you two," I said. "Say, can I borrow that ice pick?"

"Certainly! Kill! Ha!" they said.

On the stoop outside the Danes' apartment, I raised both hands high over my head so they wouldn't get trapped at my sides by the crowd. Then I shuffled into the stew, toward Bill Izzoli.

I strained and grunted, trying to get through and to stay above the crowd. My whiskers poked through the shoulders of my jacket and into my skin. The crowd was so tight, the only movement was at neck level and above—heads bobbing on necks, deep, viscous kissing, beer cans in beer hats draining quickly through clear pipes into collegiate mouths. I was immobilized. I screamed, but everyone was screaming.

Above me people leaned out of the iron balconies, tossing things down, catching things tossed back up.

Suddenly Bill was in front of me. He was still trapped between the breasts of the woman in the leotard. He couldn't see me.

The leotard lady then removed her bra without removing her leotard. She magically pulled the substantive purplish lacy thing out of her armpit. She waved it around, then slung it up to the slavering crowd leaning over the balcony.

The pitch of screaming rose as other women on the street and up on the balcony started taking off their Playtexes and Wonderbras, using the same sleight of hand, and throwing them any which way.

Bill reached as high as the breasts of the leotard lady and his own ability would allow him, but he couldn't catch a bra.

I squeezed my ice pick. I held it high overhead, with both hands, left over right, bad over good. I was right beside him. His head was the leotard lady's third breast.

Bras shot like Perseids.

Pop his head, pop it.

I began to bring my weapon down hard, with all my strength, to stick in his skull.

But my hands would not come down. Not at all. The crowd of stew kept them aloft.

A small white bra, flung from some remote part of the crowd, draped itself over my hands and my ice pick.

I looked down. The leotard lady had just two breasts again—Bill was gone. I struggled and sidled and tried to periscope myself above the crowd. Where the hell did he go? Trampled to death, maybe. What luck that would be!

No, there he was, squeezing into a cab already tamped with people.

I jumped into another cab, a gypsy, also stuffed. I recognized my fellow travelers as a local jug band, the Poot-Pooters.

"No split fares, bay," said the cabbie, whose name, according to his laminated license, was Reuben Fitzwagon. "And no stickers. Hand me that sticker."

Reuben seized my ice pick. No matter; I'd bite Bill to death if I had to. Just thinking about it made my tongue splash in my mouth like an urchin in a gutter.

The crowds and traffic forced both Bill's and my cabs in the same direction: uptown. We were a dozen cars apart.

Soon the crush of the night forced the traffic to slow and stop.

"I have to get out."

"172.50."

"What? I've been in here maybe eight minutes."

"177.50. Meter running, bay."

When Bill was dead and Mardi Gras was over, maybe I'd look up Reuben and pay his fare. No tip, though.

I yanked on the door. It opened less than six inches before the massive pickup next to us stopped it.

"Hey!" said Reuben.

I tried to squeeze out. There was less room than between jail bars.

"Let me out!"

"192.50."

I climbed across the laps of the jug band. But the doors on that side—both front and back—were pinned shut by a stalled float of a high-heeled shoe.

I kicked at the back windshield. Nothing. I tried to squeeze out of the gap in my door again. I worked my head through—it had acquired some lateral play due to its past of misuse—but Reuben incited the Poot-Pooters to yank me back in and search me for $197.50, plus his tip.

"Y'all keep whatever else y'all locate," he said.

Just before my line of sight was obscured by the jug band, I saw that Bill's cab had broken free of the jam and was again on the move. I began to thrash and scream.

"Stop! I'll have diarrhea on all of you!"

"Ain't scared," said Reuben. "Happened before, lots of times."

They tore at me. I kicked and bit and rotated. Two of them began to drool and smack their lips. In addition to being broke, jug bands are always full of THC and thus hungry: they were going to pull off my extremities and eat them like hot wings.

I found myself upside down in the middle of the backseat, between the saw player and the washtub-bass man, grimy overalls squashing my ears. One of those merciless cannibals bit my ankle.

Something in the vinyl seat behind my head moved. I pulled it. It opened. It was one of those trapdoors that leads into the trunk, the kind that some bright car designer had thought up in order to make it easier for someone needing room to stow long things like Christmas trees or grandfather clocks.

I was skinny from the high metabolism that comes with weeks of obsessive love and a night of attempted murder, so I started to wriggle through the trapdoor. With lots of kneeing and kicking I freed myself from the snaring grip of the jug band and found myself in the trunk. One last good two-foot kick and the trunk popped open. I was finally through with the cab. And pleased with myself. I felt like Papillon, free from Devil's Island.

I ran across the hoods of the gridlocked cars like a bad guy in a movie. The crowds finally thinned enough so I could see the ground. I jumped off the last car and ran in Bill's cab's direction.

But it was gone.

I wondered if Dee was already dead. There was no way to know. No way to find her.

I dropped into the Detrebesq Hotel. It was far enough away from the more serious and desperate Mardi Gras crowds that its bathroom, a blue-minus, could be snuck into without much trouble. I would sit down there and relieve myself and think.

Someone had taken the stalls away, so there were just three naked commodes sticking out of a wall, like in a Marine barracks. Any normally private moments in a normal bathroom with normal individual stalls would here be at large. I decided to downgrade this restroom to a red plus.

Then the urgency of my situation came upon me hard.

This was it. I'd failed. This was the end. Appropriately, the end was in a gross bathroom.

There was a kid sitting on one commode—eleven years old or so— reading paperbacks, and a tattooed guy on another, who kept alternating between sitting on, and kneeling before, his toilet, apparently unable to decide whether he needed to shit or barf.

The middle toilet was unoccupied. I couldn't even get an aisle seat.

I rested my forehead on my arms to think.

The tattooed man finally chose to barf.

I noticed that the little kid next to me had a whole stack of paperbacks with him. They were at his feet, atop a little hillock of wadded-up toilet paper he'd obviously built himself to function as prophylaxis between his books and the revolting tile floor.

They all looked like true crime: garish pink and green covers, or black and red. I squinted to read the titles. He was reading *I Shant Quit Ripping Them*. And on the hillock were *Gilles de Rais* and *The Red Devil: Andrei Chikatilo* and *Richard Kuklinski: Mob Enforcer or Serial Killer?* and *Milwaukee Brain Sucker: Jeffrey*

I stopped breathing. Why hadn't I thought of this before?

I ran to the lobby, found the pay phone, called information: local. The 411 gods smiled.

"Hello?"

"Jeff Dahmer?"

"Who the fuck might this be?" said a weary voice, surely tired of crank calls.

"Jeff, hey, this is Jerome Coe! You sound exactly the same!"

"Uh, hey, what's up, wait, who?"

"Jerome. Remember, from Duke's? Hey, sorry about the serial killer stuff. Pretty rotten luck to be a namesake to that guy."

"What're you gonna do," he said, unsteady, defeated—the same way he used to talk when Dee was with Bill instead of him. "Who is this again?"

"Jerome Coe. We used to sit in Duke's and talk about invading Stamford."

"I did that with everybody. But I remember you. Mental guy with the huge pimple mountain on his forehead? How the hell'd you find me, bro?"

"I heard Dee was here in New Orleans, and I just figured you guys got together after Bill went to Walpole. Look, that's why I'm calling—you know Bill escaped, right, and he's in town somewhere? I think Dee's in danger and—"

"She broke up with me. She really fucking broke my heart this time, bro. I don't care anymore. I can't even barely move."

"Bill might kill her, though! Like Leigh!"

"Coe, right? Listen: she can take care of herself. She's tough as nails. The woman must've been hardboiled in gasoline, bro."

"What about the cops, then?"

"You're kidding. Right?"

"Well, where does she live?"

"No idea, bro. A web, maybe."

"Where's she work?"

"Probably still dances."

"Where?"

"MoneyMaker."

On Canal I spotted an acquaintance.

"Hey, remember me?" I said to the bum in the wheelchair. "Couple Halloweens ago? I traded you my knife for some clothes?"

He tried to roll away, but I grabbed the arms of his wheelchair.

"Say, can I have my knife back?"

"Fuck away, the fuck off me, man!"

"I just want my glass knife! I'll buy it. Twenty bucks."

I had to pinch the bill between my teeth so I could use both hands to keep him from rolling away.

"It's in the side saddle, man. Damn. Gonna give me a heart attack! Get away!"

The knife seemed unused. A little old blood, my own. A snug cardboard sheath had been fashioned from what I recognized as a high-school French textbook: *Son et Sens*. I couldn't remember what that meant.

The glass edge was still supernaturally sharp.

Again I ran, down Dauphine, which was far less crowded than the other northeast-to-southwests. Halfway down I turned right.

I squeezed my way across the street and went into the MoneyMaker.

It was bizarrely empty. Even though the crowds were murderous outside, the MoneyMaker was almost entirely deserted. It was as dark as Hy's. The only light was the stage, where a naked, fifties-pinup-girl type was dancing. More like shuddering, really.

A small man, the only patron I could see, sat right up at the edge of the stage, the front half of his body lit by the stage lighting, his back half dark. Like a shapeless moon, far from the sun.

A bar was barely visible in the back, lit by a low red glow, like in a darkroom. There seemed to be a bartender back there, floating in the red murk.

There was no evidence of Dee.

The whole room smelled of sour milk and burnt hair. It was an old smell, part of the room, in the walls. It was the weather of the place.

The dancer's eyes grew round, bulging, pupils perfectly centered. Her face was blue. She was garroting herself with her own hair. Her tongue came out. She crumpled slowly to the stage, coming to rest in an unnatural, mortal position that suggested she'd really died. Like the busted posture of a ledge-leap suicide.

I could feel the floor under my feet, but couldn't see it—just unreflecting black. My feet disappeared into it, like I was wading in coal smoke.

I sat down in the back of the bar, in full darkness. I waited. I watched for Dee. For Bill. For anything. I felt fully invisible, invincible. I watched the dancer's cold blue face. She was older than she looked at first—at least fifty-five.

Suddenly she was up on her hands and knees on the stage, smiling, pink, flirty. She was facing away from the little moon man. She wiggled her rear end and spread her legs. She looked coyly over her shoulder and between her legs. She tossed her hair over one shoulder, then the other. The moon man slid a dollar across to her, folded lengthwise like a little tent. She reached between her legs, picked it up, wadded it into a ball, and flicked it toward the brass pole, which was covered in oily fingerprints clearly visible in the stage light. At the base of the pole were about fifteen wadded-up dollars.

She backed toward the moon man a little, still on her knees, and flattened her chest against the floor. She reached back and grabbed the long heels of her high-heel slippers. The soles were dirty and scratched and studded with little stones and flecks of glass. She moaned. She pulled her feet back until her calves splayed against the backs of her thighs. The moon man did not move except to occasionally drink his beer. Even at a distance she was visibly wet, dripping. She gasped and coughed and pulled hard on the heels of her shoes. Makeup ran with the sweat on her face. The left side of her face was pressed to the wooden stage. She stuck out her long tongue and licked at the stage. She pulled harder at her heels, until the toes of her shoes were twisted against her hips. She gasped, squeaked, pulled harder. She shut her eyes, bared her teeth, and froze still. Her gums began to bleed.

"Mama!" she said. "Mama!"

The bartender turned around.

"Okay, baby," called the bartender from the bar. "Let it go. Let it go. Good for you."

The dancer let out her breath, a whistling scream. Blood sprayed, a pink vapor in the spotlight. She opened her eyes. She fell forward onto her belly.

The moon man drank beer. He slid two bills toward her, but she didn't move. He grabbed her ankle, pulled her toward him, leaned over, and with a pair of gold scissors, snipped off a generous lock of her hair.

Someone applauded. I couldn't tell where it was coming from. It was slow, deep, and powerful—two seconds of silence between each cherry-bomb clap.

Bill.

Fuck.

He must have come in during the show. He was sitting at a table a few feet from the stage. I took out my knife and experimented with grips. Overhand, stabbing? Like Norman Bates? No, that felt wrong. Underhand, right in the breadbasket. No—a big, wild, lateral, navel-splitting swipe, a machete through the sugarcane. Hmm. There wasn't any hurry now—Bill was twenty feet away. Better get it right. Maybe try to shorten him! That would be something. I could mail Bill's head to Dewey—he could pick it up at the post office along with whatever the newest commemoratives were. Dewey would like that. He'd like to see a mask of surprise on the monster's face. He'd like the chance to drop-kick Bill's tiny, murderous head into Boston Harbor.

As I quietly experimented in the deep dark, the bartender came from behind the bar, climbed onto the stage, picked up the tiny stripper like she was an old tire, and then carried her off, accidentally knocking her legs into the pole—one of her little high-heel shoes fell off and landed on the stage. The moon man climbed up. He had on lipstick and rouge and blue eyeshadow. He retrieved the wadded-up dollars and dropped the shoe into the pocket of his long coat, the kind Jackie Onassis used to wear. He climbed back down.

"Come on!" shouted Bill. "Next! Come on! Bring on Penny! Penny, haul your deep roomy hairy pussy onto this fucking stage!"

The bartender emerged from backstage, where she must have dropped off the exhausted dancer. Dee was still nowhere to be seen. Stay away, Dee, just a few more seconds.

"Penny ain't here," the bartender shouted at Bill.

She climbed off the stage and headed back toward the bar. Bill jumped up and followed her. He was half her size.

Now was right.

I stood up. I had decided on the wild swipe, but neck-high and back-hand, like Laurence Olivier's evil Nazi at the end of *Marathon Man*.

The door opened.

"Cigarettes, cigars, cigarettes."

Julie. Dressed for work. Of all places, here. Please, no. She walked past me with her cigarette tray. I sat back down, staying hidden in the dark coal smoke of the blackest corner of the MoneyMaker, lost. It was supposed to be just me here, alone, full of murder. Just me. It was why I'd left her by herself at the hostel.

"Oh, yeah," said Bill, returning from the bar with two bottles of beer. "I need smokes. I'd've bought some this morning if I knew *you* were selling."

"Do we know each other?" said Julie.

She was smiling.

All of me stopped.

"Sure we do. You threatened to set your boyfriend on me this morning," said Bill. "Suck out my eyes. 'Member?"

"At the hostel? That was you?"

"I couldn't forget you," said Bill.

"Well, well. Fancy meeting you here. Having a nice time?"

Sweat soaked into the cardboard hilt.

"Fancy fucking A right," said Bill. "You know that old chick that gets on her knees and screams for her mama?"

"Ozie. Sure, she's something."

"Yeah. And she was the only pussy here, till you walked in."

"You're very sweet. But you don't count Penny?"

"Ain't here yet, the slow bitch."

"Come on, I'm almost done tonight. Walk with me on my last round."

"Serious? Shit. *That* was easy. These Southern girls get right to the point, hey dude?" said Bill, addressing the moon man, who showed no sign that he'd heard.

"You got that right," said Julie. "So how about it? Want to go?"

I began to carefully shave the hairs off my arm. The glass whisked against my skin.

"You know I do, but I'm busy here right now. Been in town a day, and I got business here. *Bidness.*"

"Busy? You don't look busy."

"You don't look busy either, baby," said Bill. "You ought to get up on-stage and put on a show for us Boy Scouts."

"Me, oh no, I'm just a poor cigarette girl."

"C'mon, I'll buy you a drink," said Bill. "Two drinks. Four drinks. Six drinks and some fucking beads, if you climb up there and rub it on the brass pole."

"Mama wouldn't like that."

"Mama doesn't like anything," said Mama, from the back of the bar. "But I don't care what you do, as long as you wipe down that pole with Fantastik when you're done."

"Come on," Julie said to Bill. "Let's go to your hostel. This club sucks."

After I finished shaving with the grain, I went against it, for a perfect glacé finish. Ah, like peeling Elmer's off your fingertips. Now, the other arm.

"I just can't do that right now," said Bill. "Like I said, I'm busy. Need to have a little *talk* with Penny."

"I'll have you back before she gets here."

Bill turned away and looked up at the empty stage.

"Come on," Julie said. "You think *Ozie* gets wet? Now or never."

I'd always had this one thick, long, abnormal whisker that stuck straight out from my Adam's apple like a More 120. It had always been easier to uproot than cut, so long as there was a pair of needle-nose at hand.

"My my. Tell me more."

"Come with me, then."

"Rub it on the pole."

"Tell you what," said Julie. "I'll do a quick dance, right on that stage, if you take me out for eight drinks right after. *Right* after. I hate this bar."

She looked at him like I'd never seen her look at anyone. She turned back and forth slightly at the hips. Bill looked back at her, shelved his tiny chin in one hand, then stroked his white goatee with his finger and thumb.

"Okay. Do it. Make me stand proud."

"We'll leave when I'm done?"

"Wherever you want to go. But not for long. I gotta be back here. Like I said, I'm a fucking busy man."

Julie put down her cigarette tray and took off her long white gloves. She climbed onstage and went through the curtain in the back. I dropped my head back and set the edge of the knife at the base of the big bad whisker.

There was no music. Julie came out with her eyes closed. She stood next to the pole. The moon man became attentive. Bill lit a cigarette and leaned back in his chair. Julie took off her pillbox hat and dropped it onto the stage. She sat down, crossed her legs Indian style, and lit the first cigarette I'd ever seen her smoke. With the cigarette still in her mouth, she pulled her top off and tossed it near the pole, where its tiny white buttons clicked on the stage. She took another drag. She kicked off her boots, my boots, Teddy and Dino's gift to me. Then she crossed her legs again and took another drag. She didn't take notice of anyone. She didn't look at Bill or the bartender or the moon man. She didn't look my way.

I let the blade slide and felled my whisker. How cleanly it schussed through! Glass is the answer. It was good enough for the Aztecs. I started in on my sideburns. A few stiff, curling whiskers scythed off and vanished in the dark.

As if she were all alone, undressing in private to go to bed or get into the tub, Julie took off her bra and dropped it onto the stage. She relaxed and lay on her back, wiggled out of her red velvet skirt, then pulled her panties down to her calves. She pulled them off the rest of the way with her little toe, on which she wore her puzzle ring. She sat up, cross-legged again, hunched over, smoking, looking at nothing, waiting for the bathtub to fill, alone, in her own house.

Bill moved up and sat right next to the stage. I'd finished my sideburn and started on the whiskers under my chin. They audibly sheared off, tiny *tk tk tk*s. The knife sometimes slipped under the skin, causing little threads of cooling blood to coil in my lap. I shaved the tricky, grayish whiskers under my lip.

Julie stubbed out her cigarette on the stage. Then she lay back again, rolled onto her side, and appeared to go to sleep.

"No deal," said Bill. "That was a fine tease, and my cock is fucking chumming, but I need a little more. Scoot thisaway."

Julie stayed in the sleeping position, but pushed herself toward him.

Bill stood up and walked my way. I could slice at nothing but my own face.

He passed by without seeing me. He went to the barroom door and locked it. He returned and made himself comfortable at the stage. Julie really looked like she was sleeping. I had seen her sleep. Once.

"Can't have somebody walking in on us, can we?" said Bill. "Closer, beautiful, come on."

She slid a little closer.

"You owe me some drinks," said Julie.

"You owe me one," he said, then reached over and grabbed her ankle and pulled her toward him. She slid noiselessly on the dirty stage.

Just under the nose and around the very corners of my mouth was always the toughest to do thoroughly, and I always got a rash no matter how careful I was, or how much cream I used, or how much vitamin E oil I slathered on after. Even steaming my whole face with a hot towel like in forties movies didn't help.

I took a breath and started at the top of my excellent philtrum, with the very tip of the knife. The whiskers came off, one wire at a time. Soon I'd shaved off my whole mustache. Julie was on her back with her knees in the air. Bill's face was between her legs. I opened my mouth wide, to stretch the corners, which made it easier to scrape off the whiskers there. Those in one corner of my mouth came off without any slips, but I was careless with the other corner, and the blade cut into the taut skin, sneaking in a good quarter inch. Bill reached under Julie's thighs, grabbed her elbows, and pulled her hard into his face. She lifted her head. Sweat rivered in the creases of her neck. Her mouth opened, and she made short, hitching gasps. A lock of hair had fallen across her face, but she couldn't brush it away. She breathed rapidly, the lock of hair billowing and cupping across her lips.

I finished up my other cheek and sideburn, and then smeared the blood from my slit cheek and the other nicks all over my face, as an aftershave. I felt for stray whiskers, mowing them down as I found them.

My mouth felt odd, like it wouldn't shut. Like I was drooling. Blood ran down my throat and I choked and coughed a little, but nobody seemed to notice—Julie was in the middle of a high, crying orgasm, and Bill's blond head was squeezed between her thighs, her heels digging into his shoulder blades. He held her arms so tightly they were crimson above his grip and blue below.

Bill worked his way out from between her thighs and tried to hold them open as he hunted for the drawstring of his parachute pants. He pulled her closer to him, roaring through his clenched teeth as he tried to free himself. She said *no, no, wait, no,* and then she pulled herself up by his shirt and whispered in his ear. He stopped his struggling and let go of her.

"Come on," he said. "Fucking come on!"

Julie dressed quickly in her top and skirt, leaving her underwear by the brass pole. She pulled on my boots. Her cigarette tray sat open at the edge of the stage. The moon man was peering into it like it was a plate of hors d'oeuvres.

Bill dragged Julie off the stage by her wrist. They headed toward the door, then stopped.

They were right before me. I stood up. I was so clean-shaven I could've impressed an army drill sergeant. The dark hid me. With my thumb I felt the edge of my friend the glass knife one more time, then drew back to slit Bill open like a lumpfish.

But instead I sat back down in the shadows.

Before they were out the door, Bill called back to the bartender. "Don't fucking mention this!"

"Certainly not, sir," said the bartender. "Have a sloppy screw, you two.

"Hey, wait!" she shouted suddenly. "Fantastik my pole!"

But Julie and Bill were gone.

The moon man selected a Cohiba from the tray Julie had left behind.

I sat comfortably in the dark and considered the foul act of shaving, how I'd hated it all my whiskered life. But now I didn't mind it at all— what a difference a sharp knife made!

To preserve the edge, I returned it to its French-book sheath and slipped it into my pocket.

The moon man finished another bottle, then climbed onto the stage to collect Julie's panties and bra. He dropped them into his pockets along with the other dancer's shoe.

I'd done a good deal of futile running today, and I deserved a beer, god-dammit. I stood up and crossed the floor of the MoneyMaker Gentleman's Club.

"Young man, I didn't even see you come in," said the bartender. "What happened to you?"

"Cut myself shaving. Can I have a Lite?"

"You may," she said. "You should be more careful with the razor. I admit it looks like a pretty close shave, though—the scattered wounds notwith-standing."

She put the can in front of me and opened it with a frothy, satisfying, beer-commercial *pbsht*.

"Thanks," I said.

"Six fifty."

"Wow," I said.

"Mardi Gras vices, Mardi Gras prices."

"I hate Mardi Gras."

I pushed her a twenty.

"Can't change that, unless you'll take quarters," she said, looking over at the moon man drinking beer and playing with his cigar. "*Somebody* here keeps using all our damn singles!"

The moon man did not react to the reprimand.

The bartender gave me a roll of quarters and the rest in lesser coins. I tried to pick them up but my hands had gone numb.

"I have a glass knife," I said. "Would you cut my throat with it? I can't seem to make my hands work."

The slit at the corner of my mouth had started to scab over, but it popped open again and began to bleed. The bartender reached over and dabbed at my mouth with a cocktail napkin.

"Sorry, on parole."

Presently the door to the bar opened. I had no interest in turning around to see who it was. If it was Bill or some other member of the felonry, let them have at it. Who cared now?

"Hey, Penny," the bartender said over my shoulder to whoever had just come in. "Get onstage, lady. You got fans waiting. *Fan.*"

"Where the fuck is he?" said the voice behind me named Penny. "He's supposed to be here. He fucking swore on his short Dago life he'd be here."

"Stepped out," said the bartender. "Back in a minute."

I turned around and was not terribly surprised to see that Penny was in fact Dee Marrat. She was dressed as a sexy librarian—dowdy, Peter Pan–collared blouse worn so tight that the slits between the buttons over her bosom spread open like serpents' eyes; heavy, matronly skirt hemmed just above four-inch cherry acrylic high-heel shoes; chained granny glasses low on her nose, black-lined green eyes staring over the rims at me. She looked just like, and nothing like, Leigh.

A needle of atonement poked at the guilt—the reality of Dee's being alive hedged Julie's horrifying treachery. I jumped off the barstool and ran over to hug her.

"Jesus *Christ* I'm glad you're okay!"

"Hey, whoa, don't touch me!" she said, stiff-arming me and making an ugly, un-Leigh-like face at me. "That blood all over your fucking face?"

"I... we've been looking for you for a while," I said, suddenly afraid, unsure. "We've been trying to warn you that Bill Izzoli is here, in New Orleans, to... you know, to hurt you. He was just here, you just missed him, but he'll be back. We have to go to the cops! Get you to a safe place!"

"He was *here?*" Dee said, addressing the bartender. "MamaDawn, who the fuck is this?"

"Fuck if I know. Razor Goodnews?"

"Well, *Razor*, Bill is here to *fuck* me, not fuck me up, and every fucking whack Leigh got with that bottle was a show of mercy, compared to what she deserved. She'd had that coming her whole life, that rancid, prude cunt—oh, fuck you. I don't even know who you are. Beefalo! Beefie! Throw this fucking rag out of here."

The moon man stood up and headed my way. He looked like Annie Lennox.

"You sit down, Beefie," said MamaDawn, in a steady voice of chilling finality.

Beefalo paused.

"You know, I do remember you," Dee said to me. "You *are* a crazy fuck. You chased my car down Magazine in the rain."

"I thought you were Leigh," I said, the needle broken, the yolk repairing its skin. "I thought Leigh was alive. I loved her."

"Beefie, get him. You can hurt him if you want. Do it, and I'll let you cut off a lock of my ha-a-a-air!"

Her singsong enticement animated Beefalo, who grabbed me around the neck with both hands. A sour odor of heavily uric piss and old tobacco ash rose off the cuffs of his jacket.

"I was trying to warn you. I was trying to help," I said, before Beefalo closed down my esophagus.

"Whatever Beef starts Bill'll finish, you weird tumor."

"Let go, Beef," said MamaDawn. "Now!"

Beef let go, but left his hands circled around my throat, haloed a quarter inch above my skin.

"Bill's bad, you know—he's dangerous," I said, forceless, exhausted.

"Go sit down," said MamaDawn.

Beefalo didn't move, but a tic of uncertainty fluttered under one eye.

"Do as you're told, Beef," said Dee. "Get him."

"Beefalo," said MamaDawn, "Sam I Am has pointed out to me that you are his least favorite customer. Do you want to talk to Sam I Am?"

He shook his head.

"Fuck, Dawn, let Beefie at least tie him up and throw him out."

She paused. Nobody moved. The blood was gluey on my face. My skin itched.

"Okay," said MamaDawn finally. "But I'm *this* close to getting Sam I Am to talk with everybody. Everybody."

Beefalo smiled and advanced, then proceeded to try to tie me into some kind of sailor's knot.

"Ow," I said. "I went to some trouble to warn you, Dee Marrat... Ow!"

"Wasted your time, fuck. Beef, try putting his arm *under* his knee and then *over* his foot."

"You know," I said, "Bill just left to go have sex with my girlfriend? They left just after he'd finished eating her out on that stage, *your* stage, while this demon and I watched it all. Few minutes ago. Ask her—ask MamaDawn, Dee. She watched it, too. Ow."

Dee whipped around to the bartender, who lied expertly. Beefalo was not questioned at all, as he was preoccupied with his knot. Dee turned back to me.

"Liar!"

"No, sorry," I said. "Bill watched my ex-girlfriend strip, then he went and locked the door to the bar—locked *you* out—and came back and went down on my girlfriend. I was shaving."

She screamed again, closer to my face.

"He's probably fucking my girlfriend right now, right this minute," I continued. "Ask him, Dee, when you see him next. Ask him if he ate out, then fucked, a certain Julie. You know her, the cigarette girl? Bill'll tell you, too, just before he bashes your head in and they bury you next to your sister."

I yawned. *Ow!* The cut pulled open again.

Beefalo had given up on the knot—he must've forgotten it over the years. He folded me up instead.

He took me outside. The shivering screams inside the MoneyMaker vibrated sharply over the din of Mardi Gras. Then the door fell shut.

Beefalo tossed me like a fishing net against a piss-soaked wall a few times, until the lights snapped off.

○

"Guilty!" shouted Knops and Dik when they opened the door to let me in.

"No, he got away," I said.

"You have many new trauma," said Knops, examining my face. "Dik, Neosporin."

Dik ran off.

"You will get another chance to kill," said Knops, whacking me on the back and rubbing my shoulders.

"Kill and kill again," said Dik, who had returned and was now icing my face with Neosporin gloplets. He paused for a moment and gestured to their comfortable divan. "Rest, my Jerome. You are fag."

"Almost!" said Knops. "Fagged, Dik. *Fagged out*."

"Fagged out."

"Yay," said Knops. "Jerome, lie."

"Okay. But just for a minute. Can I use your new telephone?"

"Here comes the bride! All fat and wide!" Dik sang as he brought me the phone. "Where is the groom! In the toilet room! Here is phone. Select these buttons and then press that button."

"Thanks, Dik."

"Where is the ring! In the toilet thing!"

I dialed.

"Hostel."

"Hey, Tommy?" I said. "Carolyn around?"

"Nope."

"What about Julie?"

"What, you don't want to talk to *me*, Jerome?"

"No, it's not that, I—"

"You sound weird."

"Cut my mouth. Hard to talk. Hey, have you—"

"Well," said Tommy, "why don't you just listen then? I never got the chance to..."

"Have you seen this guy Bill who's staying at the hostel? I'm sure you know him. Short. Scary. Curly blond hair—a wig. Parachute pants."

"...share some of my thoughts with you."

"Tommy, shit, he killed someone I knew a long time ago and he's an escapee! And he's with Julie and—"

"Death follows you around like a fat little puppy, doesn't it?"

It did, kind of. I didn't say anything.

"You know," said Tommy, "you left that night without your cinnamon rolls."

"I did not hurt her. I loved Marta."

I sneezed. My cut opened up. I sneezed again, spraying a pink mist of blood on Dik's phone.

"Why, bless you! You know I had to hide in the woods for two nights with a broken rib and road-rash down to the fucking bone because of you? Then I got busted and spent a week in a fucking chicken-fried hayseed Alabama jail until my parents came down and got me out."

"Good."

"I came here to murder you, Coe. You're lucky I met Carolyn first— I didn't really care about you after that. Imagine my surprise when it turned out she knew *you*. Then your silly bitch and her fat ass make their appearance, which I'd like to point out really complicated shit for me."

"Good."

"The only reason you're alive is so Carolyn doesn't get hurt. But I'm almost done turning her against you. I'm a pretty fucking good liar. So look out!"

"You wouldn't be holding any cards then, Tommy. There wouldn't be anything stopping me from telling her that you're a monster, a fucking bona fide fucking DSM-IV 301.7 Cluster B sociopath."

"Careful. Any idea what I'm capable of? Who I'm capable of taking my frustrations out on?"

"I'd kill you if you were here. I'd poke your blue head with an ice pick."

"And your fat-ass 'girlfriend'—you haven't even fucked her yet, I heard— and she hates your guts. She had some fairly negative things to say about you when she came in after you left her alone on the porch today."

I paused. Then I laughed.

"Yeah, I guess it is funny. So look, Coe, I gotta check in a couple of Guitar Wolf who don't fucking speak English, so I'm hanging up on you. Bye, cocksucker."

I brought Dik his phone.

"I got a little blood on your new toy, guys. But I cleaned it up."

"You have many effluences," said Dik. "Have this new Fresca."

"I need to say good-bye, you guys."

"Good-bye," said Dik.

"Bra, where are you going?" asked Knops.

"I don't know."

I took out my remaining cash and counted it down.

"$289.50," I said. "I guess I could go anyplace."

"Outlet mall," said Knops. "Go to big-ass outlet mall, in Tucumcari. Polo. Guess. Tommy. J. Crew. Everything, bra."

"I'm leaving for good, I'm afraid. I made a few more mistakes in judgment, and so I'm moving on."

"Your new bride will accompany you."

"No. She won't."

From somewhere in the apartment came a *beedlenoop beedlenoop*.

"Telephone call!" shouted Dik, who jumped up and ran into the kitchen to get it.

"Is nice to have phone," Knops said to me. "Dik splurge at Erril's with own moolah."

"I thought Cecil gave it to him," I said.

Knops stopped, like a frame of movie film. He looked up at my chin.

"What?" he said.

"Oh. Shit. Wait. Knops. I meant to say—"

Knops turned and went into the kitchen. He took the phone out of Dik's hand and expectorated a rope of vulgar Danish invective, then tried to fraction the *beedlenoop*ing telephone by slamming the oven door on it.

Dik held his head in both hands, then threw up, while Knops howled and slammed the oven door. I caught the words *Cecil* and *No*, but most of the fight they roared in that low, filthy, merchant-marine Danish.

Then Knops pointed at me.

Dik looked at me. He came toward me, a sickened monster with murder in his teeth. He stopped before me and yanked the Fresca out of my hand.

"Go."

"I don't see you come by here too much lately," said Nyelle, who was restocking a shelf of inch-thick bridal magazines a little ways down the candy-and-reading-material aisle at K & B.

I was looking at the spinner rack of romance novels but there wasn't anything new.

"You got blood on you a lot," said Nyelle, thoughtfully. "Most girls don't like blood on they boyfriends.

"Signets and Harlequins in tomorrow afternoon," Nyelle added, after I'd spun the nine books on the romance spinner for the hundredth time.

"Oh, okay," I said. "What about Regency?"

"They come in Tuesdays, but nothing come in on Mardi Gras Day," said Nyelle. "I can't stand Mardi Gras Day."

"Me neither."

"They got it everyplace, just about, they just call it something different. Can't get away, don't even try. Shrove Tuesday in Canada, Terça-feira Gorda in Portugal, Vastlapäev in Estonia..."

"Mexico, too?"

That was where I'd decided to go.

"You know they do."

I wandered around the K & B and shopped for my trip to Mexico.

I loaded a couple of fistfuls of Slim Jims and some ibuprofen into my basket. Instead of a romance novel, I picked out a coloring book and some colors. *Little Mermaid*. It qualified as a romance, I figured.

"How many jerkies you got," said Nyelle, as I stevedored piles of Slim Jims out of my red basket onto the counter.

"About forty," I said.

"You special-order razor blades from Germany come in, too," said Nyelle. "Want me to get them?"

"That's okay. I'm trying a different kind of shaving."

"Look like you need some practice, bay."

"I'm going to have to learn all over again."

"You the only man I know who don't buy nothing but jerky and head-ache powders and romance books."

"Too bad you're out of romance," I said.

"You got that right."

My apartment was untouched since I'd been there last.

I did have a lot of blood on me.

I washed and inspected my shaving. I had shaved pretty close, and the slice in my cheek wasn't really that bad, though I should've had stitches. It would serve as a fine reminder.

I lay on the bed and carefully chewed Slim Jims and colored. I ate eleven Tums. I had decided that Tums would be a good way to measure how cruddy I was feeling: sixteen would be death's-door hopeless. Maybe I'd go to Mexico and find a cave to live in. I'd name it Sixteen Tums. I'd have to look up how to say *sixteen* in Spanish. And *Tums*, too, though I suspected it was just *Tums* everywhere.

Coloring was harder than I'd remembered. I'd bought felt pens, and even though I was being careful, the paper soaked up the color, spreading it out-side the lines. It was infuriating, and I wound up tearing the Little Mermaid into tiny, satisfying bits, then started to reread a romance that I hadn't liked or finished when I'd frst tried, determined to enjoy it this time.

I read twenty pages and judged it even more intolerable than before. I fell asleep meditating on how I would destroy the book. Submergence, hurling, stompering, division, interment, putting to sea. Auction. Fire. Yes, fire. Very complete, final. Whole. Fire, fire, fire, fire

I woke croaking and sweating. The room was dark, but I had no memory of getting up and turning out the light. I had little memory of anything recent at all.

I was on the verge of recalling when I saw a shadow under the door, interrupting the yellow light from the hall.

Then, rapid, strafing knocks.

"Jerome!" said Julie.

"What," I said, without moving.

"Oh *god* am I glad you're there!" she said, sounding giddy and drunk. "Open up. I got him. I motherfucking *got* him."

I opened the door.

Julie was wet with sweat, alive, shining, smiling, crying, dirty, almost breathless. The tiny scar of the spider bite was like a beauty mark on the apple of her cheek. She had a few spatters of blood on her white cigarette-girl blouse, the one she'd stripped off and then so hastily put back on after she'd *come* for him.

She said, "It's just us now, for real."

She ran up and hugged me. I pushed her away.

"Jerome?"

"What. The fuck. Are you doing. *Here?*"

She stepped back and studied me like she was waiting for a subtle punch line.

"After you left..." she started. "Oh no, what happened to your mouth? Did Bill do that?"

She reached up to touch my cut. I slapped her hand away.

"After I left *when?*" I shouted, stepping forward into her wet face.

"Don't you yell at me! What the hell is wrong with you, Jerome?"

"Oh, give me a break. Come on, when I left *when?*"

"When we were sitting on the steps of the hostel," said Julie, suddenly weak. "When Tommy and Carolyn came in for work."

"When?"

"At the hostel," Julie said, little pops in the back of her throat. "You and me sitting on the stairs. Remember? When he came out and walked past us, at the back of the pack of Danes. Remember? When you didn't tell me it was him. When I threatened to sic you on him. When he looked at me and licked his lips. Remember? When you suddenly got mean and cold and distant. Remember that? Do you remember that that was the last time we saw each other? Huh? *Remember, Jerome?*"

"Yeah. Right before you went in and cursed my name. To Tommy, of all people."

"Okay, I was mad," she said. "Mad that you ran off just at the very instant we'd gotten rid of fucking Bill and Dee and Carolyn and Tommy, the instant we were officially together, the instant I'd gotten what I'd been praying for for so long. I'm sorry about that. I didn't know at the time that you'd gone after Bill. You should've brought me. That was the *deal*, Jerome. Cosa nostra, right?

"But I figured out how to find him on my own. I got the number for the post office in Allston where you lived and just asked the postal lady that answered if she knew Duke's and what had happened to it, and she said it was called Connie's Pint Bar now. I got the number. And there he was.

"Dewey told me that Dee was a dancer, semi-famous, and went by the name of Penny Candy."

"Penny Candy," I said.

What's your stage name, Julie?

"I knew who he meant. I knew Penny Candy. She's a dancer from the MoneyMaker. I sell her Marlboro Lights sometimes on my rounds. I don't like to go into that creepy place at all, except Penny tips well."

Right after she'd talked with Dewey, Julie'd called the MoneyMaker. Ozie, the tiny fifties-pinup-girl-type stripper, had answered and told Julie in her preposterous slutty toddler voice that Penny wouldn't be in until later, that she didn't know what time, that she couldn't tell time too good, that MamaDawn had to tell the time for her, but MamaDawn couldn't right then because MamaDawn was busy looking for her glasses, which she'd dropped in the ice maker.

"I was so excited," said Julie. "I had a plan. I was going to be able to fix everything. I got my cigarette tray and uniform, and headed down to the MoneyMaker fast as I could."

Julie told me that she'd only wanted to divert Bill, to get him out of the MoneyMaker before Dee/Penny got there. Julie said she'd done a *hey, big boy* sort of come-on, and had finally lured him out with a promise of having a few drinks with him.

"Thank god Dee wasn't there yet. I bought a bottle of tequila and kept him occupied, out of the MoneyMaker and out of the Quarter for a couple of hours, but eventually he said..."

"Occupied," I said, laughing, bleeding at the mouth.

"...he needed to go back. He said he was busy with shit. We'd gotten drunk. Then I—"

"What? Come on now, Julie. You guys take a carriage ride around the charming French Quarter?"

She started crying, her voice hitching.

"Fuck. Fuck. Jerome, I did it for you, Jerome, I really love you, I didn't know what else to do to keep him away—I thought if I saved Dee for you, then you'd..."

"Then I'd what?" I said, with the ugliest possible tone of junior-high contempt I could summon.

"...that you'd like me again. That it would clear the way for you and me to be together. Fuck, I'm still drunk. Oh god, it was only two hours ago."

It.

"What the fuck makes you think I don't like you?" I said, leaning back and lowering my voice to a cruel pitch. I relaxed, hands behind my head. I hated myself, I hated everyone.

She stood and yelled: "Maybe because you don't show it? Because you never tell me? You never even tried to kiss me? Why didn't you fall in love with me? I'm neat. I'm cute. I love *you*, Jerome, and I've loved you for a long, long time, longer than you know. I just wanted you to love me back, you selfish, teasing prick. But you only fall in love with ghosts, Jerome, the dead, the missing, the unknown, the buried, the imagined. I wish I was a fucking ghost. I want to be a phantom. I want to watch you over my shoulder, chasing *me*."

She came at me with both fists. She hit me with windmills, fists closed. There was no anguish this time, just rage. I didn't try to stop her, and couldn't have even if I'd wanted to. It hurt. She stopped when I didn't resist.

"Get off me."

She climbed off my chest and sat down on the floor, cross-legged, like she had onstage.

"I do love you—I did, I was infatuated with you, *was*, was obsessed with you, but you *are* a ghost now, Julie. Just a tricky phantom now, full of lies."

"I'm not lying!" she said.

"Huh. Not lying."

"No!"

"Oh," I said, not sure if the liquid running off my face was blood or tears or drool or sweat or salve or all. "What about the MoneyMaker? I saw you strip for him. That's right, yes indeedy! Did you know that? I saw him eat you out. I saw you come. I *heard* you come!"

She stopped rocking.

"Oh. No."

"Yes. And I can't imagine what you did with him after you left. How you kept him *occupied*."

"I—"

I was so disgusted I couldn't even laugh.

"I killed him!" she cried. "To save Dee, because you care for her so much. I did it for you. For you and me. I didn't want to hurt you. I don't ever want to hurt you. I was trying to stop him from going back to the bar. I didn't want him to touch me—I did what I could to stop him. It was all I could think of! And when that quit working... I fucking murdered—"

"Like a widow spider. Sure you did."

"He was jogging down Iquem, on his way back to the French Quarter to kill Dee, and he wouldn't stop. He kept looking over his shoulder and saying *I got business you slit leave me the fuck alone* so I ran after him and jumped on his back. I choked him, and he fell and hit his head. There wasn't anyone around. I hit him with a sign that had been knocked down. Then I hit him again. His wig came off like I'd scalped him."

"You daytime-soap-opera *bitch*."

I sat down, shaking. There wasn't anything left to do now. Maybe get some sleep, deal with my cuts, move. I put my head on my knees. I couldn't look at her.

"How did this happen to us?" she said, quiet but strong. "Oh, I was so careful for so long!"

"Long? Three months is long to you?" I said, without looking up.

"No. Years. I met you in the newspaper."

"What?"

"There was a picture of you a couple years ago, in the *Picayune*. When you were at the Luncheonaire. You were so weird and cute. I loved you right away, like I'd never felt before. I cut out your picture and kept you in my bra."

"Are you kidding?"

"One hot day, I got all sweaty and the newspaper fell apart. So I went to the Luncheonaire to spy on you from way across the store. Every day. Then you were gone, and the lunch counter closed. I looked for you. I hunted. But you were gone. I thought I would *die*. I thought about you every day. I never saw you.

"Then you saved me, Jerome. In a thrift store. You saved my blood from spilling on the ground, you caught it in your hurt hands. I followed the little drops like bread crumbs all the way across the Upper Ninth and found you on the banks letting my blood run clean into the river."

"You—" I'd never told her about that. "I—"

"I followed you home. I followed you to the French Quarter on Halloween. I sat on your lap and you held me around the waist and I can't tell you how hard I was in love. Never like that in my whole life."

"If that's true, you left me at that bar, by myself! That's you in love? Oh, fuck you!"

"I was in the *bathroom*, Jerome!" Julie yelled. "And I was trapped in there by that stupid fucking riot! And when it was over, you weren't outside waiting for me. You left *me* alone. I would've waited for you!"

"I—"

"Next day I go to the library, find your old picture on microfilm. Carolyn is in the picture, the caption says she works at a hostel, I go there, find her. I say casually I think I saw you at the Luncheonaire once and she says Yeah, maybe a long time ago and I say So what happened to that place, what happened to that kid that worked there, the grilled-cheese guy, Oh that guy, she says, who fucking knows, he was crazy, and I say, Oh, ex-boyfriend, and she says Like hell, no friend of mine, in fact I have a bone to pick with old Jerome Coe, and I ask What and she tells me, tells me about the whole night, tells me like she's been holding it all in so long and wants to tell someone so bad and it all comes out, and all of sudden she's crying, right there at her desk and I say It sounds like Jerome was trying to protect you, go find him, you'll feel better.

"She says How can I find him, and I tell her I'll help, that I know everybody, I'll find out. Of course, I already knew."

"You stalked me."

"Don't you judge *me* on stalking, you bastard."

"Why?" I was bled out now. "Why? *Why* go to all that fucking *work*? You could've just told me!"

"I had to stage everything. Carolyn said you were pathologically shy and weird when it came to women. You would've run off."

"I'm not that shy. Besides, you have a fucking boyfriend! Why would I run?"

"That's exactly what I thought you'd think, and that's why I invented

Vishy. I made him up. A cockblock. You would've freaked and run off to another country if I just came up to you and said Hi, I'm Julie, your stalker, and I'm in love with you, and once you saved my blood and anointed a river with it so we have to be together forever, kiss me, fuck me, Jerome, live with me, *save* me. So I created Vishy, I made him out of all the parts I thought would keep you near me, a mental Frankenstein boyfriend. He worked. He kept you at exactly the right closeness. He tempered us. He cushioned the fragile you and me.

"One day I go to tell Carolyn I found out where you live, and we all came up with this plan to freak you out. Then, just like that, we're at your apartment and we've got you pinned to the floor. You were so warm between my legs, and so terrified even though you pretended you weren't, and I swore that I would never let anything happen to you, *ever*, and that you'd never have to be afraid again."

"Good work. Look how it all turned out. You filled me up with your terrible lies and made me fall in l… you broke my fucking *heart*, Julie."

She turned and uncrossed her legs. She pulled off her boots, my old Teddy and Dinos. She stood up unsteadily and went to the corner of the room and found her old shoes, her official cigarette-girl shoes, the ones with the little buckles, that I had not touched but had thoroughly memorized in the long hours when Julie and I weren't together.

"Wanna know about the best sex I ever had? When we were in bed, at my place, you touched me, kissed me without touching my lips, then when you went downstairs to the bathroom, I didn't even have to move or touch myself, I just thought about you, and just like that, I came and came and came and came."

She stepped into them, her mary janes. She picked up one of my boots. She reached inside, deep into the toe, and pulled something out. A wad of paper. She let it roll off her palm onto the bed. She dropped my boot, turned her back to me, and left, pulling the door closed behind her. The shadow under the door disappeared, and soon there was only the dull amber light there.

Miranda was badly wrinkled but hardly smudged. The fixative Coryate had used was pretty tough stuff. I wadded her back up again. I put her in my mouth, chewed her to a mess, and swallowed her back with warm beer.

VIII

Then it was Ash Wednesday. Early.

I walked to the bus station and arrived at 5:15, right as it opened. I bought a ticket to Matamoros. I felt calm. I was calm. I should have been suicidal, but I wasn't—maybe it was because I'd been preparing all along for Julie to never work out. And she didn't. Not in the manner I'd expected, but who cares?

My bus didn't leave for an hour and a half, so I headed to the French Quarter to use the ATM there. I had $440 to my name, and I wanted it all.

On the way, I passed the MoneyMaker. Maybe Bill and Dee and Julie were all there. And the old stripper and Annie Lennox and MamaDawn, all of them on the stage in a slurping daisy chain, wiggling like mosquito larvae. Well, good.

I bought a *Times-Picayune* to read while I waited in line for the cash machine. I wanted to check the murder tally for Carnival.

There'd been fourteen killings on Fat Tuesday, a twenty-two-year low, according to the article, which was written in a tone that seemed distinctly disappointed. But at the end of the story the reporter perked up a bit, suggesting that many bodies may be found today and tomorrow, so the Crescent City is sure to stay ahead of Atlanta and Gary, Indiana, as America's Murder Capital.

Among the confirmed murderees there was no mention of a tiny, bewigged, bludgeoned white man. Of course not. I knew Julie didn't have it in her to kill someone, even someone like Bill. Fuck, yeah. Kill, no. Lie about both? Looks that way.

I withdrew my cash and started back to the bus station. I didn't want to pass the MoneyMaker again, so I took a parallel street several blocks outside the Quarter. I'd never been here before. Little kids ran around scavenging coins and beads before the street-sweepers came and sucked up everything worth scavenging.

I came upon a long, wide street of boarded-up businesses and houses. There were no people. There weren't even beads or bottle caps on the ground.

I still had plenty of time, and the bus station was only eight or ten blocks, but I hurried down the middle of the street—the blank, somehow mocking neighborhood frightened me.

I noticed a tiny, glimmering object on the pavement. I stopped and crouched down to see.

A fly. It was crawling, sluggish and tentative—cold, probably—across the street. Its body was silver, with a bare tint of lemony green, like fake gold. It stopped. I poked it with a twenty. It wouldn't fly away. A wind I couldn't feel ruffled its wings, and it came to life again and continued across the street, toward a dirty blue plastic tarp that partly covered a low pile of molded planks and crumbles of cement and an old uprooted STOP sign, bullet-punctured, bent, and pink from sun. The wind flipped the edges of the tarp, allowing peeks of the interior ruin of softer rot and the torn stem of the STOP sign.

I watched the crawling fly. About halfway to the pile of junk the fly disappeared into the glare of cold sunlight.

I walked over to the junk pile. My fly had joined many others—hundreds, thousands of busy, lemony, argentine machines.

I obeyed the STOP sign for a moment, then lifted the tarp.

He looked the same. A living, cunning smile, now moving with flies instead of threats. In his skull, above one ear, running from his eyebrow to the back of his head like the band of an eyepatch, was a narrow, deep interval, red-black, flyblown. Nearby, the blond wig, collapsed and blood-stained. I let down the tarp. A puff of flies bellowed, then settled.

I was pinned for a full minute by confusion and uncertainty and the adhesive nothingness of the neighborhood, before I finally turned and ran back the way I'd come.

There was a small crowd around the door of the MoneyMaker. A few cop cars and a white van with ORLEANS PARISH CORONER on the side idled grumpily.

De Trie and Ucille were there. They went inside. Presently, they came back out with MamaDawn, whose hands were cuffed in front of her. She sat on the curb while an EMT took her blood pressure.

Then Ozie came out of the strip club. She headed away from the crowd, toward Louis Armstrong Park. She paused for an instant to light a cigarette. I caught up to her.

"Hi, Ozie," I said.

"Oh hi, hi! Who are you?" she said, beaming and smiling at me while we walked.

"Jerome," I said. "I've seen your show."

"I'm Ozie," she said. "My show is faaaan*tastic*!"

"It's a great show. Say, what happened back at the MoneyMaker?"

Ozie walked fast, and I had to hustle to keep up. Her legs scissored like a sandpiper's.

"That's MamaDawn's house. I do my show there, for people. Look at my money."

Ozie stopped abruptly and pulled the foot of an old fishnet stocking from her purse. It was filled with wadded-up dollars. She dangled it in front of my face.

"Ha, ha, I have more money than you-oo."

"You do have a lot. I have more though, look."

I showed her my pile of twenties.

"Wow! Can I have some?"

Her upper teeth were dentures, perfect, white; her lower teeth an old, crowded cemetery.

"No, I need it to start my new life in Mexico," I said.

"That's okay. I'm going on a better trip, to Arkansas. My husky Snowball is there, at Winnie's cabin."

"Ozie, any idea how to say *sixteen* in Spanish?"

"*Dieciséis.*"

"I'm going to Mexico to live in a cave. And I'm going to name it 'Dieciséis Tums.'"

"That's gay. Nobody names their caves."

"When are you leaving for Arkansas?"

"Duh! Poopyhead! Right now!"

"Oh, you're in a hurry, huh," I said.

"A *big* hurry, buster. But I can give you a show. I'm very wet right now. You can fuck me, too, after, wherever you want, any hole. You're very cute. Souvenir panties, too, one hundred smackeroos."

"Won't that make Beefalo mad?"

"Oh, ho *ho*! Beefalo's fucked!"

"Why's that?"

"Um, duh? Because the cigarette lady told Penny that Penny was safe now because that little clapping Bill was dead from murder. Penny got mad and told Beefie to get the cigarette lady, so Beefie hit the cigarette lady on the wall and she's a light bulb now. And that made MamaDawn mad and she got old Sam I Am and old Sam I Am talked to Beefie. Beefie can't come see me again."

"Light bulb." There were tiny red speckles on her face. Spatter. "Like, *broken?*"

Ozie took one last drag and threw her cigarette on the street. She ground it out with her tiny high-heel slipper.

"Firestarter! Firestarter!" she said, pestling the cigarette to powder.

A block away, the door to the MoneyMaker opened. Two EMTs carried a body out on stretcher. It was covered with a white sheet. Blood had made it through the sheet in places and was spreading along the cotton fibers, forming large diamond-shaped stains.

A round woman with a three-ring binder came out of the club and stood next to the stretcher. She opened up her binder, balanced it on the covered body, and then scribbled notes on a couple of the pages. Then she lifted up her binder and looked on the other side.

"Fuck!" she said, and wiped the blood that had gotten on the back of the binder onto a clean bit of sheet.

"Hey!"

The round woman and an EMT didn't seem to have heard me. They loaded the body on the stretcher into the van. I ran toward them. The coroner slammed one door to the back of the van. I ran. She slammed the other door, but it wouldn't catch.

"Stop," I said, but no word came out.

She slammed the door again. Still there was something in the way. She slammed again and again.

Stop

She slammed it one more time, putting all her body behind it. Something black came out of the van and landed on the street. She kicked it up onto the sidewalk. She climbed into the van and drove away.

Stop

On the sidewalk, a black shoe, shiny, with a strap and a silver buckle. It was mangled and scuffed from the slams of the van door. It lay on its side, a spoonful of drying blood spilling out of it into a crack in the sidewalk.

Tadpoles, an explosion of them. I fell onto the sidewalk, I crawled, blind, yelling, feeling around for her shoe, but it wasn't there, the morning passed, afternoon came, the tadpoles wriggled off. I had crawled blocks and blocks. I went back to the MoneyMaker, but her shoe was gone. Her blood had been washed away. I sat on the curb and waited for my heart to stop, but it wouldn't.

On Canal was my old friend the bum in the wheelchair. I was sure he thought I was a rotten human being for all the lives I'd let slip away, and especially for giving gifts and then taking them back. Clothes and knives. But he didn't roll away this time. He looked tired. He had a big bandage on his head, covering one eye. I asked him what happened, but he looked at me without saying anything.

"Well, my friend," I said, "I'm not going to Mexico after all, so this is for you."

I showed him my bus ticket and all my money.

"But I have to keep twenty," I said. "I have to go to K & B to pick up some last-minute *matériel* for an offensive I just thought up. Wanna hear about it?"

He said nothing. I looked over his head—this was exactly the kind of scenario in which bubbles usually began to appear, with their sage strophes and mind-readings—but there were none.

I rolled up the twenty and stuck it behind my ear, like the schoolkids did with their bus transfers.

I tossed the ticket and the rest of my money into his lap. But he just looked at it without moving, so I picked it all up and dropped it into his coat pocket.

"I know what you're thinking," I said, but I meant it colloquially, not that I actually knew: there were still no bubbles. "You're thinking, This clown'll turn up later and take it all back, at the worst possible time. Well, you're wrong, though I can understand why you'd be skeptical. I hereby promise: I won't bother you again."

It was getting dark. People who hadn't partied enough in the past two weeks started coming out of buildings and houses and hotels and were soon on the street prowling for more. Among them were others who had been holed up for two weeks to avoid the whole carnival and just now were feeling safe to venture out and get a few supplies.

I had gotten lost—a great feeling—but I soon found myself on a recognizable street again. There, up ahead, was the Smart Harriet.

I didn't go in, of course. I looked in the window, the same one I'd looked out of at the people on the street, back when I had the feeling that things were just starting, when I'd first come to town and I knew only Carolyn and Ioanna. She was refilling the coffee cup of a man eating a king cake at the counter, a little hill of king-cake babies at his elbow. It looked warm in there.

I stared, waiting for a bubble of collective opinion, like a big down comforter tacked to the ceiling, to deploy over the heads of the Smart Harrieters, but none did. It was damn lonesome without my bubbles.

According to the clock over the makeup aisle at the K & B it was four a.m. I tried to remember what the rules were about buying alcohol this time of night. I hoped Nyelle was working, as I felt she interpreted the complicated liquor laws a little more favorably than the other clerks. I walked up and down the aisles, but she didn't seem to be around. In fact, there was no one around at all.

A new variety of Slim Jim had emerged on the market: Tabascoflavored. I put six in my basket, which had a black leaf of old lettuce stuck to the bottom. K & B didn't even sell lettuce. Normally I hated things stuck to the bottoms of shopping carts and baskets.

But it would be okay today.

I loaded a roll of masking tape and some baggies in with my Slim Jims. I also found a romance, a new series by a publisher I hadn't heard of. According to Quentin Bohner, Method #6, in his chapter "Easily Obtainable Lethal Vapors," worked fast, but not so quickly that one wouldn't risk boredom or accumulating a quorum of second thoughts; so one might as well have something to read. Lucky the baggies were clear. I hoped they wouldn't fog up on the inside.

I hoisted my basket up onto the counter where Nyelle usually was.

A figure emerged from behind the photo-developing counter, holding a tall, narrow jar of cocktail onions. He walked leisurely over to my checkout counter, picked a cocktail onion out of his jar, popped it into his mouth, and began to ring me up, wordlessly, using his non-cocktail-onion-getting fingers to depress the register keys.

"Pint of tequila, too," I said. "The one with the yellow label."

"Can't purchase spirits before six a.m."

"You mean you can't *sell* spirits," I reminded him. "But I can buy them."

"Okay then," he said, getting a pint down off the shelf, adroitly using only his pinkie and ring finger. "$16.45."

"Where's Nyelle?" I asked him as he was walking off toward the photo area. He stopped. Awesome forbearance slowly turned him back around.

"Why," he said, not looking at me but at my forehead, "do you ask?"

"Well, she's usually working now."

"She has moved on, sir."

"Oh. I wanted to say hi, bye."

"Well," he said, again addressing my forehead, "say what you want, but Nyelle can't hear you, because Nyelle is not here, because I fired her narrow ass."

"You did? Why?"

"I fired her and threw her out my house. That's why."

He gave me a receipt and walked away.

"Can I have some matches?" I called after him, but he ignored me. I took some from the matchbox fishbowl by the Tic Tac rack.

Nyelle came in.

She didn't see me. She walked right to the photo-developing area and, to the empty store, boldly pronounced herself due her last paycheck.

"Pay me now, mother*fucker!*" shouted Nyelle. "You owe me two weeks. You heard me?"

The cocktail-onions man emerged from somewhere.

"Checks won't be in till Friday," he said, tearing open a bag of Skittles.

"I know the checks ain't in," said Nyelle. "But I said pay me. Now. In green money, motherfucker."

"Checks—"

"And let me worry about tax and FICA. That make $390.85. Mother-fucker."

"Nyelle, go on, now," he said, funneling Skittles into his mouth. "Come back Friday."

"I'd like to share something with you. If you don't pay me what you owe, right now, I'm gonna walk these aisles and sweep shit off the shelves. Remind yourself you put Clamato and fragrances on the same shelf. Maybe I start there."

"You'll remember from when you were employed here that we don't keep that kind of money on hand."

As forecast, Nyelle started in the mixers-and-perfumes aisle. She'd cleared half the shelves before the man could react. She paused for a second to confront him again.

"Nyelle, babe, please! There's no money here! You know it's in the drop safe! Come on, now!"

"Get it out the machine."

She gestured in the general direction of the ATM in the back of the store.

"You want me to give you *my* money?" he began, assuming a haughty, sarcastic tone, which he soon regretted: Nyelle immediately resumed clearing shelves, this time using a toilet plunger to boost efficiency.

"Better hurry!" she shouted over the crashing and popping.

He started at a saunter, but then took off at a sprint. He returned with a handful of cash.

"Here's four hundred. Now please get out of my K & B drugstore," he said wearily.

Nyelle accepted the money and leisurely counted it out while the store filled with the odors of Eau My Goodness and Veldt-Fresh Tide.

"I need a few things first," she said.

She came over to the register and picked up a red basket.

"Hey, baby," she said to me. "You look even worse than you did Mardi Gras Day."

"I know."

"You need a new romance."

"Yeah, I just picked one up. *Plank of Passion*."

Meanwhile Cocktail Onions was waving his arms and moaning and begging her to please leave, to which she paid no attention.

Nyelle headed down the magazine, paperback, and candy aisle, which caused the man to redouble his panicky wavings and pleadings. But Nyelle merely paused at the romance-book spinner.

"I need a few books, too," she said. "I'm going on a trip."

"Bus?"

"No, no. My parraine give me his car. I'm driving out this town. Going to Austin, Texas, to enroll in the Vogue College of Beauty."

"You're leaving?"

"Had me enough," she said, adding several decibels to the last word in order to enlarge her declamation to the whole of the store.

"When're you going?"

"Right now, baby. Right now. Today. I got a few errands to run, then I'll be up on the I-10 west."

"Oh."

We studied the spinner. Whimpering could be heard in the background. Every so often some shaken-up bottle exploded, or some automated toy, activated by the fall, barked or oinked or sang *Iko Iko*.

"This is starting out pretty good," I said, handing her a copy of the romance I'd picked up. "If you like pirates and stuff."

She flipped through it.

"Mmm, I don't care for all they keelhauling and yardarms and shit. I like contemporary romance."

"Look, there's a whole new publisher," I said. "There'll be something."

"You right."

"Lordsake, please go," said Cocktail Onions, holding a broom with green plastic bristles dripping with syrup. "Please. Lord."

Nyelle turned around and tipped over a corn-nuts display.

"You between lady friends?" she said to me, when the noise ceased. "You usually got one around."

"I'm between."

"Let me tell you something. You don't look so good. I think you ought go home and get back in bed."

"I'm kind of between apartments, too."

"Well, where you stay?"

I didn't say anything.

"Look, why don't you go lie in the backseat of my car. You rest while I run around. I drop you off anyplace you want before I get on the high rise."

"Oh, I don't know. I still have one last errand to run. And it's way over in the Quarter."

"Go on, now," she said, digging the keys out of an enormous white leather purse and gesturing at the door. "Do like I tell you. The only car out there, silver Bonneville. Push all that shit off the seat onto the floor. I be along shortly."

The dents had been knocked out. It had been repainted a shimmery silver white. It had new blue-wall tires, tinted windows, and a fifteen-foot CB antenna bent in a long arc from bumper to bumper. The entire inside had been gutted and reupholstered in white leather. Antique Mardi Gras beads, pale and delicate, hung from the rearview mirror, which was at least a foot and a half long. But the Pontiac had the same smell, bare and faint as it was, of ancient cigarette dirt, rotting and salt-splattered fake down coats. Of iron oxide and sulfur, of my own blood and shit. I cracked a window.

I moved Nyelle's round white suitcase carefully onto the floor of the backseat, put my bag of supplies next to it, then lay down. It was dawn.

I woke up. We were parked on a quiet street bordered on one side by a long, high, white stone wall. Nyelle was gone. There were grocery bags on the floor up front, and dresses in dry-cleaner bags hanging from hooks by both back doors, blocking out most of the late-afternoon sun.

I peeked out of a curtain of black and red dresses. On the side of the street opposite the white wall separating me from the river was a row of camelback houses surrounded by well-honed iron-spike fences.

A key in a lock. The front passenger door opened. Two long arms entered through the curtain of dry cleaning and placed a large pink stereo on the seat.

"Be good," said a deep voice.

"You know I won't," said Nyelle.

"I know it."

Nyelle climbed in the driver's side.

"Eeek!"

"Hi, just me," I said.

"I forgot you was here, you been so quiet. You scared the ginger outta me, bay."

She started the car.

"I'm through with my errands," she said. "Took me all day. You ain't stirred even once, even when I drove over a mattress I didn't see in the street until it was too late."

"Pretty worn out."

She looked at me in the rearview mirror and gave me a long, hard stare.

"You looking even sorrier than you did twelve hours ago. What am I gonna do with you? I can't bring you to Texas."

She stared. Her hand squeezed the gearshift, ready to pull it down into drive.

"Will you take me to the Saint Louis Hotel? In the Quarter."

She studied me.

"Here I thought you broke and homeless and all but alone. But guess what, you gonna stay at the Saint Louis. Bellhops and room service and heated pool. Mmm. You a mystery, bay. Maybe I give up romance and start on mysteries."

At the hotel Nyelle climbed out and gave me a hug.

"Got money?"

"A little."

"How much little?"

"Three dollars and fifty-five cents."

She tried to give me a twenty.

"Everything costs more in Texas," I said. "Better keep it."

I sat in the darkening courtyard of the hotel and watched the people walking along the square of balconies above. As it grew darker the restaurant and lobby indoors began to fill with diners and people ready for an evening in the Quarter.

A waiter came and lit the candle on my table. I told him that I wasn't having anything right now.

I waited an hour, and then went to find the bathroom.

It was bright and clean, as I remembered. The steel walls of the stalls went all the way to the floor, and the doors shut perfectly—no gaps or misalignment or other eccentricity. The level of privacy was unsurpassed. According to Q. Bohner, one needed only fifteen private, uninterrupted minutes for this particular method to work.

I went back to the courtyard, but a couple had taken my table.

I stood by a palm tree near the glass wall separating me from the restaurant.

Oh, there.

I wasn't sure I'd remember what he looked like, though I'd seen *Che!*

"Mr. Sharif?"

He was eating a salad and a perfectly round roll that steamed when he tore it open. He chewed for a moment, and then wiped his mouth with a vast starched white napkin.

"Yes."

"I was a friend of Julie's. My name is Jerome."

"Yes."

He bit into another roll. He looked worn. He paused every few seconds to take a breath. He touched his heart.

"Okay?"

"Yes. Sit down."

I sat across from him. Between us on the table in a slender crystal vase was a flower, a kind I'd never seen before, lolling, red-orange like the muzzle of an overworked machine gun. I was glad for the flower, as it blocked his view of me.

A waiter came and handed me a menu.

"Nothing for me," I said.

"Red snapper with asparagus," Omar said.

Before the waiter left, Omar handed him the vase and flower.

"I can't see you, Mr. Coe," he said. "Roll?"

I buttered a roll and tried to stuff the whole thing into my face at once, opening the cut on my mouth. Fortunately it bled on the inside only, so the blood ran down my throat instead of my chin.

"All right?"

"Yeah," I said, coughing.

We both brought our hands to our hearts at the same time and breathed deeply.

"Bypass," he said, smiling.

"Psychosomatism," I said.

"Julie mentioned you often. In her letters, and on the telephone."

"She did?"

"An excellent letter-writer, Julie. Few letters are written these days. Yes?"

"I never get letters."

"You must write them to get them."

He finished his salad.

"Julie used the word *love* in her letters, often, did you know? For me, sometimes, but most for you."

I thought of the bathroom, its white walls.

"No. I didn't."

"Do you know what I'm thinking?"

"What?"

"You can't see? As you say, my bubble?"

"Not now, no."

I ate another roll.

The waiter came with the red snapper and asparagus. We sat in silence while he ate. When he finished, he patted his breast pockets.

"Ha! I quit smoking. Old habits, et cetera."

"Have you... seen her?" I said.

"Of course."

"How did she look?"

The waiter came again with a dessert menu, and asked if we would like coffee.

"Have a cup of coffee. I know you to be a drinker of au lait."

"I just wanted to see you," I said, "to tell you that everything that happened was my fault, I loved her very much, but I never told her, and now it's too late, and it's my fault."

"There is the matter of the police."

His eyes were extraordinary. I could understand how people fell in love with him.

I wasn't afraid of the police. I would escape them, too.

"I suppose there is," I said, glancing down at the floor to make sure my bag of supplies was still there. "The matter of the police."

"*Matters*, I think, is the more appropriate word."

"Sir, how did she look?"

The waiter brought our coffee: chicory au lait, like Café du Monde. Better.

"She was bloodied, Jerome," he said, carefully tapping sugar into the china cup. "Her hair had been cut off, crudely."

He tapped once more. Three grains of sugar fell into his milky coffee.

"She was barefoot."

A few tadpoles began to crowd the whites of my eyes.

"I wanted," he said, "to kill you, did you know that?"

"I didn't know," I said, thinly. "I won't stop you."

"Melodrama," he said, stirring his coffee, slowly, like a 33⅓-rpm record playing. "I want you to see her, too."

"See her? Oh, no, I can't do that. I have to go to the—"

"Why did you come to me here?"

"To tell you what I'd done, and tell you I'm sorry."

"I want you to see her."

"I couldn't!"

I picked up my bag of supplies and headed for the bathroom.

He yelled across the restaurant.

"I had her brought here, Mr. Coe, afterward. She's here. Go see her."

Something hit me in the back. I turned and looked down. A room-key card.

"You have her *body?*"

"215. Then you can go to the *bathroom.*"

Omar Sharif sat down heavily, one hand over his heart, the other shaking over a tiny china cup.

The elevator opened onto the second floor, across from a gilt mirror under a brass chandelier.

I was dirty, especially my face. The cut on my mouth was black and plum and barely scabbed.

A withering loneliness came over me at the thought of Julie's hair, cut off and stolen.

I shut my eyes and considered the air that occupied the second floor of the hotel. It was watery and heavy, and rolled around on the floor and walls and ceiling, unsure of what temperature to be. It had odors, both faint and powerful, anemic and pungent, of mold and rot, of steak, of yellow fever, of cigars, sex, shit, of Chanel No. 22, of pillows crackly with starch, of hundred-year-old beatings, of hashish. There may have been a million dead on the second floor of the Saint Louis Hotel, or none—the air, rich as it was, betrayed nothing.

At 215 I raised my hand to knock. I let it fall and laughed out loud.

I sat down. I smelled under the door. Old coffee. The powdery base note of industrial carpet cleaner. A sugary, vegetable decay.

"Julie," I said.

Farther on down the hall, the motorized crunch of an ice-maker.

I stood up, slid the card into the lock, and opened the door.

The lights were off. It was medievally dark and cold. I shut the door behind me and stood still, next to the closet by the bathroom. I sat down and listened to the silence, and to the simple, comfortable ring of my own cowardice, until the central heating clicked on. I waited for the breath of the heat to reach me. I gathered my supplies. Then, having known all along that I would not look at her body, I left.

To avoid Omar, I headed quickly toward the emergency-exit stairs at the opposite end of the hallway.

Up ahead, an open door cast a reddish light into the hall. As I passed, I glanced in. I stopped.

In the bright room was a Mr. Pibb machine and a Coke machine and an ice maker. There was a sturdy brown box on a stand, a change maker, with a little red light lit up next to a sticker that read NO CHANGE WHEN LIT. A rejected dollar bill stuck out of it like a tongue. There were ice cubes on the floor, melting in neat little puddles. Crouched on the floor by the Coke machine was a woman wrapped in a soft white oversize robe, its hem and the ends of its sash curled on the linoleum tiles and soaking up the icy water. A sleeve of her robe was rolled up, her arm stuck up in the guts of the machine. In the fluorescent silence of the room, it seemed like the machine was exhaling her; like she was a breath of frost. She braced a bare foot against the Coke machine and pulled. Without a sound, she fell back on the floor, Cokeless.

She stood up. Her face was bruised. She had a long, even slice from just under her nose across the apple of her cheek, bisecting her old spider bite. Her hair was savagely uneven, long, loose strands resting on the collar of the soft robe. Her right eye was bruised shut. She wore a silver puzzle ring on one toe. The compressors in the cold-drink machines went off, went on, went off. She turned and looked my way.

"I know how to get a Coke out," I said. "Want me to get you one?"

She nodded.

Quietly—ghosts vanish like pheasant if you startle them—I found the ice scoop, tipped the Coke machine back, and stuck the scoop under.

Beneath the machine was nearly two dollars in change. I bought a Coke for each of us.

"Are you a ghost?"

"No," she said. "Are you?"

"No."

"Tell me you love me," said Julie.

"I love you."

"Open my Coke for me."

"You're dead. Beefalo murdered you. He broke you like a light bulb. I saw you, dead, on a stretcher."

I opened her Coke.

"He hit me with a chair and he broke a bottle that he cut off my hair with, he stole my shoes and put them on and said *Oh god oh me oh perfect* and then took down his pants but then Dawn shot him with Sam I Am. Got an awful lot of blood on me."

She held her Coke to the breast of her robe. Hollow pips of bursting bubbles. Then, a magnificent nosebleed, a wide red ribbon, stealthy, lovely, quiet.

ACKNOWLEDGMENTS

I would like to thank my family for the unconditional love and support they have given me over the years, and also for the crying-shoulders, cheerleading, and advisories that every single one of them—my parents, Bob and Cathy Cotter, my sister Melissa Dempsey and her husband Brian Dempsey, my sister Karen Cotter and her husband Joe Etherton, and their families—have graciously and repeatedly supplied during the writing and rewriting of this book.

The following people were also constantly in mind as comfort and inspiration and anchorage: Jude Spaith, Sialia Rieke, Linda and Peter MacNeilage, Rodger Friedman, Ann Enzminger, Kate Dillon, Christine Horn, Eli Horowitz, Jordan Bass, Angelica Delgado, Maria and Keith La Ganga-Harmon, Jane Simpkin, Ileen Goldsmith, Amber and Jazzy, Eric Rossborough, Zara Steadman, Big Poppa E, Hilary Thompson, Jennifer Boyden, Ruth and Steve Jones, Jane Stone and Don Walker, Harriet and Al Evans, and Don Sanders.

And, most of all, I thank the beautiful Annie La Ganga, my special lady friend evermore, whose bright and sudden appearance in my life nine years ago is all that will ever really matter.